# SURVIVAL OF THE FITTEST

Book 1 of the *Crossroads* Trilogy

*By Jacqui Murray*

From the *Man vs. Nature* Saga

"It is not the strongest or the most intelligent
who will survive but those who can best manage
change."

— *undetermined*

# Other books by Jacqui Murray

## *Dawn of Humanity* trilogy
*Born in a Treacherous Time*
*Laws of Nature (coming Winter 2021)*
*In the Shadow of Giants (coming Winter 2022)*

## *Crossroads* trilogy
*Survival of the Fittest (Book 1)*
*The Quest for Home (Book 2)*
*Against All Odds (coming)*

## Sequel to *Crossroads*
*Coming 2023*

## Cro-Magnon trilogy

## *Rowe-Delamagente* Series
*To Hunt a Sub*
*Twenty-four Days*
*Book 3 (coming 2026)*

## Non-fiction
*Building a Midshipman: How to Crack the USNA Application*

## Education
*Over 100 non-fiction resources integrating technology into education available*
*from Structured Learning LLC*

# Praise for Jacqui Murray

Born in a Treacherous Time, *from the* Man vs. Nature *saga*

*"Murray's lean prose is steeped in the characters' brutal worldview, which lends a delightful otherness to the narration ...The book's plot is similar in key ways to other works in the genre, particularly Jean M. Auel's The* Clan of the Cave Bear. *However, Murray weaves a taut, compelling narrative, building her story on timeless human concerns of survival, acceptance, and fear of the unknown. Even if readers have a general sense of where the plot is going, they'll still find the specific twists and revelations to be highly entertaining throughout. A well-executed tale of early man." —Kirkus Reviews*

\*\*\*

*Move over Jean Auel (*The Clan of the Cave Bear*) for Jacqui Murray. I went to bed right after dinner last night because I had to finish this book and would have stayed up all night to do it. What a fabulous read. – Amazon reader*

\*\*\*

*What a treat to read a fiction work that goes so far back into prehistory. I enjoy reading prehistoric fiction in general, but this is a rare gem. The author successfully combines facts with imagination to create a believable story about our ancient ancestors. We are given a peek into a distant mirror of a people who reflect our own hopes, emotions and fears. – Amazon reader*

\*\*\*

Born in a Treacherous Time ... *follows the life of one, early hominid called Lucy. She is intelligent and curious, a healer amongst her people, but neither she nor they "talk" the way we do. They do verbalize, but communication is a fluid blend of sounds, body language and signing. Although Jacqui Murray has gone to extraordinary lengths to re-create authentic hominids of the era, it is the personality and courage of Lucy that I remember most. She is a remarkable "heroine" and a distant ancestor I'm proud to claim. – Amazon reader*

\*\*\*

Born in a Treacherous Time *is a brilliantly researched book with an interesting and realistic storyline. I have read all of Jean Auel's books and enjoyed them but I found the first book,* The Clan of the

Cave Bear, *to be the best by far. Why you may ask? The answer to that question is because it was realistic. I appreciate that in a historical book of this nature. I loved this about* Born in a Treacherous Time. *The story line and interaction of the various group members with each other rang true to me. Jacqui Murray's depiction of the group and their suspicion of anyone who has any progressive and different characteristics or qualities makes perfect sense. This type of attitude still prevails in many small towns and villages today. – Amazon reader*

*\*\*\**

*I've never read prehistoric fiction and wasn't sure what to expect. … I was immediately pulled into Lucy's world, and though her goals and motivations are in sync with her time period of 1.8 million years ago, her desires are those of humankind today: shelter, food, protecting our children and loved ones, contentment. It's because of these basic desires that we relate to Lucy so easily and want to see her survive the harsh conditions of the time... That, combined with Murray's smooth prose and well-paced narrative, makes this book an enjoyable and original read. – Amazon reader*

*\*\*\**

*Thanks to Murray's book* Born in a Treacherous Time, *I view the world and the creatures within it (including humans) with new eyes. The main character, Lucy, is one of our foremothers, long long ago. Murray uses intense research and just as intense imagination to envision what it was like during prehistoric times, when beings on two feet needed to survive a harsh yet hauntingly beautiful world. Murray's prose is fully detailed and imaginative as she shows the language development between beings, and the empathy and compassion that is there... I highly recommend this fascinating fictional look into prehistoric times. – Amazon reader*

Published by Structured Learning LLC
Laguna Hills, Ca 92653

*This is a work of fiction. Names, characters, places, and incidents, are the product of the author's imagination. Any resemblance to actual persons, living or dead, events, or locales, is entirely coincidental. The publisher does not have any control over and does not assume any responsibility for author or third-party websites or their content.*

Printed in the United States of America

ISBN 978-1-942101-35-2

# Table of Contents

## Part Three: China and Java

## Part Four: Middle East

# Characters

## Xhosa's People

*Ant*
*Asili*
*Bone*
*Cloud*
*Ngili*
*Nightshade*
*Shadow*
*Siri*
*Snake*
*Stone*
*Xhosa*

## Rainbow's Splinter Group

*Bird*
*Hecate*
*Mbasa*
*Rainbow*
*Starlight*
*Tor*

## Pan-do's People

*Lyta*
*Pan-do*
*Sa-mo-ke*
*Wa-co*

## Hawk's People

*Clear River*
*Dust*
*Hawk*
*Honey*
*Talon*
*Water Buffalo*

## Big Heads

*Thunder*
*Wind*

# Author's Non-fiction Introduction

*Homo erectus,* the star of *Crossroads,* is a highly-intelligent prehistoric hunter-gatherer who outlasted every other species of man and spread throughout the Old World of Europe and Asia. He possessed a sophisticated ability to reshape stones into intelligent tools, cross waterways, solve new problems, and make complicated plans. He was smart enough to face-off with dangerous situations and adventurous enough to want to try.

This stalwart predecessor to whom we are today survived in a myriad of environments, ate almost any food, made primitive spears to hunt, and used fire (or not, depending upon the expert you talk to—some of mine do because of their cold habitats). Their communication was robust and sophisticated but rarely verbal. Instead, they shared ideas, thoughts, directions, and more with a complicated collection of body movements, facial expressions, sounds, and hand gestures. This sort of "body language" even today is responsible for about half of communication. In this story, I refer to it as "motioned" but it's synonymous with the dialog tag, "said".

*Homo erectus* individuals were more comfortable on the ground, on two legs, than in trees and adept at imagining what they couldn't see. Their vast differences from earlier *Homo* species continues to fascinate paleoanthropologists. For example, their skulls are the thickest of any human species. They left a homeland they dominated and traveled to the far corners of Eurasia. They were a violent people, well equipped to survive a treacherous world and eager to do so. While the first iteration of man, *Homo habilis,* was timid and shy, you'd never accuse their successor, *Homo erectus,* of that.

To honor their dispersion to all corners of Eurasia, the trilogy *Crossroads* follows five tribes who eventually come together in the Levant 850,000 years ago. Xhosa and her

People are from East Africa, Pan-do from South Africa, Hawk from Gesher Benot Ya'aqov in Northern Israel, Seeker from Indonesia, and Zvi from China. They all flee their homelands for various historically accurate reasons, some because man's next iteration, *Homo sapiens*, is determined to eradicate them. When thrown together by circumstances, they put aside differences, trade knowledge of skills and techniques, and are willing to compromise to achieve the greater goal of finding a new home.

**Survival of the Fittest** is Book 1 in the *Crossroads* trilogy and covers how they come together. Book 2 follows their journey West when the combined group must flee what they had hoped would be a new home. Book 3 shares their new life in what we now know of as Gran Dolina, Spain.

The references to Lucy in Xhosa's dreams are from **Born in a Treacherous Time**, where Lucy and her small *Homo habilis* group are forced to leave their home to escape an invading tribe of *Homo erectus*. When Xhosa is threatened by an unbeatable enemy, Lucy helps her find a path to the future.

Both the *Crossroads* and the *Dawn of Humanity* trilogies explore early man's struggle to become who we are today. Together, they are part of the *Man vs. Nature* saga which chronicles how the family of man survives from inception to present day. The characters all share the particularly human drive to survive despite extreme adversity, well-equipped predators, and a violent natural environment that threw everything possible at them.

Here are questions I often get from readers about the *Crossroads* trilogy:

- **Why are some animals capitalized and others not?**
  *Not knowing any different, early man feels they are equals to animals— maybe inferior but definitely not superior. They believe animals are like themselves—able to plan, make tools, and evaluate circumstances—and respect them.*

- *Why are Others and Uprights capitalized?*
  *Others when capitalized refer to* Homo erectus *not in one of the five groups.* Uprights *refers to all species in the genus* Homo *who walk upright on two legs. As with animals, this indicates Xhosa's respect for them.*

- *I don't understand the use of the term "People" (or why it's capitalized)*
  *'People' in this trilogy is the name applied to a group organized around a leader—like Xhosa's People and the Hawk People. It identifies the community of shared common experiences, culture, and beliefs. It would be akin to the term "Americans" or "French" for people who live in those geopolitical territories. Since there were no nations 850,000 years ago, they are simply the People.*

- *Their speech is too sophisticated*
  *These early humans were highly intelligent for their day and possessed rich but rarely verbal communication skills. Most paleoanthropologists believe that the "speaking" part of their brain wasn't evolved enough for speech but there's another reason: Talking is noisy as well as unnatural in nature and attracts attention. For these early humans, who were far from the alpha in the food chain, being noticed wasn't good.*

- *What is "strong" and "weak" side*
  *Paleoscientists guess that even 850,000 ago, early man had a preference for right-handedness. That would make their right hand stronger than the left (though they didn't identify "right" and "left") so they would see their right hand as the "strong side" and left as the "weak side".*

- *Why are these characters so violent?*
  *That answer is simple: If humans weren't violent 850,000 years ago, we wouldn't have survived. We weren't the apex predator at that time. We had thin skin, short claws, and teeth that were useless for defense. What we did have that those who would prey on us didn't was a thoughtful brain (well, the beginnings of one).*

- *I am not reading these books in order. Does it*

**matter?**

Survival of the Fittest *is the first in the* Crossroads *trilogy, which is the second trilogy in the* Man vs. Nature *saga. Each trilogy is a stand-alone story; each book also is a standalone story. They can be read out of order, but some find the reading experience enhanced if the three books in each trilogy are read consecutively.*

- **What is a "hand of Sun's travel"?**

  This is the amount of time it takes Sun to travel the distance of a hand held up to the sky. It's about fifteen minutes for a finger or an hour for a hand (four fingers). This is one of the ways earliest People measured the passage of time.

# Introduction

No one told the heroes in *Survival of the Fittest*—Xhosa, Pan-do, Hawk, Wind, Rainbow, Zvi, Seeker, and Spirit—that they were the leading edge of man's dispersion across Eurasia. Their willingness to journey into the unknown marked man's flexibility, adaptability, fungibility, and wanderlust—hallmarks of an evolutionary fitness that would challenge Nature for control of the world.

As you read this book, keep in mind that these characters are 850,000 years old. They are pre-everything civilized. Their rudimentary culture fits some definitions of this complicated word because they share behaviors and interactions, cognitive constructs and understanding, but it doesn't fit other more thorough attributes. Xhosa and those like her don't wear clothes, don't marry, and haven't discovered religion, art, or music. They don't bury their dead—why would they? Other animals don't. They have no social norms, traditions, societal rules, or judgmental attitudes toward others. They wear no tattoos, jewelry, or adornments. They don't count past two. They prefer descriptions to proper nouns.

Everything in their lives revolves around two simple goals: survival and procreation. To accomplish these, they have become some of the smartest, cleverest animals in the kingdom. How else could they survive a violent world where an angry, disruptive creature like Nature ruled?

# PART ONE: EAST AFRICA
*850,000 years ago*

# Chapter 1

Her foot throbbed. Blood dripped from a deep gash in her leg. At some point, Xhosa had scraped her palms raw while sliding across gravel but didn't remember when, nor did it matter. Arms pumping, heart thundering, she flew forward. When her breath went from pants to wheezing gasps, she lunged to a stop, hands pressed against her damp legs, waiting for her chest to stop heaving. She should rest but that was nothing but a passing thought, discarded as quickly as it arrived. Her mission was greater than exhaustion or pain or personal comfort.

She started again, sprinting as though chased, aching fingers wrapped around her spear. The bellows of the imaginary enemy—Big Heads this time—filled the air like an acrid stench. She flung her spear over her shoulder, aiming from memory. A *thunk* and it hit the tree, a stand-in for the enemy. With a growl, she pivoted to defend her People.

Which would never happen. Females weren't warriors.

Feet spread, mouth set in a tight line, she launched her last spear, skewering an imaginary assailant, and was off again, feet light, her abundance of ebony hair streaming behind her like smoke. A scorpion crunched beneath her hardened foot. Something moved in the corner of her vision and she hurled a throwing stone, smiling as a hare toppled over. Nightshade called her reactions those of Leopard.

But that didn't matter. Females didn't become hunters either.

With a lurch, she gulped in the parched air. The lush green grass had long since given way to brittle stalks and desiccated scrub. Sun's heat drove everything alive underground, underwater, or over the horizon. The males caught her attention across the field, each with a spear and warclub. Today's hunt would be the last until the rain—and the herds—returned.

"Why haven't they left?"

She kicked a rock and winced as pain shot through her foot. Head down, eyes shut against the memories. Even after all this time, the chilling screams still rang in her ears...

The People's warriors had been away hunting when the assault occurred. Xhosa's mother pushed her young daughter into a reed bed and stormed toward the invaders but too late to save the life of her young son. The killer, an Other, laughed at the enraged female armed only with a cutter. When she sliced his cheek open, the gash so deep his black teeth showed, his laughter became fury. He swung his club with such force her mother crumpled instantly, her head a shattered melon.

From the safety of the pond, Xhosa memorized the killer—nose hooked awkwardly from some earlier injury, eyes dark pools of cruelty. It was then, at least in spirit, she became a warrior. Nothing like this must ever happen again.

When her father, the People's Leader, arrived that night with his warriors, he was greeted by the devastating scene of blood-soaked ground covered by mangled bodies, already chewed by scavengers. A dry-eyed Xhosa told him how marauders had massacred every subadult, female, and child they could find, including her father's pairmate. Xhosa communicated this with the usual grunts, guttural sounds, hand signals, facial expressions, hisses, and chirps. The only vocalizations were call signs to identify the group members.

"If I knew how to fight, Father, Mother would be alive." Her voice held no anger, just determination.

The tribe she described had arrived a Moon ago, drawn by the area's rich fruit trees, large ponds, lush grazing, and bluffs with a view as far as could be traveled in a day. No other area offered such a wealth of resources. The People's scouts had seen these Others but allowed them to forage, not knowing their goal was to destroy the People.

Her father's body raged but his hands, when they moved, were calm. "We will avenge our losses, daughter."

The next morning, Xhosa's father ordered the hunters to stay behind, protect the People. He and the warriors snuck into the enemy camp before Sun awoke and slaughtered the females and children before anyone could launch a defense. The males were pinned to the ground with stakes driven through their thighs and hands. The People cut deep wounds into their bodies and left, the blood scent calling all scavengers.

When Xhosa asked if the one with the slashed cheek had died, her father motioned, "He escaped, alone. He will not survive."

Word spread of the savagery and no one ever again attacked the People, not their camp, their warriors, or their hunters.

While peace prevailed, Xhosa grew into a powerful but odd-looking female. Her hair was too shiny, hips too round, waist too narrow beneath breasts bigger than necessary to feed babies. Her legs were slender rather than sturdy and so long, they made her taller than every male. The fact that she could outrun even the hunters while heaving her spear and hitting whatever she aimed for didn't matter. Females weren't required to run that fast. Nightshade, though, didn't care about any of that. He claimed they would pairmate, as her father wished, when he became the People's Leader.

Until then, all of her time was spent practicing the warrior skills no one would allow her to use.

One day, she confronted her father. "I can wield a warclub one-handed and throw a spear hard enough to kill. If I were male, you would make me a warrior."

He smiled. "You are like a son to me, Daughter. I see your confidence and boldness. If I don't teach you, I fear I will lose you."

He looked away, the smile long gone from his lips. "Either you or Nightshade must lead when I can't."

Under her father's tutelage, she and Nightshade learned the nuances of sparring, battling, chasing, defending, and assaulting with the shared goal that never would the People succumb to an enemy. Every one of Xhosa's spear throws destroyed the one who killed her mother. Every swing of her warclub smashed his head as he had her mother's. Never again would she stand by, impotent, while her world collapsed. She perfected the skills of knapping cutters and sharpening spears, and became expert at finding animal trace in bent twigs, crushed grass, and by listening to their subtle calls. She could walk without leaving tracks and match Nature's sounds well enough to be invisible.

A Moon ago, as Xhosa practiced her scouting, she came upon a lone warrior kneeling by a waterhole. His back was to her, skeletal and gaunt, his warclub chipped, but menace oozed from him like stench from dung. She melted into the redolent sedge grasses, feet sinking into the squishy mud, and observed.

His head hair was sprinkled with gray. A hooked nose canted precariously, poorly healed from a fracas he won but his nose lost. His curled lips revealed cracked and missing teeth. A cut on his upper arm festered with pus and maggots. Fever dimpled his forehead with sweat. He crouched to drink but no amount of water would appease that thirst.

What gave him away was the wide ragged scar left from the slash of her mother's cutter.

Xhosa trembled with rage, fearing he would see the reeds shake, biting her lip until it bled to stop from howling. It hardly seemed fair to slay a dying male but fairness was not part of her plan today.

Only revenge.

A check of her surroundings indicated he traveled alone. Not that it mattered. If she must trade her life for his, so be it.

But she didn't intend to die.

The exhausted warrior splashed muddy water on his grimy head, hands slow, shoulders round with fatigue, oblivious to his impending death. After a quiet breath, she stepped from the sedge, spear in one hand and a large rock in the other. Exposed, arms ready but hanging, she approached. If he turned, he would see her. She tested for dry twigs and brittle grass before committing each foot. It surprised her he ignored the silence of the insects. His wounds must distract him. By the time hair raised on his neck, it was too late. He pivoted as she swung, powered by fury over her mother's death, her father's agony, and her own loss. Her warclub smashed into his temple with a soggy thud. Recognition flared moments before life left.

"You die too quickly!" she screamed and hit him over and over, collapsing his skull and spewing gore over her body. "I wanted you to suffer as I did!"

Her body was numb as she kicked him into the pond, feeling not joy for his death, relief that her mother was avenged, or upset at the execution of an unarmed Other. She cleaned the gore from her warclub and left. No one would know she had been blooded but the truth filled her with power.

She was now a warrior.

When she returned to homebase, Nightshade waited. Something flashed through his eyes as though for the first time, he saw her as a warrior. His chiseled face, outlined by dense blue-black hair, lit up. The corners of his full lips twitched under the broad flat nose. The finger-thick white scar emblazoned against his smooth forehead, a symbol of his courage surviving Sabertooth's claws, pulsed. Female eyes watched him, wishing he would look at them as he did Xhosa but he barely noticed.

The next day, odd Others with long legs, skinny chests, and oversized heads arrived. The People's scouts confronted them but they simply watched the scouts, spears down, and then trotted away, backs to the scouts. That night, for the first time, Xhosa's father taught her and Nightshade the lessons of leading.

"Managing the lives of the People is more than winning battles. You must match individual skills to the People's requirements be it as a warrior, hunter, scout, forager, child minder, Primary Female, or another. All can do all jobs but one best suits each. The Leader must decide," her father motioned.

As they finished, she asked the question she'd been thinking about all night. "Father, where do they come from?"

"They are called Big Heads," which didn't answer Xhosa's question.

Nightshade motioned, "Do they want to trade females? Or children?"

Her father stared into the distance as though lost in some memory. His teeth ground together and his hands shook until he clamped them together.

He finally took a breath and motioned, "No, they don't want mates. They want conflict." He tilted his head forward. "Soon, we will be forced to stop them."

Nightshade clenched his spear and his eyes glittered at the prospect of battle. It had been a long time since the People fought.

But the Big Heads vanished. Many of the People were relieved but Xhosa couldn't shake the feeling that danger lurked only a long spear throw away. She found herself staring at the same spot her father had, thoughts blank, senses burning. At times, there was a movement or the glint of Sun off eyes, but mostly there was only the unnerving feeling of being watched. Each day felt one day closer to when the People's time would end.

"When it does, I will confess to killing the Other. Anyone blooded must be allowed to be a warrior."

She shook her head, dismissing these memories, focusing on her next throw. The spear rose as though lifted by wings, dipped, and then lodged deep in the ground, shaft shivering from the impact.

Her nostrils flared, imagining the tangy scent of fresh blood as she raced down the field to retrieve it, well beyond her previous throw.

"Not even Nightshade throws this far," she muttered to herself, slapping the biting insects that dared light on her work-hardened body and glaring at the males who wandered aimlessly across the field.

"Why haven't they left?"

Another curious glance confirmed that the group looked too small. She inhaled deeply and evaluated the scents.

"Someone is missing."

Why hadn't her father asked her to fill in?

Irritation seared her chest, clouding her thoughts. A vicious yank freed the spear and she took off at a sprint, wind whooshing through her cascade of hair. Without changing her pace, she threw, arm pointing after the spear, eyes seeing only its flight.

Feet pounded toward her. "Xhosa!" her father's voice. "I've been calling you."

She lifted her head, chest heaving, lost in her hunt.

He motioned, "Come!"

What was he saying? "Come where?"

"Someone is ill."

It all snapped into place. "I'm ready."

She knotted her hair with a tendon and trotted toward Nightshade, newly the People's Lead Warrior. One deep breath and she found the scent of every male who had earned the right to be called hunter except Stone. He must be the one sick.

Nightshade nodded to her, animated as always before a hunt, and motioned. "Stay close to me."

Nightshade's approval meant no one questioned her part—as a female—in this hunt.

A deep breath stifled her grin. "I will not disappoint you, Nightshade."

And she wouldn't. Along with her superior spear skills and unbeatable speed, her eyes possessed a rare feature called farsight. Early in their training, Nightshade had pointed to what he saw as a smudge on the horizon. She not only told him it was a herd of gazelle but identified one that limped which they then killed. From then on, he taught her hunting strategies while she found the prey.

Xhosa and Nightshade led the hunters for a hand of Sun's travel overhead and then Nightshade motioned the group to wait while he and Xhosa crested a hill. From the top, they could see a brown cloud stretching across the horizon.

Xhosa motioned, "This is a herd but there are no antlers and the animals are too small for Mammoth." A breath later, she added, "It's Hipparion."

Nightshade squinted, shrugged, and set off at a moderate lope. If she was wrong, the hunting party would waste the day but he knew she wasn't wrong. Her father joined him in the lead with Xhosa and the rest of the males following. Nightshade chose an established trail across the grasslands, up sage-covered hillocks, into depressions that would trip those who didn't pay attention, and past trees marked by rutting. At the end of the day, they camped downwind of the fragrant scent of meat and subtle Hipparion voices.

Sun fell asleep. Moon arrived and left, and finally, Sun awoke. Everyone slathered themselves with Hipparion dung and then warily flanked the herd. When they were close, animals on the edge picked up their scent and whinnied in fear, pushing and shoving to the center of the pack, knowing that those on the outside would be the first to die.

Xhosa pointed to the edge of the field but Nightshade had already seen Leopard, lying atop a termite mound, paws dripping over the sides, interested in them only to the extent they meant food. Xhosa imagined the People as Leopard would see them.

"We look benign, Leopard, with our flimsy claws, flat teeth, and thin hide, but we can kill from a distance, work together, and we never give up a chase that can be won. You, Leopard, can only kill when you are close enough to touch your prey—and you tire quickly.

"Who hunts better?"

Leopard answered by closing its eyes, rolling over, and purring.

The battle began and ended quickly, the hunters killing only what they could carry. They sliced the bodies into portable pieces and slept curled around each other in a copse of trees. When Sun awoke, they left for home, shoulders bowed under the meat's weight, leaving the guts for scavengers. Xhosa hefted the carcass of a young Wild Beast to her shoulders. The animal had crossed her path as she chased a Hipparion mare and her colt. One swing of her warclub, the Wild Beast squealed and died. It provided more meat than the colt and would be a welcome addition to the People's food supply.

Sun was almost directly overhead when her father diverted to a waterhole. The weary but happy group dropped the meat and joined a scarred black rhino, a family of mammoth, and a group of pigs to drink. Xhosa untied the sinews that held the Wild Beast to her shoulders and splashed awkwardly through waist-high cattails and dense bunchgrass. Broad-winged white-bellied birds screeched as they swooped in search of food and a cacophony of insects chirruped their displeasure at her intrusion. A stone's throw away, a hippo played, heaving its great bulk out of the water, mouth gaping, snorting and grunting, before sinking beneath the surface. Within moments, the air exploded with engaging dung smells.

Her feet burrowed into the silt as she pulled the tendon from her hair allowing it to tumble down, covering her back, too thick to allow any cooling breeze to penetrate but like Cat's pelt, it kept insects from biting and warmed her in the rainy times.

Nightshade stood close by, legs apart, weight over the balls of his feet. One hand held his spear, the other his warclub. Even relaxing, he scanned the surroundings. When his gaze landed on her, there was hunger in his eyes.

Her breath caught. That was his look for females before mating but never for her. She flushed and splashed water on her head, enjoying the cool bite on her fevered skin, gaze drifting lazily across the pond. Sun warm on her shoulders, breeze soft against her body, scent of the People's meat behind her, the whisper of some animal moving in the cattails—she wanted to burst with the joy of life.

Like that, everything changed.

"Big Heads," she muttered and ticked them off on both hands. "Too many—more than our entire group."

Her father had predicted trouble.

She studied the Big Heads, their swollen top-heavy skulls, squashed faces, brow ridges rounded over beady eyes, knobby growths under small mouths for no purpose she could imagine. Their chests were small, legs long, and bodies lacked the brawn that burst from every one of the People's warriors, and their spears, unlike the People's, were tipped with a rough-hewn stone about the size of a leaf.

She strode to her father, head throbbing, throat rough and dry. He acknowledged her presence by moving a hand below his waist, palm down, fingers splayed, but his gaze remained fixed on the strangers, thoughts unreadable.

After a breath, she motioned, also low to her body, "Why do they constantly grunt, chirp, growl, and yip?" No animal this noisy could survive.

Her father said nothing, calmly facing the strangers he considered enemies, arms stiff, spear down but body alert in a way he hadn't been a moment before. Xhosa wondered if this was what her instincts had been screaming.

Slowly, the Big Heads confronted her father's stalwart figure. One pushed his way through the group, muscles hard, piercing eyes filled with hate. Someone else shouted the call sign Thunder, making the male who must be Thunder snap a call sign—Wind—as though he'd eaten rotten meat.

"Those two must be the leaders," her father motioned. "And brothers."

Both were the same height with thick straight hair that hung past their shoulders. Thunder had a scar that cut his face, making him look resolute and intolerant. For the other, face smooth and young, the word "hopeful" popped into Xhosa's thoughts. Why, Xhosa had no idea, but something told her Hopeful Wind wouldn't win this battle.

As if to prove her right, the Big Heads behind Thunder flexed their arms, waved their spears, and bounced to a rhythmic chant. Someone beckoned Wind but he walked away, head down.

A purr made Xhosa jerk. A hungry Leopard stalked the People's meat. Xhosa started toward it, to protect it, when a scream punctuated the air.

Xhosa snapped toward the sound. One of the People's warriors clawed at a spear lodged in his chest, blood seeping between his fingers.

"They threw that all the way across the pond—Father, how can they do that?" No one was that strong.

"Run!" Her father bellowed.

Over her shoulder, Xhosa heard the pounding of retreating feet but she never considered it, not with the mass of bawling Big Head warriors plunging into the shallow pond, spears thrust forward, rage painting their faces.

"Why do they attack, Father? What did we do?"

He shoved her away. "Go! Get our People to safety! I will slow them!"

"No," she answered softly. "We stay together! *We*, Father. I stand with you!"

His eyes, always soft and welcoming, held hers for a moment as though to object but instead, offered the faintest of smiles and then confronted the onslaught.

Xhosa broadened her stance, picked the closest Big Head, and launched her spear. It flew true with such power it penetrated the male's throat and into the next warrior. Both fell, dead before they hit the water. When a Big Head spear landed at her feet, she seized it, warclub in her other hand, throwing stones in her neck sack.

"I am blooded!" she screamed. "I do not flee in fear!"

Her scalp tingled and her eyesight grew vivid as everything about her grew stronger, harder, and faster. One enemy after another fell to the skill of Xhosa and her father. Her chest swelled with pride. No one could beat them. These creatures would soon withdraw as did all the People's enemies.

She buried a spear in a young warrior's thigh. He screamed, tears streaming down his cheeks.

"You were never stabbed?" With a snort, she yanked the weapon from his leg, eliciting another anguished howl. He was not much older than she. Maybe he too fought his first battle.

She threw the bloody spear at another Big Head who collapsed, blood bubbling from his mouth. Out of spears, she hurled stones from her neck sack, dropping one warrior after another, her barrage so fast no one could duck.

But there were too many. One moment, her father brandished his deadly weapons. The next, the Big Head Thunder appeared, obsidian eyes blazing, white scar pulsing. He caught Xhosa's eye and sneered as if to say, *Watch what I do to your Leader.*

A bellow came from the Big Head Wind, "Thunder! Stop!"

But Thunder jeered. "You are weak, Wind!" And he drove the spear's stone tip into her father's chest, twisting it as he did.

Xhosa's hands flew to her mouth as fury burned through her. Her father, the one who believed in her above all others, pled, *Go.* With the spear thrusting grotesquely from his body, he slammed his warclub into another Big Head who made the mistake of considering her father a walking dead. A loud crack told Xhosa the warrior's chest had caved in. Xhosa started toward him but Nightshade grabbed her.

"You can't help him. We must get the People to safety!"

Body shaking with rage, she shook loose and squared off to Thunder. "I will destroy you! As I did the one who killed my mother!" She gripped her warclub, head high, body blazing with fury, never wavering.

His eyes widened in surprise. He hadn't known.

Her father hurled his last spear and impaled a charging Big Head as another clubbed him. He legs collapsed but he kicked ferociously, tripping one and another before they overwhelmed him, pummeling him with clubs until he no longer moved.

Nightshade forced her away. "We leave our meat. They will let us go," or scavengers would take the food.

To her horror, she chose life over her father and doing so, abandoned her belief in fairness. Her father saw the Big Heads first and let them be. Xhosa would never make that mistake.

# Chapter 2

A blinding flash and a boom overwhelmed every other sound as Xhosa fled, blotting out the pounding feet, the screams, and the anguished cries of the injured. Within moments, a surprise storm swept over the land like a giant waterfall.

As Nightshade predicted, the enemy chose meat over the sure destruction of a dispirited People with no defense except warclubs and throwing stones. Without their Leader, all turned to the Lead Warrior. He stepped up without hesitation, driving the group at a grueling pace despite the storm until they could continue no longer. Then, all except Nightshade curled against a cliff, huddled together for warmth, and slept.

Xhosa stayed with Nightshade knowing her farsight was more important than ever. She dug her fingernails into her arm, letting the pain drown memories of her father, the evil Thunder, and the mystery of his brother Wind whose hope—if that's what it was—surely became a casualty of the battle.

As she watched, shivering, one thing was clear. Nothing would ever be the same.

The sky growled like Sabertooth, its voice bouncing off the hardscrabble land as though agreeing with her.

The next day, the discouraged hunters left as Sun awoke, hurrying along their backtrail, straggling toward the relative safety of homebase. When they crossed onto their land, Nightshade left warriors at the boundary with orders to kill anyone who tried to cross.

Scouts watching from the People's tall bluffs spread the word that the hunting party returned without meat. When Nightshade led the bedraggled group into the homebase clearing, every groupmember froze in shock, knowing this meant their Leader was dead.

When a Leader died or simply became too old, the designation passed to his son. Lacking one, it went to the most capable warrior as determined by the Primary Female. If several males qualified, a challenge would follow. The Primary Female held authority over all families, as the Lead Warrior did over males. Born before Xhosa's father, her wisdom and experience imbued daily decisions and discussions.

Every warrior, hunter, and female slept that night expecting Nightshade would be the next Leader.

With Sun a hand above the horizon, the People gathered with the Primary Female. She spoke with a mixture of body movements, gestures, and vocalizations, sharing the story of the People.

When finished, she asked a simple question. "Who leads our People?" And squatted, waiting. Sadness drew her features down. Clearly, she never thought it would be her duty to preside over the choice of a new Leader.

Two older males rose, both strong warriors with much loyalty among their peers, but when Nightshade stood, they dropped and slapped the ground to signify approval. Nightshade was young but admired as a masterful warrior, a successful hunter, and the favorite of their dead Leader.

"I am ready. I won't fail the People," Nightshade motioned.

The Primary Female allowed a heavy sigh. "Does anyone challenge this warrior?"

Her hands were neutral, giving nothing away about her feelings. When Xhosa rose, like mist from wet hot-season grass, everyone snickered except the Primary Female. A wisp of a smile touched her lips.

"I too am prepared. Nightshade, I challenge you."

Nightshade glared, though he kept his head down so no one would see. He should be the next Leader, after the death of Xhosa's father. Never did the powerful male consider that Xhosa would challenge him but he should have. Her mother's raw courage was legendary, as potent as a she-cat defending her cubs, as vicious as any warrior protecting the People.

The only time he'd ever seen Xhosa cry was at her mother's death.

That child was no more. The adult Xhosa bristled with the strength of her mother and skills of her father.

Nightshade grew up in awe of Xhosa's commitment never to let what happened back then happen again. No other female—or male—had that passion. He became obsessed with her rebellious spirit and courage, her tenacity to learn warrior skills though few would help her. He wanted her as his Lead Warrior, fervent to harness her fearlessness for the People.

When he was Leader and she Lead Warrior, then they would pairmate.

That was his plan. He never thought he would be fighting her for leadership.

# Chapter 3

When neither Xhosa nor Nightshade deferred, the Primary Female rose.

"We solve this as we did when Xhosa's father became Leader." She placed stones in a pile in the center of the clearing. "There are this many challenges. The winner of each gets one. Who collects the most leads our People."

Grunts of approval filled the air. Of course, Nightshade would win. The warriors would get their pre-eminent Leader and the People would be secure.

"First, the cliff challenge."

Without pause, Primary Female shuffled to a towering precipice that edged the homebase. Her hair more white than black, she moved prudently, hunched over and leaning heavily on one of the warriors, a spear serving as a walking stick. This cliff was one of the steepest in the People's territory. Of those who tried to scale it, most fell to their death. The Primary hobbled past the only path to the top, one that was treacherous but doable, and stopped a long spear-throw and another and another farther away. There, she folded onto her haunches and closed her eyes.

Xhosa kept her face impassive but inside, she blanched. This spot was considered impossible to scale and since no one had ever tried, no handholds existed.

"Nightshade and Xhosa. Select a position no farther from here than a spear throw."

Xhosa strode to her strong side, Nightshade to his weak. He tipped his head, shoulders back, arms hanging loosely, with the relaxed assurance of one who knows he will prevail.

She snorted. Nightshade thought he would win this one because he could hang by his fingers longer than any of the People but so could Xhosa—and unlike Nightshade, experience taught her that strength wouldn't win this challenge. One day while exploring, Xhosa had discovered a family of Climbing Gazelles. They moved sure-footed and quick up a cliff steeper than the one before her, springing from one safe spot to another, clawing at the tiniest protrusions and leaning in. With leg strength and an astounding lack of fear, they completed impossible moves that should have ended in death.

From that day, Xhosa practiced being Climbing Gazelle. Many falls helped her master the technique she hoped would beat Nightshade.

The Primary scrutinized their selections and motioned, "They are equal."

The People stomped, marking the beginning of the challenge.

Nightshade jumped upward, quickly a full body-length and another ahead of Xhosa. He seemed to make decisions when he must, not before. Xhosa had a different approach. She stood still, ignoring Nightshade and the People's whispers, only her farsighted eyes moving to study the bluff. One by one, the protrusions and ledges that would enable her climb and the slippery areas that would cause trouble burned themselves into her thoughts and she built her plan.

By the time that was done, Nightshade had moved well ahead but his lead wouldn't last. Xhosa could see that the course he followed would disappear well before the bluff. If he didn't adjust soon, his only choice would be to reverse course and find another route.

Once started, her ascent went quickly as she grabbed handholds exactly where they'd appeared to be from the valley floor. Time and again, her arms and legs stretched to their full length, her body tight against the jagged cliff, while her toes gripped the thinnest of ledges and her fingers found almost invisible protrusions.

She paused for a breath as her eyes fixed on a seam in the rock an arm's length away. From below, its color had appeared faintly different which meant it was softer than its surroundings. With a determined prod, it crumbled so she sidled over and tunneled out ledges and then sprang up, one leap at a time, as Climbing Gazelle would. The seam disappeared at a narrow shelf, offering a welcome rest while reconstructing her next steps from the image drawn below.

"There you are," she greeted her next hold.

A precarious bounce allowed her to grab a ridge as narrow as a finger. She gripped tightly, leaned into the cliff, regained her balance, and again leaped, gripped, and stabilized, over and over. Her fingertips shredded and bled but it didn't even slow her.

By the time the People below shrank to the size of her thumb, fatigue caused her arms to spasm and her fingers to cramp. Just in time, there—exactly where it should be—appeared a shelf that should be wide enough to hold her entire body. She grabbed it, pulled up, arms trembling, and peeked over.

And almost lost her grip.

A massive black-and-orange snake examined her with its huge unblinking eye. She froze, body dangling by her fingertips, hoping he slept.

His tail shook.

A cutter was in her neck sack but could she reach it while dangling by one hand?

She'd talk to him first.

"Snake. I need this spot or I die. Go to your family. I don't want to hurt you."

It twisted toward her, menacing coils level with her face, tongue tasting the air. She transferred her weight to one hand, preparing to snatch the snake with the other and fling it away but that proved unnecessary. He must have decided this odd creature who smelled of dirt and sweat presented no peril so slithered away, leaving behind a musky cloying scent and a smooth flat rock for her to sit on.

After a long calming breath, Xhosa hooked her legs over the narrow shelf, rolled onto it, and leaned back against the cliff. Her muscles quivered and sweat poured from her body. It was time to rest.

Panting, she peered down at Nightshade. He had realized his mistake and adjusted his path but again, picked a dead end. Frustration made him scowl.

"There's a nice path not too far below," Xhosa muttered to herself while chewing a root from her neck sack. "But do it soon."

Xhosa felt the stirring of worry but shook it away. Her future would be defined by the choices made today. Those couldn't include helping her competition.

Rested, she gave a hard push with the balls of her feet and snagged a one-handed hold, but her foot slipped, wrenching her leg as it slammed against the cliff. Tears blurred her vision as she swung by one hand, flailing for a new hold, found it, and hung on until her heart slowed.

Bit by perilous bit, fingertips bleeding, she clawed her way up, holding onto tiny protrusions while searching for the next.

"I'm close," she huffed much later, as Sun fought a losing battle with ominous dark clouds. Both she and Nightshade must be off this cliff before rain made it too slippery.

A glance at Nightshade showed him on a good path upward but his hands glistened with sweat which meant he could slip. An arm's length away but out of his view was a patch of green.

"Nightshade! Around that rock—moss to dry your hands!"

He ignored her or couldn't hear.

She shrugged and returned to her climb. Close to her was a wide crack. She swung, grabbed, and tucked herself securely into its tunnel. When she looked up, she couldn't believe her luck.

"It goes all the way to the top." An intoxicating mix of ecstasy, fatigue, and relief filled her. "I made it."

By pushing her feet against one wall and her back against the other, Xhosa scuttled up to the lip and over the bluff only moments ahead of the rain. Eyes closed, her head tipped of its own accord and rain filled her mouth, drenched her hair, and cooled her neck. Red welts covered her arms and thighs from stinging nettles in the tunnel. Her knees throbbed from being slammed against the rocks. Her fingernails were broken and bleeding from scrabbling for purchase, but the climb was over.

When breathing no longer meant wheezing, she peeked over the edge and gasped.

Nightshade was stuck, trying to hang on until the rain ended.

"Nightshade!" His eyes canted up. "That crack—there—it will take you to the top!"

He took a moment to find it and then clambered over and up, finally crouching beside her. She handed him a piece of pain bark to chew and took one herself. Numbness seeped into her shredded skin, deep body wounds, and overstrained muscles. The gaping cut to her thigh, from something in the crevice—that would take more than bark.

"That's one for you," Nightshade motioned. "There are two more."

The next day, Xhosa's pile held one rock.

Primary Female motioned, "For the next challenge, each of you must kill a Wild Beast. Alone."

Xhosa blinked, her gaze on the Primary Female, ignoring every warrior and hunter sure this monster would end her challenge. For Wild Beast was a monster, its robust muscular body as tall as Nightshade with massive hooved feet, a head the size of Warthog, sweeping long horns, and a powerful tail that could fling a hunter to his death with one sweep. Predators underestimated this magnificent creature at their peril.

Despite this, the advantage was Xhosa's. While Nightshade often hunted in a group where males funneled prey to others who killed it, Xhosa was not allowed to join. At her father's insistence, she still hunted the great prey—Wild Beast, Oryx, and Buffalo—but alone.

"Many predators hunt without a partner or pack, Daughter. Be like cheetah stalking, like keen-eyed Eagle and vigilant wolf."

She became good at it.

Xhosa and Nightshade were delivered to the border of the People's territory. One headed to the strong side, the other the weak. Within a finger of Sun's travel, neither could see the other.

Xhosa speared a hare, slung it over her shoulder, and then tracked a noisy Wild Beast as it rooted in the brush, oblivious to the downwind intruder. She dropped the hare's still-warm body at the base of a tree that would be in Wild Beast's path, sliced its belly open to perfume the air with the pungency of death, rubbed leaves over her body to screen her scent, and scrambled up the tree. There, she waited, spear ready, for the Wild Beast to investigate the odor.

A hand of time passed before the monster plodded toward the tree. It was smaller than some, only as tall as Xhosa's hips and with a broken horn.

"You have survived battle, Wild Beast. You are a worthy opponent."

It sniffed the tantalizing smell but approached cautiously, browsing on grass and shoots in its path, distracted often by smells it eventually discarded as less interesting than the hare, not understanding Xhosa was in a hurry. It finally shuffled under her tree to lick the hare's innards. Xhosa cocked her spear but bumped into a branch which threw off her aim and she impaled only the ground. With a bellow, the Wild Beast fled and in doing so, stepped on her spear.

Xhosa dropped from the tree, angry and annoyed.

"I can't hunt without a spear."

By the time she felled a sapling whose trunk was taller than her head and as fat as her arm, smoothed off the nodes and bumps with tree sap, and sharpened the tip, her body shook with anger. Sun had already peaked and now moved toward the horizon. The rules of the challenge required spending nights with the People. Unless Nightshade tackled problems like hers, he was already finished.

Nothing to do but chase after the Wild Beast.

Its snort gave its position away. Xhosa hurried after the sound, staying downwind, but every time she zigged to get in front, the creature swerved away. Xhosa began to fling rocks, hoping it would become annoyed and attack but it didn't. If anything, it ran faster.

Xhosa growled and stabbed her spear into the ground but then froze, staring into the distance, now understanding its motives.

"It leads me from its calves."

Wild Beasts had few calves and were fiercely protective of them. What Xhosa should have done was target a male, not a female, but it was far too late in the day for that. The only recourse was to keep chasing this one.

Wild Beast, unlike antelope or gazelle, must drink every day so no surprise it veered toward a river. Xhosa advanced quietly through the dense sedge and cattails along the water's edge, staying within a spear throw of the animal, hoping to spear Wild Beast while it drank.

"If you give me another chance, Wild Beast, I won't miss."

When it stepped up to the water's edge, breathing deep and labored, mouth open to gulp a drink, Xhosa threw. It would have hit Wild Beast's throat but the monster caught her scent, snorted, and jerked. That sent her spear into its haunch, not a killing spot. With a bellow, it fled, galumphing awkwardly, spear bouncing wildly. Again, Xhosa was without a weapon and no time to make a new one.

"Time for a new plan," she panted, throat tight, desperate to kill this beast.

That's when a trick her father showed her popped into her brain.

Not far from here was a cliff, so shrouded by bushes that no animal would know it was there until it was too late. Xhosa often scaled this cliff using the vines that hung down. If Wild Beast would chase her to the edge, she could leap off the bluff and grab one of the vines while Wild Beast plunged to its death.

The plan was perfect except the vines weren't there. They were much further down the cliff. She blew out, frustrated, but brightened as another idea formed.

Since Wild Beast drank nothing at the last stream, it would make its way to the closest pond. Xhosa dropped another dead hare at the water's edge and submerged herself to wait. Soon, it would be dark. If this didn't work and Nightshade also failed, both would try again tomorrow.

Xhosa's arms and legs stiffened from the cold water, making it almost impossible to hold her spear much less throw it. This must end soon or Wild Beast wouldn't be the only prey.

Just before giving up, a family of Wild Beasts approached. The female caught the bait's scent and padded toward it, pausing often to sniff.

"Keep coming… a few more steps."

The female bent over the fragrant meat, snuffling, ears tweaking, something telling it this food should not be lying here, that the predator must be nearby, but hunger overcame fear. It dipped its head, jaw spread to snap up the morsel as Xhosa exploded up and forward. Her throwing stone hit the female behind the eye and it toppled over, bleeding and stunned while its family bolted. Xhosa bludgeoned it with her warclub until it breathed its last breath, grunted at its weight on her shoulder, and hurried toward homebase. When it got too heavy, she tied a vine around her chest, attached it to the carcass, and hauled it behind her.

Sun was nothing more than a glow on the horizon when homebase appeared. Nightshade helped her drag the carcass in and dropped it next to his, already partially eaten.

"I didn't expect you to complete two challenges, Xhosa, much less win one. I am impressed." This from the Primary Female with grudging nods from several males. "Now sleep. The next challenge will decide the winner."

Xhosa collapsed, eyes closing, her last image of Nightshade's pile with one stone in it.

# Chapter 4

Xhosa awoke as fatigued as when she went to sleep but dragged after a large group of warriors as they set out on the last and most treacherous challenge. The group jogged for a day and another, leaving the People's territory far behind. Xhosa memorized the landmarks that would guide her home, glancing back often to see their position in relation to the point of departure.

The morning of the third day of travel, Nightshade was led toward Sun's rising place and Xhosa the opposite. They traveled until Sun slept, taking no breaks to eat or drink. When Xhosa arose the next morning, she was alone in an unknown valley. Lush stalks of grass bent gently in the breeze. Slow-moving mammoth, tails flicking, grazed on the undulating stems. In the distance, Hipparion galloped. Eagles circled overhead, preying on rodents. Steep, rugged cliffs as treacherous as those from the first challenge, surrounded the area.

Her task was deceptively simple: Survive until Moon disappeared and then make it back to homebase before Nightshade did. The first to reappear would become the new Leader.

According to the rules, Xhosa brought only what a hunter would on a day trip. Everything else must be created from resources in this area. That included a handaxe, choppers to remove meat from bone, a spear, throwing stones, and a new neck sack because hers had split. The sack required a dead animal with an unchewed stomach.

The search for water took most of the morning, trotting over open savanna punctuated by scrubby ridges and dry washes which led finally to the damp edge of a stream. She drank her fill and then swamped herself, watching the steam rise from her overheated body.

Her stomach's growl interrupted the glorious cool feeling.

"I guess food is next."

She collected a handful of throwing stones from the stream, climbed a tree, and waited. It took a while but a family of pigs finally passed, headed for the water, trailed by a lone wolf, yellow eyes bright with hunger. He killed the largest piglet but fled when the female charged him, raking him with her horns. When the mother and her remaining babies left, Xhosa harvested the carcass's stomach for a new neck sack and ate her fill from the still-warm meat.

It was late, time to set up a camp. The cliffs that edged the savanna looked promising. Heading toward them, she collected vegetables, healing herbs, seeds, vines, and a cast-off antler to use for digging or as a spear.

The hair on her neck rose. Someone was watching her.

She melted into the grass, looking for moving leaves, listening for animal calls or the flap of ground-dwelling birds as they fled.

Nothing.

"It must be the strangeness of this new area."

With a shrug, she found a cave that looked perfect— small enough for warmth but not big enough to interest cats with families, wolves with packs, or wild dogs. The front was soft ground rather than hard cliff rock and the weeds grew around it with abandon, both perfect disguises for the trap she had in mind. Inside, the floor was swathed in scat, clumps of fur, chewed bones, and debris. Claw marks scored the walls from previous inhabitants. Spider's webs hung on the corners of the entry, sparkling in Sun's light. The interior reeked of wet, dung, musky hide, rotten vegetation, stale air, and body odor from another Upright.

None of that worried her. She dumped the pig carcass in the rear, saw no light from another entrance, and then collected rocks that would seal off the entry and protect her from the cold night air.

Again, her neck hairs tingled. Keeping her eyes down, her side vision searched but picked up no movement or shadows. Still, her senses screamed. Casually, she walked into the brush as though to relieve herself but instead, circled the area. The only prints were old and smudged, probably the Others that left their stench in the cave but nothing that would make her hackles rise.

With the last of the day's light, she sharpened the antler. Tomorrow would be spent digging a pit and finding out who else traveled this area.

When dusk deepened to full dark, she rolled boulders across the cave's opening and curled beside the entrance, antler in hand. A chill draft made her shiver but her thick hair warmed her. A wolf howled and a mammoth trumpeted. Bushes rustled as night prowlers crept from their lairs to investigate the new smell.

Only the strong survived alone at night. Such was the way of life.


He recognized this female Primitive, the one who had stood boldly with her Leader, fighting as skillfully as any warrior, fleeing only when another male dragged her away. She had called the dead Leader "father" and he called her Xhosa.

What brought her out here, alone?

Wind crouched on his haunches, watching her work. Her legs, longer than any other Primitive, made her his height. Her slender body curved in at the waist with prominent breasts like females of his group and decidedly unlike other Primitives he'd seen. Her ebony hair extended below her shoulders, glimmering like an iridescent waterfall. He needed to touch it, feel it in his hands, against his skin. He sniffed, wondering what scent it carried.

Something about this female made Wind want to be close to her.

Wind fought with his brother the day this female's Leader died. The Primitive unmistakably wanted peace. He saw Thunder's warriors first but did nothing more than watch. Thunder took that as a sign of weakness. After the Leader's death, as his tribe fled, Thunder had wanted to chase them but Wind convinced him they would risk losing the fresh meat.

Wind couldn't help but be impressed by this one called Xhosa's strength. Few females could roll that massive boulder over the mouth of the cave. Odd there was no fire. His people built them for warmth, cooking, and to scare away predators.

Finally, Wind left, wondering how long she would remain. Maybe he should make contact.

The next day, Xhosa excavated a pit in front of the cave, disguised it with branches, and sprinkled dry leaves at its edges. No one could get by without being heard. Defenses complete, she knapped cutters and choppers from the river rocks, and collected berries, pausing often to listen. Something other than the old Upright prints caused her senses to spark to every sound and smell.

As Sun began the downward path to its sleeping place, Xhosa washed the pig's stomach with silt and sand, and then rubbed it with salt to keep it from decaying. Next, she pierced small holes in the top and wove a tendon through that would circle her neck and allow the sack to rest between her breasts. By the time it was finished, Sun slept and the sky was dark.

The nights came and went, each with a smaller Moon as it lost pieces of its brightness. During the day, she scoured her surroundings for signs of Big Heads or Others. The impressions discovered the first day were useless, leading only to a rock bed, exactly where she would hide from prey. Just to be safe, she scrubbed her backtrail with dirt, dung, and water.

One night, on her usual tour of the area, fresh Big Head tracks crossed in front of her cave.

"He's probably passing by, nothing else," but the frown on her face, never absent since that first day, deepened and her stomach coiled into a tighter knot.

"I leave tomorrow. I need only survive one more night."

The next morning, she pushed aside the boulder and squatted to await Sun's glow. Sleep had been restless, her thoughts filled with worry, her senses pricking to every sound.

"One sliver of Sun above the horizon and I leave."

Out of the corner of her eye, in the dark recesses of the cave, something moved. She snatched her spear while pivoting and howled.

A Big Head, spear raised, eyed her.

Outside, from a distance, someone yelled her call sign. Why was Nightshade here?

The momentary distraction allowed the Big Head to score a searing cut to her shoulder. She yelped, heat scorching her body, which gave him time to drive another spear into her leg. The pain was nothing compared to the retching agony when he yanked the spear out.

"I'm coming, Xhosa!"

"Go towards Sun, Nightshade!" Hoping he would understand.

The Big Head leered at her, confused, rotting teeth stinking even from this distance.

"Xhosa is it? I've heard of you."

A high-pitched yelp and muted thump confused the Big Head for a breath and then he roared with laughter. A smile crept across her lips, so subtle the Big Head missed it.

"I guess help will not be arriving, *Xhosa*. You are mine!"

He circled her, jabbing and thrusting as he tested her proficiency when injured.

She confused him again by yelling, "Nightshade—raise your spear!" Then flew out of the cave, almost tripping when her wounded leg sent pain lancing down to her toes. The Big Head was so intent on catching her, he failed to notice what was under—or not under—his feet. With a snort, he leaped, trying to grab her arm but instead crashed through the tattered foliage that covered the pit. His startled cry ended with a squeal and a wet oomph.

Muted grunts and chirps came from the pit and then Nightshade's voice.

"I skewered him although if I hadn't, that antler you embedded in the bottom would have. Your warning was appreciated."

Her body shook with relief that Nightshade was safe and unharmed. "Why are you here?"

"This same Big Head crossed my area, headed your way. He looked ready for battle as though he knew exactly where you were. I should have known you need no help."

Xhosa panted. "I'll get a vine."

"I can get out. You go. With that leg and shoulder, I'll still beat you."

Nightshade, of course, must prove himself the worthiest to lead the People, which meant working alone. She limped away, slowed by the gash in her leg and wincing as heat burned deep into her shoulder. It took longer than it should have, trying to hide from anyone who had been hunting with this Big Head.

Xhosa washed the blood from her injuries and coated them with honey harvested from a nearby hive. Next, she slathered the wounds with mud layered with moss and wrapped everything with leaves.

She paused, ticking off the sounds, but found nothing worrisome so continued homeward. As Sun approached the horizon, it took everything she had to clamber up a tree to an abandoned nest. Her knee throbbed from groin to toes, her shoulder was stiff, her arm numb, and her leg threatened to blow up.

None of that kept her awake.

The next morning, a search for her backtrail revealed that time and rain had erased it.

"That doesn't matter. Fire Mountain never moves."

Keeping the massive landmark to her weak side, she staggered homeward, each day harder than the last. Her thoughts became blurred, her leg grew to twice its normal size and so stiff, it wouldn't bend. After a day, she simply dragged it behind her. When that no longer worked, crawling did, one armed because her wounded shoulder locked in one position. Her teeth chattered but the skin on her forehead was hot to the touch. She finally collapsed, thoughts so jumbled that moving forward became impossible.

Someone—friend or foe, it didn't matter—grabbed her arms and dragged her away, scraping her bare skin over the dry rough earth. When the ground smoothed, they stopped and someone applied moss and herbs to her wounds before darkness took over.

Consciousness was momentary before she sank back to darkness but one of those times, she smelled the sure scent of Nightshade, sleeping by her, before oblivion again took over. The next time, he was staring at her, worried, finger brushing her hair, and then again, sleep overcame her.

When her eyes popped open this time, something felt different. Her body ached, all over, but not with fatigue. Nightshade lay by her, eyes closed, skin pale.

She nudged him and his eyes burst open. Her spirits rose just from the sight of his familiar face, his assured expression, and the strength radiating from his body.

"How did you get out?"

Nightshade rubbed his eyes, still locked on her. "The Big Head's body hardened in death. I tilted it up against the wall of the pit and used it as steps."

A giggle bubbled out before she could bite it back. "No enemy can outsmart the People's new Leader. You deserved to win, Nightshade, and you wouldn't miss the rear entrance."

It took a moment for him to respond. "I await your direction, new Leader of the People. My warriors are at your disposal."

The next day, Xhosa got the first of what would become chronic burning head pains, one with no wound to treat, but one she wasn't entirely unprepared for. Another female warrior Xhosa respected as much as any had warned her.

Her name was Lucy.

# Chapter 5

Swallowing the bile that rose in her throat, Xhosa pushed to her feet. The fact that Nightshade had barely a scratch from the last challenge wasn't lost on her or the People. Today, she must show that their new Leader was strong and ready, despite her battered appearance. To that end, she would practice with the warriors. Even damaged, she expected to beat all of them in battle skills and endurance.

That would have to wait.

Nightshade joined her, cold gaze studying the far distance. "The scouts report no Big Heads during our absence but I must check. Will you join me?"

A glower was his answer and then she turned away, hiding a wave of nausea. Physical discomfort mattered nothing compared to the security of the People. The two spent the day exploring every corner of their land, paying special attention to spots where someone could hide, pausing only when she needed to rewrap her wounds. They found nothing unexpected.

The next day, despite sleeping little thanks to her aching shoulder and leg, Xhosa trained with Nightshade's warriors, ordering them to treat her as they would any warrior. In every drill—spear throwing, stones, running, and strategy—they fell to her prowess, including Nightshade's Second, Snake.

That done, she walked among the People, answering questions and helping where needed. Her goal was to measure their acceptance of a female as Leader. To her surprise, no one questioned her competence, toughness, or ability to lead. Her courage and mastery in the challenges garnered their full acceptance especially since Nightshade would remain Lead Warrior. Every warrior was blooded with scars, mended limbs, jagged knuckles, and memories of death, but none more than Nightshade. His reputation for ferocity first, questions later brought a clarity badly needed to counter the violence of the Big Heads. Under his leadership, warriors would not quit until the enemy died. Driving them from the People's land was no longer good enough.

What no one said but showed in the People's eyes was the expectation that Nightshade and Xhosa would rule as a team. Xhosa encouraged this, talking with Nightshade often and in full view of the People. Today, though, she led him to a secluded spot where their hand motions couldn't be seen.

"The Big Heads won," in the battle that ended her father's life, "yet they leave us alone. Why?"

Nightshade curled his upper lip. "They know you and I— we are as unbreakable as a cliff. Rather than fight a battle they can't win, they gather their forces to await the right moment. That will never arrive, not while I'm here."

Xhosa's stomach tightened. "How do you know this, that they are growing in size?"

"From scouts I send deep into Big Head territory."

She clenched her fists. "Nightshade. Their weapons are strong—"

"Our warriors are stronger, Xhosa. Never doubt that."

His hands spoke with a quiet confidence that left no room for fear. He pivoted to leave but she stopped him.

"Nightshade. Know I consider you a co-Leader in everything but name. You provide a counterbalance to me. You spot issues I miss. I welcome that."

He had never shown anger that she won the leadership. In discussions, he spoke his mind but deferred to her. He seemed satisfied to be her Lead Warrior but how could that be? His entire life had been preparing for leadership. Now, short of her death, it would never happen.

He cocked his head, face a mix of curiosity and insult, and left.

She observed him as he went about his duties but saw nothing that made her worry. He performed without complaint, without hesitation, and with a full sense of authority.

"There is nothing there."

# Chapter 6

Xhosa bent forward, panting from the torturous ascent. Between ragged breaths, she snuffled in the damp smell of Fire Mountain. A group of children charged across a clearing, stomping their feet and tossing their heads like Hipparion. Some plodded in perfect rhythm with those in front while others flawlessly replicated the pronking leap of Antelope with its arched spine and stiff legs. In this way, they learned to confuse prey on a hunt by walking and thinking like them.

She studied the People's territory with satisfaction. One side was protected by the Rift and the other by a waterhole. Beyond those, oversights like this one allowed scouts to see a day's travel toward the horizon, providing plenty of warning should enemies invade. It stretched from one range of hills to another, filled between with rich grassland edged by berry bushes, fruit trees, melon patches, and a variety of tubers, rhizomes, bulbs, roots, and corms. These fed the People well in the absence of meat. Nightshade's warriors and scouts patrolled constantly, marking the borders with urine and feces and allowing no one entry except to trade for females or children. This was the richest of all territories and must never be taken for granted.

Nightshade caught her eye and bobbed his hand level to the ground. She dropped without a thought and just in time. At the edge of the People's territory, Big Heads passed one of the many boulders that marked the People's border, moving as though this was their territory. No Others, only Big Heads, acted this way.

Since her father's death, Xhosa had relentlessly but subtly stalked this enemy, searching for their weak spots. They hunted fearlessly with no respect for boundaries. The stone-tipped spear wasn't their only unusual weapon. Often, she saw them use a fire stick to set the grassland ablaze and force a frightened herd over a cliff. Big Heads at the bottom would then harvest the meat, never sharing with others—something Coyote and Eagle always did.

"Xhosa."

Her call sign was quiet as Nightshade joined her, both hidden in the grass.

"Big Heads killed the Others that used to live there," and he pointed to where the enemy collected.

A cold chill ran down Xhosa's spine but Nightshade seemed unperturbed. In fact, respect for their power tinged his movements.

He continued, "Soon, we must clash or lose our territory. I will follow this group to see what danger they pose."

"I join you."

They waited as the Big Heads killed a handful of birds and chased down a pig. Finally, the group left, leaving an easy-to-follow trail of noise. After a hand and another of Sun's movement overhead, Xhosa heard a buzz like a hive of angry bees. She crested a hill and immediately ducked, biting her lip to keep from gasping.

"Big Heads—that buzz is their voices!"

During the day, the People vocalized to communicate call signs or warnings. Only at night, when well-protected by the bramble barrier, did they use voices, but not the constant uncontrolled barks, chirps, hoots, howls, and yips of these Big Heads.

The encampment abutted a hillside as would the People's but there the similarity ended. Their people covered the land in front of her. She opened and closed her hands too many times to track. For the People—it took only a hand of hands to tick off everyone.

A youngster caught her attention as he took food to an elder, her legs shriveled like desiccated twigs. Why feed anyone who could no longer work? The elder chattered a string of the odd Big Head noises, patted the child with a dry wrinkled hand, and he ran off, giggling.

Nightshade pointed to the warriors training rigorously with the long-throwing spears. To the tip of each, they'd affixed a stone, like a pointed chopper. "How do they attach that?"

He licked his lips and leaned forward, his agitation building the longer he watched. He didn't answer—or couldn't.

As Xhosa prepared to leave, a male touched a burning torch to a mound of twigs and dry weeds. Instantly, they burst into flames but no one fled. Instead, they gathered around the fire, hands out, smiling.

With that, the two slipped away, their footsteps obscured by the crackle of burning branches, both lost in their own silent thoughts but with the same inescapable conclusion: The Big Heads needed more room.

# Chapter 7

"We have to leave, Nightshade."

Xhosa hated that her motions were stilted and worried and that her insides cramped with fear, but what she had seen—so many Big Heads, so well armed—made her want to run. No wonder her father had hoped for peace with these creatures, up until the day he died.

The day they killed him.

That horrid thought rattled around inside of her. *But my job as Leader is to protect the People. Doesn't that mean sometimes, it's better to run than fight?*

Her hands were damp with fear, partly because of the Big Heads and partly because she just didn't know what to do.

Nightshade glanced at her, his face filled with recrimination, jaw so tight his teeth ground like rocks rumbling down a hill, but he said nothing, simply headed home, never looking back the entire time. At homebase, he sent his most trusted scouts with instructions to find the People a new home. They would go every morning until they found one.

For the rest of the day, every time his eyes found hers, it was as though he had sized her up and found her disappointing. Truthfully, she disappointed herself. What she wished to know was, the day her father died, did he stand and fight to allow the rest of his warriors and hunters to escape or was he frustrated they hadn't stood with him?

Xhosa walked to the stream at the edge of the clearing and washed the heat from her body. With her sweat stink gone, a new one made her eyes water.

"What's rotting?" She muttered, sneezing, just as a distraught mother grabbed her arm.

"My son—his leg—it's worse," her eyes pleading.

In her panic, she raced off but all Xhosa had to do was follow the fetid stench to a grimy squalid pile of sordid flesh and bones.

"Ant," Xhosa motioned dispassionately, swallowing the sourness that rose in her throat. "You look awful."

Though one of the People's newest adults, Ant wouldn't get much older if the boil on his leg didn't stop weeping gooey yellow puss. He deserved it of course—who would wade into a feces-laden stream with an open sore? His excuse had been that a rhino chased him. He survived but the formerly benign wound grew into a pustule the size of his palm and now much larger with a smell so awful, no one would go near him.

Xhosa stooped, cutter in hand. "I must rupture it."

Not waiting for Ant's approval, she told the mother to keep her boy from moving and abruptly stabbed the pustule until it broke open. Ant howled as a bloody foul-smelling mucus squirted out. Xhosa patted it with moss until the gush trickled to a stop, leaving a crater of raw weeping tissue.

Ant whimpered and Xhosa scowled. "Be quiet. This is your fault. You irritated Rhino."

"I wanted a drink of water, not her calf!"

She ignored him while stuffing the last of a particular blue flower into the wound, layered it with honey, and sealed the whole thing with leaves.

"Mother of Ant, keep this damp with honey. I will look for more of the blue flowers but it may be too late."

The old female clutched her chest, tears wetting her cheeks, but Xhosa had no time for her. She handed Ant the shredded pulp from inside a brilliant orange bark. "Eat this. It helps the fever," adding as she left, "and the pain."

When far enough the boy wouldn't see, she beckoned Nightshade. "Ant will die without more of the blue flower," and motioned where it grew.

"That's on unclaimed land." A smile flitted across Nightshade's face. He loved a challenge.

Xhosa, Nightshade, and handfuls of warriors left the next day when Sun awoke, planning to return well before Sun slept. One of the warriors carried a dead gazelle for trade in case the blue flower's location was controlled by an Other tribe.

Xhosa led the group along a dry riverbed, past the caves where subadults learned skills, and skirted the tree where the elders talked while pounding and chopping roots. As they left the People's land, Xhosa executed a careful sensory search, probing the shadows for movement and searching for noises out of sync with Nature's own. All seemed well so the group continued toward the shimmering narrow band of the Great Waterhole. The blue flower lived in the forests along its edges.

The group continued in silence, each stepping in the prints of those in front of them, crouching to remain below the grassline as much as possible. They passed a family of graceful Giraffid, their delicate necks rising high above the mammoth and Wild Beast that browsed close by. A youngster limped, gashes left by Cat's claws still fresh on its hind leg. Nightshade brushed a single digit over his hip, motioning, "We should kill it and harvest the meat."

"We first collect the healing plant. The carcass will be here or won't when we finish."

Nightshade frowned. "We skip a sure hunt to heal the wound of a boy too stupid to protect himself. He will never be able to defend the People!" Nightshade had no patience for stupidity. That the boy was innocent mattered not at all.

Xhosa held her hand behind her, palm to the ground—*Wait*—and scrambled up a hill to check the forward path. And think. She remained motionless for a breath and another, head pivoting over her surroundings, mind churning. Killing Giraffid would be easy but then, they wouldn't have time to harvest the healing plant. Ant would die.

It didn't take long. Nightshade wouldn't like her decision but he wasn't Leader.

She beckoned him and headed toward the blue-flowered plant. "If a predator kills Giraffid, we scavenge the carcass on our way back."

Nightshade dropped to the end of the column. Protecting their backtrail was a good job for him. His reflexes were like Cat's, his hearing like Owl's—no one would surprise them.

Today was hotter than yesterday and that worse than the day before, the land's way of saying the wet time had ended. A white haze shimmered in the sky like a mist. The thump-thump of their feet frightened a family of bush pigs as they scooted across the trail. The group pounded beyond a copse of trees, down a treacherous defile, and under a jutting ridge.

Around midday, they moved away from the cliffs to ground filled with sagebrush and bunchgrass. She stopped just beyond a termite mound where Leopard slept, searching the landscape, looking back along their backtrail, a frown wrinkling her face. Fire had burned a thicket of trees that always provided a restful break in trips past. Her nose flared at the acrid aroma of scorched meat—some animal died in fire.

"This way," she motioned to Nightshade.

Their shadows shortened to the length of a hand by the time they came across a mud-filled puddle. The warriors smeared the muck over their bodies while she monitored the surroundings. In the distance loomed both Fire Mountain and a nearby cousin. Their flanks met in a deep gully that disappeared below the horizon. Xhosa compared this to the mental image from her last trip and searched.

There! The dry creek bed twisting amid stalky grass at the foot of a boulder bed, and a spear's throw from that, the skinny-stalked, small-leafed blue-flowered plant swayed in the shallow breeze as though to catch her attention.

She raced over, leaving Nightshade and the warriors resting in the shade of a baobab. It was a large patch with so many flowers, roots, and stems that they filled her neck sack. A welcome breeze lifted her hair, carrying the smell of dust and carrion—

And Big Heads. No other creature had this stink.

She raised her arms high and motioned, "Down!"

Another breeze and the odor disappeared but no one moved. Her leg twitched as ants poured over her foot. She bit her lip to distract herself. Sweat dripped down her face, tickling her neck.

Nightshade crawled to her. "We take a different route back," and they diverted toward the waterhole where her father died but Big Head stench was strong here. Sun's glare bounced off the sparkling surface making it impossible to see so she squirmed around to get a better view. A pair of mammoth blocked her view as they threw trunkfuls of water at each other, flaring their giant ears and trumpeting their contentment.

When the behemoths plodded away, a flash of movement and a glint of light on the opposite shore caught her eye. Xhosa tightened her grip on her spear and tried to focus.

"Big Heads," Nightshade motioned, his shoulder touching hers, body reeking of energy. "Let's see what they do," and he took off up a hillock with oversight of the waterhole. Xhosa huffed and followed.

The dry grass crackled beneath her steps. Insects chirruped and squeaked their displeasure at the intruders, these noises concealed by the Big Heads non-stop chatter.

Nightshade and Xhosa peered below. Big Heads filled the shore, eyes on each other, ignorant of those watching. A dangerous stillness settled over Xhosa, part of her wanting revenge for her father, another part knowing this was not the time. Sweat dripped from Nightshade's steaming body, plopping loudly against the hardscrabble ground. A snake wriggled across Xhosa's hand and into its hole to escape the muggy heat.

The pounding began inside her head as she focused on her nemesis, her mind starting to tingle but before a plan could pop into her brain, the Big Heads left.

She motioned to the warriors and all followed, traveling deep into strange new territory. When the landscape changed from crater-pocked grassland to wooded flatland, Xhosa breathed a sigh of relief and oriented herself to this new terrain, marking her position relative to Fire Mountain, Sun, and the distant scent of Great Waterhole. Over there, on her weak side, trees crowded against their neighbors. A baobab tilted over a cracked wadi as though pushed by Mammoth. Subconsciously, a map formed in her head populated with these landmarks. This was the same way she found roots, scavenge, fruit trees in bloom, and periodic waterholes, and knew how to avoid where other bands lived and predators slept. It happened without thinking.

She scanned for broken branches and impressions, sniffed for urine and feces that would mark this as Big Heads' territory, but found nothing. They too traveled outside of their home.

Finally, a faint dampness in the air beckoned like the mist before a storm and the Big Heads veered toward a pond. Xhosa settled downwind, hidden by tussock grasses and cattails.

Nightshade motioned, "They don't know we're here. We should attack." Tension edged his movements.

Xhosa stiffened. Nightshade must have seen it but misunderstood.

"This will not be like last time, Xhosa," meaning the attack that killed her father.

She nodded once, not sure this was the right decision.

As they prepared, a Big Head youth sprinted out of the brush that edged the water, panting, face glowing, muscles bulging across his bronzed chest. His head hair hung to his shoulders, straight like Xhosa's but lighter in color and damp with sweat. He jabbered Big Head words, using his fingers to tick off how many of something excited him. The Big Heads screamed to their feet and sped off, Xhosa and Nightshade right behind.

As they rounded the last tree in the thicket, the Big Heads were already flanking a Hipparion herd, exactly as the People would. The paleohorses bolted, ears pinned back in fear, manes flying, snorting damp clouds of saliva as the Big Heads flung their deadly stone-tipped spears. Some Hipparion fell as others reared in terror. Panic filled the whites of their ebony eyes. Sweat washed from their loins and muscles rippled, driving them on as the Big Head warriors butchered those that fell, their frightened whinnies not slowing herdmates.

When finished, hunters severed pieces from the still-bleeding bodies and carried them away, leaving the rest to a smaller group of Big Heads.

Nightshade motioned. "This is our chance."

He never considered failure. Fighting meant winning and he trained his warriors to be more vicious, ruthless, and violent than those they faced. If they refused to give up, they would prevail.

Usually, he was right.

She sighed, seeing more clearly why she hadn't yet pairmated with this strong, loyal warrior. Yes, she must establish herself first, as Leader, and definitely, carrying a baby would slow her down but one reason overshadowed all others: Leadership had changed Nightshade. The male who grew up with her once considered violence a means to an end, the end always peace. Sometime following her father's death and after Nightshade lost the leadership to her, he forgot that. Peace became what killed her father, a weakness to be avoided. It showed in his mating. Many females refused him rather than suffer the painful bruises and stinging slaps, sometimes broken bones. It frightened Xhosa. Not only did that attitude disgust her in a pairmate, it didn't serve the People.

Nightshade might be right, that violence was the answer, but her father's voice spoke as though standing beside her. *"Confront them in our territory where you know every trail, waterhole, and predator."*

# Chapter 8

Nightshade pushed. "The meat is unprotected. We steal it as they stole ours. While I distract them, you grab it."

Xhosa wanted to say no but he'd already left. The hill he headed toward did provide good coverage and her position allowed easy spear shots. Tree-tall boulders would protect their exit.

There she waited as did the warriors. Sun moved a finger across the blue sky while she inhaled the humid air, as quiet as snake in the shade of a rock on a smoldering day. She looked where Nightshade should be but saw no shadows, no awkward sway of grass, no telltale animal responses to an intruder in their midst. Nightshade and Nature were one.

Suddenly, the Big Head yips increased and they picked up their spears as though to leave.

"If he doesn't start soon, it will be too late," Xhosa muttered to herself and then tensed. The Big Heads weren't leaving. In fact, from the edge of the clearing, Nightshade's blind spot, many more arrived.

She hooted Cousin Chimp's warning call, one Nightshade would hear and heed, but it was too late.

A whoosh, a thunk, and a Big Head collapsed. The group twisted as one toward Nightshade's hiding spot, their muscles tense, faces dark. Xhosa identified a Leader and flung a palm-sized stone at the sensitive spot above his ear. With a smack and a hiss of air, he crumpled. When their rage switched to her, she roared and sprinted forward, spear in one hand and a missile in the other. Her warriors charged with her, screaming, brandishing clubs, and unleashing a hailstorm of rocks. They would grab part of the meat and flee, forcing the Big Heads to stay with what remained.

That didn't happen. Part of the Big Heads flooded toward the attackers while the rest guarded the meat. Xhosa heard a wet *thwump* and one of her warriors fell, fingers clasping a Big Head spear. She bent to help him—Ngili, a name popped up—but he pointed, warning of a Big Head spear flying at her. Xhosa ducked as it scraped her hair and loosed her last stone, crushing his nose and embedding itself in his forehead.

*This isn't working. There are too many.*

She warbled the command to flee. Nightshade grabbed Ngili and Xhosa led the warriors past the tilted baobab and the cracked wadi, beyond the chimps screeching about the smell of fear that filled their territory. Xhosa's breaths became ragged gasps. Her chest burned, and her head pounded but never was resting or slowing a consideration. Her callused feet moved lightly, almost flying. She could run forever though not at this speed. The scree slopes ahead would hide their tracks. Her calls exhorted the warriors forward even as the Big Heads threatened to overrun them. One of their strange spears whizzed by, its stone tip digging a deep groove in her arm. Her mind conjured up her father, never quitting despite the odds, never giving up on his warriors.

With a lurch, she stopped and whirled to face the charging Big Heads.

"Here. I. Am!"

Warclub ready, head up, she widened her stance, howling while waving a handful of branches, hoping the Big Heads would be too far to know it wasn't a weapon. The lead Big Head skidded to a stop and shoved an arm out in front of the rest. He tipped his spear down, gripping it so hard, his knuckles whitened against the dark hair of his hands. His body glowed in the sunlight, slick with sweat and tight with muscle.

"Wind," she remembered.

When the bloodthirsty rabble behind him pulled up in a ragged line, roaring and bouncing, brandishing weapons, fear stumbled across Wind's face and then kindness.

*Impossible.*

Xhosa aligned herself with him, spear too toward the ground, and used hand motions he would know. "You killed my father."

He stepped away as though hit. "You confuse me with my brother. I am sorry for the death of your Leader."

He was as tall as she with broad shoulders, muscle-bound chest, straight black hair that hung well below his neck. His scarred hands spoke like the People.

"You sent your warrior to kill me, in the cave—"

"No! That cave—he wanted to use it for hunting. If I had known you were there, I would have told him to avoid it, and saved his life." His face froze, stricken, as his eyes turned inward. "He was a friend."

Sadness filled his eyes but quickly disappeared. "When he didn't return, we tracked him to that cave, to the pit. My warriors—they call you divine." He bobbed his head back. "They do not want to kill you. They want to possess you."

What did he mean—*divine?*—but she wouldn't ask.

"It was you I smelled watching."

"Yes. I am Wind. I have been searching for you. My dreams told me to protect you, to make up for the death of your father. "

Her thoughts flashed to her own dreams of Lucy. *That's impossible.* She examined his face and body, analyzing the movements he used to communicate. There was no denying the truth in his words.

"We—my people—we wish you no harm. But we do want you to leave."

She stuck her chin toward his weapon. "Yet you attack us."

As though surprised at the weapon in his hand, he tossed it aside and repeated, "I am not here for that."

"Tell that to my warrior, Ngili," but her hands spoke softly.

Nothing about him screamed danger. In fact, the cast of his eyes, the quiet authority in his bearing, the way he balanced on the balls of his feet as though relaxed but ready to spring—everything declared truth.

Before Wind could explain further, a figure shoved him aside. This male bore Wind's build, same color hair and skin, same stance, but also a white scar across his cheek as though from Cat's claws. His nose hung crookedly which only added to the sense of menace that pervaded his presence.

"Go, Thunder! I can handle this!" From Wind.

Laughter rolled like a snarl from Thunder's mouth. Fear coursed through Xhosa, from her ears to her toes, but she kept her face blank. Without willing it, her body prepared to fight or flee.

"My brother Wind is weak. He would save you. I want to dominate you. We are more vicious than even your warrior, Nightshade. You can't defeat us."

Xhosa faced Thunder. He looked her in the eye, blood coating his chest, carrying his body like a warrior used to winning fights.

"Yes. We can."

Her hands moved with sureness, her words clipped. She had never seen a male who could throw a spear faster with more accuracy than hers. A blink was all the warning he gave as he launched his spear. Her first thought flashed to how anyone could be that quick and then she lost herself in the weapon, detached completely from her imminent death. Like a butterfly drawn a flower, the spear slowed the closer it got to her chest.

A warble made her shift and Nightshade batted the weapon from the air, his reflexes so fast his rival gasped. That's all Xhosa needed and she launched her spear. It embedded deeply into Thunder's arm, the tip poking out the back. Thunder's face reddened with rage.

"Oh, you've never been beaten by a female? Get used to it, Big Head!"

Thunder's anger overflowed like lava from a volcano. He threw his head back, raised his arms, and howled. Nightshade yanked Xhosa away.

She squirmed free. "No! We must stay—our warriors need time to flee!"

"Your warriors have fled. They need you alive!"

With a last glare at Thunder, Xhosa pivoted and fled. She looked back once and saw Wind watching her, a smile playing around his lips, preventing the Big Head warriors from advancing despite his brother's injury.

Finally, Thunder howled, "You are a frightened hare awaiting your destiny! And we shall deliver it!"

Xhosa sprinted until her legs felt like logs, disconnected from her body, finally stumbling forward onto her outstretched arms. Nightshade caught up, an injured warrior over his shoulder and another he dragged by the hair.

"They won't follow. They want the meat."

His chiseled face radiated energy and passion. Her people feared neither death nor combat. It was part of life. Children battered playmates, clubbed them over the head, banged them in the chest with rocks and dull spears, brutally yanked their fragile child limbs. That was play. Unless children toughened, and quickly, they fell to predators. A favorite game involved using any means necessary to keep an object away from competitors. The entire purpose was to prepare children to be adults.

Although, nothing equipped her to combat a quicker predator, smarter and more agile than any she'd ever seen. If her band became their prey, they would lose everything her father fought for.

She set a fast pace, no slower than the fleeing Hipparion, with no stops to eat or rest. When the group reached home, they would leave, move as far from these Big Heads as possible.

# Chapter 9

It wasn't until they reached the safety of the People's territory that Xhosa allowed her exhausted warriors to rest. They collapsed, wheezing, skin damp, faces slack, glazed with fear and fatigue. While Nightshade sent scouts to cover the backtrail and talked with his Second, Snake, Xhosa strode from one warrior to the next, providing salve for pain, filling wounds with honey and covering them in moss dabbed with sap.

A young warrior caught her attention, his face ashen, lips colorless. A broken spear dangled from a wound in his upper arm. Without warning, she yanked out the shaft and staunched the bleeding with honey and crushed leaves. He grunted but didn't move.

"Where's your neck sack, warrior?"

Each warrior—in fact, every one of the People—carried a neck sack stuffed with choppers, cutters, travel food, a handaxe, and healing herbs. No neck sack meant he had eaten nothing all day.

He patted a gash on his other shoulder, crusted with blood. "A spear broke the vine. I couldn't retrieve it."

She handed him dried berries and a stout root. "Eat."

When finished tending injuries, she moved off by herself to observe unobtrusively and undisturbed. Instead of the idle chatter that usually followed a hunt, there was only silence. Everyone looked frightened, mouths open as though asking, *How did this happen?* Many stared at the ground while others watched her, wondering at her first loss so early in her leadership.

Xhosa didn't wonder. Cold fury raged in her body. The violence to her People—her father's People—ate at her until everything beneath her skin hurt. A low pounding in her head became louder until there was no other sound.

*I must do something or explode.*

A warm wind whipped across the landscape and fluffy white clouds floated over the light blue sky. Ignoring her fatigue, discouragement, and the still-dripping gouge in her arm, she closed her eyes, soothed by the voices of the birds and the chirruping of the insects going about their daily business as though a major assault hadn't just ended. After a finger of time, Nightshade joined her.

"The warriors need you."

Her mood was as dark as the worst of her fighters but that didn't matter. She stood in front of the warriors, head up, eyes looking at each warrior.

"Warriors, feel no shame that we faced a stronger adversary. Instead, savor the pride in a battle well-fought. Rest. Eat."

Nightshade might have berated them but that wasn't her way. Happy grunts replaced the murmurs. Xhosa ran down a mental list of warriors, ticking them off on her fingers.

"Nightshade, did Ngili survive?"

He shook his head. "Ngili was young. He ignored the lessons we taught him."

Xhosa agreed. After one more glance, she and Nightshade left the warriors and hiked up a brushy slope to a berm where they could study the landscape. Worry furrowed Xhosa's brow and tension knotted her insides.

"Is the Big Head Thunder right, Nightshade? Did they already win?"

Her hands spoke so low on her body that Nightshade missed the question. Xhosa didn't care. The answer to the question was meaningless. What she wanted was to protect the People.

She spread her arms in front of her, palms up, waist-high.

"This is our home, Nightshade." Her eyes glittered with exhilaration. "There the trees knocked down by migrating mammoth. There in the open woodland, Giraffid browses. Beyond that, the river flows, dry this time of year but overflowing during the rainy time, and surrounded by the most succulent, delicious vegetation."

She stopped, unable to continue, her throat tight. The earth fed them well after Gazelle and Hipparion and Mammoth migrated to avoid the searing heat. The People consumed the food closest to homebase first and then moved outward. When finding it took longer than a day, they moved outward again or relied on less-desirable food like grass, seeds, and acacia gum. This was why their land must be so large, spread so far.

"This, what we see, my father fought for. It is the only home many of the People have known their entire life. Here—here!—we are the strongest."

She slapped her chest, eyes moist.

Nightshade curled his lips up. "If you ignore the clouds of biting flies, so impenetrable we can scarcely see and so small they fly into our ears and nose. Sometimes, I wonder if they are stronger than us."

He paused, face reflective. "The worst part of this day, Xhosa, was losing the injured Giraffid."

Xhosa chuffed a laugh. "I saw no sign of its death. It survives despite what should be a fatal injury."

A weight tumbled off her shoulders. The People could be Giraffid.

A familiar sound rang from a copse of trees beyond the spiky tussock grass that marked an underground pool, Cousin Chimp calling his family. He did this every day at this time. Life continued.

She breathed evenly, shallowly, waiting for the beat inside her chest to slow, and then motioned, "Can this Thunder drive us away?"

Nightshade hooted to deploy the scouts along the forward path and the backtrail before answering.

"These Big Heads are unlike Others. That makes them a challenge." A quiet intensity filled his eyes as he looked back on their traveled trail, as though he could see the enemy. "They entered our territory. We responded with strength. They will respect that."

"We can leave, peacefully."

"We cannot run, Xhosa. They entered *our* territory. They take *our* plants, kill *our* animals. They want to own what is *ours*."

Xhosa stiffened at his anger but continued, "Wind wants to help us."

Nightshade barked, "Wind is not Leader. The one called Thunder leads."

"Would Thunder risk lives to assault such a powerful People as us?"

Nightshade exhaled in frustration, as though he spoke to a child. "They are not like us, Xhosa. Do not expect them to live by our rules."

Xhosa stood straighter, forcing her shoulders back. "You forget, Nightshade. Sabertooth, alpha over all animals, tolerates others as long as she dominates. As did my father."

She looked into the distance, hands softening at memories of how her father allowed others to hunt the People's land. He said it protected the People. If the surrounding tribes were well-fed, they wouldn't attack and it provided a buffer from Others that might.

Nightshade's hands chopped, frustrated. "Thunder wants nothing less than to replace your father."

Xhosa took Nightshade's face in her hands and gently forced him to look at her. "My father often talked about wanting to get along with Big Heads. It's why we moved to this homebase between a pond too deep to cross and a cliff too steep to climb."

Nightshade's shoulders sagged. "That's not what Big Heads want to do."

She started to argue but he interrupted. "Do not worry, Leader. I have a plan."

# Chapter 10

They followed their backtrail through the same scree slopes that brought them out, up and down the humps and trenches of eroded riverbanks, past the remnants of a recent hunt where a few desultory vultures picked old shreds of flesh from yellowed bone.

Each warrior shouted his call sign before entering the homebase. Within moments, the camp exploded with excitement. Pairmates greeted warriors, children the hunters. Only Ngili's female remained alone. Nightshade approached her and motioned something quietly. She blanched. Her head fell and her chin bounced on her chest as a keening shriek escaped her lips.

Xhosa dismissed it. Ngili wasn't the first or last to die. Illness, injury, and the boldness of their lives killed equally, invariably. Only aggression forestalled death. The more aggressive, the longer life lasted.

She needed to show the pairmates of the injured how to care for the wounds.

"Mulch these leaves and smear them over the wounds. Wrap them in leaves, layer on mud, and let them dry." "Soak this moss in honey…" "Chew this bark and force him to swallow…"

Next was Ant, the boy responsible for today's hunt and Ngili's death. It shocked her how much worse he was since morning. The ulcer now stretched heel to shin and a thin sheath of bloody tissue covered it. When she pressed, pain flared in his eyes and his face paled.

Once he could breathe again, the boy gasped out, "Where is Ngili?"

"If he lives, Big Heads will enslave him. We can do nothing."

Either way, a warrior died due to Ant's stupidity. The People cherished each individual, valued their contributions to the whole. Though crossing into another band's territory was dangerous, it was worth the risk if it cured Ant. Otherwise, it was a waste.

She motioned to Ant's mother, "Here is more of the blue flower," and described how to care for the wound with it, and then motioned to Ant. "Ngili died to save you. His work has become your work. Be more careful next time."

As she left, Nightshade joined her.

"Rest," and he motioned toward a rotting log deposited by some long-forgotten flood. From there, she watched the children play their version of today's battle. Though rough, it prepared them for the rigors of being an adult. At one point, the group ganged up on one weak child. They rained blows on him, bleeding his nose, bruising his arms and legs, cutting his lip open, but he never gave up. He kicked them in the groin, the chest, slammed rocks into the sensitive parts of their heads. In the end, they caught all four of his limbs and pummeled him until his father called him away. Children defended themselves or died. If this scrawny boy added nothing to the People, he should die before using their resources. Life was about the challenge. Survival awarded itself to those smart enough to grab ahold.

Nightshade crouched on his haunches and extended a moist broad leaf to her.

"Where are the scouts?"

She didn't say it but her Lead Warrior understood. "They will not be ambushed."

Xhosa felt calmer but no less adamant about the decision to leave. Without looking at him, she motioned, "We must go far from these Big Heads."

"Take this." Nightshade handed her a leaf blade brimming with roots, bulbs, corms, rhizomes, baobab fruit, and crunchy seeds.

"I thought the seeds were gone until the wet time." Where did he find these?

As she crunched one bite after another, images floated about in her thoughts, of the females collecting dry pods, beating them with sticks, and then winnowing seeds from pod fragments—all while too many of her warriors were grievously injured and Ngili lost his life to the Big Heads.

With a lingering glance, as though he wanted to say something and decided against it, Nightshade left. Watching his solid muscular body move confidently across the clearing, she wondered again about her feelings for him. He was completely devoted to her, would gladly take on the responsibility to feed both her and their children. Females pairmated after they bled but as Leader, no one forced her. Nightshade mated often, fathered many, but never called a female "pairmate" or the children "family".

She cocked her head as Owl rose, carrying a shining snake into the trees. It bit into the wriggling creature even as it fought for its freedom.

Why did Nightshade wait for her?

She winced, pressing her palms against her temples. Nightshade stood across the clearing, eyes on her, head tilted, a curious smile on his lips.

"Go," he motioned. "Take care of yourself. Nothing will happen that I can't handle."

Xhosa rose and her world spun. At times like this, pain grinding into her temples and forcing her eyes closed, it was a struggle to maintain an appearance of vigor. Everyone thought she liked the quiet, which was true, but it was time to share the truth with Nightshade.

"Come," her hand beckoned him while her feet headed across the plateau in the center of the homebase. She nodded to several females as they gathered their children, waved to a warrior patrolling the perimeter as he melted into the growing gloom, pleased to see Ant totter from the communal food to Ngili's mate.

Away from the People, Xhosa squeezed her eyes closed, willing the pain into submission, but it never listened. Nightshade gripped her arm as someone inside her head banged mercilessly, trying to escape. She stumbled and he steadied her. His hand pulled a pod from his neck sack.

It stunned her. "How did you know?"

"It is my job to know." When he saw her concern, he added, "No one else does. There is no need."

She laid the pod on a flat rock and slammed it with a hammerstone until the seeds popped out. These, she pulverized into mush, ate, and then waited for the numbness.

Is this what it means to have a pairmate?

Her finger found a black dried-out toe, the only remaining piece of her father. Even in death, he gave her courage. The band settled in for the night as she inhaled Nightshade's presence, letting it sink into her pores, wishing it would wash away the horror. Stars twinkled, grasshoppers chirruped. Children ran their last races of the day, threw their final game of toss. Someone thumped the ground with open hands, the pleasant rhythm that calmed everyone and announced the start of grooming. Others hummed, hands too busy to beat the earth.

Her parents had been happy together, maybe what she felt with Nightshade. They read each other's minds, did for the other without being asked. No matter the load, neither seemed
burdened. When her mother died, her father changed.

The pain receded to a dull thrum above her cheeks and below her forehead.

"We underestimated our rival, Nightshade, as Others do us."

"We saw them fight only once before."

She acknowledged but continued, "I fight like Cat—stalk prey carefully, watch for any trace. How did I miss the clues, Nightshade, telling me to withdraw?"

"Big Heads are weak. You mistake their far-throw spear for strength. We will learn to attach a stone to the tip."

"How?"

He brushed over that. "Our warriors are excellent with weapons. They will figure it out. Today Xhosa, our archenemy learned we are not easily defeated."

Then why did Xhosa feel that today's conflict ended life here, at their homebase? In truth, she and Nightshade talked often of moving. Scouts went out every day in search of a new home, the urgency inspired by both the ruthlessness of the Big Heads and changes in the land itself. When her father first brought the People here, every type of animal traveled their territory, usually to visit the abundant waterholes. Today, dusty trails led past desperate-looking junipers to ever-shrinking ponds and lakes. They relied on rain but every season, it started later and ended earlier. The pond a young Xhosa dangled her feet in didn't even touch the toes of her adult legs. The underground streams that used to run just below the surface now required a day of digging. Herds that left to escape the heat returned smaller.

Not just the animals and the water had changed—the earth itself seemed angry. The mountains exploded and the land split open more often and more violently.

Still, it always provided. Grasses, seeds, berries, and nuts, the People took only what they needed, leaving plenty to reseed for the next time they harvested. They ate cossid larvae, eggs, nuts, scorpions, and termites holed up in their massive mounds.

The evening air cooled their weary bodies. Nightshade brushed a finger over her smooth face. Blotchy white sweat glistened against the shine of his black skin, his hair heavy with trail debris.

"There is one other option," she motioned, watching him out of the corner of her eye.

He looked away. "That is a desperate move, to be considered only when nothing else is possible."

She leaned her head against his chest, enjoying the sound of his body beating, slowly and rhythmically, much like the beat in her ears.

Nightshade motioned, "Come."

By the time they crossed over the brambled barrier, built every night for protection, her head no longer pounded. She squatted by Nightshade, grooming the fleas, ticks, and lice from his hirsute hair as he did hers.

As they finished, a whoop sounded from the males guarding the perimeter. Xhosa snagged her spear, as did Nightshade, and raced toward the noise.

It must be the Big Heads.

**PART TWO: SOUTH AFRICA**
*850,000 years ago*

# Chapter 11

Pan-do urged the ragged remnants of his vibrant community onward. They wheezed desperately, muscles screaming, bodies starved for water, but he refused to slow. The hairless enemy with the vaulted heads and broad flat faces who threw a death stick farther than was possible would not stop their pursuit because his People were worn out.

They had been crossing these wide open lands for more than a moon, up and down steep slopes, sloshing through shallow rivers, cowering in open grasslands that provided little protection. The terrain was nothing like the limestone caves and forests that had been his home most of his life. And he missed the gentle kindness of the Hairy Ones. Though strange looking Uprights—short-statured and long-armed with pear-shaped chests and noses that flattened against their faces—they had welcomed his People when they had nowhere else to go, offering sanctuary and asking for nothing. Before living with them, he had considered them more like Cousin Chimp than Others though larger, more mobile, and more intelligent but as the Moons came and went, he got to know them as hard workers who respected his People and were always willing to teach them new skills.

Soon the shared hunting, gathering, childminding, and knapping became a way of life. Together, the tribes excavated bulbs and roots, extracted termites from logs, scavenged meat, and sniffed out water. Pan-do's People were skilled fighters but the Hairy Ones knew nothing about combat. When handfuls of Moons passed without violence, the People's warriors no longer practiced those skills. Why waste the time when attacks never occurred?

That mistake almost destroyed them. When the vicious hairless ones decided they wanted the caves, the combined group had no defense other than to flee. The Hairy Ones ran well but only short distances so soon, one by one, the Big Heads picked them off until only Pan-do's People ran onward, for their lives.

Pan-do led with his pairmate Ah-ga and his daughter Lyta, with no real idea where to go. The forests and cliffs gave way to rolling grasslands marked with prickled bushes and deep-rooted trees, and then an infinite flat, dry monotony, a limitless scrub waste without landmarks or water, the only living animals being the People trudging onward.

Finally, when it was impossible to believe the enemy would continue to chase, Pan-do motioned, "We rest."

His People collapsed where they stood. Scouts who explored the front- and backtrail reported no trace of the big headed-hairless ones. For them to continue the chase risked losing the caves and the surrounding lush lands to another invader. Still, every day while the People rested and replenished supplies, Pan-do sent scouts. One day, breathless and skin damp with sweat, they stumbled into the temporary camp.

"Big Heads—many—a day's travel."

Without a thought, Pan-do and his People moved on, this time away from the gentle salty tang that had guided them, its familiarity bringing comfort because it scented the air of their homeland. Maybe something about it kept the hairless ones following.

Finally, a handful of days later, Pan-do stopped, once again hoping—believing—he had lost the enemy. His People were exhausted and dejected. If they didn't find safety soon, they would give up.

Ah-ga, his pairmate, motioned gently, "Are we finished running? When can we go home to our caves?"

*No and Never,* but Pan-do wanted to phrase it more positively, maybe shape their flight as a great adventure. As he struggled with that challenge, his daughter, Lyta, flicked her fingers toward their old homebase. "Bad lives there. Good lives ahead," and she flicked toward the flat horizon.

Pan-do smiled.

"It's decided—I will share the good news with the rest."

Pan-do's People accepted Lyta's strange antics because what she heard and saw often saved lives.

He rose to leave but motioned to Lyta, "Do you know how far? Before we're safe?" Though her visions often included no details, Pan-do hoped this would be the exception. Rather than answer, she twirled off to pluck a dry flower from a broken stem.

Ah-ga gazed at the flat brown bumps that grew daily. "Maybe she means those mountains."

Mountains meant cliffs which meant caves so Pan-do adjusted their direction, still keeping Sun's waking place to his strong side, sleeping nest to his weak. By the time Moon came and went once and again, two things happened. A bright star appeared in the night sky over their forward path and all trace of the hairless ones disappeared. Sure, the scouts uncovered the familiar long narrow Upright prints with the prominent bump at the top and a deep indent at the bottom, but few Uprights were enemies.

Lyta happily skipped, arms overhead, eyes alight with excitement.

"I will meet him ahead."

While Pan-do had no idea what she meant, warmth and joy filled him as it did every day spent with his daughter.

With the immediate threat stemmed, Pan-do let everyone stop at a river to bathe and refresh. Water ran high on the banks creating swampy pockets and secluded inlets perfect for the children to play. The mud provided good opportunities for the hunters to trap game.

"Pan-do!" His pairmate Ah-ga had just finished bathing with Lyta and the child raced up to the dry shoreline. He would have watched Lyta until she was safely away from the water and any dangers it held but a wide log was floating toward Ah-ga, with eyes on top. Before he could scream, *Crocodile!*, treacherous teeth flashed dripping white saliva, and snapped shut on Ah-ga's leg. She bellowed in surprise and pain. With a yank, the crocodile knocked her down and started dragging her into the depths. Her fingers clawed at the shoreline but it was all sand and silt.

"Ah-ga! I'm coming!"

Fury powered his steps as spittle flew from his lips and a muscle twitched beneath his left eye. He had only his spear—his warclub left behind while they bathed—but it didn't matter. He would have attacked with no weapons.

The croc was a monster, as long as two of the People. Boney plates covered its back and left no space for a spear to penetrate. Still, Pan-do strode into the water and slammed the dull end of his spear into the croc's head, aiming for his sensitive nose but missing. His goal was to force it to release Ah-ga and attack him. That didn't happen. The croc slapped Pan-do away with a violent swish of its tail and continued dragging Ah-ga into the sludgy current.

Pan-do scrabbled forward on his knees, head spinning.

"Pan-do—stay there," Ah-ga ordered in her I-have-a-plan voice. She knew he couldn't swim and the croc was already too far into the lake. Ah-ga gulped in as much air as she could just before the croc dove, spinning, leaving a trail of blood from her bleeding leg. Usually, a crocodile kept its prey underwater until it suffocated but this time, it surfaced, hissing as Ah-ga beat its head and snout with a massive rock she must have pulled from the river bottom. She slammed it over and over, bludgeoning every sensitive part.

Finally, the creature let go with a deadly sigh and she kicked away with her one good leg, dragging the other. Pan-do extended his spear to Ah-ga so he could pull her to shore but the croc pounced again, this time closing his great jaws on her remaining good leg. She howled in pain but managed to adjust the spear in her hand and jab its sharp point into the croc's unblinking eyes and throat, all the while screaming and bellowing to disorient the animal.

With a final low-throated bark, the crocodile released Ah-ga and she scrabbled up the shore with only her arms. The crocodile wanted no part of this vicious prey and slid soundlessly back into the river. Pan-do splashed to his pairmate and pulled her out of the water to the drier edging ground. One leg had been mangled to a pulpy red mass and the other bitten to the bone, leaving the shape of the croc's snout in the skin.

Sa-mo-ke, his Primary Warrior, sprinted to Pan-do. He took one look at Ah-ga, gulped as though to keep from throwing up, but what he had to say was worse than what he looked at.

"They found us! We must run!" He tensed at the sight of Ah-ga's shattered legs and damp white face, before continuing, "I can lead the People. You get Ah-ga to safety."

Ah-ga waved Pan-do away. "Leave me in that burrow," and she started to crawl toward a small animal den. "When I am healed, I will catch up."

Pan-do shook his head. This female was life itself. Without her, he might as well quit. He motioned to his Lead Warrior, scarcely beyond childhood but blooded by Big Heads. His face shone with the light of youth mixed with the wisdom of age.

"That is a good plan, Sa-mo-ke. We cannot escape carrying a crippled member. I stay with Ah-ga. When she recovers, we will catch up. Lyta—go with Sa-mo-ke."

Lyta's eyes glistened with unshed tears but she agreed. "I will see you again, Father. Don't worry," and she left moving at the only speed her uncoordinated legs could go. Finally, as they disappeared from sight, he saw Sa-mo-ke throw Lyta over his shoulder like the loin of Gazelle, and no heavier.

Pan-do hefted Ah-ga into the den she had found. After placing her gently on the dirt floor, he disguised the entry with brush and treated his pairmate's wounds with moss, sap, and plant roots.

"I need bark from the shedding tree for the fever. And pain."

He got no further than the mouth of the den when he saw it. "A dust cloud. They are here."

He pulled back into the shadows away from the mouth of the den, spear clutched tightly, shielding Ah-ga with his body. Within moments, he heard pounding steps and smelled the stench of their bodies. They weren't likely to notice this hole. It was too small for anyone's interest. They picked up the trail of the fleeing People and followed. When they were gone, Pan-do emerged cautiously, sniffed for any remaining enemy, but found none. Still, as he harvested the bark, he stayed in the waist-high grass as much as possible, ready to drop out of sight at the slightest noise.

The days passed as he applied moss and honey to Ah-ga's wounds, harvested bark often for pain, and brought water in his cupped hands so she could drink. Still, his pairmate got worse until cysts filled with slimy green puss that smelled like offal covered her legs. He ruptured the cysts, re-applied the poultices, but it did no good. Her skin burned so, he submerged her entire body in the cold river, head in his lap. He shivered so hard his teeth chattered, warmed by the heat radiating from Ah-ga's skin.

One night, his shaking hands pouring water on her fiery body, dripping tears, her chest fell and didn't rise. Pan-do dropped his head to her breasts and shook with sobs.

"How do I survive the pain of life with you?"

Unexpectedly, the wind whispered, *Lyta.*

He tipped his head to the sky and loosed a long, mournful howl.


As many days passed as fingers on both hands before he caught up with his People. No one asked about Ah-ga. All knew why he arrived alone. Lyta took his hand. Sa-mo-ke greeted him with relief. Pan-do's lips were badly swollen, as was his weak eye. The strong one, the color of a blackberry, had nearly closed. Sadness leeched from his body

Pan-do motioned, "You did well, Lead Warrior. Few seasoned males could have done what you did here."

Sa-mo-ke shook his head. "Many died so those you see here could escape. The injured—most we had to abandon."

Pan-do had seen the bodies, ravaged by Coyote and Hyaena. "Victory requires sacrifice, Lead Warrior."

Lyta tipped her head upward and Sa-mo-ke motioned, "There's a bright star Lyta insists will guide us. It hangs over the fire-breathing mountains."

"Lead."

He pushed the group as hard as he dared, keeping a brisk pace and avoiding all animal trails. That meant fighting their way around clinging brush and struggling up and down steep ridges. At night, they slept in hollow trunks, nests like Cousin Chimp, or holes lined with grass and leaves for warmth. Though the air felt warmer here, when Sun slept, it became as cold as their homeland.

One night, their only protection was against a cliff wall and under a weak-looking overhang. When most had finally fallen asleep, the ground shook violently. The People ignored it until chunks of the roof tumbled down and buried groupmates. Everyone rushed out just before the rest of the overhang collapsed.

Pan-do huffed. "This place confuses me. The mountains spit fire to keep us warm but shake the land until it almost buries us!"

They spent until Sun awoke salving cuts, applying poultices to scrapes, and chewing shredded bark to numb aches. When Sun awoke, they left, dodging berms and lakes, plagued by the constantly shaking earth. It was like nothing Pan-do had ever experienced. Water became their biggest worry. Every morning, Pan-do and groupmembers licked the night's dew from the leaves and Spider's webs. A good day would be when Lyta caught a water scent in the air. Often— usually—it was a dark spot at the base of a cliff. Then they dug until the ground turned to mud and they could squeeze the water into their mouths.

For days and then a moon, and then another, they crossed dull brown terrain under thin wisps of clouds, saturated in the smell of Fire Mountain's anger, breathing in the muggy air that threatened but never delivered rain. Bored and dejected, Pan-do crested yet another hill.

In front, like a massive herd, stretched a vast swaying field of grass. In the dark shadows on the edging cliffs were caves. He waved wildly to the struggling group and ran toward them, oblivious to any danger. It helped that Lyta hobbled along with him. If she had sensed danger, she would have told him.

Sa-mo-ke stopped him before he entered the first cave. "I go."

Pan-do nodded anxiously. When his Lead Warrior returned with a smile, the People bedded down for the night, satisfied for the first time in hands of days.

The next day, Pan-do sent scouts to explore what could be their new home. When Sun prepared to sleep without their reappearance, he became worried. Before he could decide whether to wait or follow the scouts' tracks, Sa-mo-ke sprinted into the camp, winded, face drawn and smudged with dirt.

"Others head this way."

"The Hairless Ones?"

Sa-m o-ke shook his head.

Pan-do set his mouth in a firm line. "We will explain we mean no trouble. If they desire we leave, maybe they can guide us to unclaimed territory."

# Chapter 12

Morning arrived with such hope and magnificence that Pan-do couldn't help but smile. Lyta seemed to agree. For the first time since their trip began, she wasn't flicking her fingers or twirling or frowning. Calm bathed her body, a sure sign this site was good. Maybe their trip ended here.

"Leader," Sa-mo-ke motioned. "I go to see if the warriors from yesterday left."

Pan-do nodded and Sa-mo-ke led a small group into the tall brush around the caves but he wasn't even out of sight before stumbling backward, pushed at spear point by rough-looking warriors.

Sa-mo-ke motioned, "I found them."

Pan-do offered a wan smile. "They look friendly."

He glanced at his daughter, wondering how she missed this danger but everything about her remained peaceful, almost expectant.

No one stood out as an obvious Leader so Pan-do turned to the one in front and lifted his hands, palms up, in a universal sign of friendship.

No reaction. In fact, the male's eyes remained flat with no curiosity about the group he threatened, as though he did this often.

"Maybe they don't understand."

"They understand," from Lyta, her eyes alight, voice like birdsong.

These Others were similar to Pan-do's People except for the longer heads, flat receding foreheads, and the massive bony ridge that shaded their eyes.

"No stone-tipped spears," Pan-do motioned to Sa-mo-ke. His Lead Warrior offered a faint nod but kept his gaze on the intruders.

Lyta tapped her fingers against her leg replicating the in-and-out breathing of the warriors. In the mass of fear-frozen bodies and troubled faces, she alone seemed content. This enemy—they must wonder at her presence as he—who must be the Leader—greeted armed strangers. They couldn't know that this fragile female with the ethereal beauty was his early warning of danger.

Finally, with a flurry of shuffling and jostling, an elder warrior shoved to the front, grunted something unintelligible, and then sprinted from the clearing at a ground-eating pace. Lyta hobbled after him and Pan-do matched her labored speed knowing she could go no faster. She began to slap her thigh in rhythm with her steps and soon, everyone trotted to her beat, including the Others.

Sun burned a brilliant and blinding white as they crossed a grassy plateau, past fruit trees and bushes filled with berries. A stifling heat rose from the baked earth, swamping the People in sweat. Some collapsed but when threatened, were dragged onward by groupmembers. Sun was almost to its well-deserved rest when finally, the Others chirped and strange females and children materialized around them. Lyta slowed, searching the new group as though expecting someone.

"There are more Others here than I can tick off on a handful of hands," Pan-do muttered to no one.

Lyta sniffed and limped away, following a scent. One of the warriors prodded her with his spear, albeit hesitantly. She responded with a brilliant smile and mimed, "Water..." cupping her hand as though to drink.

He pointed ahead and Lyta slipped in among the crowd. When Pan-do tried to follow, the Others' warriors stopped him. No one noticed—or cared—that Lyta drank her fill from a large lake and then scooped up a handful of water, elbowed the spear-carrying warriors aside without spilling a drop, and approached her father.

"Give that to Red-dit, Lyta."

Sa-mo-ke laughed. "I see it's not just us. Even these who don't know your daughter do as asked."

Lyta trundled toward Red-dit, one of the pregnant females, her stomach so large, crouching was impossible. The female drank gratefully.

Lyta shuffled up to Pan-do with a sigh. "He's not here."

Before Pan-do could ask who "he" was, Sa-mo-ke motioned, "Where do they sleep? I see no caves or trees."

Pan-do looked around. He too had expected caves but there was only a clearing protected on one side by a soaring cliff and the other by a lake.

"A good question. No matter their size, sleeping in the open is risky."

He swatted at a flying insect. "How do they stand these creatures?" and he slapped another, this time connecting. "They bite so deeply, they draw blood." He brushed several from his eyes and clawed one from his nose before giving up. "I need Hipparion's tail."

The Other warriors hadn't moved, still staring at Pan-do's group. He unclenched his fists and grinned, refusing to be intimidated. His hand motion for "friend" again got no response.

He murmured to Sa-mo-ke. "They are waiting."

"For what?"

"Their Leader. He must be the only one who can make the decision."

The gray night turned inky black, Moon showed its face, and still, everyone waited. Only Lyta's soft humming broke the silence.

Finally, the wall of warriors parted and a massive muscular male as dark as Panther pushed forward. His neck melted into his shoulders, wide and corded. His nose, broad but flat, protruded from a sculpted face. Power radiated from every part of his body. His arms hung ready, one with a spear and the other a handaxe.

"He must be the Leader," Pan-do motioned quietly.

A tall, lithe female joined him. She moved with the silence of sunlight, her wealth of hair glistening as it swayed to her steps, neck pale in Moon's muted glow, bearing straight and proud. Between her breasts bounced a sack, stuffed full. She towered over the male by a head, gracile in build where the male Leader was short and thick boned. Like the dark male, her spear filled one hand and a handaxe the other.

"The Leader's mate," Pan-do whispered under his breath.

Lyta shook her head and shuffled forward, gaze locked on the female. Pan-do tugged her back. He kept his weapon down and again tried the motion for "friend". She stared at him, betraying neither comprehension nor confusion. If he interpreted her facial expressions, gestures, and grunts correctly, she was more curious than threatening. If he misread this, Lyta would tell him. Risk made her scream.

The dark male puffed his chest and stepped to within an arm of Pan-do. This close, Pan-do saw both his youth and the battle scars he wore with pride. A warrior's warrior. He seemed to think that his blooded body and aura of command would intimidate Pan-do into giving respect not yet earned, but he had the wrong adversary for that. Pan-do had lost a home, friends, and a lifelong pairmate. What else could this male take?

He twitched, thinking of Lyta. She was his weak spot. He allowed a glimmer of respect to touch his face.

"Nightshade." The male pointed inward.

"I am Pan-do. These are my People," and he motioned around himself.

Nightshade dismissed Pan-do, moving on to Lyta. Her beauty and sincerity captured every male. Unlike the dark coarseness of most People who spent their days in the sun, Lyta's fawn-colored skin remained both flawless and smooth. Most saw a weak female who would bend to their will but nothing was further from the truth. Lyta never aligned with anyone's wishes except her father's and that only because she felt he needed her.

When Nightshade extended a hand toward her, Lyta jerked away, swallowing, but never lost eye contact. She was neither frightened by his power nor intimidated by his self-aggrandizement. Pan-do heard her sniff and saw her mouth tighten. He smelled it too, deceit, as potent as the stench of carrion.

Nightshade seemed not to notice and moved on to Pan-do's bone-thin warriors, few with the musculature of the Leader's well-fed fighters. Finished with his assessment, he fixed Pan-do with a querulous stare, some decision made. What that was, Pan-do had no idea.

The warrior's mate stayed still, one muscular arm lose at her side, the other lightly gripping her spear. Though obviously a skilled warrior, comfortable with battle, the look she gave Pan-do seemed unsure.

"I am Xhosa," she spoke and motioned her call sign. "You enter my People's territory."

Pan-do knew he failed to hide his surprise when her lips tugged into a faint smile.

"I am Pan-do, Leader Xhosa. This is my daughter, Lyta, and my Lead Warrior, Sa-mo-ke."

Xhosa studied Lyta who studied Xhosa. The subadult's hands perfectly reproduced Xhosa's call sign and then she motioned, "I've never met a female Leader."

Xhosa studied her for a breath, raised an eyebrow as though to acknowledge the statement, and then turned back to Pan-do. "Why are you here?"

Images of blood and destruction flashed across his mind, the ravaged body of his mate, the butchery of the friendly Hairy Ones, the horror of the deadly spears. *We are outcasts trying simply to survive.*

That was none of her business. Yet. "We flee violent Uprights who infest our home like a disease. We seek a new homeland far enough from them that we are safe," and he again motioned to his People.

Faintly, certainly not expecting an answer, Lyta rephrased the question to Xhosa. "Why are you here when danger surrounds you?"

Pan-do stiffened and his eyes widened. That explained why the Leader's warriors were constantly alert, hair puffed, weapons at the ready though fatigue seeped from their eyes and muscles.

"What perils face us here?" He muttered to himself but motioned to Xhosa, "Do not be alarmed by Lyta. She sees detail better than any warrior."

Xhosa fixed on Lyta. "Everything you see is our home, young one. You intrude."

Though the words might sting, they were softened by the twinkle in her eye.

Pan-do jumped in. "She intended no disrespect. My daughter can only speak the truth. My People appreciate her honesty but it is challenging for those newly met."

He hoped his openness would relax the Leader but she didn't react. He swallowed and dipped his head once. Was it the difference in language?

"She understands," Lyta sang, in a low mellow voice. Xhosa gave her a funny look, not unfriendly but tinged heavily with curiosity. Nightshade jerked but some of his warriors hid smiles. When his gaze settled again on Lyta, it held none of the earlier warmth.

"Shhh, Lyta."

"Shhh, Lyta," she repeated, stomping her foot.

Nightshade hardened further. Lyta made an enemy.

When Nightshade stepped closer, Pan-do smelled a rotting tooth. The warrior motioned, "You lie, intruder. You are hungry. You don't take time to treat injuries. What enemy chases you to our territory?"

"We don't lie," Lyta sang.

Pan-do offered a faint smile without removing his attention from the warrior in front of him. How much should he tell? Would this male appreciate that Pan-do brought knowledge of an unknown and dangerous opponent or value the protection afforded by a larger group?

"We travel for many moons from our home. There, Endless Sea surrounds us on two sides and salt rather than sulfur fills the air."

The quizzical looks around him said this place he described was not one they understood. He would explain it later.

Nightshade crossed his arms and widened his stance but Xhosa relaxed. Her posture, words, in fact everything about her was designed to evoke confidence without coercion.

She motioned, "But you are chased. By whom?"

When Pan-do described the hairless bodies, vaulted heads, and unusual spears of his enemies, her face paled while Nightshade's darkened.

She motioned, "How far away do you live, man-called-Pan-do?"

He pointed at Moon and ticked off every finger on both hands. "This far."

He thought the vast distance would please her but her face whitened further. She seemed about to say something but didn't.

After a moment, she straightened her body, bumped her nose up, and motioned, "You escape nothing. They are here, too."

# Chapter 13

"They cannot stay!" Nightshade's Second, Snake, shouted, stabbing his spear into the soil.

"Quiet!" Nightshade hissed, "This is not your decision!"

Xhosa and Nightshade left Snake bristling and moved away from the strangers.

"Snake is right, though, Xhosa. We should kill the males and claim the females and children as ours. The warrior Samo-ke is too weak and the Leader Pan-do too kind." This last he motioned dismissively, like a flaw to be expunged. "They would not serve us well. And what if their Big Heads followed them?"

A melodious voice interrupted. "We weren't. Followed."

Lyta bounced on her tiny feet, eyes locked on Xhosa. Why would her People keep such a frail creature who couldn't walk well? Her only contribution seemed to be her ability to notice details and hear lies.

Pan-do flashed his teeth and motioned to Xhosa, "Lyta learned your words on the walk here from our camp. And the tiny details she notices include sounds."

Which stopped Xhosa. Was Lyta's skill like Xhosa's farsight but different than what is seen? Xhosa found herself staring into the distance at nothing, wondering about this far-thinking skill.

Lyta whispered something to her father and he motioned to Xhosa, "Her suggestion is you move further away if you need privacy."

Xhosa responded with a noncommittal one-handed gesture. Her back was to Nightshade so she didn't see his response but felt the burn of his anger, rising like steamy heat from Fire Mountain's vent. He gripped her arm and guided her behind a boulder.

"Why would Big Heads follow them this far? Are you thinking they want to band together with ours to fight us, Nightshade? No animal does that —Sabertooth never joins a strange pack to attack a herd."

Nightshade's shoulders bunched. "We know they gather warriors from far away, much more of them than the group who lives here."

Xhosa's head began to hurt, a rumble that would soon squeeze her temples and cheeks like Cat's jaws. She must ignore it, continue as though nothing was wrong.

She motioned, "Pan-do beat the Big Heads. His strategies may be helpful—"

"I need no help from these weaklings," he growled as he snatched a flying insect from the air and swallowed it. "Pan-do fled rather than defend his home. I don't want warriors who would do that—"

"Our strength, warriors trained by you, could retake what he gave up."

Nightshade fell silent so she continued, "There's another solution, Nightshade. We leave, take the path marked by my father."

Nightshade took a long halting breath, mouth tense, but his shoulders drooped. As Leader, it was her decision, not his.

Nightshade and Xhosa stepped around the boulder to observe the newcomers. Lyta was busy carrying handfuls of water to the pregnant females. Sa-mo-ke was motioning to Pan-do, arms waving over the motley group of males around him. All looked dispirited and tired, their warclubs chipped and spears dull.

As they watched, Sa-mo-ke's gaze found Nightshade. He turned to him, stance strong, feet wide, spear and warclub in hand.

"That one," and Nightshade pointed at Sa-mo-ke, "is the only warrior worth saving. The rest must be trained or destroyed."

Xhosa shrugged, not caring either way, but a hunch made her think these males were stouter than Nightshade expected.

"There is a reason they survived on the run against countless enemies for so many moons, Lead Warrior."

She glanced toward Lyta, hobbling between the lake and her People, never spilling a drop of the precious water, face radiating what could only be described as happiness. "Something about the girl Lyta intrigues me."

Xhosa and Nightshade approached Pan-do. As though to prove her Lead Warrior's point, Sa-mo-ke emitted no scent of fear. In fact, Xhosa saw nothing but confidence and power.

Xhosa motioned, "Come, Pan-do. Tell us about this far away homeland of yours."

The two groups gathered behind the bramble barrier and Pan-do enraptured everyone with stories of his People. It didn't take long to decode his calls, chirps, body movements, and hand motions. They sounded like those of Coyote when angry or Wolf playing or Cousin Chimp calling friends. The words that made no sense were those related to locations like *limestone cave* or unknown animals like the *white-headed black-winged bird*. When she asked about Fire Mountains, Pan-do said they didn't live in his homeland. Her many questions about how Big Heads fought and why Pan-do's People lost would wait until they could speak privately.

Bellies full, Sa-mo-ke and Pan-do joined Nightshade's warriors patrolling the camp while Xhosa escaped to the quiet of a boulder. She chewed on pain bark while listening to Panther cough as he neared his prey, Owl hoot a warning to a hapless rodent, and Wolf's chilling howl answered by pack members.

When the ache in her head had dulled sufficiently, she joined Pan-do sitting on a ridge that overlooked the People's land.

"You discovered one of my favorite spots, Leader Pan-do. I often come here to soak in the night's guidance."

Pan-do smiled. "Another similarity in our leadership."

"Are you not sleepy, after such a challenging day?"

"I am too excited to sleep. For the first time in many moons, my People feel safe." He studied her. "They are, aren't they? Your confrontation with those you call Big Heads and we call Hairless Ones has ended?"

She ignored the question. "Tell me more about your homeland."

"It was beautiful with high plateaus, woodlands, and waterholes stuffed with fish. My father lived there as did his. It rained often but the caves we shared with the Hairy Ones always remained warm and dry." He paused at Xhosa's confusion. "They are Uprights but not Others. They are more comfortable in the trees than the open grasslands that you enjoy."

As he spoke, his daughter squeezed against him, leaning her head on his shoulder. He absent-mindedly petted her hair as he continued.

"Their legs are shorter than mine, arms longer, heads smaller, actions slower, and dense fur covers much of their bodies."

Xhosa nodded. "I know of them but haven't seen any since I was a child." No need to explain that one named Lucy often visited her dreams, at least not yet.

Pan-do continued, "During the last hot time, many waterholes dried up and didn't refill when the rain returned. The air—it became so cold, we shivered all the time despite the protection of our caves. When the one you call Big Heads arrived, they wore animal skins—"

"They pretended to be animals?"

"No. We could see they were Uprights. We thought they wrapped their bodies in the hides for warmth—as do animals—but came to realize it was to trick us. They knew our respect for all animals would mean we trusted those who honored them by wearing their skins. By the time we realized we were wrong, it was too late."

Xhosa peered into the darkness. "We too respect animals. They struggle to survive this land as we do. When we lose one of our People to Cat, we know Cat must eat. We raise our children as Wolf does—to be strong—and as Hyaena does, to be patient."

Pan-do chuffed. "Then you'll enjoy this story. Early in our travels, we came to a wide river. As I pondered how to cross it, Cousin Chimp arrived, stared, and left. I thought nothing of this. Why would he know how to cross when I didn't? A finger of Sun's travel passed before Cousin Chimp returned with a stick. Imagine my surprise when he moved down the shoreline, toward me, and marched into the river, stabbing the riverbed as water rose to his calves, his hips, even his waist, but there it stopped and Cousin Chimp walked across."

Pan-do grinned. "Cousin Chimp taught me that to cross a river, I need only find where it is shallow. Me, I saw everywhere as deep."

Silence fell between them but a comfortable one. Xhosa wanted to hear about the girl's farsight but wasn't sure how to ask.

She glanced at Lyta, eyes closed but Xhosa doubted in sleep. "Lyta is different."

Pan-do showed his teeth. "Yes, in a good way. A walk with Lyta becomes an adventure. Her hand explores the roughness of a tree's bark, the brittleness of scrubbrush, and the bounty of seedpods. She will bump into everything around her just to hear the noise and then reproduce it."

As if to prove his point, Lyta jumped up, cocked her head, and stepped in rhythm with the chirring of grasshoppers.

Pan-do laughed. "Walking in rhythm with sounds sooths her. It can be Cousin Chimp, insects, the thrum of raindrops, the rush of wind, or a grass fire. Anything aural, Lyta can repeat. Her imitations of bird chirps are so exact that they come to her voice."

"Why does she flick her fingers?"

"That calms her, as does twirling and swaying."

Lyta tapped her feet to an insect's chirrup.

"Lyta likes you, Xhosa. That means more than you can imagine. One of her traits—as you say, that makes her 'different'—is her ability to smell evil and dishonesty. No one can hide it from her. I've never been led astray when following her instincts."

Lyta stared at Xhosa and flicked her fingers.

"She finds neither in you, Leader Xhosa."

Xhosa looked away to hide the warmth that flushed her face and neck. Pan-do's honesty was unusual in a warrior as was the trust he placed in the youngster Lyta. It would be incomprehensible except that her own father had treated her that way.

"Where is your pairmate, Pan-do?"

The Leader blanched and finally whispered, "Dead."

He shook as Wolf does to throw water from his fur. "I have a story to entertain you before we sleep." Lyta settled at his feet. One by one, others of both groups joined her, sensing something fun about to happen.

"Long ago, I stumbled on a carcass not yet chewed by Eagle or Coyote. Hunger made me eat from it even though the predator responsible for the kill undoubtedly remained close. Was the risk of starving to death greater than becoming someone else's meal?" He shrugged. "Obviously, I lived."

Everyone awake squatted by Pan-do, attention fixed on the storyteller, mouths open. Even Nightshade listened intently.

Pan-do continued, "I'd not been there long when a porcupine began to eat at the forelegs—I was at the hind legs. I considered his arrival fortunate for he would alert me to danger. Soon, in fact, his quills stiffened and he raised his head. I watched as a coyote and another approached from different directions."

He yawned. "But I must sleep."

"What happened?" A child yelled as another giggled. "How did you escape?"

Pan-do responded with his own laugh. "Think about what you would do and tell me."

When Pan-do tucked in with Lyta, exhaustion from the long travel and the new Others finally catching up with him, his daughter motioned, "Xhosa didn't tell you the truth. The conflict with the Big Heads isn't over," and she fell asleep. It took Pan-do much longer to drift off, struggling with why Xhosa would hide that from him and what it meant.

Xhosa liked the new Leader. He was smart with common sense that protected his People as the prickled barrier did sleepers. His mildness might be out of step with the treachery of this land but it balanced Nightshade's ruthlessness.

One point they agreed on was the importance of keeping their People safe. Her father would want to help Pan-do.

# Chapter 14

The next morning, Nightshade explained to Pan-do that if he was to stay with the People, his warriors must be trained. Pan-do agreed, telling Sa-mo-ke that learning under the guidance of a fighter like Nightshade would be an honor. Nightshade scoffed at the praise, explaining he must forge their sloppy fighters into an effective and domineering weapon before the Big Heads invaded.

Sa-mo-ke stiffened. "Will that be soon?"

"Soon enough. Knowing how to fight will make the difference between slaughter and survival. Now go with Snake!"

Xhosa grimaced as Nightshade huffed his displeasure as the scraggly group advanced toward the practice field. "Can you train them in time?"

Nightshade's face hardened. "Each day, Pan-do's warriors will be more prepared than the day before. Whether that is long enough, no one knows."

Nightshade left and Xhosa joined the rest of the males and females knapping scrapers, choppers, handaxes, cutters, and the other tools. Some would be used to slash attackers; others, like the sturdy blunt-end cleaver, to cut tissue and bone. Knapping was a complicated task that often required an exacting length, breadth, and thickness. The most challenging tool was the handaxe, a flat cobble longer than a hand with a narrow rounded point and broad base that must be flaked to a sharp edge on both sides. The hard rocks required for this tool were mined only in quarries by Fire Mountain so beginners practiced with pond stones. Completed tools were gathered in a communal pile to be loaded into individual neck sacks.

Too soon, Xhosa's shadow became a tiny sliver and her hair a soggy mat. Her back ached, her hands throbbed, and her eyes burned from the dust. She walked around, unbending her stiff legs, and nibbled at dried berries. Her muscles more relaxed, she picked up another stone, uncovered the story it held, and began.

Nightshade glowered at the group in front of him. The People's warriors defeated Pan-do's in every skirmish not only because of superior skills but because of their dogged stamina. At the end of the first day, he fed only those who chased down their own food. The rest—which included all of Pan-do's—slept hungry. Snake, Nightshade's Second, admitted they were good hunters but slow so the People always got to the prey first.

As the days passed, Nightshade recognized one of the true strengths of Pan-do's warriors: They never quit. Each morning, they awoke energized, yesterday's disappointments forgotten. They fought tenaciously, hunted vigorously, and sprinted until they collapsed. No amount of failure defeated them.

Then, one day, the rhythm changed. Dirty-gray clouds gathered overhead until they blocked the sun. Nightshade ignored the imminent storm saying battles occurred in rain or sun. He paired up warriors who would fight until one lost. But no one gave up, even as the sky switched from dark to stark white, despite the deafening crashes of thunder that drowned out all senses, continuing when a huge tree at the edge of the field burst into flames and hurled burning embers over the fighters.

This impressed Nightshade but it didn't end there.

All battles finally ended in a draw except the one between Sa-mo-ke and Snake. Despite a brutal contest, neither would quit. Every time Snake thought he defeated Sa-mo-ke, the tough male escaped. Finally, Snake showered Sa-mo-ke with a ruthless series of blows and headbutts. Sa-mo-ke's eyes blackened and swelled and his lips turned red with blood but he wouldn't stop. Finally, what had to be the end, he tripped over a sharp rock and fell, slipping in the mud, wincing as a deep gouge ripped through his leg.

Snake set his feet in the slick soil, fists poised for the final strike and smirked, "Give up."

Sa-mo-ke leaned heavily against one arm, his blood mixing with the rain. No one would have thought less of him if he quit but instead, he fixed Snake with a defiant glare.

"You give up, Second of Xhosa, and I will let you live."

Blood covered his skin. His strong arm hung uselessly, unable to hold the warclub or spear, but he showed neither fear nor resentment.

Snake stiffened with rage and growled, "You have lost but you won't admit it!"

Sa-mo-ke didn't blink. "You are to blame for what happens next."

Snake howled and swung his club for what he thought would be the winning blow but something flew from Sa-mo-ke's hand. It slashed a deep groove in Snake's upper arm. He dropped the club so his hand could staunch the bleeding. Sa-mo-ke leaped to his one good leg and charged—well, hopped, swinging his warclub weak-handed at Snake's exposed chest. It smacked into the warrior's muscle-bound chest sending both of them splashing into the mud. Snake lay there stunned, staring a "what just happened" look at Sa-mo-ke.

Neither got up. The fight was over.

Nightshade couldn't believe what he saw either. "What cut him?"

Sa-mo-ke showed him a specially-designed cutter, rounder than the usual choppers.

"Show me how it works."

Branches of fire cut the sky and then a rumble. Rain poured down in sheets, saturating all of them with freezing pellets. Sa-mo-ke whisked them from his eyes as he pushed to his good leg. He spiraled his body, ignoring the pain in his bad leg, digging his toes into the squishy mud. As one arm crossed over his chest, he flicked his wrist and flung. The projectile sliced the wet air and embedded deeply into a tree's bark.

Sa-mo-ke motioned, "I held back on Snake. I wanted him to learn a lesson, not lose an arm."

Snake pushed to within a hand of Sa-mo-ke. "Teach me how to do that." The statement, though growled, came out a question.

Sa-mo-ke handed Snake one of the throwers. While all other warriors left, bedraggled and sodden, the two practiced. They finally straggled into camp, Sa-mo-ke's eye watering, Snake's black and swollen shut, both with cheekbones in varying shades of purple, blue and yellow, feet making sucking sounds as they trudged along the muddy path. Their heads bent together, sharing something that made both break into loud guffaws.

As days passed without the Big Heads, the females of both groups foraged together while the males trained. Because Pan-do stayed away from the warriors' practice, Xhosa got to watch him with his daughter. She always seemed happy. If he comfortably blended leadership with fatherhood, why couldn't she?

It was time to tell Nightshade she would pairmate in the new home.


"Ouch!" Pan-do yelped as he pricked a finger on the bramble bush collected.

The children giggled.

"Here." One of the females—Mbasa, Pan-do remembered—wrapped a leaf around his fingers. "The sleeping barrier must be as thick as I am tall so no animal can leap over or crawl through."

He smiled his thanks. "You are Nightshade's pairmate?"

"No. I bleed but am still learning to mate. He wishes only to pairmate with Xhosa." She motioned this as though everyone knew. The bruises on her legs and arms belied her smile.

"Pan-do—what happened?" A young voice shouted from across the clearing.

Pan-do searched. Two eyes stared at him, wide and curious, mouth open.

"With what?"

The youngster shouldered his way past the crowd and skidded to a stop in front of Pan-do. "When the coyotes tried to take the carcass that you and porcupine ate?"

Many ears perked. Even the warriors wanted to hear the answer

Pan-do snickered. "What would you do?"

"I would have fled!"

"As did I, young one. Besides, my belly was full."

A chuckle rippled through the crowd but his daughter stiffened and stared into the distance.

Nightshade motioned to Pan-do. "I see why you refused to share that answer."

Pan-do motioned, "What do you mean?"

"It makes you look weak and stupid."

Pan-do refused to allow this warrior to rile him. "Knowing when to confront an enemy is often the most difficult—and wisest—decision."

"I heard how you run from enemies. Do you ever confront them, Leader Pan-do? Or is that never the "difficult and wise" decision?"

Nightshade didn't wait for an answer.

Pan-do watched as his warriors left to patrol with Nightshade's. The fact that Sa-mo-ke liked Nightshade despite the male's obvious animosity toward Pan-do didn't bother Pan-do as much as what he himself had done to anger the Lead Warrior. He hoped to find out tonight.

He hid in the darkness outside of the sleeping area and sniffed for Nightshade's scent. Instead, he got a sharp cutter pressed into his throat, hard enough to draw blood.

"If I hadn't smelled you, Pan-do, you would be dead."

"I didn't try to be quiet—" he lied.

"But you should. Always. You no longer live in your safe caves with mild-mannered Hairy Ones. Here, danger always stalks."

"I was looking for Nightshade, Leader Xhosa."

She released him and motioned, "He prepares. Conflict comes."

Pan-do shivered. "My daughter feels it, too."

When Xhosa said nothing, he left. As he lay next to Lyta, Pan-do smelled Nightshade's sweat, heard his unique footsteps.

"Bad man," Lyta hissed in the darkness. "Evil."

"What do you mean?"

"Don't trust him. Xhosa shouldn't either," and closed her eyes.

# Chapter 15

Xhosa awoke the next morning, anxious from a dream of the Hairy One Lucy, her pairmate Garv, child Voi, and a friendly blue-eyed wolf named Ump. This was the first time since her father died that Lucy had visited Xhosa's dreams. Last night, the ancient female fled for her life, following landmarks Xhosa recognized as well as cairns that must be her father's.

Xhosa swallowed the pain bark and then kicked a sleeping Pan-do as last night's scouts thundered into camp, breathless, sweat pouring from their bodies despite the cool morning.

"One and another and another..." The ticks against her fingers matched the expected number and she breathed out.

Snake stood by Nightshade, still wearing a leaf poultice from his skirmish with Sa-mo-ke, listening to the report of the Lead Scout.

"Big Heads are on our borders..." He wheezed, gulping, and continued, "A day, maybe two…" He collapsed to his knees, crushing a hand-sized spider, face red.

The scouts began to talk over each other, hands flying, bodies bobbing, until Nightshade bellowed, "Quiet!" He motioned to Rainbow, the adult tasked as the Second on this outing. "What did you find?"

Rainbow's ready smile, liquid eyes, and flashing white teeth got him much attention from the females but not the males. They responded to prowess and Rainbow was weak, whiney, and indecisive, one who delegated duties rather than do them himself. Nightshade tolerated him because he was disposable.

Rainbow saw a chance to shine. "They amass a huge force in our territory."

Rainbow spread his arms, warming to his listeners. "But as Lead Warrior Nightshade asked, I have found us a new home, away from this danger. It is far from here, rich with herds, awash in grass, and with no trace of Big Heads."

As he talked, Lyta's nose twitched in disgust. "Can he not smell that where he wants us to go takes us right into the Big Heads' camp?"

Nightshade paced. "Where you speak of, Rainbow, we were there when Xhosa's father lived—"

Rainbow interrupted, "It is replenished, Nightshade. Grass abounds. Mammoth and gazelle are heavy with young."

Nightshade glowered but the subadults who had scouted with Rainbow eagerly bobbed their heads. "Take your scouts, Rainbow. Watch the Big Heads. Tell me if anything changes. We leave tomorrow's tomorrow."

Surely he didn't consider Rainbow's suggestion. When she caught Nightshade's eye, she smiled to herself.

Nightshade motioned to Pan-do, "Come with me!"

Without waiting for agreement, he left.

Xhosa licked her lips. Two days! That was barely enough time to replenish her healing plants. Cousin Chimp scolded her as she ran from the camp. Birds took up the protest in harsh chatter. A fat, old, near-sighted pig crossed her trail and froze when it picked up her scent. A hard-thrown clod of dirt hurried it out of her way.

A hand of Sun's travel overhead, while Xhosa dug out the root ball of a deep-rooted plant hoping to prevent damage to the nodules, the animals fell silent. Xhosa froze, her senses alive. Beneath her, she felt the rumble of steps. One Upright, maybe two, close by, and then a bush rustled. She peeked over the grass and gulped down a gasp.

It was a Big Head warrior.

He smelled her, head rotating, a tightly-gripped warclub in one hand and a stone-tipped spear in the other. Xhosa crawled backward but her foot hit a ground-nesting bird. It screamed and launched. The Big Head snapped his head up to the bird while the other pivoted her direction.

It was Wind.

# Chapter 16

Pan-do pretended surprise when Nightshade invited—ordered—they hunt together. Last night, Lyta heard the Lead Warrior argue with Xhosa.

*"I don't trust Pan-do."*

*"I can take care of myself, Nightshade."*

*"I will make sure of that."*

Hunting with Nightshade gave Pan-do the opportunity he'd missed last night.

The acrid tang of sulfur made Pan-do sneeze. "Is it always like this?"

Pan-do rubbed his nose. The dark clouds of dust and cinder from Fire Mountain drifted over everything. If he was to stay here, he must get used to it.

Nightshade ignored him.

As always, the Lead Warrior carried his warclub, a thick weapon as long as his forearm, wide at the top and tapered to a narrow knob where he could hold it. They avoided animal trails as they scrabbled among prickled bushes and over a rock bed, trusting the hard land to conceal their tracks from any Big Head scouts. They crossed a sequence of rolling hills, skirted a herd of gazelle, and dodged a family of pigs snooting for food. Nightshade moved quickly, not waiting for Pan-do, never checking that he followed, seeming not to care. Pan-do though, hardened by moons of travel, easily kept pace. In fact, he slowed down so he wouldn't pass Nightshade.

After ascending a steep incline, dodging massive boulders lodged in craters, and leaping over gaping cracks that cleaved the land, they arrived at a vast plateau far from homebase.

"Show me your tools," Nightshade ordered. Pan-do did as asked. The Lead Warrior pawed through them, picking out a sharp cutter sized to Pan-do's hand. "Sa-mo-ke has one like this?"

"Of course. All my warriors carry these."

"Where's the hand axe?" At Pan-do's quizzical look, Nightshade handed him a flat cobble from his own neck sack, longer than a hand with both surfaces flaked to a sharp edge. It took Pan-do a moment before he recognized his people's version.

"Here. Ours flange in the middle and narrow at the ends. Watch," and he deftly swung it in a looping motion using both ends to pulverize a root faster than Nightshade's tool.

"Hmmph."

After a moment, Nightshade snatched Pan-do's spear, not without a grimace from Pan-do. He lost it once in a flash flood, finally discovering it high in the branches of a tree. Spears took many days to shape, perfected to the individual hunter, and finding wood hard enough took time.

Nightshade stabbed it into the hard earth. Pan-do cringed but remained silent. He would resharpen it.

"This might suit your tree-thick homeland where prey is close but not the grasslands."

It was time to stand up to this warrior. "Let's see who can throw further."

Pan-do gripped his spear where long experience told him it balanced perfectly, stretched his weak arm forward as though pointing, and flung. It flew like a bird, finally settling into the undulating grass.

Nightshade's expression betrayed his surprise. He lifted his spear above his shoulder and level with his ear, fidgeted briefly for the balance point, spread his feet beneath his body, and hurled with a stutter step to add force.

He grunted in satisfaction but Pan-do knew that wouldn't last. When Nightshade found his own spear, he frowned.

"I missed yours."

"No, not yet." Pan-do proceeded one stride, another, and another, until he bent and picked up his spear.

Nightshade gasped. "How did you do that? With that distance, you can hit a monkey in a tree."

Pan-do grinned. "And I do."

Nightshade harrumphed and left, Pan-do scrambling after him. They crossed sign of grouse, hare, and a pig but Nightshade continued. The warrior sniffed what could be gazelle tracks, fingered them, and moved on. Pan-do required no test to know they were too old but kept silent. Nightshade probably considered this training. The next prints that caught Nightshade's attention were topped by deep pinpricks, one for each of Pan-do's fingers.

"Wolf. He's outside his territory. "

Pan-do sniffed. "There's no urine or excrement to warn other's away," which meant he hunted alone. "If he downed an animal, we can steal it," but the tracks meandered off. Whatever he trailed escaped.

Each sign, Nightshade appraised and rejected until Pan-do motioned, "Are we looking for a particular animal?" He got no answer.

Sun moved a hand and another overhead before they rested at a waterhole. A small herd of Hipparion drank alongside a black rhino and a Sabertooth cat. On the shore, a Chalicothere browsed the top sprouts of an acacia. Nightshade motioned Pan-do to a second trail that led to the water. They would wait until a weak animal left and then one of them would drive it to the other for the kill.

As a Hipparion herd wandered off, thirst quenched, one female limped after them, favoring her rear leg. Before long, she fell far behind.

Nightshade motioned, "We move between her and the herd."

Coyote hunted this way as did Cat and her cousins, but Hipparion's hooves would be fast and deadly, despite its injury.

Pan-do motioned, "Rather than confronting Hipparion where it is strongest, I'll go above it, to that bluff—"

"It's upwind." Nightshade motioned.

"When I cover my body with Hipparion dung, it will think I am from its herd."

"No one can throw that far, from that bluff." Nightshade based his comment on the distance Pan-do threw a spear in their contest but Pan-do wouldn't be using a spear.

"I'll use a rock."

Nightshade huffed. "From there, you are skylined where anyone can see you. That compromises us. You must kneel."

His hand movements became stiff and angry. He clearly objected to questions.

"Of course," Pan-do might have spit this out. Any subadult knew this.

Nightshade almost sputtered as rage colored his face. "Go, Warrior. When you fail, never question me again."

"I am not questioning you, Lead Warrior. I am suggesting. If my method works, it will be safer for both of us. If it doesn't, you kill Hipparion."

Ignoring any response, Pan-do picked up several palm-sized stones and showed them to Nightshade. "These focus power on one vulnerable body part like the head, the eye, or under the ear. And unlike a spear, the supply is limitless. I've felled many animals this way."

He clambered up the bluff after coating his body in Hipparion dung and then signaled to Nightshade. The Lead Warrior's projectile missed by a body length—as Pan-do expected. The Hipparion snorted and kicked, jinking away from Nightshade and toward Pan-do. When the animal got close, he hurled a missile, hitting the animal mid-forehead. It froze for a breath and then crumpled. Pan-do flew down the steep hill, chopper in hand, intent on killing the stunned animal before it recovered. By the time he got there, Nightshade had already sliced its throat.

They disemboweled the carcass, sheered away the haunches and ribs, and shared the rich blood. As they trotted home, heavily burdened with meat, Nightshade opened up, sharing his closeness to Xhosa, her mastery as Leader, and the problems they had with Big Heads.

After that, both fell into a comfortable silence, scanning the area, searching for dangerous smells and out-of-place colors. Pan-do snatched a hare and eggs from the nest of a ground-dwelling finch, filling his neck sack. It bounced heavily against his chest. One egg broke and dribbled yoke down his chest.

# Chapter 17

When Pan-do and Nightshade trotted into camp, Nightshade hefted the Hipparion carcass high to the celebration of his warriors. Pan-do said nothing when Nightshade took credit for the kill. He simply added the hare and the bird eggs to the meal. It was more important to get along than claim credit.

He realized he hadn't questioned Nightshade about the conversation he'd overheard. That was probably for the best. Better to bring it up first to Xhosa.

Lyta hobbled to him. "Xhosa is still gone."

"Gathering her healing plants?" He scanned the group but no Xhosa. "Sa-mo-ke! Come!" and he raced away, Nightshade a step behind. Before they'd gone far, Xhosa appeared, running at a ground-eating pace.

"Big Heads are here. We must go tomorrow when Sun awakes."

Nightshade took her arm. "Tell me what happened."

She explained where they were and what happened. "When I tried to sneak away, Wind heard me but blocked sight of me from his brother."

Nightshade stared, stunned. " He saved your life?"

"Yes, and there's more. Thunder told Wind the warriors would meet here in a day. Wind was furious he hadn't been informed but Thunder called him too weak to trust."

"How did you get away?"

"I waited until they left."

Nightshade sent a scouting party to the field where Xhosa ran into Thunder and Wind while Pan-do and Xhosa informed their People the departure would now be when Sun awoke.

That night, Lyta slept but Pan-do couldn't. He ended up again with Xhosa. She made room for him on her favorite boulder and then fixed her intense eyes on him, either waiting for him to speak or building her own courage to say something difficult. He twitched uncomfortably as her fingers tugged a strand of hair that fell over her breast, running it through her fingers over and over,

Finally, she turned away, gaze fixed on the dark night. "I'm glad you are with us, Pan-do. Your warriors, Sa-mo-ke and the rest, have become skilled defenders. But I sense a problem."

He couldn't hide his relief and let the confession tumble out. "This is not where our new homeland should be. If not for the Big Head threat, we would leave."

"I have felt the same about this area. Big Heads or not, we would leave."

"Why?"

"You told me that where you lived, your waterholes shrank from one wet time to the next and that the herds birthed fewer babies. This area too changes and has for a long time. My father, before he died, provided the People with a plan.

"When I was young, he left, taking with him his best warriors, promising to return with good news. He was gone this many Moons," and she ticked fingers off on her hand, "before next I saw him.

"He told how he and his warriors shadowed the Rift, traveling inhospitable land that required full neck sacks. It finally narrowed at a land bridge. Once across, Others attacked. My father and his warriors escaped across a river and continued until they came to another river. On its opposite side, the land was lush, rich, and green. He called it our new homeland. As he returned on his backtrail to the People, he placed cairns. He told me that if necessary, I need only follow them."

"It is a good plan." From Nightshade. Though he approached from behind, his appearance startled neither for his scent preceded him.

He continued, "Pan-do did well today. The distance he covers with the spear, his ability to throw while kneeling—he can teach my warriors much."

"As you did mine," Pan-do responded.

Out of nowhere, Lyta appeared. "Come, father. I must show you," and she dragged Pan-do to a swampy alcove beneath a ledge. "Flowers. One, another, another," in fact, a bed of brightly colored blooms.

Nothing made her happier than the patterns created by petals. She forced a handful at him and stuffed more into her neck sack. Pan-do allowed it, knowing it would do no good to resist. He preferred flowers to the red-and-yellow snake she brought to him once. It took all his patience to explain how some patterns must be avoided. Despite her assurances that the snake wouldn't hurt her, Pan-do insisted it must be returned to its home.

"Give these flowers to Xhosa," and Lyta flitted to her ground nest.

With her safe, he left to patrol the homebase's perimeter for the last time. Somewhere along the way, he dropped the flowers.

Hushed shuffles interrupted his walk. Pan-do stopped, ears pricked, searching for the source of the noise. So absorbed was he that he almost missed Xhosa. The swish of her hair in the night breeze was all that gave her away.

*Why does she leave camp alone?*

He traipsed after her.

Quietly, invisibly, she climbed to what appeared to be a familiar plateau. Here, Moon's brightness revealed her pain. Pan-do blinked, shocked. Did the Big Heads injure her? Strangely, in her hand were Lyta's flowers. He stared at his empty hand, aghast, but wondered why Xhosa picked them up.

Xhosa sniffed, licked the petals, and to his surprise, swallowed them and then closed her eyes, extinguishing their lively sparkle. There she sat, motionless, the only hint of wakefulness the occasional movement of her hands. No animal—only Others—could sit so long without falling asleep. He did this too.

*Darkness helps her strategize.*

Finally, the deep lines etched across her face smoothed, her shoulders relaxed, and her fists unclenched. She rolled

Lyta's flowers in her fingers and then stuffed what remained into her neck sack. Rather than leave, she picked a rock from a pile and chucked it with her weak hand, the movement stiff, without the fluidity of mastery. That didn't stop her throwing over and over until her weak hand became as effective as her strong.

When he settled to sleep by Lyta, he came to an unwanted decision: Not only did his daughter consider Nightshade "bad" but that spot deep in his own body that warned of a threat burned like a brushfire. He must stay. He couldn't abandon Xhosa to the Big Heads.

Or Nightshade.

Xhosa selected a stone from those piled on the ground, planted one foot, and released the missile with a snap of the wrist.

It missed the entire tree.

"Again," and set up the next stone. It whooshed, landing closer to the tree. What did her father say? *Look at the target before and after you throw.* Another rock, this one nicked the bark. By the time the projectiles ran out, they dependably hit where aimed.

She rested and wondered what appealed so about Pan-do. He couldn't protect his People as Nightshade did but somehow commanded respect from his People. When her father led, it was like that. In those days, she would listen to the insects chirp, watch the night sky brighten and dim, hear the wind blow the leaves, and feel its soft caress. Was there no longer time for that? Would it always be about death? Big Heads killed for no reason. All other life, be it plants, animals, birds, or insects, killed to survive.

Coyote's baleful cry floated on the evening breeze. She too wanted to cry. The idea of leaving this place—her father's home—upset every part of her.

Her head rumbled, the pain tolerable thanks to the flowers. Where did they come from? She dismissed the question, gazing up into the night sky. Time remained to practice before Sun awoke.

# Chapter 18

Nightshade shook her. Sun glowed softly, not yet awake. It was early.

"The scouting party is back!"

A panicked voice drowned out whatever came next. "Big Heads!" Nightshade and Xhosa sprinted toward it. The scout bent over, mouth open as he sucked in air.

Xhosa put her hand on his back. "Ant—what happened?"

He looked up but couldn't focus. Blood dripped from a gash on his arm. He carried only his club, no spear. Xhosa crouched and held his face in her hands.

"Warrior—calm down. Tell me."

His gaze grabbed hers like a lifeline. "We scouted as far as the field that becomes one with the sky. There, the Big Heads appeared."

"How many, Ant?" This from Pan-do.

Ant opened and closed both hands many times and drew a line from his cheek to nose. "That man, the Leader."

"Thunder," Xhosa murmured.

Ant's chest heaved. "We hid our trail ..."

Nightshade shook him. "When will they get here?"

Ant trembled from fatigue, too drained to talk so Sa-mo-ke stepped forward, sweat streaming down his body despite the cold morning. He pointed upward.

"There," meaning when Sun touched that point in the sky.

*Two hands.*

Nightshade looked around, searching. "Where is the Lead Scout, Rainbow?"

Sa-mo-ke motioned, "He returned early, sick. I replaced him."

Nightshade grunted and headed out with the People's best warriors toward a bluff on the border. When Big Head's dust cloud appeared, the People would have to flee. Xhosa weighed her choices. The People's land would be strange to

Big Heads while her warriors knew every corner, every hideout.

A chill ran down her spine as she remembered Wind and Thunder. Had they been here for Moons? Was it now also familiar territory to them? In weapons, too, did the Big Heads have the advantage with their stone-tipped spears? Death did not worry her. It would come when it came, as it did with her father, but she wasn't prepared to fail her People.

Sun moved only a finger before a bloodcurdling shriek broke the air and Nightshade burst into the camp. "They are here."

Xhosa snatched her spear and warclub, as did every male and some females. "Warriors! Slow them! Primary Female—get the females and children away!"

Hordes of Big Heads poured from the brush, screaming and pumping their weapons in the air. Xhosa met them head-on, wielding her warclub with deadly accuracy. She plunged her spear into the chest of one, yanked it from the male's spasming body, and flung it again at a Big Head prepared to skewer Ant. She swung her club with her strong hand as she hurled stones with her weak one, stunning one after another with deadly shots to their temples, throats, and eyes. Blood sprayed over her face and chest but there was no time to clean it off. Her wealth of hair circled her body, entrancing the attackers as she bashed their legs from under them.

She battled even as wave after wave of Big Heads spilled from the surrounding brush. The enemy fought like seasoned warriors, the nob under their mouths jutting high in arrogance, disdain curling their lips. To her side, Sa-mo-ke grinned as leering Big Heads surrounded him. He swung his club in a circle, smashing into ribs, arms, and shoulders until he broke free.

But it didn't matter how many the People brought down; more poured forth. Xhosa warbled the retreat call as she slashed a warrior's neck sending a fountain of blood over the warrior next to him. He fell but two replaced him. Watching, like Leopard on a termite mound, lurked the scarred Thunder, vicious grin aimed directly at her.

She tried to retreat but couldn't find an opening. Thunder howled, lips split wide, eyes fixed on her, surely expecting to see her destruction.

"Xhosa—I'm behind you!" And there was Nightshade, exactly where she needed him. They stood back to back, he covering her as she him, fighting their way out of the deluge of enemies, one spear thrust and club-swing at a time. Once they cleared a path, they caught up with the main group of warriors. She caught a glimpse of Rainbow at the front of the retreat, leading the females and children away.

"Sa-mo-ke! Get out!" she called to Pan-do's lead warrior, again surrounded by Big Heads. He swiped sweat from his forehead with the back of his arm, never removing his eyes from the enemy. Step by step, they advanced on him as he fought like a she-cat. Xhosa wondered how Sa-mo-ke kept upright. She shoved toward him but Big Heads had boxed him in.

"Pan-do—he needs help!"

Both flung one stone after another at the advancing Big Heads. Some collapsed; others toppled into their own warriors, slowing them enough that Sa-mo-ke escaped.

Still, Big Heads flooded forward in an uninterrupted wave. They stepped over their dead, caring nothing for life or the loss of it. The People fought ruthlessly, buying time for others to escape. The trail of blood, entrails, and feces assaulted Xhosa as she flung rocks the size of squash into a group of charging Big Heads. She warbled to her warriors, encouraging them, her call echoing above the grunts and screams.

Even this withdrawal, Nightshade had planned. As they withdrew, the People cautiously avoided the Lead Warrior's tricks. The Big Heads, blinded by what must look like a chaotic exodus, hit every one of them. Some fell screaming into debris-covered holes the People had excavated, impaling themselves on sharpened stakes that lined the bottom. Others stepped through matted grass into beds of snakes. Most would find these traps if they looked closely which the Big Heads didn't, thoughts only on killing.

As Xhosa fled, following her People to safety, the Big Head onslaught slowed, wary of what else could be hidden.

"They got what they wanted," she muttered to no one. "Why risk chasing us?"

Still, she set a ground-eating pace, moving to the front of the People where she waved her warclub over her head, motioning to the Rift. They never traveled in it because the danger of flash floods was too great but today, it was an escape the Big Heads wouldn't expect, especially with dark clouds gathering. Somewhere up the valley, it rained, filling the rift with water, rushing toward them.

Death by Big Heads or drowning? If descending into the valley discouraged the enemy, the People could climb back out before the flood arrived. And why would these invaders further imperil themselves when they now claimed the area's richest land? No, they would let the People go as they had when they stole the meat long ago.

She led the way, sliding down the long vines they had strung over the cliff, and dropped to the Rift floor, followed by everyone else. The last to descend cut the vine at the top and then monkeyed his way down. If the Big Heads tried to descend, the People could pick them off.

The Big Heads didn't follow, chose instead to cascade spears down on the People from the cliff's precipice. A female fell, dropping her child who screamed, a spear through its young chest. Several elders, moving too slowly, collapsed, spears piercing their chests. No one could stop to help without becoming a target themselves. Pan-do, Xhosa, and Nightshade dispersed among the frantic group. Bellowing and flinging their arms forward, they exhorted them to hurry.

"Nightshade," she panted as she caught up to her alpha warrior. "Beyond this narrow part, the Rift expands. We'll be too far from the cliffs for their spears to hit us."

Nightshade nodded and pushed his warriors relentlessly, the pace one that would soon exhaust everyone.

"Run or die!" His voice spurred the People on, mothers carrying exhausted children, subadults supporting tottering elders.

Nightshade sniffed and peered over her shoulder and his eyes popped open. "Fire!"

The Big Heads spears were now tipped with fire. They exploded into flames and fed by the dry scrub, soon covered the narrow tunnel that moments before was their escape route. If they couldn't outrun the fire, they would die.

"Faster!"

Xhosa had never seen anything like this. How did they command such a deadly force? Nightshade, though, showed neither fear nor worry. In fact, he glowed with excitement, energized by the challenge. His breathing increased and muscles tensed. She watched, enthralled, as everything touched his senses in his search for escape. He was never as prepared as when danger intruded.

Pan-do appeared calm, hustling his People, calling, ordering. Leading. When Lyta failed to keep up, he hoisted her to his shoulders and carried another youngster in each arm as their mothers juggled other babies. Still, he outpaced everyone.

Xhosa and Sa-mo-ke pushed from the back of the crowd, driving children and elders faster than they thought they could run. The screams of those who couldn't keep up pierced the air, their burning bodies pyres, arms spread with no one able to help. Xhosa forced families to grieve their losses later.

Another female, Mbasa, one of Nightshade's many mates, hung back with Xhosa and Sa-mo-ke. A wail made Xhosa shiver.

"My baby! I dropped him!"

Mbasa didn't hesitate. She plunged into the conflagration, seized a wailing infant too small to crawl, and flew back to the mother.

"I can carry her, Red-dit. You take your other children."

Xhosa fumed that Mbasa would jeopardize herself for a tiny child, pleased it worked, and shocked at her speed and bravery. No female moved that quickly.

Well, except for herself.

Mbasa cast a quick glance at Xhosa and offered a shy grin.

Finally, every one of the People cleared the bottleneck. The area they crossed now was heavy with dust. Without sagebrush and bunchgrass to feed it, the fire died out. The Big Heads lined up along the Rift's lip knowing if they tried to descend, her warriors would cut them down. Instead, they shook their spears in victory, bouncing rhythmically, their raucous shouts jeering the People onward.

Still, Xhosa forced everyone forward. The dark black clouds ahead told her they would soon meet a new enemy. She ran until her heart drummed in her throat and threatened to burst through her skin and then ran more. She heard fatigued grunts but no male would quit when she didn't.

When the Big Heads were finally well out of sight, the group stumbled to a stop and collapsed around her, filling their lungs with air, quivering muscles refusing to resume. Nothing, not even the storm raging up the Rift, persuaded the exhausted People to continue.

"Xhosa. Look," Nightshade motioned.

Fire cracked in the distance. That meant rain, which brought floods. She peered up to the lip of the Rift. That's where they needed to be but how to get there?

"My father built an escape but I don't know where it is."

She hadn't even searched, thinking it would never be needed.

"Here," Pan-do called from ahead and fingered a succession of tiny ledges that would serve as hand- and footholds.

She barked, "Everyone. Leave your spears—if you still have one—and warclubs. They will get in the way."

"No, they won't." This from Nightshade.

"We can make new ones."

Pan-do motioned, "Or we can connect them to our feet and arms with a sinew and drag them up with us."

Xhosa stared into the distance. "Untie them if it fails."

She attached her spear to her ankle, warclub to her waist, and started the climb, motioning everyone to follow.

Nightshade and Pan-do came next. Rainbow pushed Sa-mo-ke out of the way and ascended immediately after the Leaders.

As rapidly as possible, the People clambered up the steps her father's warriors laboriously dug into the hard wall. Dust sifted into Xhosa's nostrils as she tested each new position, tugging and yanking, before committing. Eagle squawked.

"Eaglets, in the nest," and she veered away. No sense presenting themselves as a threat to the tearing claws of a mother Eagle.

Sunshine gave way to a cloud-choked sky that quickly became a cold drizzle. Xhosa sped up, afraid it would become rain. The faster she went, the more the spear dangling from her foot swung wildly. She wished she had tied it to her waist with the warclub. People screeched when hit by loose spears and howled when it was a club. A child's wail ended in a splat. That was the first but not the last. Risk was part of escape.

Rainbow lagged a full body length behind the Leaders, panting and whining to anyone who would listen.

"Rainbow. Move faster!"

He ignored her.

"You are too slow," she barked. "Let the others pass," but he trundled clumsily on.

She heard Pan-do encourage his People as Lyta voiced her beautiful calming bird-song. Though clumsy on flat land, she moved with the agility of a mountain goat up a route by her father.

Xhosa let her People pass. She would be more useful in the rear, encouraging those frightened. Rainbow pushed past her without a glance, wheezing, dampness matting his hair and dripping on those beneath him.

As Xhosa started again, a female screeched, "My child!"

Xhosa lurched her head upward, spotting his falling body, knowing she would have only one chance to save him.

# Chapter 19

A howl erupted as a mother snatched frantically for a tiny hand and missed. The boy screamed, bounced off those below him and slammed into the cliff before continuing his downward plunge. His fingers grasped someone's hair but couldn't hold on. Most of the People spun away, afraid they would die with him if they tried to help, but Xhosa never considered that. His body flew by, hands flailing, eyes wide with horror, mouth an O. She snatched his hair and leaned into the cliff, fingers anchored to an outcropping. His momentum yanked her arm down but her grip held. A squeal escaped his mouth when he smacked into her legs with an oomph.

"Calm—you are safe." The boy shook uncontrollably as tears streamed down his cheeks. "Now, climb onto my back and put your legs around my waist."

"I can't—I will fall!" he whimpered.

"You must or I leave you here."

Out of nowhere, Lyta scampered to Xhosa. One hand secured to the wall, she stretched the other out to the boy. "El-ga—is that your name?" When he nodded, Lyta continued, "Do as Xhosa asks, El-ga. I'll help you."

The boy visibly relaxed, sniffling but nodding, and scaled Xhosa's legs, up over her hips, and with Lyta's help, wrapped his legs around the Leader's waist.

"I'll stay with you," and Lyta smiled at Xhosa.

Xhosa breathed out and began again to climb, El-ga clinging to her, tiny fingernails digging into her skin. The wind stiffened and the drizzle hardened into rain. Finally, Nightshade motioned everyone to halt and he cautiously pulled himself over the top and disappeared from view. After what seemed forever, he motioned the line up and over the lip.

Xhosa pulled herself over as Nightshade hoisted El-ga off of her, his mother crying with relief. Lyta scampered to her father who crushed her to his chest, tears filling his eyes.

Xhosa closed her eyes and breathed in deep ragged gasps. When she finally forced her breathing to slow, her senses searched the new world—carrion, a wolf pack, water, blood, and at her side, Nightshade's sweat.

What she didn't smell was Big Heads.

She opened her eyes. A stark plateau flowed in front of her, stained a patchwork of dull colors with few trees to break the whip of the wind. But there was no time to rest. The rain had become a torrent as if a whole river was lifted into the sky and dropped on them.

"This way!" Nightshade shouted above the roar and the People took off at a sprint.

Xhosa dipped her head against the force of the rain, feet sloshing through puddles that deepened with each step. Without expecting it, she tumbled into a cave, stinking of urine and decayed tissue. The floor was coated in bone shards and molted fur but it was dry.

Xhosa stared into the darkness and felt a slight breeze.

"I'll check the rear," and left Nightshade grunting something to his warriors.

She traced the uneven crumbling rock, ducking at times to avoid low ceilings. She slipped on a slick spot, jammed her fingers into a fissure to hold her balance, and felt the tickle of Spider racing for safety. Often, she brushed away strands of Spiders' webs that caught on her face and in her hair. She peered down each tunnel but discovered no predators so returned to the group.

"How many spears did we lose?" She motioned to Nightshade and Pan-do.

"One, and no warclubs," from both.

"I told my people to abandon theirs rather than fall," Rainbow whined.

His use of the phrase "my people" brought a searing glare from Nightshade but Xhosa responded levelly, "I see you did also," nodding to his empty hands.

"Carrying them was dangerous," he growled a pitch too high.

Xhosa didn't hide her disgust.

She mentally ticked off everyone who should be there, and then, with a frown, again.

"Someone is missing." She shuttered her eyes, seeing every member move across the horizon of her mind. A hole appeared.

"Primary Female—where is she?"

"I saw her," from Lyta. She swayed, anguished. "A spear in her chest."

Xhosa felt no sorrow. The elder lived a full life serving the People. The question was who would step up to serve as Primary Female? Someone would. That's how it worked.

"Xhosa." Pan-do touched her arm. "Thank you for saving El-ga. He is Wa-co's only child and she is without a pairmate."

"Of course. Anyone would."

"But no one did except you. You never pick the safe path over the right one, do you?"

In fact, Xhosa didn't know how to.

The People settled on their haunches, arms wrapping their legs for warmth, as the gale transformed the dry Rift valley into a roaring killer. Torrents of rain pounded the ground like a stick against a hollow tree trunk. A booming crack echoed as a chunk of the cliff gave way. Bolts of fire fractured the sky joined by thunderous roaring that echoed off the cave walls, often drowning out the pounding rain.

They ate travel food, tipped their heads to drink from the curtain of water falling across the cave's opening, and waited for Sun. When Xhosa ventured outside to relieve herself, a wolf trotting along the edge of the plateau glanced her way, its fur soaked, a squirming rat in its mouth.

The People slept curled together against the cave wall. When a bedraggled wolf—maybe the same one she'd seen earlier—stumbled in from the storm, pale yellow eyes dull with hunger, tail tucked between its legs, Nightshade chased it out and added guards to the entrance.

The next morning, the relentless freezing rain and gusting wind had ended, leaving damp plants and sparkling promises.

She took stock of her dejected and frightened People. Migration was normal but not flight. Everyone knew they could never go home.

Nightshade approached, looking as rested and energetic as she felt tired. "The scouts found no Others and no Big Heads."

"How are your warriors?"

"Several of the injured can be treated. Others are missing, dead, or will wish they were when the captors finish them. We are fine, Xhosa. The People are many and our warriors skilled. Others will avoid us."

"Weapons?"

"Few have spears—they are in the bodies of dead Big Heads. We can make new ones. Most have warclubs." He paused, eyes darting among the group, telling her he felt the same as she.

They hadn't seen the last of the Big Heads.

Before continuing, she must deal with injuries. The first that caught her attention was Ant, hobbling on his re-injured leg. The crater still covered much of his calf but the skin had healed.

"Xhosa!" A distraught voice interrupted. "My son! Please—he needs help!"

The boy, barely old enough to walk, winced as he displayed a hand-sized bruise on his thigh, swollen and a raw shade of crimson-purple. Xhosa pawed through her neck sack without finding what she needed. She motioned to the mother, "Find bruisewort. Lay it over the wound and wrap it in a leaf."

The female left to search outside the cave for the plant. Her son whimpered.

"Stop whining. You are a warrior," Xhosa motioned but handed him a piece of bark. "Chew. It tastes bad but helps. Tell your mother to strip more of this from the white trees when she finds them."

She spent most of what passed for morning in the gloomy cave treating the injured, salving burns with seedpods, treating cuts with moss and spider webs, and using stems when she ran out of the pain bark.

Just as she began to wilt, Nightshade provided a welcome break. "Nothing lives in this area except prickle bushes, scrub, and scorpions. The ground is so hard we can't even dig out the roots and bulbs."

"Any water?" She carried a small amount of succulents in her neck sack, as did everyone, but they would soon run out.

"Just what's left from the rain."

"We leave when the People are rested. It must be better ahead."

Pan-do beckoned her, "Xhosa."

She snapped her head toward him. His People were also her responsibility. She forced herself to breathe in and rolled her shoulders back, wondering what problem she must solve.

"Come watch. The children invented a game."

A group of youngsters stood in a tight group, laughing as they kicked each other's feet. Xhosa couldn't stop from smiling especially when Pan-do joined the play, making the children squeal with joy. The females, content their charges were occupied, gathered together, giggling and hiding smiles.

Xhosa felt the tension evaporate from her shoulders. She long ago lost the ability to play. Her mother's death focused her on a goal, to be a warrior, and that took all of her time. Until her father died, she held an absolute belief that he would take care of her until she could achieve her goal. Tranquility bathed her as she understood he still did. His cairns, the path to their future home—even now guided her.

Pan-do left the children to their play and whispered to Xhosa, "Our worst injury if we don't heal it is fear, Xhosa. Our People look to us—you and I—for leadership. We must provide it, even if that's a game to make them laugh."

Xhosa wished for Pan-do's gift. He didn't worry about what was out of his control. His people were fiercely loyal to him in no small part because they enjoyed their lives. She compared this to Nightshade across the cave. Scarcely controlled wrath darkened his handsome features. Anyone looking at him would consider the People's future bleak.

She noticed the female Mbasa, the one who rescued the child from burning to death. Her singed hair clung to her head like cattail fur. Her chest blazed a fiery red, blistered from breasts to hips. She'd slathered her body in mucous to sooth what must be wrenching pain but her face showed nothing. Somehow, the brittle dry hair, the resolute attitude, and the weeping burns made her look fiercer and more competent.

"If older, she would make a good Primary Female."

In one hand, Mbasa held a spear, really just a stick. Xhosa headed over to show her how to release the weapon hidden within but Rainbow got there first.

"Here's how to sharpen this, Mbasa."

With everyone busy, Xhosa took the opportunity to think. Nightshade wanted land with no Others but Xhosa thought settling near Others, while unusual, would facilitate trade and safety. Eventually, the People's natural dominance would prevail without the need for violence.

For the rest of the day, families groomed, murmuring among themselves, and reassuring each other the worst was behind them. Nightshade left with a hunting party and Snake with the scouts. Rainbow helped anyone interested to knap new tools and sharpen spears made from whatever branches were available.

Lyta appeared, eyes on the group gathered around Rainbow. "Do you want to know what they say?"

Xhosa almost said no but nodded, curious. She didn't trust Rainbow. While she applauded any who took initiative, something about Rainbow—his too-fluid movements, the set of his mouth—told Xhosa he wanted as much to be seen as a Leader as to be one.

Lyta rattled off, "*Where we go—is it safe from enemies?*" They sounded worried.

"Rainbow answers, '*I can keep us safe.*'"

That disturbed Xhosa.

"I don't like him, Xhosa-friend-of-my-father, though he treated Mbasa kindly."

# Chapter 20

As darkness took over, Nightshade trudged in with nothing more than several drowned birds and a piglet. These, he tossed into a communal pile and strode toward Xhosa and Pan-do. As earlier, his eyes sparkled and he bristled with energy.

"What is the plan?" Nightshade motioned.

Pan-do unconsciously crossed his arms over his chest. Xhosa thought this tension had been overcome when they hunted together. She ignored that for the moment. Decisions must be made.

"Tomorrow, we continue along the Rift until we are far enough the Big Heads will not take up the chase again. That shouldn't be far. They need to stay in our former homeland to protect what they stole."

With no objections, the People ate the meat brought by Nightshade and shared the roots and plants dug up by the females. From the edge of the group came a faint hum that quickly flowed like a smooth river across the crowd. Lyta, of course. She stood alone, eyes closed, as the beautiful sounds rolled from her mouth.

"The People need to hear from you, Xhosa," Pan-do murmured with a grin. "Start with our successes."

Xhosa stretched to her full height in front of her People, hair covering her like Leopard's pelt, legs wide, arms open and inviting. "We outsmarted the Big Heads."

"But they still chase us." This from Rainbow, desperate to show himself as a Leader.

Nightshade retorted. "This land is barren. If they enter, we will easily see them and kill them."

Pan-do motioned, "Our neck sacks carry sufficient food but continue to collect what you find. Eat what you want."

"I found these!" A child shrieked as he popped a handful of berries into his mouth.

Xhosa grimaced. "Those give you the rear-end squirts and a belly-hurt."

Another child squealed, hands and lips stained with the berry juice, and spit out a mouthful. Xhosa flared her nostrils. "Eat these roots," and she held up a yellow light-green plant. "They are everywhere. Pick them whenever you see them.

Nightshade motioned, "Watch for knappable stones and sticks—anything that could be a tool. Those without spears, find slender trees or branches to shape into new weapons."

Xhosa waited until the group became silent and all eyes latched onto her.

"Never have we abandoned a homebase. When we migrate, we always come back but this time, we must find a new home."

Rainbow stood. "I know where we must go. I have seen it, rich with herds and few Others."

"That is the home of the Big Heads—"

Rainbow interrupted. "They now live in our old homebase. Their old land is now open to whoever wants it."

Xhosa kept her hands calm. "There are too many of them to abandon it. They will keep both." She paused to look around. "We either choose a challenging path without Big Heads, the one laid out by my father, or the easy one Rainbow describes which is also the home of Big Heads. Everyone speak your mind."

Her father allowed no discussion but that wasn't her way.

One warrior asked, "What is it like up there?"

"Dry at first, according to my father, with no herds and few grassy areas, but it ends in a vast sea rich with food and water."

"We can fish," someone offered.

"Are Others there?"

"Or Big Heads?"

An elder stood. "None of you remembers the journey to our last home. It was like this, much grumbling, worries we would never find a new home, and then it became the best home we ever had. I am content with Leader Xhosa's decision."

Xhosa waited but got no more comments, until Rainbow stepped forward.

"I explored the land to Sun's sleeping nest. I saw no Big Heads there—"

"No, that's not true," Nightshade interrupted. "Xhosa and I have seen their massive size, as many as would cover the Great Waterhole. We have talked often as a People of leaving, going where Big Heads aren't. This is our time to do that."

Nightshade's hand motions, augmented with clicks and snaps, made it clear he bristled at Rainbow's bald bid for leadership. She and Nightshade both saw Rainbow as a disruptive force but his ability to speak well and relate to others made him dangerous.

Lyta chirped the sound of a night bird.

Rainbow continued, "Your own father told us travel further along this Rift was perilous. Why not go where we will find mother mammoth filled with babies, grasslands flowing with food—"

"And Big Heads." Nightshade interrupted, voice commanding, presence dominating. "Do you not listen?"

Rainbow frowned but thoughtfully as though he led the discussion. "But we are powerful, Nightshade. They split their forces. We will have no problem defeating them. You know that."

The group buzzed when some of Nightshade's warriors nodded at Rainbow. The Lead Warrior clenched and unclenched his fists, his face redder with each breath.

Sa-mo-ke motioned to the dissenters, hands high and strong, "My People know first-hand that there are many Big Head tribes, all vicious. Even if Rainbow is right, that this particular Big Head tribe is not as powerful, there are others, especially for those entering the heart of their territory."

Snake stood by Sa-mo-ke. "I too prefer the unknown to Big Heads."

As the debate continued, Rainbow emerged as the voice of the opposition, offering a safe choice if not a good one. Xhosa shook her head. Rainbow held much promise as a warrior but lacked basic common sense. When still a subadult, he had challenged Stone, huge even then, taunting that the galumphing oversized male the size of a baby mammoth was too slow. Stone walked away, laughing, so Rainbow blindsided him and broke his jaw. Most warriors would quit but not Stone. He pivoted, his entire being spewing fury and revenge, hand tight on his warclub, and swung so hard it broke Rainbow's shoulder. The smaller male squealed as his knees buckled. Stone roared, spittle spewing over Rainbow, and stomped on Rainbow's hand, smashing his fingers. Words slurred, he ordered Rainbow to stay down. Every warrior left with Stone.

Both males healed, leaving Stone with a crooked smile that made him look meaner.

It was time for Xhosa to exert her control as Leader. She prepared to interrupt the warrior talking—something about pregnant females suffering from the difficult travel—when Nightshade did it for her.

"That direction, where Rainbow would lead you, offers no cover if—when—you are pursued by an enemy. Here, the Rift may be harsher travel but it provides many ravines for hiding. It cuts between promontories as well as boulder beds that offer concealment."

With this, many warriors closed on Nightshade.

Ant moved in front of the crowd. "Of course what Leader Xhosa proposes is dangerous, but Big Heads are worse. And when did we ever run from danger?" He sat, everything said.

Murmurs filled the audience. Nightshade proved many times he could keep the People safe.

Xhosa motioned to Pan-do. "What of you and your People?"

He rose to his feet and addressed the gathering. "My People have traveled for many moons. We are never sure of security or food. When we don't find it, we move on." All listened without making a sound. "Here's what you should be thinking about. What will you do when faced with a problem no one's ever seen? Who will guide you wisely when those who did so in the past are not there? You survive by staying together under the right leadership. The size of this tribe makes us strong."

Into the silence, Lyta's voice sang, "The size of our tribe makes us strong. He speaks the truth."

Pan-do's group murmured agreement.

Nightshade added, "Rainbow cannot protect you."

Rainbow bristled. "No, Nightshade, you are wrong. You yourself declared me a warrior." Rainbow's voice came out a whine. "But we need not all make the same choice."

Rainbow's divisive message resonated with those weary of conflict, who wanted to live peacefully as they had their entire adulthood. Her father, when he led, destroyed invaders. As a result, peace prevailed. Resources and ideas were shared. Conflicts became distant memories. Rainbow thought this peaceful life existed everywhere, not understanding it depended on one man's indomitable will.

She dismissed him. Many of the People would accept the difficult route without question. The warriors would stay with Nightshade and the females and children with those who protected them.

She spread her arms wide, palms down, and all eyes rotated to her. "We leave tomorrow. At the foothills, those who wish can go with Rainbow. The rest of us will travel along the Rift to the fertile land promised by my father. Each will decide for themselves at the separation point."

# Chapter 21

The rain ended and the People started their journey, searching for food, healing herbs, and water along the Rift though there was little to find. Rainbow tried to insert himself with the Leaders of the migrating group and was shunted aside. He dropped back, walking with Mbasa until she left to join Red-dit.

With each passing day, stomachs growled louder, throats parched drier, and spirits sank. Only Pan-do's People remained upbeat. Not only were they experienced with endless walking but Pan-do had gotten them through much worse.

The closer they got to the point where the two groups would separate, the more intense the heat, the air almost too thick to breathe. Sweat poured down Xhosa's forehead, over her brow, and flattened her copious hair to her skin. Inviting glimpses of the sun-soaked grass where Rainbow would go taunted. Her path, a slight bend in the opposite direction, was—well, stark would be too kind a description. The land sneered at them with lofty jagged spikes punctuated with bubbling green pools and clouds of steam that burst from the many vents.

Xhosa joined Pan-do as they rested one day in a tiny sliver of shade cast by a boulder. Every part of his body was damp with sweat but his eyes remained bright and relaxed. He greeted her and she smiled vaguely, enjoying the quiet of her feet and the slight breeze cooling her body. Her eyes stared ahead, shoulders drooping as she chewed her lip.

Pan-do touched her arm. "No one thinks the journey will be easy but your father didn't give up. We will do no less."

She wiped a hand across her brow and pushed a stray hair out of the way. "I can't imagine what made him continue, Pan-do."

Their shadows had become long and dark by the time they arrived at the spot where they would separate. Xhosa walked along the column telling the People to stop for the night. The boulder they crowded around would protect them from unexpected attacks though the scouts had uncovered no evidence of Uprights or animals. The children collected brambled bushes and ate what food they carried before falling asleep.

Clear cloudless skies greeted Xhosa the next morning, promising another sweltering day. She strode toward the valley that marked the People's path and then crouched on her haunches to wait. Within moments, Rainbow strutted toward her leading a larger group than Xhosa expected. Some showed deep concern, others grinding fear, but most simply uncertainty. Children clung to parents and adults huddled together. No one wanted the People to separate but Rainbow's arguments convinced many that heading away from this desolation presented the only chance for survival.

She motioned, "Rainbow are you sure of what you do?"

Without hiding his disdain, he strode toward a vast swath of lush green savanna. With a shrug, Xhosa set off along a route bounded on one side by the Rift and the other by scree slope. Nightshade joined her as did Sa-mo-ke, Snake, Ant, and most of the People's warriors. Next came Pan-do, his group led by Wa-co and El-ga, the child Xhosa rescued.

It surprised her when Mbasa, one of Nightshade's mates, chose Rainbow. Judging by the deep purple and orange bruises on her arms, chest, and legs, Nightshade beat her often, including last night. This worried Xhosa but not enough to intervene. With the People, if a male punished a female, the family alone must stop it. Mbasa's parents were long dead, both taken by Sabertooth Cat.

Xhosa wasn't surprised when many of the pregnant females chose Rainbow's easy route. She secretly applauded this. The arduous travel would slow them down which would hold up the entire group.

"Rainbow," Xhosa called after him. "Your group is too small. You are vulnerable."

He flapped a contemptuous farewell but some of his followers glanced back, fear whitening their faces as the enormity of their choice washed over them. One subadult—

Bone—scampered toward her, deserting a friend who chose Rainbow because the new Leader promised he would become a hunter.

Xhosa couldn't help but ask herself why so many rejected her leadership. Did she not explain herself well? Was it a mistake to allow Rainbow to speak? How many more setbacks would there be before her People found a home like their last, where they lived—thrived—side-by-side with Sabertoothed Cat, Wild Beast, and Mammoth, sharing food and respect.

Most worrisome was whether they had in fact left the Big Heads behind.

She kept these dark thoughts to herself and resolutely headed away from those who had abandoned the People. Within a finger of Sun's passage, her group descended into a bleak valley and lost sight of Rainbow. The crunch of loose pebbles beneath their feet loudly announced their presence but Xhosa saw no trace of life. By the time they reached the bottom, her eyes burned and her throat ached from breathing the parched air. To her strong side, steaming vents, boiling lakes, and molten lava lined her passage. Explosions of fire and sizzling embers showered down, so bright, she had to shield her eyes while slapping at the cinders that scorched her skin. To her weak side stretched a massive bubbling lake, the color and consistency of vomit. On its shores grew beds of finger-sized spikes, sharper than any rock Xhosa had ever seen. Among these white and yellow spires gurgled a clear liquid Xhosa first hoped would be drinkable but instead, was so toxic, it blistered her finger.

"Keep moving!"

The People moved guardedly, so treacherous was the passage. One child died when the ground beneath his feet dissolved, sending him tumbling into the miasma. His mother grabbed for him but got only a savagely burned arm for her effort. His screams fell silent as the boy sank below the green fizzing surface.

Finally, the boiling ponds were behind them, replaced with dusty brown ground so hot they had to wrap their feet in leaves to avoid blisters. The wind pummeled the People, forcing parents to carry their small children or watch them blown away. Thankfully, this soon gave way to a cooler crusty white substance that stretched as far as she could see.

Xhosa sniffed and exclaimed, "Salt!"

Xhosa had offered Rainbow some of the People's supply but behind her back, he took all of it. Without this sparkling white stone, they would die. To come across this so early in their travel was an amazing find.

The bristly blocks shredded the leaf wrappers on their feet but spirits soared. No one had ever seen a salt patch this immense. Quiet happy chatter accompanied the labor of digging it up, breaking it into chunks, and stuffing it into neck sacks.

Nightshade approached Xhosa. "The scouts find no Others, no Big Heads, but also no dust from herds, no sign of carrion eaters, and no trace of water."

"The food we carry," in their neck sacks, "will last."

As the days passed, not only did they find little water and less meat but the trees that provided homes to the beetles, ants, slugs, and birds that could feed them went from sparse to gone. Everyone rationed supplies and sucked pebbles. No one complained. Most of the weak had gone with Rainbow.

The fact that the People seemed to be alone in this desolate land didn't stop Xhosa from worrying. In her former home, birds could chirp all they wanted, insects could sing, Wolf could call to his pack and her instincts didn't twitch because she recognized each sound. But here, all the noises, scents, and shadows were strange and unknown. Without cliffs, trees, brambled bushes, or any other protection, they slept in the open. Nightshade ordered extra guards and Xhosa joined them often, unable to sleep.

It became evident that the People were completely alone. Of course they were. Life couldn't survive here.

The days passed and the column lengthened as elders struggled to keep up. Xhosa and Nightshade always led with Pan-do and Sa-mo-ke at the rear. Behind even these two, limping gamely, was Ant, still slowed by the grievous boil on his leg. The wound would heal or not. He would keep up or fall behind. Xhosa would not slow to his speed. He always caught up when the group rested and never complained when they left as he arrived, as though they'd been waiting for him.

By now, the differences between her People and Pan-do's had disappeared. Each helped the other, lending support where needed and sharing supplies. Xhosa mentally cut Rainbow from her thoughts. She could do nothing for him or those who chose his path.

After traveling for more days than fingers on a hand, Lyta joined Xhosa, her eyes as always curious about everything they passed. "Water and animal dung are ahead," and the girl skipped away.

Xhosa beckoned Nightshade and scrambled up a treacherous hill, ignoring that she was skylined to any below. If Lyta was wrong, it wouldn't matter because they would all die shortly from thirst or starvation.

Nightshade motioned, "There, trees."

# Chapter 22

The grove of trees was a glorious find. She and the People stripped the limbs of their round brown-and-green fruit and drank the pond dry. Hunters discovered an animal trail and downed two pigs. The People feasted and then rested for the balance of the day, feeling like everything would be alright.

That was before Nightshade returned. He grabbed his warclub, motioned Xhosa to follow, and hurried out of the grove, jogging until the hard ground gave way to gravelly talus. The sticky heat tickled Xhosa's scalp and chest, reminding her of the cool shade of the trees she'd left behind.

"Footprints of Uprights, watching us. Maybe a hunting party, too small to confront a group our size."

The hard surface made it impossible to tell whether these Uprights were Big Heads or Others. His lips thinned and he pointed ahead.

"I lost them at the base of the mountains."

"They probably live there rather than this desolation."

Nightshade made a noncommittal gesture. "Or knew enough to hide their steps in the scree."

Xhosa huffed. "Maybe we drank their water and ate their only food." She scratched the lice nested under her ear. "We had no choice. The People were starving."

They left the next day with Sun, thirsts quenched, stomachs full, shadows to their weak sides. Lyta matched the rhythm of trotting feet with a sonorous hum, punctuated by animal calls, tapping on her chest and slapping her leg. When others joined in, she added her perfect bird songs.

Xhosa set a fast pace but not grueling. Thanks to the abundant food and water, everyone kept up. Before Sun moved a hand overhead, the pleasant grove was far behind and they were back to a landscape of stark rolling prairies broken here and there by gullies, ridges, and hills. Xhosa squinted against Sun's glare as it bounced off the land and pounded their bodies with blistering heat. Scouts reported more of the same—thirsty grassland, no herd animals, no predators, no Uprights, and no end to the Rift.

"This looks like Lucy's path," Xhosa muttered to herself, referring to the ancient female in her dreams, but that couldn't be.

Finally, with their shadows mere slivers at their feet, she motioned the People to rest. For her, it didn't last long.

Pan-do trotted over, barely sweating despite the heat. "Come see this."

He was calm as always but breathless. Xhosa followed him to the Rift where Nightshade studied something hidden from view. When he moved aside, her face lit with excitement.

"Cairns, and they're old. See how the wind swept them smooth. These must be from my father."

Nightshade motioned, "Or someone who expected others after them."

"If these are my father's, we are going the right direction!"

Nightshade glowered. "That would mean we should be close to the first of the rivers. I see neither."

Pan-do interrupted. "That's not all I found," and he trotted into the foothills. "Prints from an Upright, maybe the same ones you saw yesterday," the mildness of his hand movements at odds with the tightness of his jaw.

She bent over. "They aren't as long and narrow as Big Heads, more like ours, but dried in the mud. It hasn't rained since we arrived.

"They travel away from us, on our backtrail." Nightshade's mouth twitched. "Why would they do that?"

No one responded.

Xhosa shared the news of the cairns with the People but not the strange prints. When they left after the brief rest, their steps were lively and hands moved in happy conversation.

When they had been moving for a hand of Sun's travel overhead, Xhosa motioned to Pan-do, "You lead effortlessly, Pan-do, despite the challenges we encounter every day."

He snatched a rock rat and ate it while dodging a deep chasm. "Nothing here compares to what we have already seen, traveling from our homebase to yours. You want the journey to end. We are fine if it continues."

He pulled a dry worm from his neck sack and offered part to Xhosa. "Soon, your People will recognize that traveling—like migrating—is what they are doing. It becomes the means to an end."

As he slowed to join a female who called him, Xhosa realized that Nightshade was like Pan-do in many ways. His stamina was boundless. His spirits never flagged, as though he flourished on adversity. He never faltered, never quit, was never happier than when challenged by insurmountable problems. He bounded forward, steps huge, arms pumping, head swiveling in search of threats.

She caught up with him later and asked, "Nothing surprises you, does it?"

He grinned. "We were too comfortable. We knew how everything worked so our days had no challenges. That is not a world I want to live in, Xhosa." He paused to study something in the distance before continuing, "I like it messy."

Xhosa furrowed her brow and tried to ignore what burst into her brain, but it must be said. "Maybe Big Heads overwhelm us in numbers and skill."

Nightshade's jaw tightened and his face reddened. "Do you blame me because they destroyed us with fire?"

"That's ridiculous, Nightshade. If you're at fault, so too am I, as Leader."

His eyes shuttered and he stared into the distance. "Fire as a weapon—Xhosa, that is brilliant! When we confront our next enemy, I will do the same!"

She pushed her lips together. *I'll ask how he plans to capture and control fire the next time we need it as a weapon.*

Sun came and went more times than fingers on her hand. The tingle of desperation that started after leaving the last waterhole grew to mind-wrenching worry by the time the scouts brought good news.

"Ahead is a Fire Mountain." That meant stones for knapping.

Xhosa tingled. Her choppers were almost gone, worn away from digging into the hard dry earth.

The scout wasn't done. "Past it is the land bridge across the Rift."

The bridge! It must be the one her father spoke of.

She called the People together. "Tomorrow, at Fire Mountain, fill your neck sacks with as many rocks as possible—make new sacks if needed," and passed out the stomachs and bladders of old kills. The durable lining that served the animals well would expand to carry many stones. She had tried the stomachs of dead warriors but though similar, they were too small.

"This may be our last chance for weapon-hard stones."

The next day, they picked their way up the scree slope of Fire Mountain, stuffing their neck sacks with as many stones as could be carried. Xhosa and Nightshade were the first to crest the rim. Dark clouds rolled across the landscape.

She motioned, "The water will be welcome but climbing over wet stones is treacherous."

Nightshade motioned, "We can cross the crater and clear the mountain before the storm arrives if we hurry."

Xhosa nodded and motioned to everyone, "As we descend, step where Nightshade and I step. Stay in line. Walk with care. Mothers, carry your children!"

They descended the gravelly slopes, shades of gray and red, into Fire Mountain's scorching interior. The air became muggy, each step threatening to blister the skin despite the travel-hardened soles of their feet. Xhosa increased the pace as she tiptoed around smoldering rocks, avoiding ground so fragile it would collapse beneath her feet. Some places, steam vented high into the air. Other spots glowed red as though molten blood pulsed just below the earth's skin, looking for a soft spot to punch through.

They dropped onto the cracked bottom without incident. The crater walls were so high, they hid the dark clouds but not the taste of dampness in the air. As she congratulated herself that no one was injured, a scream boomed and then frantic voices.

"Grab him—get him out!"

Ant—again—lay curled in a fetal ball, his injured leg fiery red, eyes bulging, drool running from his mouth as he shrieked. Xhosa leaped over a steamy vent and a bubbling mud pool while tugging herbs from her neck sack.

"His knee gave out and he fell into a fissure," Wa-co from Pan-do's group offered, mixing her voice with hand motions to be heard over Ant's cries.

"Ant. Stop screaming. That does nothing to help."

"It's on fire!"

"No, it's not. You will never become a warrior if you whine about everything," she chided as Sa-mo-ke and Snake yanked the boy further away from the bubbling fire. "Every warrior suffers worse than this."

"Leave him here." Nightshade motioned, annoyed. "There is no time to wait for his leg to heal—again."

Xhosa ignored him and searched the few herbs in her neck sack. The blue-flowered plant would be her first choice but that had been exhausted long ago. A small supply of roots for pain and sap for infection remained but nothing to salve a burn.

"Here." Pan-do handed her a thick-skinned leaf the length of a finger. "Break it and paste the mucus over the injury." He scowled at Ant. "If you whine, it hears you and rubs itself off. Plants, like People, hate whining."

Ant stared at Pan-do, confused, while Xhosa did as instructed. When she finished, Ant stood unsteadily, forehead prickled with perspiration but face a mask of determination. He grimaced with every step but refused to stop.

"Where do I find this plant, Pan-do?"

"Many places. It seals wounds and salves burns but also reduces inflammation." He grinned and added, "It even moisturizes skin."

The clouds broke as they left Fire Mountain's crater, pouring rain on the mountain while twisting wind screamed down the steep crags.

When they reached the valley, Pan-do motioned to a gray smudge just off to the side. "A cave."

A streak of fire lit the sky followed by another boom and everyone dove into the cave.

# Chapter 23

Pan-do ran out of the mucous plant so before going to sleep, Xhosa crushed leaves, dampened them to form a compress, and pasted the concoction over Ant's wound.

"Keep the salve on your leg if you want to prevent the red fingers of death." She motioned to the hulk of Pan-do's mucous plant. "Look for this as we travel."

"I will help him." Siri appeared at Ant's side. "I am alone. My children are with Rainbow."

As Rainbow's pairmate, she surprised everyone by joining Xhosa.

In the end, Ant would keep up or he wouldn't, with or without Siri's help.

The next morning, Xhosa awoke as the first faint orange glow lit the sky. Standing quietly, she breathed in the last cool air of the day, eyes locked on the land bridge that stretched across the Rift, still almost at the horizon. It would take most of the day to get there but just the sight energized her. Before setting out, everyone sucked rain from puddles and licked it off rocks.

Sun was almost overhead when Pan-do motioned, "That way," away from their path.

"Why?" She wanted nothing to slow their arrival at the land bridge.

"Lyta smells water."

Within a finger of sun's passage overhead, everyone was drinking at a small waterhole. Good cheer filled all as children splashed in the shallows and everyone stuffed water-soaked leaves into their neck sacks. Pan-do's females giggled as they evaluated Xhosa's males—warriors and subadults—for potential mates. Ant walked with the help of a stick and Siri stayed with him. He made no complaint, no whine or groan. When healed, he would be an admirable warrior. They would need every one of them to protect their new home.

Sun had moved well-beyond overhead by the time the

group stood at the mouth of the bridge. Across from them was green grass. As one, they smiled.

At the entrance to the bridge, Xhosa found her father's cairns. As though that was all they needed to see, the People raced forward.

"Stop!" Xhosa bellowed. "I go first in case it fails."

Pan-do stepped in front of her. "I appreciate what you say, Xhosa, but we should select the heaviest member. If the bridge holds him, it holds anyone."

"That would be Stone."

Stone was not as tall as Xhosa but larger in every other way. He grinned, poorly-healed jaw chronically painful but warrior attitude undimmed. Nothing about a bridge that could collapse and send him crashing to a painful death intimidated him.

The People gathered to watch as he stepped onto the bridge, bearing confident and movements steady. Without a trace of fear, he walked forward, steps sure, not running but not dawdling either. When he reached the far side, he growled his excitement.

Everyone lined up, mothers with children, males interspersed, Pan-do in the middle of the line and Xhosa and Nightshade at the end.

"One at a time. One crosses; another follows when they are safely with Stone."

It would have worked if the People continued one at a time but invariably, the next in line started before the last finished, and then several went at the same time until a stream of the People packed the bridge. No one heard the first crack. The next startled a child who jumped back and knocked the person next to him off the bridge which caused everyone else to scream.

"Stop!" and Xhosa forcibly shoved the next female off the bridge, preventing anyone else from entering the narrow opening until those already on were cleared. Pan-do stood still, partway across, a step from the crack.

"Everything will be OK," Pan-do announced after a dismissive glance at the break. "Walk calmly to Stone!"

Instead of walking carefully, they stampeded, desperate to clear what they considered a collapsing bridge. Pan-do sidestepped the broken gap and returned to Xhosa. For a long time, he stood motionless, only his eyes moving as they darted over the landscape, taking the measure of their predicament.

He brightened. "I have an idea."

He unlooped an old vine from his neck and handed one end to Xhosa.

It didn't take much to figure out his plan. "No!" Xhosa motioned wildly. "I can't risk the People's safety. We continue along the Rift. When it ends, we make our way back on the other side, to the others."

Pan-do's tranquil smile spread well-beyond his lips. "We will go one at a time." He extended the vine. "Hold this. I'll carry the other end over—"

"It is too short," Xhosa interrupted.

"We will twist the ends together until it extends all the way across."

Xhosa grunted, trying to keep her face blank.

"As the People cross, they hold the vine. If the bridge collapses, you and I pull them up."

Xhosa pushed everything from her mind. Sometimes, that simple process allowed answers to come but not this time so she twisted vines, making the final cord stronger but still not long enough.

Pan-do trotted away, dug around in the grass, and came back with an armful of dead brown stalks. "We use these to make cords when we run out of vines."

She watched as he stripped the woody exterior and exposed flexible interior fibers. He wound these around each other, twisting them snugly, adding additional fiber pieces to the ends to make the cord longer. Satisfied, he handed an end to Nightshade.

"Tug as hard as you can, Lead Warrior," and Nightshade did. He yanked Pan-do off his feet but the cord held.

Pan-do and Nightshade both grinned. "This will hold many if necessary."

Xhosa frowned. How could these simple plants wrenched from the soil without difficulty carry the People?

Nevertheless, what was her choice?

Sun traveled a hand by the time they completed the cord. Without waiting, Pan-do left Lyta with Xhosa and walked firmly, one foot after another. His first cord ran out at the crack. He placed it on the bridge, next to the end of another vine. He hopped the broken part of the bridge and continued with the second vine to Stone. This way, should the bridge crumble, those crossing would hang on vines held by different groups of people. No one group would carry the full weight. Stone clapped him on the back, almost knocking him over, and handed him an egg. Pan-do swallowed it and beckoned the rest across.

Xhosa instructed, "Hold this. It anchors you to Nightshade and I. If you fall, we pull you up the cliff. When you reach the second vine, drop this and pick up the other."

Lyta led. When no problems occurred, the People crowded forward, filling the bridge in their hunger for the food they could smell even from here. As the last of the People, save Xhosa and Nightshade, were almost across the bridge, a boom—like an explosion—pierced the air and chunks of the bridge tumbled to the valley below. A few of the People fell but most clung to the vine as they plummeted downward, even when wrenched upward and smashed into the cliff.

"Hold on!" Pan-do bellowed, motioning for the warriors to grab the vine. "Stop thrashing! We will pull you up!" Some fell, too frightened to pay attention, but most hung on until dragged over the lip.

Huffs blew from the rescued People. Food and water were thrust into their hands but Pan-do tensed, mouth open in shock, eyes across the Rift.

Alone, separated by the vast expanse of the Rift, stood Xhosa and Nightshade.

However, that wasn't what worried him.

Xhosa let a breath out, surprised she had been holding it

and relieved that the People were safe.

She swung her arms down the Rift, motioning, "We'll cross there, at the end. Pan-do—lead the people to Endless Pond. We will meet you there!"

But Pan-do didn't relax. "You face a bigger problem," and pointed behind Xhosa.

She and Nightshade turned as one and stared, unblinking, at an assemblage of Uprights, spears in hand, scowling.

"They look angry."

As if to prove her point, one howled, flinging his spear, a weak throw that wouldn't kill. Nightshade dodged it easily.

He yanked it from the ground. "We'll use their spears and our stones to hold them off until we can figure out an escape."

Two more Uprights advanced, both at a full run, spears cocked. Before the first launched his weapon, he collapsed, spear in his chest, eyes glazed in death. The next gurgled, clutched his throat, and crumpled. The rest of the Uprights retreated, mouths open, confused by what happened.

A spear thunked to the ground by Xhosa and Pan-do shouted, "The cord!"

It took Xhosa a breath to see the cord attached to the spear and figure out its purpose.

Nightshade grabbed it. "Jump on my back!"

Xhosa threw her arms around Nightshade's neck and he ran full speed over the edge of the cliff. They flew forward briefly and then dropped. Pan-do screamed and motioned excitedly but Xhosa had no time to figure out what he meant, too busy bending her legs. When they slammed into the cliff, jarring every bone in her body, they bounced. Xhosa almost let go but Nightshade seized her arm with a grip like Crocodile's jaws as they flew out over the Rift floor and bounced against the opposite cliff. And again. Somewhere in the distance was a hum like a swarm of bees and then something pricked her, nothing more than an insect bite. Below, spears clattered to the Rift floor and Pan-do roared. Then they started rising, their skin scraping over the rough rocks, arms and legs pushing themselves around the biggest projections, until finally, they were over the precipice.

She rose, body shaky, but turned toward the Uprights. Nightshade pushed close to her, shoulders strong, mouth a tight line, staring at those who would have killed them. His stance spread and he shook his spear at them, roaring.

"This is no time to show weakness," Nightshade motioned, one-handed.

Xhosa agreed and shook her spear, howling, ignoring the blood streaming down her body from more cuts and scrapes than she'd ever had.

Finally, the Uprights melted into the distance. Eyes wet, hands quivering, Xhosa thanked Pan-do for his quick thinking. Then it was time to breathe in the fragrance of this new land.

"Rest everyone. We are safe from the Uprights now that the bridge collapsed."

Over the next day and another, the hunters brought in a gazelle, Wild Beast, and a handful of birds. The scouts found Upright prints though never saw the two-legged creatures. That worried Xhosa. Why would they hide?

Every night before sleeping, the People sharpened spears, knapped tools from the wealth of rocks brought from Fire Mountain, and practiced throwing stones. Those who excelled with one hand moved to the other. Pan-do played with the children, teaching them to track, clash, and tolerate. Each day grew colder than the one before. They were busy enough during the day but at night, they huddled together to share body heat.

Without her pain bark, the pounding in Xhosa's temples intensified daily and finally made it difficult to think. Her supply of pain plants was long ago exhausted and she had found nothing to replace them.

"Nightshade. Pan-do. I will scout ahead." She tried to project power but even to her ears, her voice sounded dull and lifeless.

"The subadults can do that. We need you here," Pan-do suggested but Nightshade motioned something Xhosa couldn't see, to which Pan-do responded, "Yes. You're right."

Nightshade led Xhosa away to where they could talk without interruption. "Find the herb. If we must leave, follow our trail."

She breathed out her relief. "The People are in good hands, Nightshade," and left. Within moments, Lyta called to her.

"I will be back soon, youngster." Xhosa could barely control her temper.

"You go the wrong way, Xhosa. What you need is there," and she pointed to a lonely hill rising amidst a desolate spread of dry land the color of old wood, and then skipped back to the People.

Xhosa had no better idea of where to find the plant so set out the direction Lyta indicated. As always, with her were her spear for defense and neck sack filled with succulents, roots, and berries. Once to the crest of the hill, she crawled forward until able to peek over the seedpods to what lay beyond.

Tears of joy rolled down her cheeks.

"The tree… pain bark…." Relief washed over her body.

The descent was easier than the ascent, all thoughts of caution muted by the pain in her eyes. Finally, she collapsed to her knees at the base of the tree with the rough red bark and started to dig.

The air was cool but sweat prickled her forehead, equally from the work and the pain. She scraped, blowing shallow breaths, oblivious to the noise she made, driven by the crashing in her head and the progress of her digging. Her body was numb to the cold breeze that sprang up around her, her entire focus on excavating the hard-packed surface.

It took the rest of the day to uncover the bulky white roots and then track them to the fingertip-sized bulbs. Finally, she chopped one free, popped it into her mouth, and chewed.

"I must never run out of these again," and began to extract as many bulbs as could be found. Her first warning that she had become prey was Cat's feral scent much too close for safety.

Xhosa froze, mentally excoriating herself for ignoring her surroundings while frantically considering her options. Her spear was somewhere behind her, dropped in her frenzy, but stones filled her neck sack. A purr told her Cat was ready to attack, which gave Xhosa not enough time to remove a stone, locate Cat, and throw.

"Do you know how afraid I am, Cat?"

She kept her voice low and smooth while rising slowly. The Sabertooth panted, her thin ribs etched against her dull coat. Her teats hung, empty, and a gash still bled on her haunch. She would fight to feed her babies.

"Where are your kits?"

Keeping her voice quiet, unthreatening, she backed up, gaze never leaving Cat but at the edge of her vision, searching for an escape.

It wouldn't be the tree limbs. They were too high.

"Is being eaten better than dying at the hands of Big Heads? What do you think, Cat?"

The animal cocked its head, sniffing, trying to unravel why this upright creature showed no fear. Cat seemed exhausted but instinct forced her to continue.

There! Her spear, just a few steps away. Cat's green eyes focused on Xhosa, still not understanding, even when Xhosa calmly picked up her weapon.

Next to it lay a palm-sized rock, too small to kill but enough to stun Cat.

"Cat. If I take your life, your kits will starve." It took everything Xhosa had to hide her distress.

Drool hung from Cat's jaws and her hackles stiffened as hunger overcame logic.

That gave Xhosa a plan.

She crept toward an outcrop at the edge of an overhang. Cat observed her stealthy movements, swaying at times, paws moving unsteadily.

She repeated, "I don't want to hurt you, not with a family who relies on you."

Cat panted, skinny chest heaving, and then stiffened her legs preparing to leap.

Xhosa flung the rock at the animal's head and raced for the overhang. *Thwack!* It was a direct hit on the tender temple. Cat shook her head, spraying blood across the grass as Xhosa dove over the outcrop. She expected to find a recess below and was not disappointed.

Tucking herself into it, she rubbed dirt over her skin to conceal her smell, hoping to confuse Cat. Above, an arm's length from Xhosa's head, Cat whined, her feral odor strong.

"Go away, Cat. I'll go to my People," but the animal sniffed, padded, and inhaled again. Furry paws peeked over the edge followed by her head. Then, Cat leaped off the ledge, spun, and faced Xhosa, wedged against the rocky wall of the recess with nowhere to go.

"Leave me, Cat."

Cat's purr rumbled, too hungry to make a good decision. She snarled and leaped at her prey's vulnerable neck. Xhosa whipped her spear up but not to throw. By the time Cat realized her mistake, she had skewered herself on the spear's point, her speed driving it through her body and out her shoulders. Her momentum threw her on top of Xhosa, eyes glazed in death as her blood seeped from the gaping holes in her body.

Xhosa slit the body down the belly, tossed aside the entrails and cleaned the stomach and intestines with dirt, stuffing these with the root papules. That done, she removed a haunch, stuck the carcass in a tree away from scavengers, covered the blood-stains with soil, and built herself a nest for the night.

The return trip took longer than the outbound, the haunch more fragrant with each step. Nightshade must have smelled it because suddenly he was there. She explained where to find Cat's carcass, head drooping though her head pain had disappeared. She couldn't push away the horror Cat's kits would feel when their mother disappeared.

# Chapter 24

While Pan-do led the warriors in spear fighting practice, Xhosa and Nightshade tracked the distant lazy circles of Vulture, hoping for scavenge. They finally followed the carrion eaters to a hill that overlooked a clearing. There, below, would be whatever had died.

Xhosa gasped.

It was a small tribe of Others, their dead bodies picked over by scavengers, so ravaged that the raptors circling overhead didn't bother to land. Whatever killed them surprised them. None of the dead even held a spear.

Nightshade pointed to a footprint, not far from where they lay on the hill. "Big Heads."

A chill ran through Xhosa's body.

They hurried back to the People and let them know that tomorrow, they would move on. Nightshade posted guards for the night and the People scattered dry leaves, branches, and twigs beyond the brambled barrier that would crackle if anyone tried to sneak up.

The land that had looked so inviting from the bridge became dry and sparse as they traveled away from the Rift. Herds were thin, roots and bulbs available but only with much digging, and they had yet to find a waterhole.

Toward the end of the day's travel, the tantalizing smell of water floated on the air. Xhosa sprinted up a berm and then stopped, awed. The largest body of water she had ever seen stretched in front of her, so large, she couldn't see the opposite side.

Oddly, with no animals.

"It could be poisoned," Xhosa thought. She'd seen that, where something turned the water so bad, no animal would drink it. Those that did, died.

It didn't take long to reach the shore. A scent assaulted her that made her nose twitch and the taste from just a fingerful made her spit violently.

"Salt!"

The pond filled with it! Was it drinkable, despite the taste and smell? She ingested foul-smelling liquids when thirsty enough.

Pan-do touched her. "Salt-tasting water surrounds my former homeland. We call it Endless Sea. Drinking it kills you."

"Could this be the river my father talked about?" Surely he would have mentioned it was deadly.

"We don't even know if this has another side. I can't see it from here."

Before Xhosa could respond, Nightshade called. "Up here."

Xhosa and Pan-do scrambled up a hill further along the pond's edge, taller than the first and set back more. When Xhosa looked at what Nightshade found, her heart raced and her skin tingled. Far across the pond, close to the horizon, were verdant grasses and full bushy trees.

Nightshade pointed. "That is where we escape Big Heads."

"But how do we get there?"

A bird caught everyone's attention as it dove into the water, emerging with a fish wriggling in its bill. Satisfied, it flew toward what must be another shore.

Pan-do motioned, "Birds didn't fly across my Endless Sea because there was no opposite shore. This one, yes, we can get to the other side. We just have to figure out how."

Xhosa puckered her forehead. "Do you see those tiny brown spots, far out, touching the horizon?" They were so small, even Xhosa with her farsight barely saw them. Both males shook their heads. "They look like land, close enough together, we could walk from one to the next," and Xhosa sprinted to the water's edge. "Your chimp, Pan-do, would try."

Xhosa stepped into the water and her feet sank into the soft bottom. Water lapped at her ankles. As she continued, it rose to her calves and knees. Nightshade barked but his voice was lost in the sounds of splashing water and bird caws.

Quickly, the water touched her hips and then her waist. First, she relished the coolness but then, began to shiver.

"Xhosa—!"

"I am fine," she motioned over her head as her foot kicked a slimy twisting creature that slapped against her leg. She swallowed her fear and moved forward, mouth a tight line, spear clenched by white-knuckled fingers.

*If this doesn't work, how else will we cross?*

"Xhosa!" Pan-do called. There was no need to see his hands to catch the urgency.

"It's leveling out!" She lied when in fact, it crept up to her chest. *How do I turn around?*

She tried to pivot but lost her balance and fell head first into the pond, flailing desperately. Water flooded into her mouth and nose but as her head finally broke the surface, her body twisted toward Nightshade and Pan-do.

*Not the way I would have chosen to turn but it worked.*

One plodding step after another, wishing for a stick like Chimp's, she finally collapsed onto the shoreline and retched up a fetid liquid, brown with dirt.

"We ... must find... a different way to cross."

A day, another, and another passed as they plodded along the shore of what Pan-do had taken to calling the Endless Pond. They continued toward where Sun awoke as her father directed, but never any closer to the verdant green valleys and tiny swaying animals in the distance. The few fingers of land that extended into the water always died out. Birds crossed with impunity and small creatures—like a rat—floated away on a vegetation mat.

"Can we do that?" But everything they tried—grass fronds, big leaves, logs—all sank under their weight.

Each day opened and closed as those before it. It was a relief when they finally found one of her father's cairns, pointing them inland, away from the Pond.

So that's where they went.

As Nightshade led the People across a wide field, it started raining, gently at first but then so heavy, the dust that layered the land became sucking mud. Nightshade raced toward a cliff with a protruding overhang but Xhosa didn't like the boulder bed in front of it.

"It blocks our view. Predators can sneak up," and she led onward, hoping for better.

They passed trees with many dangerous dead branches and others with limbs too high for a quick escape. A wadi tempted her but Nightshade pointed out that in this rain, it would flood. Pan-do's sharp eyes finally located a cave. It was saturated with old coyote smell but deep enough to hold everyone. They huddled together, letting their combined warmth fill the cavernous expanse and dry them. What food they had was eaten in silence and then everyone slept where they lay. Xhosa tried to stay awake but failed.

When she woke once, the rain had stopped. Stars twinkled. Moon showed its face. Nightshade sat in the cave's mouth, facing the cold night, eyes bright with anticipation.

# Chapter 25

Pan-do woke up groggy. It took a moment to realize this cave was not home. He wrinkled his nose as the odor of stale breath washed over him.

"Hungry," and Lyta sprinted from the cave.

She had never been happier than now, traveling with Xhosa's People. Even when they lived with the Hairy Ones, Lyta worried constantly, warned him of danger, and told him often that their future was not there.

Pan-do spread his arms and reveled in being alone. Much was different from the day he committed to stay with Xhosa, in his mind to protect her, but nothing made him want to change that decision. Lyta still told him Xhosa needed protection though his daughter didn't say why.

He rolled that around in his brain. Something about Nightshade continued to disturb Pan-do, even more so the further they traveled. His thoughts jumped to that last night before the Big Heads' attack. He was sure Nightshade had enjoyed Xhosa's discomfort. The more derisive Rainbow's comments, the wider the Lead Warrior's smirk and when many joined Rainbow, Nightshade seemed energized by what he considered her failure.

Did the powerful male want to lead the People? If Xhosa failed, would he take over or simply wrest control from her? Nightshade disdained every female except Xhosa—did that mean his goal was less about saving the People than claiming Xhosa?

If coming between Nightshade and Xhosa put Pan-do at risk, so be it.

Feet hustled outside the cave. Arms waved as members chatted. Everyone was busy.

Lyta trundled inside at her galumphing pace. "We go we go we go!" and then left. Pan-do shook himself and raced after Lyta, the column of people well on its way.

Daylight drained away, replaced by comforting darkness. Pan-do tucked his daughter behind the brambled barrier and left to check the area. Others' prints were rare and Xhosa insisted their group size kept them safe. Pan-do agreed but still patrolled each night.

Finished, he crouched, at peace with the quiet. He loved the cold beauty of the land, more like the home of his youth than anywhere he'd been. Moon meandered across the glittering sky as the nocturnal sounds serenaded any who listened. Coyote howled in the distance. Crickets chirped and branches brushed against each other in the soft nighttime breeze. Owl hooted as it awoke hungry. These comforting sounds brought quiet serenity to Pan-do but another sound didn't—hushed voices that carried too far in the thin night air. Pan-do pricked his ears. One sounded like Nightshade but he couldn't identify the other.

"We must destroy.... ...the safety of our People ..." The stranger's answers, augmented by invisible motions, muffled as they moved closer together. Nightshade responded, "Yes. Do what Big ... before ..."

Voice One hissed, "Too strong... Outnumbered... Xhosa..."

Nightshade interrupted, "No. She will ... And be quiet!" He growled when Voice One answered, "*We* must ..." with an emphasis on *we*. "Xhosa is ..."

"How.... know her—"

"I know her better than you. I can keep everyone safe ..." These words were loud.

"Shhh!" Both voices fell silent, the only noise now padding footsteps as the two disappeared.

Pan-do waited until the night stilled, wondering at Nightshade's plan. If Nightshade wanted to lead and the group wanted him to—much like Rainbow—Xhosa could do nothing. Should he tell Xhosa? *I heard a broken conversation between someone who might be Nightshade and someone I didn't recognize. They were planning your destruction."*

He laughed to himself, doubting that would convince even him. That left only one issue: how to stop these two from destroying his People. He scratched the lice that nested in his chest hair. The next time Wa-co offered to groom him, he would accept.

He shook his head, not understanding why anyone would disagree with Xhosa. She was fair, open-minded, and tolerant and Nightshade thought leadership required violence. Pan–do understood why the Lead Warrior felt entitled to lead. His entire life had focused on that. The fact that Xhosa beat him in the People's challenges must have stunned him but would he weaken the group, possibly destroy it, to get what he considered his right? Pan-do shivered at the next thought that popped into his mind.

Would Nightshade kill to achieve his goal?

# Chapter 26

*Northern Africa, along the Mediterranean Sea*

Sun at his back, stomach full, Rainbow headed toward Mammoth's lows. The mostly rolling prairie was broken here and there by gullies, ridges, and low hills, the soaring spires of Fire Mountain already far behind.

Rainbow felt good, his step light, head high, arms swinging. Any doubts about his ability to lead diminished the further they traveled. For every member of the People who stayed with Xhosa, one came with him including the talented hunters and well-trained warriors that would ensure his People survived. Because Xhosa's path was so obviously arduous, it surprised no one that many females, especially the pregnant ones, joined him. New babies ensured the growth of Rainbow's People.

Rainbow's People. He liked the sound. He would tell everyone to use that call sign.

How easy it was to lead. Xhosa always made decisions sound difficult. She listened to everyone, weighed their input, balanced each against the other, but in the end, didn't she simply do what she thought best? He expedited that by skipping the listening step and simply following his instincts.

Leaders should expedite.

No, that was wrong. Xhosa gained loyalty by listening. Everyone had a voice in decisions even if they didn't get their way. It surprised him she allowed so many to leave but many of his People, even now, had nothing but good to say about her.

Rainbow's People. He would use that term as often as possible, to acclimate his People to its sound.

The new Leader stared into the distance, mulling this over as he marched forward in search of the group's new home. Yes, he saw what to do. He would encourage his People to work problems out themselves. When they came to him for advice, he would send them to talk among themselves, collaborate, and share ideas—as Xhosa did but without his involvement. When they found a solution, he would applaud their efforts.

In fact, he'd already started this. Many of his males still had not replaced their spears. Xhosa—and Nightshade— would force them to spend nights honing new weapons at the expense of sleep. Rainbow reasonably evaluated that there were no immediate threats so why risk being tired the next day, maybe miss clues that led to food? Let each male decide for himself the importance of replacing his weapons. In this way also, they would learn the consequences of good and bad decisions.

Already Nightshade's female, Mbasa, brought Rainbow food, walked with him, and slept beside him at night. Nightshade's female! She ignored him when they were part of Xhosa's People. Now, they mated whenever he wanted and she drove other females away.

He picked up the pace, jogging now, listening to the whisper of his passage through the waist-high supple grass, smelling the familiar herbs Xhosa used for healing. This terrain, with its savannahs and flowers and skittish birds, reminded him of his youth when massive herds of Mammoth, Hipparion, and Gazelle grazed everywhere, there for the slaughter. Even in the hottest of times, the People always had food though it might be limited to rodents, bats, snakes, or the huge insects that inhabited rotting bark.

Rainbow spotted a tribe of Others but as always, they maintained a respectful distance. No doubt the size of his group intimidated them. As a result, his People hunted where they wanted.

"Rainbow." Mbasa hooted his call sign and motioned, "Over that rise. A band of Others stalks a Rhino."

He paused, deciding if he should respond to the beckon of a female, and finally followed her. With Mbasa leading, he and the hunters tracked the scent and then hid as the Others killed the rhino, took what they could carry, and left.

"Scavenge what remains," he motioned loosely.

One—Tor, he thought was the male's call sign—posted hunters to alert the People if the Others returned while the rest scavenged the wealth of meat. When they left, each hunter burdened with ribs and slabs of meat, a hyaena pack moved in to clean the carcass.

Rainbow grinned to Mbasa. "No injuries. No deaths. This is how to hunt."

She nodded but seemed distracted. That reminded Rainbow that he had been annoyed.

"Tor!" He called the young hunter over. "Why did Mbasa find this before you?"

Tor gulped. "Mbasa—she is a powerful—" Rainbow interrupted whatever excuse he planned to give.

"You will become Lead Hunter of Rainbow's People someday. You must prove yourself ready."

He moved his hands with strength, tone pedantic as though teaching a child. He expected no answer—didn't want one—and sped ahead, eager to rest after such a trying hunt.

Rainbow knew what he wanted in a new home—gurgling deep streams, countless waterholes to draw prey, a quarry nearby rich with the hard stones required for tools, and herds that grazed on vast swaths of grass—what they had before the Big Heads drove them away but with each passing day, the land became drier, food sparser, and the distance between waterholes greater.

He might need to adjust his expectations.

As one Moon replaced another, he slowed the pace for the pregnant females, stopping to rest often. None of his People was accustomed to the fatigue and gruel of migrations. The last time they moved homebases was before the pairmate of Xhosa's father died. After that, the People never moved, in no small part because Nightshade's reputation for brutality drove all Others away.

"Rainbow! Starlight delivers her baby!" From Mbasa.

Another of Nightshade's mates. Rainbow had promised Nightshade leadership of his People if the powerful and charismatic male would join him. Of course, Rainbow lied but by the time Nightshade figured that out, it would have been too late to change his mind. Mbasa shattered that plan. When Nightshade saw her in Rainbow's group, he wrinkled his nose in disgust and left.

Mbasa trotted to him. "There's a cave ahead. We need a safe place for Starlight. Jackal lived there long ago. Its scent will keep others out, despite the aroma of the new birth and female blood."

Rainbow motioned, "Lead." Mbasa hesitated, as if she wanted to say more. "What?"

Mbasa motioned, a nervous shimmer in her hands, "Starlight, she's small. I worry."

Rainbow waved her away. A Leader shouldn't waste time on that—and what did he know about births.

"Take care of it," and he left, excited about this new opportunity to show leadership. Sleeping in caves rather than in the open—the right decision for a new land.

While Starlight struggled to give birth, the males explored. Not far away, they discovered a quarry, collected as many stones as they could carry, discarding the antlers, leg bones, and bone shards they had been using in place of the stone tools.

Despite the importance of the quarry, the grass here was too sparse to draw grazers so as soon as Starlight finished, her baby born dead, they moved on. Mbasa begged for a delay, to allow Starlight to rest, but Rainbow refused.

Females didn't set the tempo of travel.

Moon came, went, and came again. Scouting expeditions became rare, so sure was Rainbow that the legendary Nightshade's warriors would effortlessly defeat attackers. The group progressed leisurely and noisily. Rainbow could hear Nightshade's harsh orders in his head—*Quiet! Leave nothing of your passage!*—and stifled a grin. His People slept in, left late in the morning, and stopped long before Sun disappeared. The only problem—which wasn't significant—was they found no herds. Nor did they find Uprights. Rainbow scratched his armpit, thinking one probably led to the other.

So sure was he of their solitary travel, he missed the Others, out of sight, watching the weak strangers, preparing their next move.

**PART THREE: CHINA AND JAVA**
*850,000 years ago*

# Chapter 27

Zvi crouched by Mother on the dirt floor of the People's cave. Her old hands never stopped tugging and pounding and patting, nor did she acknowledge Zvi. The girl wriggled, bored with the assigned job, and bumped Mother's knee. The elder scowled, adjusted, and pounded harder.

Zvi pinched her lips together to hide her frustration and removed the tiny nodules from the roots. When finished, more awaited her. Always more.

"Mother." Zvi spoke as she continued her work, body flushed with heat. "I w-went to that area you talked about."

A grunt was the only reply so Zvi tried again. "Can I show you what I found?"

Mother showed no interest. Zvi exhaled without surprise. No one was ever interested in her explorations.

Except Giganto. She already missed the slow-moving Upright with fur the color of Sun. Giganto was a kind, humble, caring creature with a loving family and a closely-bound tribe. He towered over Zvi and like her, walked upright on lumbering legs. His curled hands hung to his knees ready to drop to the ground when needed to support his massive upper body. Standing, Giganto trundled, but on all limbs, he galloped, as fast as any Upright. Zvi tried moving like that once but it shredded her knuckles and they ached for days.

Giganto couldn't run like that for long so for extended flight, he swung through the trees like Monkey. Zvi loved when Giganto would cradle her in one arm while swinging one-handed, the breeze blowing her hair back in a stream, giggles of pure joy rolling from her mouth.

Zvi's hair, hanging past her shoulders, always made Giganto happy. His head hair was not much longer than the fur on the rest of his body but it was thicker, protecting him from the claws of predators—though few dared attack such an intimidating creature with his massive yellow teeth and blood red eyes. Zvi though knew the true Giganto, so shy he hid in the trees, so terrified at times he shook, and so kind he sheltered the smallest of creatures.

Giganto was the only Upright who accepted Zvi despite her blunders, follies, and stutters. Once when Zvi and Giganto were exploring, a wolf threatened Zvi. Giganto grabbed the slobbering creature by its tail and threw it aside as though straw in a wind. Another time, several of Zvi's people cornered Giganto. They considered him easy prey because of his slowness and lack of weapons, but they were wrong. The spears that reached him, he batted aside with deceptively-quick reflexes. When they continued the assault, he wrapped his muscular arms around the entire group and clutched them to his chest. He intended only to stop them from hurting him but ended up crushing the life from their bodies. He'd been so distraught afterward, Zvi stayed with him, fearing he would do something rash.

Since then, her People hated Giganto but not Zvi. During the hot times, she joined him as often as possible to forage food, which for Giganto took much of Sun's daylight. He ate mostly bamboo and it took a lot to fill him. Zvi disliked the tasteless stalks but enjoyed exploring her friend's world. When he settled to eat, Zvi would whittle the bamboo into tools. Done correctly, the edges rivaled sharpened stone and were much lighter to carry.

That all changed during the wet time. Then, without the fur that kept Giganto warm, Zvi was stuck inside her tribe's caves.

"Go," Mother motioned. "Sit with the others."

Zvi scrunched in among the tribe's other females. They gathered shoulder-to-shoulder facing the central pit that held the roots, leaves, stems, tubers, corms, and berries requiring preparation for meals. Each worked quietly, head down, pounding and chopping and cutting, ignoring her with a fierceness.

Zvi didn't understand why being the largest female made her an outcast. If she were male or foul-tempered like some subadults, her size would make her a Leader. Maybe it was her lumbering movements while others sprinted, leaving her far behind. Giganto taught her to scale trees and swing through the canopy but no one older than a child did that.

Her oddities weren't Giganto's fault. He was the one who rescued her when a rogue tribe killed her parents and left her for dead. Giganto took her to his tree nest, every day feeding and playing with her. It was the happiest time in Zvi's life, one she wished never to end, but Uprights attacked. Giganto squealed in fear, snagged her with one arm, and swung into a neighboring tree. When a spear pierced his shoulder, he dropped her. Zvi bounced, head slamming into the hard ground, and blacked out. When her eyes finally opened, Others stared down at her. Far above, in the trees, was Giganto's anguished gaze. She tried to tell him not to leave her, that he was her tribe, but her mouth and arms wouldn't move. Her best friend yanked the spear from his body, howled with pain, and fled.

For a long time after that, the simple act of talking made her head hurt. Remembering places or tasks felt like someone beating inside her head, trying to get out. The childless female who had agreed to take her soon tired of Zvi's needs.

By the time the injuries healed, her body had grown so large, groupmembers confused her with an adult and labeled her as dumb, lazy, and worthless, never realizing no one had taught her the skills. This made her cry which made everyone shun her. Even infants knew crying attracted the wrong attention.

When her bleeding commenced and no male showed interest, her adopted mother rejected her. "We must trade you, Zvi. I can't care for you any longer."

No one else wanted a huge unskilled female. When the dry time arrived, she escaped to the cool, restful, and shady world of the jungle. There, in the same nest, she found Giganto, still her best friend.

Zvi could hardly contain her excitement. The light filtered down from high overhead creating muted shadows everywhere. The branches scratched her skin and slapped against her chest but it didn't stop her from climbing the tallest tree. From there, the river flowed like a snake, coiling against its muscular currents, shimmering as its waves caught the sunlight like scales, the green meadows bathed in the humid light of a sinking sun.

That was all distraction for her real interest.

"Giganto!"

It was time to finalize their plan.

A day later, back in her tribe's cave, Zvi couldn't help but smile, despite that again they ignored her. It no longer mattered because her job was too important to be sidetracked by anyone. What she did now would decide the success or failure of Giganto's plan. Moon would arrive and depart a handful of times before all was in place but in the end, she and Giganto would be together.

"There is no bamboo for you today, Zvi. Giganto's tribe wouldn't share."

"They eat only bamboo. Without it, they starve."

"That's stupid."

Zvi thought about that. "Well, they like fruit but the monkeys grab most of it and they scare Giganto."

A giggle came from among the females. "Go, help with the deer."

It was Zvi who had chased the deer being defleshed over a cliff. Before she could trundle her way down the slope, the People's hunters claimed the kill. Zvi tried to explain her part in the hunt but no one listened.

"There's room for you here, Zvi," and one of the males—Bork—scooted over. "Watch how I remove tendons to be used for tying and carrying."

Zvi gulped back her shock and crouched, watching raptly. When he separated the hide to be scraped for skins, her mind ticked off the steps. As she worked, her muscular hip jarred one of the females.

The newly-blooded adult squealed and muttered, "Go over there where you won't be in the way," pointing to those who were pounding bones to free the marrow.

"Blood makes me sick," but Zvi scooted over.

With a *thwack*, the bone's hollow interior cracked and a long squishy tube popped out, rich with nourishment and juices. This went to the females carrying children.

"There's no room here, Zvi. Help the children shape bone picks."

"It's alright," she mumbled to no one in particular because no one listened. To her surprise, Bork made room for her among the males knapping.

"Hand me that gray rock, Zvi," and he motioned toward the pile in front of him.

Zvi did as asked. He ran his fingers over it, frowned at a dark line in the surface, and tossed it aside. Zvi pawed through the pile and uncovered a palm-sized chunk of chalcedony. Hard, almost transparent, its smooth surface felt cool to the touch. It would require time to knap but time was plentiful. Bork situated the rock on a flat surface at his feet and slammed the hammerstone into it to create the sharp flakes that became cutters.

"I can do that," and Zvi grabbed a piece of chert.

"We're running out of those," he motioned not unkindly. "Use the pond rocks."

"Where are they?"

Someone snickered. "Outside."

When Zvi looked confused—she hadn't seen pond rocks outside, Bork motioned, "That's OK, Zvi. Watch me."

When he finished one and another, he rested on his haunches and motioned, "Your name—Zvi—says you survived Buffalo."

She bobbed her head, not sure where he was going.

"Why not run?"

Any answer would come out a stutter. Then Bork would lick his lips and the stutter would get worse, finally making it impossible to talk. By that point, everyone would be laughing at her. She had tried a variety of tactics to prevent stammering—authoritative movements like the Leader, calm but assured ones like the Primary Female, self-deprecating and humble, even begging, but nothing worked.

When he waited expectantly, the only thing to do was answer honestly. "I c-can't outrun a b-buffalo. Can you?"

No one could. Of course.

As though he didn't hear her stutter, he asked, "But what made you run toward it?"

*I couldn't think of anything else to do!* Her spear was a castoff but the buffalo wouldn't know. Maybe flailing her arms, yelling and pounding her chest would frighten it.

To her great surprise, the animal bolted.

Her gaze caught Bork's. "What would you do if you were there?"

Bork shrugged. "Probably die," and then rubbed his eyes. "You earned your name, Zvi, one-who-fought-Buffalo. Wear it with pride." Most of those who heard him snickered but Bork's eyes narrowed.

Zvi had no idea how to respond so reapplied herself to the fascinating task of knapping. It was odd that everyone flaked only one side of the stone. Flaking both would make it sharper and why not all around so no matter how the cutter or chopper was grabbed, it would be sharp? It would take longer to knap but make better use of the best stones.

By the time her courage grew enough to ask Bork his thoughts on this, he'd left to scout the area around the cave in preparation for sleeping.

Everyone paired up to remove the insects, dirt, twigs, and lice that accumulated in their hair during the day. Zvi enjoyed this with Giganto but her groupmates complained that her grooming took too long. When she explained—between stutters—how fascinating the tiny bugs were that lived in fur, they laughed and refused to groom with her. Not even her adopted mother would.

Zvi swore to be kinder with her children.

The next day and every one after that, Bork invited her to join him on his daily tasks. A female doing male tasks was unusual but everyone agreed Zvi was barely female. Zvi eagerly accepted. Giganto wanted her to learn survival skills. Each day, Zvi's knapping, foraging, hunting, and spear throwing improved. When they hunted, Bork always took credit but in return, taught her how to track Hyaena, Wolf, Bear, and the big cats like Panther. Soon, not only were their tracks clear but also their voices—the greeting bark of deer, the call of the tiny musk deer, the cautionary rumble of the sambar with its treacherous antlers, the warning of Wild Pig, and the slap-slap of the giant beaver building its den. As they traveled, Bork showed how to orient her location to the sulfuric smell of the volcanoes on one side and the salty tang of Endless Pond on the other.

Partnering with Bork made him the tribe's best hunter and Mother no longer threatened to throw her out.

When Bork pairmated with a female in another tribe and no other male would partner with her, it didn't matter. She was ready.

No one noticed her disappear into the jungle, clumping away at her quickest pace, eager to tell Giganto the good news. It had been a handful of Moons but Zvi knew Giganto would be waiting. A family of Giant Panda ate at his favorite spot so Zvi leaned against a tree, whittling and sleeping, knowing when the Panda left, Giganto would arrive.

Except he didn't, and a search of his other favorite places came up empty. When night arrived, there was nothing to do but curl into the hollow trunk of Leopard's tree until Sun returned. For some reason, Leopard always draped carcasses over the boughs of this tree. It had become a reliable source of meat for Zvi, except when Leopard needed to feed her nursing cubs. Zvi wouldn't take the meat then.

After patiently searching for most of the next two days, Zvi began to worry. Did his tribe move on and he had to leave without her? When they showed up at the bamboo patch without him, her big body shook with fear that Giganto was dead.

# Chapter 28

Zvi worked the cricks from her body after another night in the confined space of a hollow tree. Giganto's family assured her he was around. All she could do was wait.

"I'll go see what the wolves are doing."

In the search for a nest last night, Zvi had seen a small wolf den dug into a hillside and tucked under a large log. Coming from inside were the growls of an adult and the whines of at least two pups. Now, Zvi quietly snuck back to it and hid in the brush where she had a good view of the pack.

"They're playing…"

In fact, to everyone's delight, the mother and father were romping and roughhousing with the pups. The yips and yelps made Zvi wonder what it would be like to live with such a loving family, in their den. Wolves were devoted to their mates and pups. They killed only for food, family, or their own protection. Zvi liked wolves better than her group but not as much as Giganto.

Which made her worry again about her friend.

*Where is he?*

She rubbed her face and trotted along the path to the bamboo patch. When Giganto finished whatever kept him busy, he would join her there. In her neck sack were bird eggs. Zvi had taken only two of the handful in the nest. If the eggs' mother was like the wolves, it would upset her to return from hunting and find all her babies gone. But Giganto loved eggs, maybe more than bamboo. His favorites were from Ostrich but the huge birds—some as tall as Giganto—violently protected their eggs, slapping with their massive wings and stabbing him with their beaks. Even Giganto had trouble stealing those.

These eggs were small but he would appreciate her gift.

Food was plentiful here in the jungle, providing a vast selection of corms, seeds, nuts, lizards, larvae, burrowing lizards, and grubs. These last were hard to spot in the cold time's moist soil, but when dry like now, fine cracks appeared above the tree roots they favored.

Zvi passed all of it, too eager to see Giganto. A cool breeze made her check the clouds—wispy, with a mix of streaks and curls. It was colder than expected.

Once at the bamboo forest, a playful huff greeted her and Zvi almost toppled over in her excitement.

"Giganto! Where were you? I worried. I have this for you," and offered the egg.

Usually, he greeted her by slamming his palms to the ground but today, worry shadowed his face and he looked lighter, less robust, as though he hadn't eaten well.

"Unh," was his only response as he gulped the egg down whole, not even chewing once. "Unnn," and he handed Zvi a chunk of bamboo.

He seldom used his voice or gestures but Zvi always understood him as he did her. She munched the woody stalk, which tasted like dry tussock grass. It would abate her hunger until something tasty showed up. As she chewed, trying to keep the distaste from her face, Giganto sat quietly, eyes staring into the distance, arms hanging listlessly. Her friend never sat still when he could eat bamboo.

"Giganto, what's wrong?"

After a succession of his mewls, chirrs, and sighs, Zvi motioned, "I feel it too. The cold lasted longer."

He waved the bamboo.

"Yes, I noticed there wasn't as much. Even the Pandas seem unhappy. Giganto—if you leave, can I come with you? I've learned many new skills since we last talked—knapping, tracking, hunting, even more. I think you and I will survive well, even with just the two of us."

The friendly giant uncharacteristically wielded the bamboo stick like a club and beat his chest, snarling and barking.

"My People–they don't appreciate the importance of sharing."

Giganto moaned, leaning tiredly on his knuckles.

"OK. I'll see what I can do. Meet me here tomorrow!"

The thought of helping her friend brightened Zvi's day so, even returning to her People didn't depress her.

The next morning, Zvi entered her People's cave as Sun awoke and asked who needed help. As expected, no one responded or asked about her long absence. It no longer mattered. Her only purpose here was to save Giganto.

Squeezing in among the females allowed her to eavesdrop on their discussions. It took every bit of restraint to remain silent—well, except for one coughing fit—when they talked openly about raiding Giganto's territory, killing his family, and taking all of the bamboo.

The next day, she again waited for Giganto at the agreed spot. A heavy mist lingered from the nighttime drizzle, dripping from the trees and forming puddles on the ground.

"I'll never go against you or your tribe, Giganto," she muttered to herself. "I will leave my People. It will work out."

When he didn't arrive, Zvi padded along the mossy forest trails, saw where he scratched his back against a tree and easily followed his prints, as deep and long as both of hers, to his favorite waterhole, but they disappeared. A warm sunny patch of shoreline called to her, so different from the bleakness of the dense humid bamboo forest.

"I'll wait." He would be here. He had promised.

A fish swam back and forth, just below the surface.

"If I had my bamboo spear, fish, you would make a good meal."

Overlaying its scales was some sort of mossy growth.

"Is that how you avoid predators, fish, by blending into the pond's bottom? Or is that greenery to make prey think you and your fins are nothing more than unthreatening green plants? That would make it easier to catch them."

The fish fixed its unblinking eye on her, snout forward.

"Why do you never blink?"

Zvi wished it would answer but all it did was open and close its mouth. When her shadow had almost disappeared, the fish long gone, Zvi too left. A bird chirped, carrying twigs for its nest.

"Where are you going, Bird? Can you spare eggs for me?" She smacked her lips thinking about their slimy taste.

A yap made her drop and perk her ears. Wolf! But not the "calling my brother" cry or the playful huffs of enjoyment. This was an "I am injured" plea. Zvi raced toward it and found a female, her leg bent awkwardly in a crack. Her cries had attracted a pack of hyaenas who sized up her desperate situation.

"Go! Leave her!" Zvi threw fist-sized rocks with enough force to stun one and another and another of the hyaenas but there were too many. Some forced her into a tree while others killed the female wolf.

Such was life. Predator became prey whether ready or not.

To Zvi's surprise, milk squirted from the dead animal's teats. Why would a nursing mother abandon her pups?

"You died trying to feed your family." Her hunger must have been desperate. "You are like me, Wolf, with no one to help you. I could feed your pups. I'm good at finding food."

Over the noise of the hyaena's slurping and chewing, Zvi heard pathetic high-pitched mewling. Several of the hyaenas heard them also and padded toward the cries.

"I must get there first."

She slithered down the tree, earning only a glance from the pack, and flew toward the plaintive yips. In front of the wolf den, one hyaena already padded forward, slowly and deliberately, to draw out the adult who must be protecting the pups. They would get rid of her first and then eat the babies.

"Argh!" Zvi bellowed and flailed a tree limb at them, making herself look as big and intimidating as possible. "Go!" and flung a rock at one of the beasts. It *thunked* off his skull and he stumbled, whining, blood dripping over his muzzle.

Another hyaena hissed.

"Leave them—it is enough you took their mother," and Zvi tossed a boulder the size of Ostrich's egg at the Leader.

It knocked him over and another one crushed his leg. With a squall, he limped away, to be replaced by a more impressive hyaena, maybe sensing opportunity in the void created by the Leader's absence. A low growl rumbled from his chest. He bared his vicious fangs. Saliva drooled from the corners of his lips as he fixed an unwavering stare on Zvi. Without a thought, Zvi pitched another missile and it smacked him in his eye. He yelped, shook his head, and pawed at the leaking blood. Zvi aimed and fired another and another. Finally, he tucked his tail and sprinted into the trees, as did the rest of his pack.

Zvi bellowed her most fulsome howl and waited a moment to be sure they left for good, and then crawled toward the mouth of the den.

"They're gone. You're safe," her voice a soothing shush as her eyes searched the dark interior for the pups.

There, one and another, huddled together at the back, shaking with fear. She gently withdrew the wiggling balls of fluff. Tails tucked, they moaned. Their eyes were still closed but they knew Zvi's odor didn't match mother. A few jabs with clawless paws, nips with toothless mouths and they gave up the defense, choosing instead to snuggle into Zvi's arms, lick her arms and chest, tasting her scent. She nuzzled them, remembering how comforting Giganto's arms were when he rescued her.

"You're OK," she soothed until their furry, round bodies stopped shaking.

Not knowing what to do for such small pups, Zvi took them to her People's cave to seek help from the Primary Female, Leader of the females and the one who would know how to care for an orphaned animal.

"Mother, look." The elder glanced up at the bundles of fur in Zvi's arms.

"Where is their mother?" She motioned while dropping her work and taking the first of the wolf pups. He mewed plaintively, pink tongue tasting this new creature.

"Killed by hyaena. These are—"

"Food. Zvi, you did well," and bashed the wriggling form against a rock, its head exploding.

"No! We must care for them—" but the Primary had already closed her hand on the last pup. Zvi swatted it away and scuttled backward, her massive feet stepping on one of the new adult females who squealed as others tried to pull Zvi down.

"Stop, Zvi! You've gone too far!"

This from the Lead Warrior, but instead of stopping, Zvi tucked the last pup into the crook of her weak arm and swung the other. Her intention was to push the warrior out of the way but her forceful slap connected with his cheek and cast him aside like the detritus of a hunt. He hit the ground hard and rolled into the central fire, screaming as his hair burst into a fiery blaze.

Zvi ran from the pained screeches and bellowed threats of her groupmates, not caring that they would never again welcome her into their midst.

Back at the mother wolf's den, Zvi collapsed, shivering. The remaining pup wriggled from her arms, yipping his excitement to be home, and scrabbled in a fruitless search for his sibling. When he forgot what he was doing, he curled into Zvi's lap.

"I'm here. No one can hurt you," Zvi promised.

The pup's nose twitched, muzzle turned up to Zvi, and he licked her. Zvi tucked him into the nest at the back of the den, built a bristle bush barrier at the cave's mouth, and settled in for the night. As they lay together, sharing warmth, Zvi listened for footsteps of her band but the only sounds were nocturnal insects and Owl's hoot as it searched for a meal. Zvi and the pup fell asleep.

When night arrived the next day and still no one came, Zvi had no doubt her people had abandoned her but it didn't feel lonely or isolated. Now that someone needed her, it felt like freedom.

"I will care for you, as Giganto cared for me. No one will hurt you. You will grow into a good strong wolf and rejoin your band."

Zvi petted the animal's downy fur until they both fell asleep.

# Chapter 29

Zvi awoke to a paw slapping her cheek. Only the slightest rosy glow showed over the treetops.

"You wake early."

The pup charged forward, slammed his tiny paws to the ground with a high-pitched squeal, and then coiled in and out of Zvi's feet. Zvi giggled but the wolf froze, head cocked, staring at his pack leader.

"You never heard a laugh, Wolf?"

Her stomach rumbled which made the pup tuck his tail and flop over.

"You and I are hungry."

She carried him in the crook of her arm while collecting roots and slugs and a tree frog, all rejected by the wolf so Zvi popped them into her mouth and kept searching.

"Where do I find something you will eat?" She grumbled and then stopped beside a familiar tree. Curled around its trunk was a thick vine. "I know this plant, pup. Its juice matches your mother's milk, well, in color. I don't know about taste."

With a snap, the stem broke. Zvi sucked the liquid out and drooled it into the wolf pup's mouth. He swallowed eagerly, licking drops of the juice from her lips. It took another and another before the pup yawned, curled at her feet, and fell asleep.

Zvi picked him up and hurried to their cave, protected the opening with small boulders and bramble bushes, and sat down by the mouth, Wolf cuddled in her lap. There, the pup slept while Zvi listened to his gentle snores.

Zvi couldn't believe her luck. She'd found a friend.

The next day, Zvi tucked the pup into her neck sack as soon as Sun peaked over the horizon.

"We have to find Giganto, Pup." But by the time Sun peaked overhead, there still was no sign of him.

"I guess he's busy again. He does that sometimes, with his family."

Zvi's stomach growled and she headed for Leopard's tree, the one place with an easy supply of meat. The pup's hackles rose as he sniffed the predator's scent and then he whimpered piteously.

"There's nothing to worry about. We'll leave if Leopard is there."

The tree was empty of both the dangerous cat and a carcass so Zvi scavenged from a berry patch and ate from a termite mound until her appetite was sated. None of those foods interested the wolf. In fact, when offered, he coughed and shook his head violently.

"I'll cut more of those vines. When you grow up, Pup, we can hunt together. I've only had one hunting partner before—B-Bork. It was much easier with both of us."

The two created a daily routine. They woke with Sun, roughhoused for a while, and then went in search of Giganto and food. Within a handful of days, the vine's milky liquid no longer satisfied Pup. His natural instinct was to eat meat but until his teeth grew in, he couldn't tear or crush even the smallest morsels. Zvi was at a loss what to do, becoming more and more desperate as the pup lost the weight he had gained and began to mewl constantly in hunger.

One day while hunting, Zvi placed the pup on the ground and waved, "Hunt!"

First, pup gnawed a root but became bored. Next, he snagged a rat almost his size but it easily escaped his baby teeth and soft claws. Zvi snatched the rat, snapped its neck, and skinned it.

Which gave her an idea.

She chewed a mouthful, spit it into her hand, and gave it to the wolf. The pup slurped it up, yipped his excitement, sat on his haunches, and wagged his tail for more.

Zvi giggled. "This will work fine." The wolf gobbled up the chewed food until he fell asleep curled at her feet. She slung him over her shoulder, paws dangling in front and back, head snuggled into Zvi's neck, and collected moss and branches. Last night, the wolf had been cold despite his fur. A nest would insulate him from the chill earth.

A sniff upon entering the cave told her nothing dangerous was there so she tucked the pup into the warm nest and petted his furry fluff as he slept, wondering what to do next. Hunger still ate at her insides but Pup was too vulnerable to leave alone.

"Food will wait. I have responsibilities." Her pack depended upon her.

The next day, when the two left the cave, again prowling for Giganto, Zvi let the pup romp.

"I hope you don't run away. I've come to consider you a friend."

That was the furthest thing from the orphan's mind. Her scent was imprinted on his brain so no matter where he bounced, leaped, nipped, or chased, he always found his way back to her. Even when Zvi hid, the wolf could track her.

As Sun dipped below the tree line, the wolf howled for the den and its lingering smell of his family. Zvi stuffed the entrance with bramble bushes and then they talked. Well, Zvi talked, the wolf listened as no one had ever before.

"I was orphaned like you…" "My mother taught me how NOT to treat a child…" "I love you…"

"Pup, I've never been so happy. You are a good friend."

The wolf pup snuggled into her chest. It helped assuage the worry that blossomed in Zvi, the one that frightened her too much to put into words.

Where was Giganto?

# Chapter 30

Zvi's anxiety grew day by day as there continued to be no sign of Giganto. Did his tribe migrate? Or was he injured?

"We need Giganto until you are old enough to hunt as my partner."

The wolf pup mewled and his forehead wrinkled.

"You will like Giganto. He's scary to some but gentle with friends. If something happens to me, Giganto will care for you. He's too big to die."

Pup looked unconvinced so Zvi explained, "Bees live in hives, termites in mounds. They travel together. I lived with my People and you with your pack. Predators avoid groups and are drawn to the lone traveler."

Pup whined.

"You're worried Giganto will reject you? He's not like that. He let me stay with him when I was alone like you are."

Pup pawed his face and sneezed. It took Zvi a moment of reflection.

"Well, Giganto's family may be frightened by a wolf but they know me. I'll explain."

Pup leaped up, sprinted around the cave, and banged into Zvi's leg.

"You're right. We will live here, in the den of your mother, with Giganto."

The next day, as the days before, Zvi and the pup searched for Giganto. The wolf stayed at her feet, instinctively remaining quiet when Zvi was. That included when they crossed paths with Giganto's family but they didn't know where to find Giganto.

After another long fruitless day, the two returned to the cave. A snarling female wolf greeted them, with bared fangs and raised hackles.

The pup yipped and leaped toward her but a swipe of her clawed paw tossed him well clear of the den where he landed on his back with a painful squeal.

"Pup!" As Zvi hurried to help him, the female wolf's mate slipped out of the underbrush. His steps were measured, head down, tail stiff, as a deep rumble rolled from his jaws, directed at Zvi.

Zvi clutched the pup in one hand and a branch in the other, swinging it as a weapon, hoping to frighten the wolves out of the den, not injure them. When two tiny pups appeared by the female, Zvi dropped the branch and fled.

"I can't hurt them, pup. They want only to protect their family."

When Sun dropped out of sight, Zvi scrabbled up a tree, losing her footing more than once, stuffed the wolf into a hole in the trunk, and fell into an exhausted sleep, wondering what to do next.

Yipping woke Zvi the next day. She'd fallen out of the tree and the pup was frantic to escape the hole he'd been stuck in all night. Zvi pulled him out, received fevered thank-you licks, and they headed away.

"We will go where the animals migrate during the cold time. They always return so it must be safe."

The rejection of his own kind seemed to wear on the pup. He plodded beside Zvi with none of his usual rambunctious energy. Often, he gazed at her with hopeful eyes as though realizing they were alone. When Zvi stopped, he leaned against her leg and huffed.

Soon, Zvi recognized the path as one Giganto had described so well, it became etched in her mind right down to the cawing of the birds and the smell of the dampness from the morning mist. They took their time traveling, the wolf pup trotting gravely at her side, head raised, ears erect and listening. When he voided, he buried it with dirt.

Zvi did the same.

She created a spear from a tree branch and stuffed her neck sack with succulents, stones, moss, leaves, and spiderwebs for healing. Wolf allowed her to hang a similar sack around his neck, this one from Gazelle's bladder and packed with more of the same.

Zvi had no particular destination and the entire hot time to get there. She took the opportunity to show the pup how to steal honey from bees and track food. Often, they located caves for their night nest, sometimes occupied but usually empty. By this time, many babies had grown enough to move out on their own.

Zvi could not believe life could be this happy, having someone to care for who loved her. They ate well and had plenty of tools and weapons. The last goal was a home.

All that changed one sunny morning. Without warning, a ball of fire careened across the blue sky and exploded in a shower of fiery embers somewhere by Sun's awakening place. A boom reverberated until Zvi heard nothing else. Pup's muzzle fell open and his eyes squinted shut as he leaped into Zvi's arms. She toppled over like a felled tree, hugging Pup to her chest and rolling up against a woody stump, determined to protect him from the hail of rocks and dirt falling from above. Despite covering one ear with her free hand and scrunching her eyes shut, the cacophony continued.

When it finally ended, her eyes wouldn't open without fire exploding in her head. Pup yipped and hissed, slapping his paws on the ground, knowing she was hurt but not understanding what to do about it.

"OK," and she leaned on her elbows, head drooping, waiting for her insides to stop churning. When her breathing finally slowed and her eyes would open without too much pain, she swiveled her head side to side. If danger stalked them, the pup was her responsibility.

"It looks normal but smells awful."

The sweet scent of jungle had been replaced with the toxic aroma of Fire Mountain exploding, though the fearsome behemoth looked undisturbed. Nor did the jungle sound as it had this morning. It crackled, like a fire raging, and the low rumble of pounding feet saturated the air. The air thundered again, this time like the roar of Mammoth. Pup howled in fear and shook from nose to tail.

Before she could decide what to do, the sky darkened with birds, raptors, bats, and insects and the ground thundered with the din of feet.

"Watch out!" Zvi scrambled backward, stumbling over a log, bracing her fall with one arm as the other gripped Pup. Leopard broke into the clearing and Pup leaped from Zvi's arms barking his high-pitched warning. His tail wagged gamely as his legs trembled so violently that when he tried to run, he fell spread-legged. The big cat flew past, never looking at the terrified animal, as did a gazelle, a warthog, and a flood of other animals.

Zvi snatched Pup and leaped into a nearby tree, cracking her spear against the trunk, and settled on a limb to watch the spectacle below. The air rang with hooves and paws, scurrying insects, and escaping rodents, nose to tail, no interest in anything but saving their own lives.

Sun moved a hand overhead by the time the onslaught disappeared.

"We must find Giganto and check on my people. Then, we escape together, with the animals."

Pup yipped and growled, unhappy with the confusion, the distant scent of fire, and more than anything, the fear he smelled from his pack leader.

Zvi petted his head and motioned, "I will protect you, Pup," knowing that if the wolf didn't understand her words, he still appreciated her tone.

Damaged spear in hand, they trundled down their backtrail. They dodged many animals too frightened to veer out of the way of this huge upright creature with the small wolf who growled in a high-pitched voice. They all eyed Zvi as though wondering whether she was lost or stupid. Zvi's home cave was abandoned with no trace of where her People went.

"It's OK, Pup. We'll find Giganto." But the closer they got to Giganto's home, the worse the devastation.

Whole swaths of grassland were burning. The blast blew down entire stands of trees, roots naked to the air, limbs tumbled together in giant frenzied heaps. The sky was so opaque with smoke, it blotted out the Sun and clouds. Zvi tucked the pup into the crook of her arm and coughed, swallowing the cinder and ash sucked in with each breath. The further they went, the worse the carnage until it made bile rise in her throat.

"This must be where the fireball hit."

The pup whined, head nuzzled into Zvi's chest, tail wrapped around his body.

The metallic smell of blood fought with the fresh stench of feces. Bodies littered the ground like refuse, crushed by trees or boulders tossed as though pebbles. Normally, Hyaena and Coyote would scavenge the eyes and tongues but today, they were untouched.

Zvi felt the first stirring of panic.

"This isn't Giganto's group, Pup. Maybe he survived." Kind, trusting Giganto—he must be alive.

Zvi darted from one usual haunt to another—Leopard's tree, the bamboo forest—but all were destroyed, nothing more than charred wood and tinder.

"There!" It was Giganto's troupe, lumbering away. She grabbed one by the arm. "Where's Giganto?" but he brushed her aside, as did the next and the next. "Where are you going?" she begged but no one bothered to answer. They shambled onward, heads hanging, arms loose.

Zvi ended up alone, with Pup, trying to decide what to do next when something caught her attention.

"Giganto…" Or what was left of him. Crushed by a boulder, arm pleading for help that never arrived, flies buzzed his blood-laden body.

# Chapter 31

Zvi threw up while the wolf flapped his ears, sneezed, and coated Zvi with warm licks.

"Why didn't I find Giganto sooner?"

He badly wanted to go away, with her. They had planned it all out. Tears sprang to her eyes.

"Pup," she murmured, voice buried in the animal's fur. "We are too small a pack to survive."

The wolf pup wriggled out of Zvi's grasp, dropped to the ground, righted himself with a terrified yip, and sprinted away.

"No—that's the wrong direction!" Zvi screamed as the pup pronked through Giganto's stumbling band, every one of them oblivious to the tiny creature dodging their massive feet. He dashed past escaping panda bears, boars, and Giganto's small orange cousins. No one cared.

Zvi chased after the wolf pup, frightened that he chased the scent of his pack, hoping he didn't.

"I know..." pant, "you recognize ..." pant pant, "...we are different. I just hope ..." wheeze, "...you still want me."

If he left her, she would be completely alone.

Zvi careened after the tiny creature, easing beyond a blockade of brittle thorny branches, dread sending prickles of fear down her long arms, frantic that every dead bundle of fur in her path would be Pup. Blazing orange flames lit the ridge above her, eating their way toward them. Balls of fire leaped from tree to tree, the dry branches filled with sap, setting off booming explosions in the canopy.

"Argh!" she barked in fear, almost stumbling into a yawning crevice so deep, no one could survive. Her gaze darted through the chaos, but no Pup.

A plaintive yip echoed from somewhere.

"Pup! Where are you?"

Another cry, this one more hopeful as though he recognized her voice. Zvi leaned forward, looking over the crumbling edge of the gaping crevice that had almost been her end.

There clinging to a ledge was the wolf.

"I told you it wasn't safe," she motioned as evenly as possible.

Pup answered by mewling, as though to say, *I now understand.* He leaped up as far as his short squat legs allowed and fell back to the rocky shelf, digging his claws into the dirt-laden wall of the crevasse.

"How do I get you out?"

It was too deep for Pup to claw his way up, too tall for Zvi to reach down.

Zvi found an undamaged bamboo pole about the size of her wrist and motioned, "I'll drop this to you."

Once it settled on the ledge by the wolf pup, he sniffed, snorted, and then batted it with a growl. When it didn't fight back, he licked the tough exterior and tried to chew a piece lose.

"It isn't food, Pup. I want you to scratch your way up. Can you do that?"

Pup huffed, slapped the cane with a paw, tasted it one last time, and then fixed pleading eyes on his pack leader.

Zvi shook her head. "I have to crawl down to rescue you—is this how it's going to be? Well, there's no other option, is there."

She looked around, hoping for a vine or an alternate path to the ledge, and saw something.

"I'll be right back."

Much to Pup's distress, Zvi pulled the pole up and wedged it between two trees. Holding a pup-sized boulder, she hung by one arm from the bamboo. It bent but didn't break.

She raced to the cliff, coughing. "The smoke is thicker, Pup. We must hurry." If this took much longer, neither of them would be able to breathe. "I'll drop this to the ledge you're on and come get you."

The mixture of hand motions and soothing sounds calmed the wolf. He plopped to his haunches, panted heavily while wagging his fuzzy tail over the dirt. Zvi clutched the pole in her big hands and let it guide her down until her feet touched the ledge. Pup leaped into her arms, almost pitching her over the edge, licking her with his rough tongue and burying his snout into her ample neck.

"I would never leave you, Pup. We are pack."

She held his shivering body against her with one arm, wrapped her legs around the pole, and tried to haul them both upward one handed but for every forward movement, they slipped back, their combined bulk simply too heavy. Even grabbing roots to steady herself did no good because they came loose.

Zvi canted her head. The smoke was thicker already and the reek of fire heavier. Whinnies and screeches were everywhere as was the stench of burning flesh. Her throat tightened and her chest contracted. Her vision darkened at the edges. Was this her day to die? Abandoning the wolf would free both of her arms to climb up the pole.

She couldn't live with herself if she did that.

She closed her eyes and became Eagle, soaring overhead safe from the fire, floating on quiet wings high above the tiny wriggling wolf, tail wagging furiously, head nestled into the chest of the bumbling female. Eagle dipped for a closer look and cawed in fright to see the red earth steadily crumbling below the ledge.

Eagle's farsight easily surpassed any other living creature and she zoomed in on the shaking figure and the tiny wolf who would never get any older if his trembling pack leader didn't do something.

"The tendons!" Always wound around Zvi's neck, fibrous and stretchy like the Gazelle they came from.

With a swoop, Zvi snapped back to reality. Fingers stiff with fear, she unlooped the tendon and secured the wolf to her chest. The pup's nails dug into her skin but it didn't hurt. Nothing about Pup could bother her. He was her pack. Now, with both hands free, Zvi clawed her way up the cliff, over the lip, and the two fled.

Smoke rolled over them like a fog bank, but despite the stench, Zvi picked out the scent.

"That salty smell is Endless Pond. We must stay in front of it."

Pup snorted happily and cavorted as though to say yes.

The deeper they traveled into the unknown, the better the air but the land continued to shake. When exhaustion stopped Zvi, the two curled into the roots of a tree and slept.

The next day, Pup greeted her with an exuberant lunge. Zvi endured his roughhousing until he loped outside to do his business. Then, Zvi licked at her many bloody scratches, the result of Pup's unrestrained play, and smiled, watching as Pup marked the boundaries of his pack's nest.

"It's time to leave, Pup. Here, it still smells of cinder."

He perked his ears and cocked his head before galumphing after his pack leader. As Zvi searched for food, Pup dodged and pranced, huffing at anything that could mean danger.

"Stay close to me!"

Which he didn't, though he marked his path with continual yapping and barking. Zvi lurched forward, calling, hoping he didn't go so far that his voice no longer carried. Finally, she rounded a corner and found Pup, hunched at the base of a tree over the unconscious body of a child as though guarding it. The youngster was an Other but much smaller than Zvi with bark-colored skin, scrawny legs, and massive brow ridges. Blood clotted in deep gouges on his chest and raw angry burns dotted his arms.

None of that bothered Zvi. Her plants would heal those. What almost scared the courage out of her was the snake next to the young male.

Earth chose that moment to tremble which made the snake hiss, thinking it was being attacked. It struck as Zvi tried to grab the unconscious boy, missing Zvi but biting the boy's ankle.

"No!" Zvi walloped the snake with a stick, wanting simply to scare it away.

Again, her unpredictable strength got her in trouble. The snake stilled, a deep flat groove behind its head almost breaking the serpentine body into two.

"Oh, snake! I know you intended no harm," Zvi wailed but there was no time for regrets. The boy would die if something wasn't done, and quickly. She dropped to her knees and sucked the poison from the fang marks, spit it out and repeated until the only taste was blood. Pup panted heavily, so close his fur tickled her face.

The youngster was too small and vulnerable to recover on his own so Zvi slung him over her shoulder, Pup prancing at her feet, and hurried to a hyaena den they had passed earlier. She approached warily, sniffed, and threw a dirt clod inside. When no growl answered, the small group shuffled across the threshold, Zvi ducking to avoid the roof, the boy in one arm and her makeshift spear in the other.

Pup growled.

"It's empty, well, except for molted fur and old carrion bones." She laid the boy in the path of a breeze. "Watch him, pup. I need plants," and left.

Despite the strangeness of the area, Zvi located the necessary herbs, mulched them, and applied a salve to the youngster's wound. Other leaves, she pounded into a flat compress, soaked in water, and laid across his burning forehead. When Sun slept and the air cooled, Zvi moved the youngster to a nest of moss, leaves, and boughs at the back of the cave where the day's heat had collected. Zvi sat at his side, knapping tools accompanied by the wheezing sound of the youngster's labored breaths.

Sun awoke, shining hazy light through the murky sky, but the boy remained unconscious.

# Chapter 32

A day and another passed. Zvi found abundant carcasses of animals who ran so hard, it killed them. Zvi collected one each morning with whatever nuts or berries were available and then tended the youngster. Nothing she tried helped, no matter the herb or root or bark, and he remained unconscious, breathing shallow, skin damp.

This morning, Zvi ducked into the cave carrying a dead hare and a water vine. To her surprise, the boy was not only sitting up but giggling, the wolf licking his neck, enjoying the taste of his stale sweat.

Her eyes popped open and her cheeks burned with excitement. "You're awake!"

He turned a red, tired gaze to Zvi while petting the wolf. "Blue eyes in a wolf are unusual. I can't believe you have a wolf for a friend. I often thought wolves must be sociable with their grinning mouths and wagging tails." He winced. "My head—what happened? And my leg prickles."

Pup nudged the youngster as Zvi smiled, happy the stranger spoke her language. Well, the hand signals helped a lot.

"First, d-drink this," and inserted one end of the water vine into the boy's mouth.

He gurgled, swished noisily, and swallowed. "How did you know about these vines? I haven't seen you here. You look nothing like the local tribes. Which is good because—"

Zvi interrupted his gush of words. "My name is Zvi. What is your n-name?"

"Seeker," and he started to rattle on about how much he liked Zvi's name but she interrupted again. "E-eat this. You must get your strength back," and handed the boy named Seeker a chunk of raw meat. Zvi didn't know how long they could stay in this den but had decided to remain with him—Seeker—until he recovered.

"Mmm..." The boy chewed, his face lighting up. "I recognize the taste."

Zvi drooped. "It's s-snake. I killed it by accident."

Seeker stopped mid-chew and looked her up and down. "Yes, you're large enough to do that. I'm not. My family loves snake but they're too fast for even the fleetest hunters in my tribe. One bit my mother..."

His voice trailed off at the sight of the fang marks on his ankle.

Zvi flushed. "It's my fault, Seeker. I saw the snake and was trying to get you away when earth shook and threw Snake against you. It bit out of surprise, I think —why would it hurt you? When I-I h-hit it so it would let you go, it d-died."

Seeker looked his own body over from chest to toes, faltering at his tingling leg, and then motioned, "Why am I not dead?"

Zvi wouldn't look at Seeker. "I sucked the v-venom out. I didn't know what else to do." Fear washed her body. Saving Seeker at the expense of Snake—was it right to interfere with the animal's meal? "It was defending itself, as I m-might. I honored its sacrifice by using its b-body for food."

When Seeker looked confused, Zvi explained in increasingly broken sentences about finding him unconscious. "Do the b-bites hurt? I can give you b-bark to ch-chew."

Seeker thought for a moment and answered, "No. Not at all."

Zvi showed Seeker how she washed the bite, crushed the plant leaves and rubbed them over the snakebite, and then covered it with a compress to minimize the swelling.

"Thank you, Zvi. Do you know why my vision is blurry?"

That upset Zvi, greatly. She blundered killing the snake—that was obvious—and it blinded her patient.

"Maybe from the sn-sn-snake bite. The blurry vision I-I mean." The wolf panted, curious eyes fixed on first Zvi and then Seeker.

Zvi took a deep breath and continued, "But I d-don't know if numb-numbness-ness is ... is ... is... "

"Normal?" Seeker finished for her. His gaze fixed on hers. "You wonder if numbness is normal from a snakebite?"

Calm replaced Seeker's rambling. "Excellent question. Hmmm… I don't know the answer to that either."

Pup panted, resting his muzzle on Zvi's foot as she motioned, "Few-few of my tribe… ever… survived… Snake's bite."

After a pause, Seeker, motioned, "How did you find me?"

"Oh, I didn't. It was Pup."

Seeker's heavy brow puckered and his head cocked. "How did you befriend a wolf?"

Zvi explained about the explosion, the fires, fleeing, finding the wolf, and then how he led her to Seeker's unconscious body. Seeker interrupted here and there with a clarifying question but grinned at Pup and seemed impressed with what Zvi thought was a pretty bumbled attempt to help.

While talking, she cut a ring around each of the hare's hind feet, slit the pelt, and then peeled upward until it bunched like a collar around the neck. One swift blow chopped off the head, making it easy to pull out the offal and the edible intestines. Then, Zvi tossed pieces to everyone and she devoured the rest.

By the time her explanation of how Seeker came to be in the hyaena den ended, they had finished eating and Zvi no longer stuttered but Seeker's cheeks were red with heat and his eyes glassy so she covered him with wet leaves.

Seeker smiled. "How do you know what to do for sicknesses, Zvi?"

She flushed. "I wasn't allowed around my tribe's healer but Giganto—my friend—taught me."

When Seeker remained silent, Zvi asked, "Why do you wear such a small animal skin around your waist?"

"It is called a loin-skin, to protect my sensitive parts from being scratched and cut while climbing. Your people don't?"

Zvi shook her head. "We rarely climb."

Seeker tilted his head up and asked, "Zvi, would you look outside for the stars? I lost them after the explosion. If they left, I must too. They guide me." His browed furrowed and he chewed a corner of his lip.

"Pup—stay with Seeker while I check." Pup scuttled closer, eyeing the new pack member hopefully, muzzle open in a smile.

Zvi walked outside and tipped her head. There, glistening overhead, was a field of stars, sparkling and shining.

"Good. Seeker doesn't need any more upset."

She chopped another water vine for Seeker and dumped the end into his mouth while delivering the good news.

Seeker threw up.

The wolf licked up the vomit and sat, swishing his tail against the dirt floor, hoping for more.

"I drank too fast, that's all. I know better."

The pup nibbled Seeker's fingers and then twisted his head to the side. "Do you hear it, Zvi? Pup?"

Zvi strained but heard nothing. Pup slapped his paws to the ground.

Seeker's features pinched. "Do you hear Owl?"

Zvi stood in the mouth of the cave, listening, but shook her head.

"That's because Owl left, Zvi. I must, too."

"But you are ill, Seeker. Wait until you are well."

Seeker shook his head. "Everything that happened—the explosions, the fires, the quaking, and my injuries—are part of a plan. It's why Snake gave up his life for me and you and Pup were there to save me. It's why you rescued Pup."

Zvi liked that a plan explained her life—why her family died and her new people rejected her, why Giganto died.

Seeker peered out the mouth of the cave, wriggling around as he tried to stand. "You are the answer, Zvi. I've been looking for you."

"Maybe being odd is OK."

"Odd is preferable, Zvi. Without odd, change can't happen."

Seeker finally lay back in the nest with Pup curled at his side.

"No one I know would help a stranger, Zvi, especially one injured. Why did you?"

"Truth, I couldn't *not* help." When Seeker didn't respond, she motioned, "Why did you travel alone? That's dangerous."

"I didn't. The stars are my company."

Seeker startled awake which woke Zvi. The youngster sat up, then tried to stand but failed.

Zvi motioned, "It will take time to get your strength back."

"Zvi, I appreciate what you've done for me but I must go. There can be no life where there are no stars."

Zvi shook her head, trying to clear the sleep away. "I saw the stars. Do you remember me telling you?"

"But did you really see them, Zvi?" Seeker's gaze drilled into Zvi as though he saw her thoughts and memories. "I'll show you what I mean. Would you help me up?"

Which Zvi did—of course—and they hobbled outside moving at Seeker's pace, which was about the same as Zvi's normal walking speed.

Once outside, Seeker motioned, "Look up, Zvi. What do you see?"

"Stars everywhere, bright and glinting. There are more here than in the jungle—"

"But they're in the wrong position. That big one should be there, and that group," he pointed, "should be further away—Zvi, I can't stay."

Zvi's eyes brimmed with tears. Seeker thought it was her fault the stars were broken. Maybe it was. Would Pup stay with someone who could break the stars? Her hands shook so, she couldn't respond.

Seeker didn't seem to notice.

"Tomorrow," and Seeker wobbled back into the cave, wincing. "We must go."

"We?" Zvi lurched toward Seeker. *Did he say "we"?*

He continued, "Of course. You are part of this Zvi. Where the stars feel at home, there we will find ours," and then his eyes rolled up and he toppled into Zvi's arms.

"He is burning hot, Pup!" *Why is he sick again?*

Days slid by and Seeker remained unconscious. Pup brought food—mostly small rats and mice—while Zvi tended the boy. The snakebite flared swollen and red, but less each day under Zvi's herbs, and the fever abated. Still, he slept.

Zvi took the time to search for Seeker's People but no matter how far she traveled or how tall the tree or cliff she scaled, there was no trace of anyone. The two were alone.

Seeker only awoke once and then, he asked immediately about the stars. When Zvi admitted they were the same, Seeker again passed out.

"Seeker, I promise, if you recover, I will help you find the stars." A tear rolled down her face. "You must live, Seeker. Please."

# Chapter 33

Zvi awoke to the sounds of Seeker and Pup playing. As soon as her eyes flicked open, Seeker scooted to his feet.

"We must go. Pup says he will join us. We will go first to my People. I promised to return."

This was the first time Seeker had ever mentioned his family. Zvi perked up. "Where do you live?"

"Far from here, in a jungled lowland that dumps into Endless Pond. It is a long journey but beautiful. I want them to meet you and Pup, the ones who saved my life."

Zvi frowned. "I don't know that area, Seeker. How safe is it? Pup is still too young to defend himself." Fear laced her hand motions.

"I will keep you safe."

Zvi wasn't convinced but let it go when Pup woofed a high-pitched growl as though to argue he had grown.

Zvi sighed in resignation. "Even if they don't join... us... they will be happy to know you are safe."

Seeker motioned benignly, "You have traveled far from your People, too, Zvi. Do they worry about you? Should we also look for them before we leave?"

Of course Seeker connected that she too was alone. Her whole body drooped like a water-starved plant. "No. And no. After the Explosion, they didn't even t-try to f-find me... They k-killed Pup's brother and wanted to k-kill P-Pup also, even when I explained that I'm his pack."

Seeker groomed Pup, eating the ticks and discarding the twigs and leaves embedded in the wolf's fur. "If I stay home, they expect me to hunt. There's no time for that when so much of life must still be discovered!"

"What If I hadn't found you, Seeker?"

"But you did." Something offhand and hopeful emerged in his expression. "And why do you think I came this direction, Zvi? I found you, too."

Zvi blinked. When she opened her eyes, Seeker was staring into the distance. Zvi turned but all she saw were trees and a misty sky.

Seeker took long ground-eating strides away from the cave, Pup beside him, Zvi lumbering to keep up.

"Does F-Fire Mountain spew molten rock and smoke where you l-live, Seeker?"

That irascible, irritable, touchy behemoth with its many groupmembers that spread across the horizon made Zvi nervous. Her mother said they killed anyone within reach—and the burnt black shell that covered the flank of each mountain was all the proof Zvi needed.

"Of course, but I know how to keep us safe, you and Pup and I. You'll see." Seeker slapped at a biting insect that was trying to suck his blood. "Zvi, why do your words come out funny at times?"

Zvi hunched forward and curled her head to her chest, knowing what was coming. "I st-struggle. Th-that's all."

In fact, her People were so abusive about her stuttering, she refused to talk for a long while. The wolf felt Zvi's discomfort and bumped against her leg as they walked.

Seeker motioned, "Why not just say it?"

*If Seeker and I are going to travel together, I must be honest, even if it means he rejects me.*

"Well… I mean… sometimes…"

Seeker laughed. "Zvi. It makes me pay close attention. Your groupmates probably told you that, too." When he finally noticed her discomfort, he motioned, "You aren't embarrassed, are you? You shouldn't be."

Seeker, as was his habit, moved on to another topic, jabbering on about everything they passed. With each hand of Sun's travel overhead, Zvi worried more that Seeker's People would be less forgiving of her shortfalls than he. Finally, she interrupted a particularly long-winded discussion of the different tribes Seeker had met while searching for the stars.

"Seeker. What if your People dislike me? Or reject Pup?" Zvi didn't want to be forced to choose between Seeker's family and pup but the decision was easy.

"They will see what I see, Zvi. You saved my life."

The bamboo Giganto loved so gave way to lush grasslands and shallow-rooted trees, and a patchwork of plants populated with small animal communities. The farther they traveled, the faster Seeker moved. Zvi lumbered faster, arms swinging, breath shorter, trying to keep up.

"That's where we scoop termites, Zvi, and there, we pick berries. They are always sweet and plump."

He finally noticed Zvi struggling to keep up and slowed but didn't stop talking. "And there, I stole honey from the bees. I only got a few stings but my brother swelled up like a dead fish. He learned to be more careful."

Seeker filled the time with family stories like none Zvi knew existed. Zvi couldn't help but get excited about the chance to become part of this loving group,

As they broke out of yet another copse of dense jungle, Seeker bounced. "I live down there. Do you see Endless Pond? When it's antagonized, it rears up taller than trees and floods inland all the way to our camp."

His excitement overwhelmed Zvi's worry over meeting strangers. Giganto had cared for her despite their differences as did Pup. Surely others would too when they realized her size wasn't a threat. Her head filled with questions but Seeker never stopped talking so she finally tuned him out. But Pup didn't. He listened, enraptured, ears pricked, gaze locked on the boy. As a result, Seeker focused on the wolf pup until it was the two of them talking as though they understood each other perfectly.

Zvi interrupted to remind Seeker, "You know Pup is my pack."

The boy paused thoughtfully, seeming to understand not just Zvi's hand motions but everything behind them. After a quiet moment, he responded, "I love him, too, Zvi. My People will be amazed at how he hunts with us."

"My friend, Giganto. His family ... well, I wouldn't say they befriended me but... they didn't reject me ... so I know some do."

"You worry too much. Besides, I told them you'd be with me."

Zvi stutter-stepped. "How did you know that? I wouldn't have found you if not for the fireball."

Seeker waved Zvi's objection away. "I told my father I had to find you. Well, I didn't know it was *you* but the stars told me to look."

He smiled at Zvi, overflowing with love. "You are the one who can help me locate them."

Zvi pulled Seeker to a stop, a cold wave running through her body. "How long since you were home?"

"I had given up finding you, or the stars, and was going home," which avoided Zvi's question, "when I heard the explosion and... Look at that tree! The branches, so full of leaves! ... Something hit me, knocked me over. I remember hitting the ground and then nothing... Where did those flowers come from, Zvi? I'm sure they weren't here when I left."

"Seeker. When were you last home?" Zvi repeated, now sure she wouldn't like the answer.

"See that insect? The slender legs, the filmy wings—how can it fly? Oh—you missed it. I only saw it for a moment. I can still hear it though. *Bzzzz Shwirp.*" He fingered a patch of moss on a tree. "This is the right direction. Feel the trunk, Zvi—oh!" A rough-skinned frog leaped from its camouflage against the cracked and lined bark. Before it escaped, Pup snapped it into his jaws and sneezed, spitting it out as he flapped his ears.

"I guess he doesn't like frog." Seeker snatched it and ate. Pup disappeared and reappeared with a rat, his teeth embedded deep into the angry animal. He shook it until it stopped moving and offered it to Zvi and Seeker. With no takers, he devoured it in a gulp.

As they continued, Zvi put aside worry and exulted with the boy over the beauty that surrounded them, the wonder of the flowering vines that wound their way up the tree trunks, the majesty of the plant eaters and the sleekness of the predators. The smell of salt grew stronger but Seeker never mentioned it, busy chattering about whatever caught his attention. Through Seeker, Zvi thrilled at a flower's pattern of colors, a plant's shape, and how the branches protected the jungle floor from rain and heat. It excited Pup, too, and he cavorted at this new adventure and the importance of protecting his pack.

Probably—most likely—the simple joy of being alive.

"Surely your people know strangers travel in their territory."

Seeker skidded to a stop and extended his arms as though to embrace the world. "This tree is my friend. If we are separated for any reason, Zvi, come here."

That made Zvi's insides churn. Why would they need a meeting place? Zvi was about to demand an answer when Pup growled. Zvi grabbed the scruff of his neck and stopped, watching Seeker continue forward, sounding more like a bird than a boy. Pup's tail extended and a low rumble rolled from his throat followed by a whine. Seeker shouted something in words foreign to Zvi and marched boldly forward.

"We better go with him, Pup. He might need us," and Zvi hurried after her friend. Pup lagged, tail tucked.

They entered a deserted clearing, ringed with shards leftover from recent knapping, gnawed-at bones, a partially-eaten carcass, and a mound of pounded vegetation. Pup emitted a throaty growl.

"It's OK, Pup," Zvi soothed as she breathed in the urine scent marking the territory.

Seeker shouted, "Come out! I'm with my friends, Zvi and Pup!"

His family stepped out of the brush that bordered the clearing. Pup's eyes glittered and his ears flattened.

Seeker turned to Pup. "It's—" but a scream interrupted him.

"Watch out!" From Zvi

Warriors sprinted toward the trio, brandishing spears and warclubs, their shrieks so strident Zvi covered her ears. Wolf emitted a vicious snarl and leaped at the nearest male as he raised his warclub, malevolent eyes locked on Zvi. The male flung Pup away, squealing, but not before the wolf's claws dug deeply into the warrior's chest leaving a trail of blood dripping down his body. Pup righted himself but couldn't avoid the brutal thump of a warclub against his ribs. Pup flew backward and thudded onto his side, whimpering.

"No!" Seeker yelled as Zvi flung a stone at the head of a warrior, moving in to finish off Pup, and another at the one beside him. One bellowed, dropping his club, and the other collapsed. Zvi hated hurting Seeker's band but Pup needed help.

"Pup—let's go!" The wolf limped to his feet and scurried away, crying with each step. Never had Uprights struck him—much less hurt him.

"Why did you bring that creature here?" Seeker's father shouted. Spittle exploded from his mouth as he glared, rage reddening his face. His eyes narrowed to beady, dark holes. "We never allow enemies in our midst!"

"They-they are friends," Seeker mumbled, head down, trying to figure out what happened.

"His tribe lives where it is cold," his father spit out, hands shaking. "They eat our children."

Seeker's head flew up. "That's not true."

His father was frailer than Seeker remembered, and shorter. Where Seeker used to reach his chest, now it was easy to see that his mouth looked angry, dripping down at the corners. His eyes had lost their luster and his forehead, once smooth and clean, bore round dark warts.

Seeker inhaled a calming breath. "She is nothing like that," and he explained how he almost died and Pup was orphaned and Zvi saved both of them.

"Zvi and Pup and I—we have a plan. The animals are leaving, Father. Not just the herds—coyote and wolf also. The air grows cold. Did you see the fire—"

"He cares nothing about you or us," his mother jumped in. "He wants to take our home because it is warm. They drove the giant Uprights out—now, it will be us! You showed him—them—where we live! How could you do that?" Her face paled, distorted with fury. A sheen of moisture coated her upper lip.

"No Mother. Zvi healed me."

"To trick you into leading him here! Can you not see that?" She hovered on the brink of panic, breath shallow and wheezing.

Seeker's head throbbed steadily and his throat was parched. For the first time, he noticed the wrinkles in his mother's dark face, like fruit in the heat so long it loses its moisture, and when had his father's hair grown so white?

"No. He saved my life." No one had even offered him a drink.

"How?" From his father this time.

"A snake bit me," and he lifted his ankle, the scar still obvious.

Color blotched his father's cheeks. When he spoke again, his voice was glacial, eyes as narrow as the thread in Spider's web.

"This Zvi killed Snake?"

Seeker nodded, miserably. "By accident."

"And he ate it?"

Seeker's shoulders collapsed and he shuffled from one foot to the other. He knew where this led. "Zvi is a 'she'. But yes, *she* did."

Seeker's father snorted, sloping shoulders hunched and his brow ridge, like a thick branch, seemed to thicken even more over frigid eyes.

"It's never an accident with them. This one you are so fond of—who killed Snake and travels with a wolf, something no one can do—I can only imagine the influence he wields over you!"

"*She*. Zvi is a she."

Seeker didn't understand what his father meant. Never had he met anyone kinder and gentler than Zvi. She listened to him and had selflessly protected him during his sickness. Now, she joined him on this trip even though it took her the opposite direction of her intended goal. Who could ask for a better friend?

His father edged away. "You are gone a long time. We thought you dead. Come with us or go. It doesn't matter."

Seeker squinted toward the dim shadows where Zvi fled, posture slumped and tears filling his eyes. Was his friend still there?

He numbly turned back to stare at his father's retreating back. Why would he force such a devastating choice upon his son? Stay with the family who ignored his disappearance or go with the Other who saved his life and asked nothing in return but friendship.

He tried one last time. "Father. The stars are gone. I promised to return for you and I have. We must go."

His father's lumbering steps stuttered but he continued. A youngster took his hand and peeked over his shoulder at the male he knew nothing about, his smile thin and sad.

"Is that a new son," Seeker motioned, teeth clenched, knowing his father didn't see his question.

A heaviness descended upon Seeker. Silent tears overflowed as his throat tightened. In the end, the choice was easy. He would go where Zvi had planned to go before diverting to help him.

"Zvi," and a smile spread ear to ear as he pivoted and twirled, his mind sparking and pulsing in all the colors of the jungle.

"I know where you are. You promised."

Zvi never lied, not even to Pup.

Zvi's needs were simple: a home where she was respected, loved ones who accepted that her size didn't bring danger, nor did her refusal to hurt others make her unworthy. That was a lesson from Giganto—he could destroy anyone but didn't.

Her trundling run was faster than Pup who limped, favoring his damaged rear leg. When he whined, she scooped him up which made him lick her wildly, tail wagging happily letting her know he was exactly where he wanted to be.

Zvi sighed. It felt good to be with her pack, even if that pack was only one.

Finally to Seeker's tree, Zvi collapsed, breathless, round shoulders slumped, broad friendly face slack. Her chest heaved in silent sobs as a single tear trailed down her cheek. Pup pressed his body against hers, moaning as he licked his leg. They must have fallen asleep because the next thing Zvi knew, Seeker's warm body lay to her other side and Pup swarmed over her lap, claws digging into her chest, in a frenzy to reach Seeker. Zvi heard his tongue lapping as he covered Seeker with wet kisses.

Seeker motioned, solemnly, hands muted, "I was as noisy as possible, to not surprise you, but you didn't wake."

Zvi brushed a fist across her cheeks. "All Pup wanted to do was play." Her voice was hoarse and broken. "He has never met unfriendly Uprights or Others."

Seeker stared at the wolf thoughtfully. "He does look more wolf than pup. What bothers me is they didn't believe me, that Pup was not dangerous. Why?"

Zvi coughed and shook her head. "Where are they now, Seeker?"

"A butterfly! Where did that come from? ... " and he chased after it, applauding each beat of the wings. "How beautiful," and he bounced as the insect flitted madly. Pup—Wolf—bobbed with Seeker, injured leg forgotten, mimicking his pack member.

Finally, Seeker captured it with a cupped palm against a tree trunk.

"The colors are the same on both wings." He cocked his head peering on top and under the frightened insect. "There's a stripe on each leg and something fuzzy and thin that doesn't like being touched. So I won't. What do you think that means, Zvi?"

"Well, I suppose..." Zvi motioned, taking her time, knowing Seeker required no answer. After a moment, Seeker flung the butterfly up and away, to freedom.

"Zvi, we must leave. Butterfly says the stars left long ago which means life will. My People refuse to listen."

Zvi tipped her head to her friend, eyes moist. "You're staying with me?"

"Of course I am. You won't survive without me, Zvi." He dipped his head and motioned, "I won't survive without you, either. My People consider me odd. You don't, ever. Nor does Wolf. Why would I be anywhere else," and he sprinted forward.

Zvi scrambled to her feet and galumphed after the frolicking boy. "Well, Pup—Wolf—depends upon us to keep him safe, at least until he's grown."

"I no longer trust my People, not as I trust you. They called you a, never mind, and they couldn't see that Wolf is so much more than… well, a wolf. You and I—we take care of each other. And Wolf." He skipped across the clearing, trying to follow the trail of the flitting butterfly.

"And, Zvi, you never made a raft."

Zvi beamed. "Well, no. What is that?"

"You'll see, Zvi. The unknown is exciting, isn't it? I so love exploring."

Zvi pushed clumsily to her feet while Wolf scampered happily. "I was so lonely until you came, Wolf. And Seeker. I can't imagine life without you two," and spun in a dizzy circle, losing her balance and righting herself, trying to mimic Seeker's erratic movements.

Wolf romped, banging her legs as he nipped her ankles, injury forgotten. His ears bounced and his tail wagged so hard, it slapped his sides.

"You like me as I am, Wolf, and Seeker picked me over his People. It'll be OK."

For the first time in her life, Zvi felt like she fit. Looking at Seeker, arms beating like a butterfly's wings, alight with excitement—no matter how much he argued that he stayed with her to search for the stars, Zvi knew he also stayed because they were pack.

# Chapter 34

Zvi had never been this far from home though Bork had told her it was warm and wet. Well, it was wet.

"Does your loin-skin keep you warm, Seeker?"

"Not at all!" he answered excitedly. Zvi shivered against the battering wind and still wished she could cover her body in a loin-skin.

"Can you show me how to make one?"

"Why wouldn't I?"

When Sun went to sleep, Zvi and Seeker found refuge inside an abandoned den. Seeker chattered, "I wonder if the wolves left food. And what of an exit..."

Zvi found one, more of a vent, so small even Pup couldn't slip through it.

Seeker's curiosity about the world never flagged, never diminished. At one point, he finished a thorough discussion of the den, the prior inhabitants, its size and relative comfort, and moved zealously on to the water buffalo they passed earlier, why the gazelle wandering alone was limping, a hippo that slapped a crocodile, the tiger that stalked them but not this time, and pretty much everything that came to mind. To be with Seeker was to notice everything, and noisily marvel about it.

"Why do some apes swing through the trees and others walk? And why are there so many colors—it's confusing and unnecessary. And this one I can't figure out. Why does Coyote run with both feet on one side while Hipparion runs first front and then rear?"

He marched rigidly back and forth across the clearing, trying to move an arm with a leg and then switching which one. His head dropped with every measured pace and his limbs became so rigid, he couldn't move faster than a slow walk but he didn't give up, determined to be Hipparion and Hippo.

"Wolf—walk for me."

Wolf snored.

At some point, long before Seeker resolved his inquiry, Zvi fell into a contented sleep, the buzz of Seeker's movements comforting, awakening only when Sun's glow lit the front of the cave.

"Sun has returned! We can continue," but the cave was empty.

"Seeker!" Zvi got no answer. Zvi relieved herself and called again. When that failed, she shouted for Wolf with the same result.

"I hope Wolf is with Seeker. Wolf won't let him get lost."

A muted *thunk* echoed in the distance. Zvi hurried toward the noise. Wolf lay on his stomach below a tree, whining softly and pawing his head, a coconut by him.

"Wolf! Why didn't you tell me where you were going?"

At the sound of Zvi's voice, he flapped his ears.

A voice came from high in the branches. "I chased a bird what brilliant colors I thought it lost its nest."

Zvi tilted her head up. Seeker straddled a limb, a coconut in each hand.

"There are no eggs but I did locate these coconuts and befriended a snake He realizes what happened, that it was an accident, you know, before."

Zvi wanted to laugh but settled on, "Good job, Seeker, but next time you toss coconuts, aim away from Wolf."

Seeker seemed oblivious to Wolf's distress. "I watched Sun awake. What brilliance! Well cloudy but better than yesterday. There's no use sleeping when Sun is awake."

Seeker descended the tree and left to collect roots while Zvi cracked one of the coconuts.

"Wolf, do you eat coconut meat?" In answer, the pup snatched a mouse that tried to run by and swallowed it whole.

When Seeker came back empty-handed, Zvi motioned, "Drink this."

He guzzled it greedily. "At home, well, before you and I and Wolf became home, we drank coconut juice, ate the meat, used the oil to salve burns and the shell for upset stomachs," and he chattered on and on. Zvi almost missed the change of topic.

"If we're going to migrate, we need tools."

Wolf let out a yip and took off. They chased him to a dead Big-horned Gazelle, eaten to the bones.

Seeker bounced. "Look at the curve of these antlers." He fingered the spiral shape and their gnarled texture. "Each grows the same distance from the center."

He petted them as though in a trance and then noticed the defleshed bones. "What luck no one ate the marrow!"

He cracked the legs, hacked slivers from them, and scooped out stickfuls of goo handing one to Zvi and keeping the other for himself. The taste exploded in Zvi's mouth and her stomach rumbled.

"I've never had this before, Seeker. It's delicious. Only the females carrying babies were allowed to eat it."

Seeker humphed in reply as he chopped at the antler with a cutter.

When the stone tool chipped, he motioned, "We need stronger stones." Without another word, he headed toward Fire Mountain. Zvi and Wolf dashed after him.

It took most of the day and the next to reach Fire Mountain but there, on the rock-strewn slopes, they uncovered a wealth of tool-making stones. They loaded them into a new bladder sack and settled into a temporary camp tucked against a soaring cliff. There, they knapped as many handaxes as possible, the basic tool used to dispense flakes for cutting and chopping. The quiet boomed with birdsong, the breeze blowing a dry stalk against its neighbors, and a cricket chirruping. Seeker listened, mouth open, and set to work, each scrape and thwack of stone against stone in tempo with the sounds.

"That's how you chew, too, Seeker, in rhythm with your body swaying or foot tapping. No one else does that."

If Seeker heard Zvi, he didn't show it, instead motioning, "I love these proportions, Zvi—shaped like the fruit, ending in a point."

Zvi knew nothing about proportions but liked watching. To her surprise, the boy finished one face and started on the other.

"My people didn't realize why anyone would shape both sides—"

"For a sharper cutter of course. And the fat bottom makes it easy to grip."

Zvi crouched across from the boy and copied his movements right down to matching the rhythm. It was easier than the old method, though slower which didn't matter. Time was in great supply.

The piteous squeals of an animal in distress interrupted their labor. Wolf took off, Seeker and Zvi trying to keep up. Wolf stopped at a huge gazelle lying at the base of a cliff.

"It fell over the edge and broke its leg," Seeker commented as he stabbed the wretched animal in the chest, ending its misery.

While Zvi swished the internal organs in a stream and rubbed the insides with a plant that neutralized the smell, Seeker scraped the underside of the pelt clean, chopped a piece out of the center, and looped it around Zvi's neck.

"A loin-skin to cover your body, Zvi."

Zvi felt instantly warmer. "It feels like sunshine. Don't you want one, Seeker?"

"Why would I?"

Zvi cocked her head and stared at the pelt for a breath, another, and then shrugged.

"Wolf needs a neck sack," and she threaded a tendon through the holes she'd dug in the top of Gazelle's stomach and dropped it around Wolf's neck. Wolf immediately shredded it, unable to ignore the tantalizing aroma.

"I'll make another out of something he won't eat."

Then it started to rain.

Zvi, Seeker, and Wolf stayed in the cave waiting for the sky to clear, Zvi and Seeker sharing the warmth of Gazelle's hide while they completed tasks to make travel easier, each doing what she or he did best. Wolf brought them gophers and rats he caught while shedding his downy fur in handfuls, revealing a pelt that made him look more like a dangerous wolf to anyone who didn't know him.

The sky finally cleared and they continued. The jungle thickened forcing them to hack a pathway through the foliage which dulled their cutters and compelled them to spend most nights sharpening tools and creating new ones. Zvi's spear was trampled by a charging bear who wanted the group's cave. A replacement required a thin but strong tree trunk. After many days, they came upon a perfect grove and spent the next days making spears for both of them.

"You can never own too many weapons, Seeker."

These they looped over their backs with tendons.

Days passed, Moon had come and gone. Zvi couldn't have been happier though a niggling worry had begun to torment her. Seeker was outside, clapping in sync with a bird's song. Wolf had settled on his haunches, head tilted sideways, listening to his packmate.

"Seeker, you know a lot but you wander off and forget things. You and Wolf are still young," to which Wolf pushed against Zvi's leg and yipped, as though to say, *I am growing*.

Zvi touched Wolf's full neck sack, stocked with travel food and tools. This one, made from Cat's hide, he left untouched. The wolf huffed, settled his head between his paws, and fell asleep.

"You're right. I do overthink things," and Zvi too took a nap.

After many days with little progress, Zvi picked up the light scent of water, barely recognizable over the stench of decayed vegetation and scat.

Seeker responded, as usual reading Zvi's thoughts. "It's salty, Zvi. Trees can't grow there."

"That would be a pleasant change from this constant chopping."

It took a full day and another to break through the trees. What they found was unending sand along an infinite pond.

"We did it."

"Did what?" Seeker reasonably asked.

Within a day and another, Zvi saw what he meant. The water was undrinkable and meat nonexistent.

But there was food.

"Zvi. Over here," and Seeker veered to a tiny inlet.

"Fish. They get stranded when Endless Pond grows and shrinks."

Zvi bounced as Seeker might, she was so excited. They would never starve with this many fish. The trick was finding a pool that flushed into a gully which Zvi could block to trap the fish too slow to escape. That made it easy to snag the stranded fish. Wolf had his own method. He snapped at the water, burying his muzzle almost to his eyes, and always came up with a wriggling, scaly tidbit.

"Seeker," Zvi motioned between bites of fish. "Every pond has two shorelines, across from each other, but this one has no birds."

While Seeker explained about his homeland's Endless Pond with only one shore, Zvi and Wolf ate. When Wolf finished, he rolled over and scratched his back against the gravelly sand, head flopping, legs flailing inelegantly. He righted himself, ears akimbo, and stared at Seeker.

Who was still talking.

"Look at the sand flowing between my fingers, Zvi!" His head tilted, eyes wide with wonder. "It creates a mound that collapses of its own weight."

Seeker recreated the mound over and over until Zvi fell asleep.

Before Sun came and went a handful of times, they tired of fish, wishing for the moist blood of a meaty pig.

Zvi suggested, "Let's travel inland one day and walk along Endless Pond the next."

Seeker and Wolf liked that.

The days passed, one moon after another slipping away, weather cooling and then warming, their direction always toward Sun's sleeping nest. They saw no other Uprights despite watching for trace, prints, and odor, and found nowhere to settle.

That changed one morning. Zvi awoke late. Wolf was out somewhere—she never knew where—but Seeker crouched across the clearing, penetrating hypnotic eyes latched onto Zvi, hands folded in his lap, lips silent.

*That's not right. Seeker's hands are never motionless.*

The hair on Zvi's neck prickled. Footprints covered the clearing and one of Spider's webs was already broken after a full night's work. An unfamiliar smell drifted across her nose and then a slight movement in the shadows behind Seeker was followed by the blink of something shiny.

"Please welcome our company, Zvi." Seeker's hands moved serenely but Zvi's throat tightened.

A hand of warriors appeared out of the waist-high grass. They were taller than Seeker though shorter than Zvi, with heads too large and legs too long. Their chests were hidden by a huge pelt, maybe the hide of Gazelle or Cat. Arms and legs were furless but thick with muscle. Each held a spear in one hand and a warclub in the other.

"Are you hungry?" Zvi asked, hoping she hid her fear.

*Where is Wolf?*

The warriors squinted in confusion.

Seeker kept his face placid. "They ask—demand—that we go with them to their homebase." He motioned so calmly, Zvi wondered if he had an idea. "I don't want to. Do you?"

Zvi narrowed her eyes as she shook her head. "Where's Wolf?"

The strangers seemed confused by Zvi's hand movements.

"Preparing."

"What does that mean?"

Seeker didn't seem to feel that required an answer.

One warrior edged closer to Seeker, spear aimed at the boy's chest, while the rest skulked toward Zvi. Her size was easily two of theirs so they led with their spear as though that thin pole would defend them. Zvi wasn't worried. Giganto had taught her how to knock a spear from the air.

One of them jabbed, testing, at the same moment Seeker brightened and motioned, "I'll start."

He jumped up, head lopsided, twirling and waving his arms. The warriors lurched back, puzzled by these odd movements.

"The sun the sky the air enraptures all creatures. There are no warriors no enemies no way to destroy us because we are from Sun. Stop Sun stop yourself…"

He danced around his guard. The stranger tried to retreat but Seeker grasped his hand and that of another warrior. Both were so shocked, they dropped their spears.

"I get it," and Zvi too snagged a hand on either side of herself, leading the chain sidestepping in a circle around the clearing, stepping in rhythm with Seeker's rhythmic voice. The warriors grunted, gnarled hands shaking in Zvi's, too afraid to let go.

Seeker raised his arms over his head, and with them, the strange warriors, and shouted, "We welcome you!"

The warriors bared their teeth and planted themselves in wide-legged stances, trying but failing to shake free of the two who should have been their captives.

"They think we should be frightened, Zvi. I'm not. Are you?"

That was Wolf's cue. He issued a throaty growl from the edge of the clearing. Only his massive head showed above the vegetation. Hs muzzle opened in a smile, lips curled, though his eyes remained as hard as blue stone. The intruders shook like leaves in the wind, from their legs to their heads. They broke free of their captives, in the process falling over their own feet. At this point, they were as close to panic as any male could be pointing a spear at unarmed opponents.

"Wolf—we were waiting for you!"

Wolf slid from the trees, tail a rigid fur-covered stick, hackles stiff. Saliva dripped from his mouth, still bloody from his last meal.

"Meet our new friends!" Seeker's arms waved overhead encompassing the quaking warriors.

They jabbered noisily but their gazes locked on Wolf. All it took was one more paw step forward and the entire group shrieked and bolted. Seeker chased them, leaving Zvi shocked and Wolf angry. His cold blue eyes and bared fangs indicated he took his guard duties seriously. He wanted to go with Seeker but somehow knew Zvi required more protection than the scrawny boy.

"I know, Wolf. You weren't gone long and still we failed to defend ourselves."

Wolf huffed agreement while Zvi collapsed, confused.

It wasn't until Sun's descent to its sleeping nest that Seeker reappeared, dragging an entire cave lion haunch behind him.

"They called me a 'god', whatever that is. We terrified them. And they say I control Wolf." Anger flared in Seeker's eyes. "I'm insulted for Wolf. No one commands him, nor does he us."

Wolf panted his agreement and Seeker audibly sighed.

"Anyway, they told their Leader what happened and the entire tribe disappeared." He dropped the haunch. "They left this."

The cave lion looked fresh, without any white worms or green flies.

"You speak their language?"

"Not before but as they ran, they jabbered nonstop. Once I see a hand motion or hear a vocalization, I remember it. By the time they reached their tribe, I'd heard almost every word they knew."

Zvi tore chunks of meat from the haunch and passed them around as Seeker talked.

"They called Wolf 'Spirit'. According to them, that's how a god like me would control a beast like Wolf. They left to warn all of the other tribes to protect us—a god and a spirit—until we leave their territory, hoping we won't cause them trouble."

Zvi chewed a flavorful wedge of the meat once and then swallowed. "So Wolf's real name is Spirit?"

Wolf snorted and burrowed his teeth into the haunch.

# Chapter 35

From then on, no one bothered the travelers. Zvi often heard rustling but when Wolf—Spirit—growled, hurried steps stumbled away. When new tribes saw them, they whispered about the strangers who talked to the gods and controlled a wolf. Often, meat—sometimes, an entire carcass—lay across their forward path, like a gift.

"I like them afraid of us, Seeker. They're good hunters."

One night, as they settled in after a long day of travel, Seeker turned to Zvi. "The stars are frosted."

Zvi blinked, hard, as she often did at something Seeker said that made no sense. Much of his conversation was confusing but there was always a kernel of truth and intrigue.

He motioned, "The coming wet time will be cold and harsh. We must go somewhere warmer."

They continued along Endless Pond keeping Sun's sleeping nest in front. The dense forest to their strong side disappeared, replaced by grassland, plateaus, and bluffs. Seeker loved the variety. Left to himself, he would walk forever but Zvi never quit looking for a home. She wanted trees, birds, meat, meandering trails, and Others. Seeker wanted the stars. Though they pebbled the night sky, they weren't the ones that mattered to him so they continued.

After a particularly boring and tedious trek, Seeker grinned, "It is good, Zvi."

Zvi scratched under her arm, scrunched her brow in thought, but still didn't understand. "What is?"

"This. You and I and Spirit. We are different from everything around us and that is our strength. We see things as others don't."

Wolf flared his muzzle and whiffled. Zvi laughed over the supreme joy of life.

# Chapter 36

*North Africa, a third of the way between the two shores, along the Mediterranean*

This land echoed with the hooves of Giraffid and antelope, pigs and Wild Beasts, and the soft-clawed paws of Sabertooth and her cousins. The soil overflowed with tubers, corms, grasses, roots, berries, and fruit. The scouts found prints of Uprights and caught occasional glimpses, but they always slipped away, as though frightened.

The People rested often, not just when the females delivered babies but to enjoy the bounty. The moon of travel before this, through scrubby grassland with dry waterholes and scrawny herds, had been difficult but was behind them. Now, as promised, Rainbow had led them with courage and confidence to what everyone called as good a homeland as they'd ever seen.

Rainbow allowed his People to travel in the open, never hiding their presence. He claimed that their massive size would deter attacks.

Mbasa disagreed. "You allow an enemy to assess our defenses. That is a mistake."

"You're wrong—it intimidates them."

She sneered. "You know we are being followed."

He dismissed her with a wave of his hand. "One Upright, always limned against the sky—"

"Head up, feet spread, spear in hand, and he shows not a trace of fear. He is not *intimidated* by what he sees!"

"Maybe their customs are different. He could be preparing to greet us."

Mbasa turned away, hiding her disgust. "He stalks us, Rainbow."

"Well, here's what we must do," and then stopped, not knowing what he should say next. He wondered not for the first time what Xhosa would do.

Mbasa huffed, mouth tightening as though reading his thoughts, which could be true. The female had instincts like no male Rainbow had ever known. "Xhosa would send scouts."

Rainbow snorted derisively. "I was going to suggest that."

"I'll take care of it," and Mbasa sent two scouts armed with spears and stones. They were never seen again and the line stranger continued to dog them.

"Those were our best scouts." Rainbow's hand shook so he hid it under his armpit and then continued one-handed in what he hoped was an assertive, even arrogant, manner, "We must confront them."

He didn't think that was the right response but it would force Mbasa to tell him what to do without it sounding like he asked for help.

After a moment of thought, she motioned, "Xhosa and Nightshade both say a show of strength can be as effective as strength itself."

"Of course," he responded, adding derision to his tone. "That's obvious."

In fact, he had no idea what she meant. The warriors with him smelled of fear. How would they frighten anyone?

"But we mustn't antagonize him."

Her brows scrunched and her head cocked. "We need him to reveal his intentions."

"Don't correct me, Mbasa. Send more scouts—

"That will do no good! Our scouts aren't trained well enough." Her eyes flashed like sky fire.

"I didn't say scouts—warriors! They can fight back if threatened." He involuntarily gulped. "Or we could ignore him. He does nothing menacing—"

"Except hold his spear ready for battle while staring arrogantly at us. Oh, and there's the problem of our two missing scouts."

She snorted. "I followed him last night back to his tribe. It is massive," and she ticked off fingers over and over, indicating a group larger than the People had ever been even under Xhosa's father.

"How do you—never mind. Maybe they're peaceful."

"When Nightshade discovered intruders that might have a legitimate reason to be in our territory, his scouts hid their weapons. For other intruders—like Pan-do's People—Nightshade's scouts carried warclubs and spears, to show a willingness to battle. This warrior carries a spear but retrieves his warclub only when out of sight."

"But why—"

"They see us as invaders, Rainbow."

"We must show them we are friendly," though how to do that, he didn't know.

Mbasa clamped her mouth shut to keep from spitting. "It is too late," she motioned. "Our weakness has emboldened them."

Rainbow walked away, flapping his hands in a final order. "Tomorrow, send five of our best warriors. We will show our strength."

They too never returned. Mbasa stared at the crest of one of the sand hills, arms on her hips.

"He is no longer alone."

# PART FOUR: MIDDLE EAST
## The Many Become One
### *850,000 years ago*

# Chapter 37

*The Levant*

Xhosa awoke from the same dream of Lucy, evading yet another enemy determined to kill her. Her message last night to Xhosa: *You will soon face a great adventure.*

Still blinking sleep away, a squeal announced another baby's arrival. The constant walking pushed the pregnant females to deliver early. No babies so far survived.

That was good. Xhosa couldn't feed the existing mouths much less new ones.

Pan-do tossed her a leg from a hare. She tore meat from bone and swallowed, so hungry chewing would be a waste of time, but not so oblivious she missed Pan-do's shifting gaze, tense shoulders, and hand tightening on his spear.

This must be about Nightshade.

When her stomach felt less like a knot, she motioned, "What did he do?" The two males respected each other but that wasn't the same as 'like'.

"I know you two are close—"

"I trust him with my life, Pan-do," she interrupted, hands firm. "My father hand-picked him."

Pan-do squatted and picked at the dirt. "I was hidden in the dark last night. He spoke with someone, questioning your leadership."

Xhosa glared at him through cool eyes. "You heard wrong."

"You know him well, and I am new—"

"Yes, you are," and left.

How dare Pan-do try to come between Nightshade and herself. They had saved each other's lives more times than fingers on her hand. Her band destroyed enemies, not each other.

Nightshade motioned from well outside the group's temporary camp. "Xhosa—here."

When she reached him, he pointed to footprints cut deeply into the ground, facing their camp. "Others scouts. They watched us most of last night."

"We will track them."

He touched her arm. "What did Pan-do want?"

She scrutinized his tired face, lack of sleep barely dimming the strength. Mud streaked his forehead and cheeks from digging through bushes, his gaze its usual mix of curiosity and concern. The many scars collected during his tempestuous life warned of the powerful threat that lay within.

Completely absent was deceit or guilt.

"Nothing. Something about his People," and then she motioned to Pan-do, "Watch the People."

She, Nightshade, and a handful of warriors trailed the Others over rugged bluffs and into scarred valleys where nothing could survive. After two hands of Sun's travel, Nightshade motioned the warriors to halt while he and Xhosa quietly crawled up a slope and peered down at a deep canyon. Its high walls and the narrow valleys would carry the sound of feet, rocks tumbling downhill, or any other noise. Xhosa stilled her body, ears tweaked, but heard only bird voices and the occasional swish of Snake.

Nightshade fingered indents left in the ground by spears. "They went into this valley."

The scent of moisture assaulted her. Sun felt warm but in the distance, the sky blackened.

"We must return."

Before they got home, the storm hit with a vengeance. Thunder pounded and fire cut the sky. Water poured from her sodden hair, her head bowed to the driving wind, spear clenched, but her steps never slowed. When they reached the group, everyone sheltered against the cliff. The female who delivered this morning was empty-handed. The mother wanted no part of a new baby when she lacked energy for herself.

Sun shone brightly the next day. Everyone had quenched their thirst with rain throughout the night but still licked the plants and rocks clean of their glistening dew. This may be the only water they found all day.

Nightshade motioned, face fierce. "They are here again, watching. Leave the meat the hunters killed yesterday to show that we simply wish to pass through."

Despite the abandoned meat, Xhosa's scalp tingled as they traveled. How to convince their followers that her People weren't interested in this land. Everything was green and brown instead of tan and yellow and red. Rather than the expansive majesty of the baobab with its ready supply of food and water, they passed waist-high scrubbrush with thorns and no sap. In place of the tall swaying grass that hid her movements while announcing the presence of predators, brittle scratchy stalks made travel difficult and tasted like cattails. That explained the absence of Mammoth, Hipparion, and all of the mighty herds that fed predators and Uprights alike. She even missed Cat and her cousins who always guided the People to meat.

Xhosa stopped to rest and crouched, staring, pleased when a string of Others lined up on the crest of a nearby hill.

A foot scraped, Nightshade announcing his presence.

Xhosa stabbed her spear into the ground. "I have a plan."

He nodded, understanding her intentions because he knew her well.

"I go with you. Pan-do can lead the People." After a pause, he added, "I trust him."

They left the camp alone, knowing the Others would follow. Xhosa set a grueling pace, wanting the Others too exhausted to think clearly when she made her move. She crossed a stream, Nightshade steps behind, and plunged into the wasteland, smiling at the grunts and subdued hisses as those behind her struggled to keep up. The two sprinted up a hill and dropped below the bluff as though to descend but instead hid beneath the waist-high grass and waited.

Nothing. No traveling feet, insect sounds, or the Others' foreign scent. A quick bob of her head up told her why.

"They wait below," spears pointed down, faces passive. Her trick hadn't fooled them. "I will talk to them."

Nightshade tried to dissuade her but failed so walked by her, his stocky frame shouting power, her taller lithe one fearless leadership. She forced a calm she didn't feel to mask her nervousness. Her hair blew gently, covering her as a pelt would an animal.

"Wait for me, Nightshade," and she strode toward the one who must be the Leader. The Other matched her pace, pride in every step, until separated only by a spear-length.

In the hand motions of her people, he spoke, "I am Koo-rag, of Koo-rag's People. We know you flee Big Heads in search of a new homeland. If you try to stay here, we will kill you. You cannot hide. We know every crevice, every valley, every hill."

"We seek a new home where we are welcomed. Nothing more."

His shoulders relaxed, slightly.

She motioned, "We come from down the Rift, following a path my father laid out long ago. We must cross the Endless Pond. Can you help us?"

Koo-rag's eyes lit with recognition and then he smiled. "I met your father as a youth. Even to one so young, he reeked of the stallion's leadership, Leopard's cleverness, and Snake's power. I tell you as my father told yours, it can't be crossed without a boat. You must go around, through the domain of the cannibals and then across a treacherous crocodile-infested river. Few survive but it seems your father did or you wouldn't be here."

"Cannibals? What are they?" *And what is a boat?*

"Uprights who eat Uprights."

Xhosa twitched as though burned. "That can't be."

"They are an abomination. They know you are here and would overrun you except for the protection I provide, to honor your father. You lose that when you leave my territory. Move quickly. Keep your weapons in hand, ready, and Sun to your strong side. Moon will disappear and reappear," and he ticked off two fingers on one hand, "before you reach the

Crocodile River. Cross it carefully. The cannibals will not follow."

"How will I know the cannibals?"

"Their stench is nothing like you or me." He examined her. "I look for a pairmate."

When Nightshade bristled, Koo-rag crossed his arms over his chest. "He is your pairmate?" In answer, Nightshade stepped forward and tightened his fingers on his spear.

"Alright. Go," but Xhosa didn't move, too confused to turn away.

"My father, you knew him?"

"I see he didn't tell you. My People were engaged in a deadly clash with these cannibals. They had gathered a huge force thinking so many warriors could overwhelm us. We would be dead without your father and his warriors."

He concentrated on something in the distance. "He told us you would come. We wanted to repay his help with food but he asked instead that we assist you."

She waited for more but he seemed finished.

"Thank you, Koo-rag. My father shared nothing of his travel, just told us to follow the cairns."

As Nightshade tugged her to go, Koo-rag asked, "Did some from your group go toward Sun's sleeping nest?" When Xhosa nodded, he continued. "They are in trouble, trailed by both Others and Big Heads. They are sloppy and undisciplined, not worthy of your father's reputation. Once these enemies realize that you and Nightshade are not with them, they will be demolished."

Xhosa grunted and waved her hand dismissively. "They are led by a young warrior named Rainbow who refused to follow the plan laid out by my father. I am no longer responsible for them."

The next day was the hottest yet. Xhosa tied her mane in a knot and let it bounce against her neck as they traveled under the comforting protection of Koo-rag's People. The travel was grueling, over hills, down and up gullies, with no meat other than snakes, scorpions, birds, slugs, and plants.

Nightshade sent scouts, hoping to discover a way across Endless Pond despite Koo-rag's advice, but they shook their heads. The People settled into a grim-faced trudge. Moon grew and shrank. The elders reminded anyone who would listen of long ago times when the People migrated often.

When Koo-rag's people disappeared, a different tribe—probably the cannibals—replaced them. Xhosa quickened the pace which made the males wary and the females and children fretful. Only Pan-do remained upbeat. He walked with the females, carrying their children while Lyta rode on his shoulders. He offered Xhosa a smile, a nod, but kept his distance. She said nothing to Nightshade about what Pan-do told her. Undoubtedly he lied but why had he told her?

# Chapter 38

Since Xhosa refused to recognize Nightshade's treachery, Pan-do must separate from her. If Nightshade took control of the increasingly disgruntled band, Pan-do's People would suffer. Where Xhosa generally listened to Pan-do's advice, Nightshade ignored it and that bode poorly for his People.

For some reason, Lyta begged him to stay.

"Across the Crocodile River, we will meet one called Seeker who will be my pairmate. None of this can happen without Xhosa. Please be patient."

His daughter's visions often were right so he listened.

For the present.

Xhosa slowed, letting the travelers pass until Shadow reached her.

"Your cough sounds worse, Shadow. The stems I gave you no longer help?"

Her supple skin, once a vibrant brown, looked pale and drawn. Her breathing was always labored and the imprint of her bones etched her body.

After a violent outburst of wet hacking, she croaked, "I am fine. I won't hold you up, Leader." Another long cough but this time, her hand came away from her mouth bloody.

"When did this start?"

"When the Big Heads struck. One male tried to snatch my child but I pushed him away. He laughed and then started coughing. Blood speckled me. When he bent over, I fled. Soon after, I started coughing and bleeding like him. How can that be?"

Xhosa considered this before shaking her head. "Don't cough on anyone, Shadow." She handed her a hard root. "Eat this. It may keep you alive until I find a better solution."

"I will do anything. My child needs me," and her head notched up a bit as Xhosa left.

Despite the brave words, Xhosa worried about Shadow. She had been one of the growing group of females interested in the warrior skills but quit because of her cough. Treating it required purple berries or the pounded bark of a certain tree or furry stems of some flowers, none of which Xhosa had seen. Soon, the female would be out of time.

Long wisps of white clouds like cattail fur floated across the blue sky the next morning. It was good weather for what she must do.

"Nightshade. Lead the People. I must find a plant for Shadow and will catch up."

"Our scouts are not back from last night." His voice carried an unusual edge of worry. "It may not be safe. Pan-do and I will join you."

Nightshade motioned to Snake, Pan-do to Sa-mo-ke, *Take over.* Xhosa didn't know Sa-mo-ke well but Snake got his name because he was as quiet as snake, often surprising prey before they smelled him. This skill, he had taught Sa-mo-ke soon after the two fought each other. Both were never anything but brave, reliable, and loyal.

Xhosa rubbed dirt into her skin as did Nightshade and Pan-do before trekking down a well-used animal path. After evading the Uprights-who-may-be-cannibals, Xhosa found the plant Shadow needed and filled her neck sack while Nightshade and Pan-do hid. Finished, she rejoined them. Nightshade pointed toward the Uprights. They stood listlessly, eyes darting over the horizon for a finger of Sun's movement, and then left.

"They lost us and will return to their homebase. We can follow."

Within a hand of Sun's travel, the Uprights arrived at what must be their homebase. Males, females, and children worked energetically preparing food, knapping stones, and other activities Xhosa recognized but this group was much larger than the People.

Xhosa motioned, "Food must be plentiful to support so many."

Nightshade jerked. "Do you smell that?"

She sniffed in an odor like honey poured on a rotting carcass. "What animal stinks like this?"

"Upright meat. I have smelled it in brushfires. These must be the cannibals Koo-rag warned of. Look there," and he pointed below.

Xhosa's face hardened and she pressed her lips together to keep from snarling. There, in a bloody pile, lay the remains of the People's scouts who hadn't returned this morning, only recognizable by the thick frizzy hair plastered tightly to their heads, nothing like the Upright's longer kinky hair. A female sliced a chunk off the scout's thigh and chewed as though it were a piece from Pig. Xhosa gagged.

As though on command, the Uprights gathered in the clearing around a pile of dry tree limbs. Someone touched the pile with a fire stick and it burst into flames. No one moved away or seemed frightened.

Pan-do motioned, "They control fire, just as the Big Heads did."

For a finger of Sun's travel, the trio crouched, so still the insects resumed their chirps. As the adults muttered strange noises to each other, the children played a familiar activity called the Running Game. Youngsters in every tribe Xhosa ever visited played this. One child was prey and the others, predators. The prey child dodged and swerved as the predators chased him. In this way, they learned to be fleet of foot.

More Uprights straggled in, this time dragging a female and a child.

Pan-do motioned, "Big Heads take Others as slaves, raising the children as their own, but this looks different."

Without warning, they seized the female. She flailed, scratching and slapping, kicking viciously. One Upright snatched her hand and bit off a finger. Her screams became howls which made him roar hysterically. The stump pumped blood and the others fell on her, ripping meat from every part of her body until all movement stopped. Then, they cut off her legs and arms, sharing them as Xhosa would a slaughtered gazelle. That done, they descended on the child. He had fainted and was easily dismembered.

Xhosa swallowed her bile. "We must leave!" Death was noble, nothing like this ghoulish activity.

Before they could, an ululating warble rose behind them. Xhosa leaped to her feet and spun, spear in hand, in search of a target.

She need not look far. They were surrounded.

Nightshade hunkered down, jaw set, head swiveling, doing what he could to protect her from the dense circle of spear-bearing warriors. The warriors barked while stabbing spears hard enough to draw blood, herding the small group down the hill toward the revelers.

A hush fell over the people as the intruders came into view. Xhosa stood taller than the Upright's warriors by more than a head with Nightshade more muscular and Pan-do more relaxed.

Pan-do held his hands out, level and away from his body. "Do nothing. I have a plan." Almost as an afterthought, he added, "Show no fear."

Xhosa nodded subtly.

"Xhosa, if you can, slow down."

Xhosa had no idea what he had in mind but began to limp, as though her foot hurt. Pan-do reached out to help her but tripped and fell, hands catching his fall. As he pushed upright, he palmed a rock.

No—it was a cutter from his neck sack. Was he going to try to slice the cannibals as they stabbed him? She huffed, distraught. *I hope there's more to it than that.* Her head throbbed and her throat turned dry.

As they entered the clearing, Xhosa rose to her commanding height, head raised, eyes hooded, anger shining through her gaze.

"Who leads you?" She motioned, movements dripping with fury, but no one responded. She repeated her order using the gestures Koo-rag had recognized. This made them laugh.

The warriors prodded the group forward. Soon they would be surrounded and Xhosa knew what happened next. These heathens might slay her but only after many of them died. Grunting and stomping increased, dull eyes fixed on the fresh meat, mouths open, saliva drooling over their lips and down their necks.

"Stop!" Pan-do shrieked, louder than any sound ever to come from his mouth.

Everyone did, more from shock than understanding. Within a breath, they all fixed on Pan-do's hand, shaking in fear, over his head.

With all eyes on him, he motioned, "Our people threw us out—we are sick!" He slyly sliced his lowered hand with the cutter and coughed violently into it. The entire group fell back as though frightened.

"We seek a cure for the bloody cough," and he held his palm up, dripping blood. He coughed again into his hand. This time, when he removed his hand, his lips were stained red. "Please help us!"

The strangers babbled in their odd language. It didn't take knowing their words to feel their horror. The warriors backed away from the group, yammering. The Leader shouted a panicked order and everyone threw rocks and dirt clods at the captives.

They fled.

When Xhosa felt they were far enough away to be safe, she looked back at the Uprights. Everyone was shoveling the dirt tainted with Pan-do's blood into the fire.

"How did you know they're so frightened of the bloody cough?" Xhosa motioned, wiping her mouth with the back of her hand.

"I didn't. I guessed."

# Chapter 39

Moon appeared as Xhosa, Nightshade, and Pan-do reached their camp. Xhosa desperately needed sleep but first took the healing plant to Shadow.

"Mulch the stems with the bark. It will slow the sickness, give us more time."

Shadow thanked her, tears rolling down her cheeks. Xhosa was so tired, her only response was a desultory wave of her hand.

Sun finally woke Xhosa, her limbs stiff from the cold, fingers and toes tingling. Koo-rag had told the truth about the risk involved crossing the territory of the cannibals. No wonder he insisted they waste no time reaching the next river.

The People surrounded the Leaders, eager for news.

Xhosa motioned bluntly, "We must move quickly. These Uprights consider us food, as we do Mammoth and Gazelle."

A gasp rippled through the group. No one could imagine eating Uprights. As she, Pan-do, and Nightshade described what they saw, everyone drooped.

"Did we make a mistake not going with Rainbow?" someone asked.

"No. Koo-rag told us Rainbow is in grave danger." Xhosa shared only that and just to quiet the people. "We are safer here."

A few of the People grumbled but Pan-do's group never wavered in their trust for their Leader, nor did Nightshade's warriors, content that their Lead Warrior had been anointed by one everyone respected.

Nightshade motioned to the assembled group, "Carry spears at the ready. We must look too fierce to bother."

It didn't take more than a handful of days to face another serious problem. Without the salt-rich meat that comprised much of their diet, the People began getting stomach aches, cramps, and fatigue. This was usually treated with the salt blocks everyone carried but they had harvested it only one time and that right after separating from Rainbow. Those supplies, though ample, had run out.

One day, as they slogged ahead, a small herd of gazelle appeared, munching dispiritedly on the sparse dry grass, ribs etched like steps against their thin flanks.

"Meat!"

Xhosa grabbed Nightshade's arm. "Wait. Let's follow them, see if they will lead us to wherever they get their salt." Animals that ate no meat found salt elsewhere.

The gazelle moved as though each step hurt, clearly suffering from a lack of food and salt. While the People rested, Nightshade and Xhosa stayed downwind, letting the usual herd noise of crunching steps cover their sounds. The path steepened, winding among medium-sized boulders and stair-stepping hills and then into a narrow canyon.

Nightshade's face lit with excitement. "Do you smell it? Salt!"

She sniffed and found the tantalizing tang but beneath it was an unmistakable dampness. "But there's also rain. It could trap us in this canyon."

"There may not be rain but without salt, we know we will die."

Xhosa couldn't deny that truth and they proceeded forward, into the canyon. A crack of thunder echoed in the distance. Somewhere it rained. The two hurried down the narrow chasm and out the other side to a broad flat plateau covered by the stark sparkling white of salt blocks. Both sprinted forward to collect as much as possible, quickly, and then get through the canyon before the rain hit. They slammed their warclubs into the jutting blocks, splintering them into portable pieces that were stuffed into neck sacks. The clouds thickened, the air cooled, and the growing menace of rain drove them.

The first fat drops fell as Xhosa finished and raced back toward the canyon, Nightshade already on his way. Thunder boomed and lightning lit the sky. The few trees bent like grass in a storm, leaves ripped away by the blasting wind. If she and

Nightshade could get beyond the canyon, they would shelter in a cave until the storm ended.

The rain hardened to a deluge as she sprinted behind Nightshade between the tight rock walls. Cold pinched her skin like frigid fingers. She flew forward, ignoring a deafening crash behind her and a rumble that intensified with each step. Nightshade exited the opposite end of the canyon as another thunderous crack exploded.

He gasped. "Xhosa, run! The cliff is collapsing behind you!"

She dug her feet into the slippery dirt, pushing with every bit of energy that remained in her body. Abandoning the salt might save her life but would ensure everyone else's death. She tripped, plunged forward, caught herself and kept going. A deafening roar chased her down the canyon. She flew out of the narrow mouth and threw herself out of the way just as a boulder caromed off the walls, bounced out of the opening, missing her by a hand's width, and exploded into pieces.

Nightshade's eyes glistened, his face white. "A landslide. It'll block the canyon."

Xhosa knew what it cost Nightshade to show emotion.

Safely inside the cave with her sack of salt, she curled into Nightshade, shaking with relief, sharing his warmth, and fell asleep.

# Chapter 40

Morning brought clear sunny skies, the devastating storm a distant memory. Xhosa and Nightshade ignored their brush with death and ran hard to reach the temporary camp before Sun dropped from the sky. They passed the salt around, each member responsible for their own portion, and ate a meal of grubs, seeds, and salt.

"Snake, any sign of those who watch us?"

"No, but," and he paused to grin at Sa-mo-ke, "we found a mastodon just before Sun went to sleep. Its leg is broken."

The next morning, he led Xhosa and the hunters to the injured animal. Its piteous bellows soon stopped and the group chopped it into cartable pieces, eating as they worked. Its tendons were looped around necks and the stomach and bladder were stuffed into neck sacks for later use. That night, the People ate well for the first time in a moon.

As they finished, Snake asked, "When do we hunt Gazelle?"

Nightshade shook his head. "A rock slide blocks where they are."

No one questioned the decision and the People left the next day, carrying what remained of the mastodon, avoiding the caves of the cannibals and anywhere they might gather. That night and every one after, they slept where dark was deepest, where bodies weren't silhouetted against the moon's shine, and with guards posted.

Finally, as Koo-rag told her, the scent of fresh water became stronger than the salt of Endless Pond. After a handful of days, each colder than the last, Xhosa saw green trees on the horizon.

Water was close.

As Sun dipped, Xhosa shivered. She had never felt such cold.

They set out when Sun awoke, drawn to the strengthening scent of water. By the time Sun hung directly overhead, the People were splashing and cavorting in the river while scouts watched for crocodiles.

A hand slower than everyone else, Shadow finally caught up, supported by Rainbow's former pairmate Siri. The female seemed to have boundless energy—first, caring for Ant and now Shadow, all while completing her usual duties.

Many of the People couldn't swim, including Pan-do, so Xhosa found what she hoped would be the shallowest path across the river. One step in and she jerked back, shocked by the coldness. After a moment, skin numb, she shuffled forward. It wasn't until her position was as close to the opposite shore as where the People waited, with the water only to her hips, that everyone followed.

The current was strong, the bottom slick and muddy so Pan-do plopped Lyta onto his broad shoulders. From there, her view extended far in both directions.

"Look for anything dangerous, Lyta." He hadn't told her about Koo-rag's warning of crocodiles. Why worry her if it wasn't necessary?

One hand gripped her father's hair and the other his wrist as she searched the river. Pan-do grabbed for fish one-handed, catching one almost immediately, and grinned.

Which was when Lyta screamed, pointing toward what could be mistaken for floating logs—if logs could change direction.

Pan-do bellowed, "Crocodiles!" In fact, a flood of them, all headed toward the group.

Nightshade roared, followed by Sa-mo-ke and Snake, and with the combined warriors, charged the reptiles, stabbing throats, eyes, and heads, trying to drive them away. These crocodiles were smaller and darker than those in Pan-do's homeland with longer snouts and more teeth—and they swam faster. His first thought was Lyta's safety so he churned forward, strong legs plowing through the shallow water, fish forgotten, both hands now firmly around his daughter. To his side, a child screamed as one of the monsters wrenched him from his mother's hand. Another boy shrieked as jagged teeth sunk into his body and whipped him around until he stopped screaming. An older child stabbed his spear so far into a croc's eye, it came out his neck. The crocodile hissed and sank as the boy sloshed toward the shore.

Pan-do dropped Lyta on the soft grass edging the river and jumped back into the fray.

Fire knifed through Xhosa's side as one of the beast's slapped her with his spikey tail, trying to unbalance her.

"No, you don't!" She anchored her toes in the muddy bottom and stabbed, her neck tight, arms bulging. Only after blinding both unblinking eyes, its throat bleeding red into the river's current, did it back away. In the corner of her eye, she watched another child lose his life. His mother would have joined him if Pan-do hadn't wrenched her viciously by an arm to drag her away from her child. The female's shoulder would hurt but her life was saved.

"Go!" she shouted, pushing everyone in front of her toward the shoreline. When finally safe, she turned and pulled elders and children from the water, sometimes bodily tossing them out of the water. Shadow huffed her way to Xhosa, swinging a warclub at any crocodile that approached, and then stayed to help. Xhosa couldn't help but be impressed by her indomitable spirit.

When the water was clear of the People, Xhosa looked around, seeing where else she might be needed, but everyone was secure. Nightshade was the last out of the water, just behind Sa-mo-ke and Snake. All had gashes on their arms and legs and Sa-mo-ke's warclub was missing a maw-shaped chunk but they grinned, happy with one more successful battle.

Well away from the river, Lyta shook uncontrollably in Pan-do's arms, tears rolling down her face, her mouth open in a silent howl.

Xhosa moved among her People, checking injuries, passing out herbs for cuts, moss to stuff gaping wounds. Only when all were cared for did her attention turn to her own wound.

"Xhosa—come!" Nightshade beckoned from the bluff of a nearby cliff.

Time later for what surely was nothing more than a scratch. With a huff, her feet shuffled toward her Lead Warrior, forcing her thoughts to what undoubtedly was the next threat to the People. Ascending the last of the slope took most of her remaining energy though not without several stumbles and a litany of scrapes to her knees and hands. She rose, gaze reluctantly looking out over what had cost them so much to find.

After a moment, tears flowed unbidden and her voice called to those behind her, "Come, everyone! Come see your new homeland!"

# Chapter 41

Below spread a lush, navigable valley more beautiful than any Xhosa had ever seen. Sparkling lakes and profuse shrubs spotted the landscape. The swaying grass, dotted with flowers and sage, stretched across. The earthy smell of loam, sweet berries, and fragrant herbs assaulted her. Twisting ravines broke the terrain, their channels hidden beneath the tan-green layers. Elephant, Giraffid, okapi, gazelle, and ostrich wandered a mosaic of forest and savanna—more food than the People could ever eat.

Pan-do gasped while Lyta bounced and waved her arms. He stifled a laugh which made Xhosa smile.

"The animals that left our homeland came here," he breathed. "This is more than I hoped for."

Xhosa shivered, chilled as much from the freezing water as Sun's nearness to its sleeping nest. The surging wind rolled over her as silently as a hunter.

"There, Xhosa," and Pan-do pointed to a soaring craggy wall a short distance from the trees. "We will find warm caves there."

Xhosa awoke the next morning sore and stiff, taking a moment to stretch before opening her eyes. Her younger self would feel no after-effects from yesterday's skirmish.

"No wonder my father settled," she chuckled to herself.

Sun was already fully awake. Outside the cave, bustling morning noises greeted her. The grass was bright with morning dew and crunched under her feet as she trundled out to relieve herself, far away and downwind from the camp. Pan-do waved but didn't stop

Nightshade motioned, "Scouts are exploring. Then, we hunt."

The day would be full.

As Xhosa lay down that night, a handful of days into their new life, rain fell hard, whipped into a frenzy by the chill wind. The People curled against each other, safe and dry in the cave, and her thoughts drifted into darkness.

Sometime later, the rain stopped, Moon bright enough to light the cave's interior, something awoke her. Even asleep, every noise registered. The familiar and safe were ignored but this one blared danger.

"Over here," Nightshade's voice came from outside the cave, tense but commanding.

She hurried over and he pointed a direction they hadn't yet explored, heading out after shadowy smudges in the distance—Pan -do and a group of warriors.

Moon shone softly, Sun already dispersing a muted glow over the landscape. The trail of the sound led up hills, narrowing to a steep curving descent toward the valley she'd seen in the distance. White crust cold to the touch covered everything. Her feet stepped in Nightshade's tracks, squeezing through a narrow wedge between boulders. As Sun splashed across the peaks of the distant mountains, they crested a hill only to drop, pressing themselves against the cold ground.

When it seemed safe to peek out, it was to see Uprights packed together in the clearing below, more than fingers on both her hands. They were neither attentive nor alert. In fact, they reminded her of Rainbow's warriors—oblivious to what stalked them. On second look, these were Others but with more hair, squatter bodies, wider noses, and lighter skin than the People. Most wore some sort of animal wrapped around their chests. Xhosa shivered and thought these strangers must be warm—and smart.

She sniffed but caught none of Big Heads' distinctive reek so backed down the hill with Nightshade and Pan-do. Lyta materialized by her father.

Nightshade motioned, "We strike before they do—"

Xhosa shook her head. "We enter their homeland in peace."

"I agree," Pan-do interjected. "Besides, these may be scouts for a larger group."

Nightshade glared at Pan-do. "No one can prevent us from settling here." He slammed his warclub into his palm, eyes gleaming and muscles bulging in preparation. Above him, clouds sailed, frightening shapes that promised more rain. The pummeling wind wrapped Xhosa in damp cold.

Her father when young would agree with Nightshade but the older experienced Leader would try peace first.

Xhosa motioned, "We watch how they live. Maybe there is room for us."

Nightshade stared at the ground to hide his irritation, clenching and unclenching his fists. Lyta cringed and scooted closer to Pan-do.

Xhosa let her face soften and placed a hand on Nightshade's arm. "There has been enough hostility."

He blinked and nodded tautly.

Xhosa and Nightshade returned to the caves while Pan-do remained to observe the Uprights. He would howl Coyote's call if anything changed.

By the time they reached the cave, dark clouds covered the morning sky and a punishing wind again whipped the land. Children stayed in the warmth of the caves while females collected roots and stems from the surrounding area. Subadults caught rats and birds and added them to the communal meal. Everyone worked silently, not wanting the Others to find them.

Snake and Sa-mo-ke relieved Pan-do on the bluff overlooking the Others. Rather than rest, Pan-do built a natural stone barrier in front of the caves and showed the People how to sleep far enough from the opening to be invisible. Stone and Ant relieved Snake and Sa-mo-ke who were themselves relieved by Pan-do and young Bone, thrilled to do the job of a scout. Much later, Xhosa and Nightshade took their turn, lying invisibly in the waist-high grass, watching the field below. When Sa-mo-ke and Snake relieved them, Xhosa ate, groomed Nightshade, and then slept.

Sun was not even a muted glow when Xhosa awoke. She hadn't slept well, wondering if the Others would be trouble, if her People could stop running, and if choosing peace over violence was the right decision. Spear in hand, neck sack loaded with edibles and cutters, she snuck to the bluff. Nightshade and Pan-do were already there.

The sounds of the Others reached her before they came into view—brash hissing voices and out-of-place snarls. Below, they brandished spears at two odd-looking strangers. The new Uprights—or they could be Others; there was no way to tell yet—cowered, spears aimed up, trying to avoid a confrontation with the burly warriors. Both had smaller heads than the Others in front of them but broader faces, probably to accommodate their over-large mouths. On top of their heads was a ridge like the summit of a mountain from where all things go down, and at the back above their necks was an odd bump, something like the one Big Heads had below their mouths.

One of the newcomers moaned. He was huge, wider and taller than any of Xhosa's warriors, shoulders massive, legs like tree trunks, hands the size of Cat's paws. Battling him would be like a flea trying to bite Wild Beast. Even Stone would be dwarfed.

The other newcomer was the scrawniest Other Xhosa had ever seen. A pelt hung from his waist and covered his dangling parts. His forehead was broad and smooth, topped by a pronounced brow ridge. One thigh dripped pus from a deep gash. It must hurt but you wouldn't know by looking at him. Balancing on his good leg, he spun in circles, oblivious to the melee around him. Scrawny One's head tilted up, a smile across his face, limping a dizzying circle, arms out. He halted facing the hill where Xhosa hid and focused to her side.

"He sees me."

Xhosa jerked. Lyta. A sparkling smile, unusual for the girl, fixed on Scrawny One.

They'd been discovered.

"You shouldn't be here," but Xhosa's motions lacked their usual bite. Would Scrawny One let the Leader know they were there?

She couldn't risk it. "I'll talk to them," but Pan-do held her in place.

"They are waiting for someone."

Scrawny One showed no sign of giving away their presence so she crouched down to watch the drama unfold below.

Scrawny One made a noise that could only be described as a giggle and then pivoted to his friend, Massive One, the male's enormous breasts bobbing as he tried with awkward steps to match his friend's fluid movements. He carried an immense sack that would bow any other male but danced as though the burden was nothing more than feathers.

A growl startled Xhosa. A wolf sauntered out of the heavy brush and padded toward Massive One. Though still growing into massive paws, it reached Massive One's hips. Its blue eyes shining, head twisting between Massive One and Scrawny One, it seemed to wait for a command. At a slight nod from Massive One, it bared its fangs at the strangers across the clearing and then serenely sat on its haunches.

Nightshade motioned, "Anyone who controls a wolf will frighten these Others."

Xhosa flattened herself, silent and unblinking, one with the earth, No one except Scrawny One had detected her, so occupied were they with their disagreement.

Nightshade scowled. To him, careful was weak. "We can't wait any longer. We can take all of them before whoever they await arrives."

"And what of the wolf?"

Nightshade huffed, clenching his fists, and didn't respond.

Xhosa didn't want more hostility or to take what another tribe depended upon. She wanted a new home for her People, one plentiful enough to feed everyone who lived there.

Another warrior arrived, a skin covering his chest and flowing down his arms. He strode proudly, head up, muscles bulging but spear down. The circle opened and he locked onto Scrawny One and Massive One as his warriors chanted, "Hawk! Hawk! Hawk!"

The male named Hawk wove through his warriors, eyes on the odd Others, stutter-stepping when he noticed the wolf. He stopped in front of the strangers, clear-eyed, self-reliant, and unafraid. A Leader revealed a lot about himself in his face and how he walked. This Leader was exceptional.

She straightened her shoulders, avoided the grab from Nightshade, and moved down the hill, never taking her eyes from Hawk, spear snugly in hand but directed down. Her scalp tingled and her vision grew vivid. Something inside of her grew larger, harder, faster, and stronger. Behind her, as though she could see them, the People's warriors gathered along the bluff, limned against the sky. Their skin would shine with power, muscles bulging, faces fierce. Nightshade would be standing at the center, shorter but with such command, no one doubted his leadership.

Hawk tensed at the unexpected sight of her marching slowly down the hill but didn't hide his intrigue that a female would approach while the warriors remained out of spear range. He matched her stride and paused only when close enough to impale her if needed, as she could him. His posture remained straight, face impassive. Beyond the slight curl of his lips, he gave no indication of his thoughts.

Xhosa's chest tightened and her skin prickled. With a flick of her hand, Pan-do stood, Lyta with him, gaze locked on Scrawny One and his on her.

"Who are you?" Hawk's motions included familiar Other's words of welcome.

"I am Xhosa, Leader of the People," and waved a hand through the air. "We seek a new home."

"You are not from here. We know all the tribes. You crossed Crocodile River?" His motions morphed from respect to anger. "You are cannibals!"

"No!" Xhosa answered abruptly.

"But you came from their land?"

"They tried to stop us but couldn't."

Hawk looked confused, waited for her to say more, which she didn't, and then motioned, "No one can cross Crocodile

River." His hands moved softly but hinted at hardness. It made her trust him.

"Neither one could stop us. I will explain all of it at another time, if necessary."

Hawk blinked, trying but failing to hide his shock, and something else—the respect of one Leader for another who accomplished the impossible. Xhosa guessed few survived the Crocodile River. She studied him. Everything about Hawk— the alert eyes, hands that were still and relaxed as her father's would be when negotiating—spoke of energy and leadership.

"We would like to rest here. A groupmember is sick."

Hawk blinked before answering. "You may." He gestured toward Nightshade. "Your warrior. Is he peaceful as you are?"

"He is my Lead Warrior. We are loyal to each other."

Hawk grunted. "He may hunt with us, provide your food."

From behind him came a voice. "We too are hungry, Leader Hawk. We will cause no problems."

The Massive One moved toward Xhosa, the wolf at his side. He stood as tall as Xhosa but without her grace and lightness. Xhosa sucked in a breath trying to keep her face impassive.

The *he* was a *she*.

"I am Zvi. Seeker and I have traveled many moons," and she ticked off all fingers on both hands. Xhosa wanted to shake her head. That was impossible. How could two such as these survive so long alone?

"This is our companion, Spirit. We are pack." The wolf wagged its tail and panted, but remained attentive.

Zvi indicated Scrawny One. "Seeker would like to meet Lyta, the one who drew us here."

Spirit shook flies from his eyes and ears and then huffed.

Before Pan-do could stop her, Lyta raced down the hill, pulling up a shadow's length from Seeker. The boy bounced, head cocked, as though performing for Lyta.

"She will do." He moved closer to Lyta and sniffed as she did him. Both traced each other's hand movements without touching. Xhosa prepared to intervene but Pan-do touched her shoulder.

"Lyta dreamt of the boy Seeker. He comes from far away, seeking the stars and a new home. She promises I need not worry when they are together."

Seeker faced Pan-do. "The ones you know as Big Heads call the Wolf a spirit. He frightens them. Without Wolf, we would be dead. He will take care of Lyta and me. And Zvi. And you. And all your people."

Hawk shook his head and motioned to Xhosa. "This one—Seeker—makes no sense. Nor does his companion Zvi. You take them," and left, pelt swirling against his body, motioning without looking at her, "Eat with us, Female Leader named Xhosa, with your people. And the odd ones. After food, we will know if you stay."

Hawk disappeared into the mist.

# Chapter 42

Lyta walked with the newcomers, her rapt attention on Seeker as he bounced from one spot to the next, steps as flighty as a bee searching for pollen. Zvi plodded at Lyta's side, eyes also on Seeker, a bright smile never leaving his face. Spirit pranced among the group, sniffing deeply and offering the occasional huff.

Xhosa motioned to Nightshade, "What did you think of Hawk?"

Nightshade snorted. "Tell him we claim this land, Xhosa. It must be ours." His words carried an unusual hint of reproach.

How best to explain her need for a peaceful home, one built on trust and cooperation, not enforced by bloodshed?

"Hawk respects that we survived the cannibals and crocodiles. That's a good start, Nightshade. We will eat with him, observe his leadership, his people, and decide if he would be an asset to us. Having an ally makes us stronger. Never again could Big Heads defeat us."

Nightshade growled toward the newcomers. "We are saddled with these weaklings. Zvi is slow and Seeker a child—"

"What child travels with a wolf? And one with blue eyes?"

The ancient female Lucy traveled with a wolf who considered her pack. Xhosa couldn't ignore the similarity but she had never spoken to Nightshade about her dreams and wouldn't now.

Nightshade scrutinized the three. "If I saw two travelers with a wolf, I might leave them be."

"I suspect that's why Hawk has made no decision."

"How does this involve Pan-do's odd daughter Lyta?"

"Lyta saw Seeker in a dream as he did her."

When the People reached their caves, Xhosa ordered the food they had harvested be returned to Hawk which made

Nightshade furious.

"We will starve!"

"We took his meat. We show our respect for his leadership by giving it back. Besides, he promised to include you in the next hunt."

Zvi came over. "When you are ready, Spirit knows the way to Hawk."

"When was the wolf at his camp?"

"Spirit will track the Leader's smell."

As they prepared to leave, a warrior Xhosa recognized from Hawk's People showed up. His alert black eyes darted through the People, finally settling on Xhosa. He strode toward her despite the warriors surrounding her. Something in his stride made it clear he feared none of them, not even her Lead Warrior. Without looking, she smelled Nightshade's wrath, heard his hands tighten on his spear.

"I am Water Buffalo, Lead Warrior of the Hawk People. I will take you to our homebase."

Spirit sniffed Water Buffalo and slowly wagged his tail. Xhosa sniffed too. The male smelled of fear but no danger.

She motioned, "Thank you."

Arms loaded with meat, plants, roots, seeds, and berries, Xhosa's People, the two strangers, and Spirit traipsed over hills, through valleys and marshlands, and past more waterholes than Xhosa thought existed. Seeker talked nonstop with Lyta about why the ground swelled and dipped and how he'd seen this moons ago when he and Zvi and Spirit traveled in a lightly-forested area. The boy took no time to breathe or listen. Nor did he require answers. Lyta absorbed every word, even when Seeker faded into what could only be described as gibberish. The Lyta Xhosa knew never listened so long, so intently, without clicking her fingers or echoing words or humming.

Pan-do motioned to his daughter. "Is everything alright?"

Lyta's face lit up. "Seeker—he knows so much. Do you hear? He is amazing."

Pan-do shook his head, apparently like Xhosa, hearing only babble.

As Sun dropped to its sleeping nest, the air's warmth plummeted. Xhosa refused to shiver but ached for Spirit's fur coat, wondering if Seeker and Zvi slept close to him at night.

By the time their destination appeared in the distance, she was eager for whatever warmth Hawk's caves held. The Leader walked toward them giving no indication what he thought of her massive group laden with food. Even Spirit dragged a huge leg bone.

He motioned, "You have been busy."

Xhosa dipped her head. "We are good hunters."

His gaze caressed her glistening hair, long and smooth as it draped to her waist. He petted it, surprised.

"It is soft."

When Hawk's penis straightened, Nightshade growled. Xhosa ignored it, used to Leaders trying to exert ownership.

She involuntarily shivered in the cool air, snugging her hair around her body. Hawk fingered the sack around her neck. "You show us how to make these, we show how skins can keep you warm."

He started toward a cave nestled into the cliff wall. "We live there—"

He fell silent, a strange look on his face, something between worry and fury.

"What's wrong, Leader Hawk?" Xhosa asked. She saw nothing other than a well-hidden cave invisible to trespassers.

"The fire—" But he stopped. A subadult sprinted to him, breathless, frightened. The thoughtful, open-minded Leader switched to one who was fierce, indomitable—and furious.

"Leader Hawk." The subadult's hands shuffled to a stop at the look on his Leader's face and his body trembled so fiercely, his teeth chattered. What could cause such abject fear?

"Speak!" Hawk yelled, though his anger said he knew what was coming.

"The f-fire..." The subadult's hands shook so they stuttered as he spoke.

Hawk clenched his fists and forced his arms to his sides. "How did it happen?"

The boy dipped his head, gazed at his feet, shrugging. "The fire tender…" was all he could get out before breaking down.

"Go." Hawk's command relayed the fury his words didn't.

"What's on fire, Hawk? I can cover it with dirt or a boulder if it is small, or help you flee."

"It's what's *not* on fire," he spit out and then shook his head and fluttered his hand in apology. "Ours died."

"Fire is inside the cave? Why?"

He gawped at her. "You don't use fire?"

"We know grass fires and forest fires. The Big Heads used fire to chase us from our homeland."

"Yes, we use it to funnel animals but not against enemies. You must tell me more about this." He hesitated, and then motioned, "But how do you stay warm?"

"It is not this cold where we came from."

"What about safety?"

Her mind raced, trying to connect safety and fire, but got nothing. "What?"

"Animals avoid fire so we build one at the front of the cave."

"How do you get it here?" This made no sense.

"When a fire burns, we grab it with a torch." When he saw her confusion, he clarified, "a tree limb that will burn long enough to reach our cave. Subadults stay by the fire pit all day and all night to be sure the flame never goes out."

Was fire like the People? It must eat constantly?

Seeker approached, steps quiet, arms hanging. "I can help."

Xhosa had not seen the boy so calm, nor his words so clear.

Hawk jolted to attention. "How?"

Zvi answered for her friend. "As we traveled, we noticed that knapping tools with certain stones—not all—produced a tiny flame."

Xhosa had detected this also.

"But they were impossible to capture so we continued, without fire."

She pulled two stones from her neck sack. "One of the tribes showed us how two stones create fire. You need a special firestone, like this, and a striker stone."

She collected tinder and, hovering her hands over the pile, struck the stones again. And again and again. Over and over. Zvi never stopped, nor did her face reflect discouragement or defeat. After so many handfuls of tries, Xhosa ran out of fingers, a flame burst forth in the debris.

"Fire!"

Hawk gasped. He touched his finger to the blaze and jerked away, skin already blistering.

"It is like ours."

His head swiveled between Zvi and Seeker with a new respect. Nightshade shook his head while staring at his feet.

"One-called-Zvi, go with Water Buffalo and do the same magic to our fire pit."

By the time Xhosa and Hawk entered his communal cave, a huge fire blazed, eating the dry tinder and reaching for the roof. Nightshade's eyes snapped open and his muscles tightened though he didn't retreat. One of Hawk's warriors tossed tree limbs into the flames from a nearby pile. Xhosa tried to withdraw but Hawk held her arm.

"See the stones around the pit? Fire cannot burn stone or dirt."

Xhosa thought of the one that chased her People down the Rift. It burned out at the cliff, bare of plants or scrubbrush. Relaxing, she realized that inside this cave was as warm as her homeland, and more comfortable than her People's caves.

Hawk patted a spot next to him. "You rest there, as a Leader."

Xhosa nodded and motioned, "Pan-do is also a Leader."

Hawk looked surprised but motioned Pan-do to his other side and then Zvi and Seeker to Xhosa's side. Across from them stood Nightshade, Water Buffalo, Sa-mo-ke, and many of the groups' warriors. Xhosa squatted, knees touching the cave floor, butt resting on her feet. She breathed in, catching sweat, baby dung, burning wood, and ash. When everyone settled by the flames, Spirit tucked in between Zvi and Spirit, a hare in his mouth. The smell of wet fur wafted heavily over everyone.

Hawk asked Zvi, "He has no fear of fire?"

Zvi smiled. "He has known fire since a pup. It is as natural to him as me."

"Does he share what he hunts?"

"Of course, as I do with him."

"And he helps you hunt?"

Zvi's face lit up. "He can drive prey over a cliff or towards us. And he's agile—never injured by hooves or teeth. I came from a tribe the size of yours. It took all our hunters to kill enough meat. Seeker and Spirit and I do this alone."

Hawk cocked his head, intrigued, as was Xhosa. Nightshade too listened intently.

Hawk motioned, "How did you partner with a wolf?"

"Spirit was a tiny pup when his mother was killed by hyaena. When I stopped them from killing him, he allowed me to be his pack."

Spirit heard his call sign and alerted, tail wagging. Zvi patted between his ears and he settled his big head on the hare.

Hawk looked like he would ask more questions but Zvi leaned over to speak to Seeker so Hawk turned to Xhosa.

"How do you stay warm without coverings?"

"My homeland is much warmer than this, even during the rain." She rubbed her palm over the skin that adorned Hawk's body. It was Cat's fur, the entire pelt.

"Though this would also keep the flying and biting insects off."

"Here," and he tossed one to her. "For the meat you brought."

Xhosa held the skin on her lap, enjoying the warmth on her legs and chest, until Hawk bent over, his hand brushing her leg, and looped it over her neck. He smoothed her hair over the pelt, taking longer than necessary, and moved his hands to her knees.

"We put a hole at the top so it rests easily around your shoulders."

Sun warmed her body though that was impossible. It slept. "I feel it!"

Hawk guffawed and then hid it with a grin.

When he began eating, so too did everyone. They shared equally the meat, plants, seeds, berries, snails, ants, and more. As Xhosa ate, Hawk's leg comfortably pressing against hers, she paid attention to his warriors. They ate but never stopped checking the cave's entrance, ears perked for out of place sounds. One remained outside, spear and warclub ready. They were tough and devoted to their Leader, much like her warriors.

So why did Nightshade disapprove?

Hawk finished the meal and then cleared his throat. Silence fell over the group.

He motioned, "Tell us your story, Xhosa. How did you end up so far from your homeland?"

She told of her People's peaceful life until the Big Heads drove them away.

Hawk interrupted. "Big Heads—who are these?"

She described them, the oddity of their over-sized heads, their control of fire, and their far-throwing stone-tipped spears.

"I don't smell them here."

Hawk eyed each of his warriors and all shook their heads. Xhosa slumped, relieved.

"We are not without our own enemies here, Leader Xhosa." His hand moved rigidly, his body tense. Some deep part of Xhosa's brain sensed a danger greater than Big Heads, but Hawk changed the topic.

"Your People are the first to come here since I was a child. We considered the Crocodile River uncrossable. How did you do that?"

"We had to or be eaten by the cannibals. We hoped this land would welcome us."

"I am amazed so many of your People survived Crocodile River. Your Lead Warrior—Nightshade—must be powerful." He smiled at the sturdy male who showed nothing. Only Xhosa recognized his pleasure at the compliment, which made Water Buffalo grind his teeth.

Hawk motioned, "And the cannibals?"

"They killed only a few scouts."

He couldn't hide his shock. "How was that possible?"

"Pan-do," and nodded toward the Leader who had no idea he was now the topic of conversation, too busy whispering to his daughter who crouched by the wolf, one hand petting his furry neck.

Xhosa saw Pan-do as Hawk must—too slender to defend himself, muscles weak, without a basic awareness of his surroundings to notice all eyes were now on him. Hawk would consider him bereft of the commanding presence required of a Leader. His cleverness could only be judged in the context of his peaceful approach and the loyalty of his people—that they would fight to the death for him. Xhosa wondered about explaining that but decided to let Hawk discover it himself, as she had.

When the group fell silent, Pan-do glanced up quizzically.

"Pan-do tricked the cannibals by coughing into a hand he blooded with his cutter. They thought—who wouldn't—that he was sick."

Hawk jerked upright. "I know this illness."

Xhosa placed her hand on his arm. "He is healthy. It was to persuade them to release us."

Pan-do interceded, "I mimicked the symptoms I've seen in one of our females."

At Hawk's increased distress, Pan-do added, "We left her at our camp. She knows to stay away from others, whether coughing or not."

Hawk harrumphed, satisfied for the moment, and motioned to Zvi and Seeker, "I know of no one who traveled as far for as long as you. How did you do this?"

Zvi told how they fled their home after a ball of fire fell from the sky and burned everything—trees, homes, people, and animals.

"It killed my best friend, Giganto. He was taller than you, Hawk, and wider than the one called Stone, but gentle. In all the places Seeker and Spirit and I have seen, never have I found more of his kind. Maybe because he eats only bamboo."

"What is this 'bamboo'?"

When Zvi finished explaining, Xhosa motioned, "Did you see Big Heads as you traveled?"

"Similar creatures confronted us." Zvi opened and closed his hands over and over to indicate how many. "But when they saw we were protected by a blue-eyed wolf, they fled, calling him a 'spirit'. That's how he got his name."

"What is a spirit?"

Zvi chewed her cheek and gulped but Lyta answered, "A formidable invisible creature that appears out of thin air. A Spirit protects any he chooses."

Zvi looked surprised at her description and Seeker slapped his hands together. Zvi motioned, "They passed the word to other tribes and no one bothered us. Many even left us food."

"An offering to Spirit." Lyta motioned, not a shred of doubt in her movements.

The wolf cracked an eye, huffed a sigh, and returned to sleep, nose touching Zvi, paw on Lyta's lap, and tail curled around his body.

"What happened to your leg, Seeker?"

He mumbled about a snake and an injury and how dizziness made him fall and seemed to think that made sense. Zvi watched her friend as though entranced by his every move. When he finished, Zvi bobbed her head up and down.

"A snake did bite Seeker but that healed long ago. This injury happened when he fell into a crevice and broke his leg."

Xhosa regarded first Zvi and then Seeker, who busily drew his finger through the dirt at his feet. "How did he climb with such an injury?"

"Nothing stops him."

Seeker chanted, "Unhurriedly," and he leaned into Lyta.

Zvi continued, "We tied a tree limb to his leg to keep it straight and made a crutch out of two forked branches."

Xhosa was impressed. "I'll call you for broken legs."

When Zvi talked of their travels, over areas empty of people, rich with animals, and dappled in sparkling waterholes, he made it sound like the adventure of a lifetime. Nightshade was repelled but most stared in awe, intoxicated by the stories. None had seen so many different lands, such an array of tribes and Others. Xhosa had trouble believing what she heard but why would they lie?

Lyta scooted to Xhosa. "Seeker will travel until he finds the stars. Then he intends to settle with me."

Again, Lyta spoke lucidly when her topic was Seeker.

Xhosa asked, "Tell us your story, Leader Hawk?"

Hawk nodded agreeably but motioned instead to Pan-do. "First, Pan-do, tell us how you ended up with the Xhosa People?"

Pan-do rolled to his haunches and began.

"When our Leader died, I became Leader because no one else offered. During the rainy time, a small band of Big Heads stumbled into our camp, starving. We fed them and welcomed them to our territory. Others came, whole tribes, and soon they outnumbered us. It didn't take long before they insisted we leave our caves; they needed the room for more of their Others. When we refused, they slaughtered our few warriors—none with the skills of Nightshade or Water Buffalo—and we faced the decision to allow more to die or flee."

He didn't need to clarify their choice.

"When we entered Xhosa's territory, she welcomed us. As importantly, Lyta felt we were safe with her, that Xhosa would lead us along the Rift to a new home. Among our People, that is important."

Xhosa needed to ask something that had bothered her since they met. "Pan-do. Lyta's call sign is nothing like any among your People."

"All my pairmate told me was that Lyta discovered her name in a dream."

Xhosa stiffened. How could that be? "Lyta" was similar to the call sign of the ancient female in her dreams, Lucy. A hint of a smile crossed Lyta's face, as though she read Xhosa's thoughts and enjoyed her confusion.

Hawk interrupted her next question with his own. "What is this Rift you speak of?"

Xhosa motioned, "A massive deep chasm with steep, jagged walls. We didn't run into the cannibals until we crossed it, trying to find a way across the Endless Pond."

"Our Endless Pond?"

"Yes but another part of it."

Hawk turned to Pan-do. "So if not for Xhosa and her Lead Warrior, you would be dead? Is that what you're saying?"

Pan-do's face paled. Before he could correct Hawk, the Leader marched outside, beckoning. Pan-do followed, face pensive, worry lines framing his mouth. Xhosa joined them, not sure what to expect.

Without the fire to light the cave, the night sky was as black as Leopard. Even Moon and its subdued light had not yet arrived.

Hawk squared off to Pan-do, his body steady and cold. "Those unable to wield a warclub are worthless to us, Leader-named-Pan-do."

Xhosa strode to Pan-do. "He has proved his worth to me, Hawk. Without his cleverness, the cannibals would have eaten us."

Hawk heard her without acknowledgment.

Xhosa added, "My Lead Warrior, Nightshade, considers him a valued hunting partner." No need to add that despite Pan-do's skill with throwing stones and spears, Nightshade disliked him.

Nightshade approached. "I have seen him outrun prey."

Hawk perked at that, a flash of anger brightening his eyes. "We run over that hill, to the tallest tree and back. If you beat me, you are welcome to stay with my People."

He drew a line in the dirt at their feet and pulled Pan-do behind it, to his side.

Xhosa was angry. "He doesn't know the way as you do, Hawk, and it is too dark!"

Pan-do chuckled, "If I am as clever as you say, Leader Xhosa, I will figure it out."

Without warning, Hawk took off. Pan-do grinned and sprinted after him. He ran with a speed and joy Xhosa had never seen in a runner. He said for those brief steps, he could outrun his memories. In no time, the pounding feet, the rustle of bushes, and the occasional hoots of disturbed animals disappeared.

Lyta bumped against Xhosa. She expected the girl to worry but heard only a yawn.

"He will win. He always wins," and sauntered over to squat next to Spirit.

Xhosa shivered despite the skin. By the time Moon appeared for its nightly travels, the pounding of fast-moving feet reappeared, two sets, one measured and smooth, the other clomping erratically as though the owner could barely continue. Slowly, the blurry smudges took shape in the darkness. Pan-do was in front and Hawk close but hunched over, driving forward on willpower alone, breath nothing more than labored wheezing.

As they came within a spear throw, Hawk closed the distance and the two crossed the finish line together. Hawk doubled over, chest heaving. Pan-do sauntered over to his daughter and Spirit, his brow damp but breathing calm.

When Hawk recovered, he motioned to Pan-do, "You are a worthy opponent and welcome to the Hawk People." His face showed no anger and much appreciation for a well-fought skirmish. Without another word, he re-entered the cave and crouched at his original spot by the fire.

When Xhosa rejoined him, he leaned toward her. "You are right. This Pan-do is clever. He sees in the dark, never stumbled, and made less noise than I. He is also smart enough to know not to embarrass the one who may provide his future.

"I like him. My warriors may be stronger but he is clever."

As Pan-do squatted beside Hawk, the Leader beckoned, "Tell us how you see in the dark!"

Pan-do's face flushed, not from the run but with embarrassment. Spirit settled next to him, licking his skin with a gusto.

"I heard the bushes sway and felt the change in the air when rocks rose in my path but really, all I did was follow you, Leader Hawk. You showed me how to get there. Then, I knew how to return."

He fixed Hawk with a straight-forward, honest gaze. "You are fast. It was close."

Hawk guffawed, face bright with pleasure. "People of Xhosa and Pan-do, you may stay, in your caves or with us."

Xhosa wanted to hear Hawk's story but he made it clear the meal was over.

Just outside of the cave, Hawk caught up. "The coughing illness of your female—it killed many among my People before we discovered a treatment. Tomorrow, we go to harvest the herbs."

With that, he re-entered his People's cave and its warm fire.

Xhosa headed back to the People's cave, wondering at the feeling inside her body. Hawk's confidence, his conviction that he was right, even his open-minded attitude, were traits she had admired in her father, but this other sensation—it frightened her. Never, not with Nightshade or anyone else, had her body tingled as it did now.

Then there was Seeker—he made no sense. His relentless need to "find the stars" drove him onward despite Moons of travel through strange and dangerous lands. Didn't he know they were overhead?

With a mental flick, she dismissed the question. What pushed him—and his friends—mattered nothing to her.

Nightshade joined her. "What do you think about these Others—Seeker and Zvi?"

"It is not up to us. If Hawk accepts them, so too shall I. The one called Zvi and her ability to make fire—I think Hawk wants that."

Nightshade scoffed. "He wants more than a stone that creates a flame."

Xhosa tried to see his face but his head drooped. "We must be patient."

"Of course. I will get to know Hawk's warriors. If the time comes they reject us, I will be prepared to conquer them. This will be our home, Xhosa, of that you can be sure."

She placed a hand on his arm. "He *will* accept us. I feel it, Nightshade. Together, we are more commanding than either alone."

"The People are already commanding!" and he stomped off. Xhosa stared after him, wanting to call out but instead, pressed her lips into a tight line. Did he think a Leader of Hawk's physical strength and charisma, with the unquestioned loyalty of his people, would replace her Lead Warrior?

If so, he was wrong.

As her thoughts drifted into darkness, warm under the mammoth skin, something pulled her back from sleep. She slit her eyes to see Seeker dancing in the moonlight wearing only the loin-skin, eyes closed as he bounced on the balls of his feet, crooning something Xhosa couldn't make out. If the cold bothered him, he hid it. His naked body glowed like the white rhino on a moonless night. Never was anyone so happy.

At his feet, the wolf Spirit danced with him, huffing, nipping at his pack member as he might a sibling. And

From Pan-do's cave, a pair of dark eyes watched with occasional giggles.

# Chapter 43

Hawk nudged Xhosa awake.

"You killed many animals. Their hides must be treated before they spoil. Water Buffalo will take your females to our cave. My females will explain how to turn skins into coverings for your people.

"Seeker and Zvi will take your Lead Warrior Nightshade and others to harvest firestones."

Xhosa rubbed her eyes. "I thought Seeker and Zvi were going to teach you hunting with the wolf, Spirit."

"That will wait. Your female must be cured or allowed to die. I won't risk infecting my People," and he left, heading toward the open fields, not bothering to see if she joined him.

She did. Shadow was her responsibility. Nightshade glanced her direction, unconcerned. Lyta trailed after Seeker and his large friend Zvi, going with Snake and a mix of males toward Fire Mountain. At Lyta's side, his head up to her chest, was the blue-eyed wolf, ears perked, nose twitching, keeping pace with these new members of his pack. Pan-do watched them go, relaxed, maybe because Spirit would guard his daughter?

There was much to learn from these new people.

Hawk was almost out of sight, hidden in a crevasse similar to Xhosa's Rift. He paid her no attention, head constantly moving, nose flaring. His face spoke of wisdom with his world, trusting while not trusting.

They arrived at a pristine pond and stopped by a healthy sapling.

Hawk motioned, "We will make a spear and attach the stone tip used by your enemy Big Head."

Xhosa furrowed her brow. "I don't know how, nor do you."

"We can figure it out."

Xhosa studied the tree. Green wood weapons didn't last long but this one was supple and straight. Good spears had been fashioned out of worse.

Hawk pulled an unusual chopper from his neck sack. One end curved exactly as her People's did but the other end wrapped in a pelt. This allowed Hawk to grab it without blooding his hand. He chopped down the sapling and cut it to his height, which was Xhosa's height. Next, he smoothed the nodes and twigs and scraped away the bark from the spot where he would grip it. That done, he flattened the tip and handed it to her.

"Now we attach the stone."

Xhosa thought about the Big Heads' spears and then dug into her sack for a palm-sized hand axe, one end whittled to a point and the other flat. Using a thin sinew from around her neck, she snugged the stone against the spear tip and wrapped until the tendon completely covered both.

This was close to a Big Head spear so she lifted it above her shoulder, balanced, and threw it into a tree stump. The tip fell off on contact.

Hawk picked the pieces up and rotated them, head cocked, gaze intense. "We should split the top of the spear and push the stone into the notch."

Hawk chopped into the end of the spear, forced the stone into the groove, and then wrapped the shaft with a tendon from the top of the groove to the bottom. This time, when thrown, the spear embedded deep into a tree stump, the tip remaining firmly connected to the shaft.

Hawk's eyes lit up and Xhosa wanted to shout but controlled herself. Still, between the two floated the meaty satisfaction of solving a problem together. Xhosa's belly tingled all the way to her neck. To cover it, she sucked up a mouthful of water and swished it slowly around in her mouth.

Hawk drank his fill and then speared fish for a meal. What they didn't eat, they stuffed into their sacks and then continued the search for the healing herb. They stayed on the pond's bank, now and then splashing through sedge beds. With Sun well over their heads, they arrived at a river. Sunlight glinted off its rippled surface as it curled over the land.

"The plant lives across."

As Xhosa flitted between excitement they were almost there and concern about crossing, he pointed out a bigger danger than the river's depth and width: a waterfall.

Her excitement melted away. "There's nowhere to cross."

Hawk headed to a tree the thickness of his waist that straddled the gorge. Xhosa had seen it and dismissed it, thinking it had fallen there in a storm.

Hawk tied his spear and warclub across his back and wrapped a fat tendon over the trunk. He grabbed it with both hands, crossed his legs over the log, and shuttled across, face up to the sky, oblivious to the raging water and sharp boulders below.

Xhosa gasped. Falling meant death. If he somehow survived, he would tumble downstream and over the waterfall. If that too didn't kill him, who knows what waited at the bottom.

Falling was not an option and he didn't fall. He wasn't even winded as he reached the other side and motioned her forward.

She hesitated, eyeing the narrow trunk and the treacherous rocks. Hawk shouted something, muffled by the roar of the roiling river but clearly telling her to hurry. She smiled to hide her fear but suspected it was more grimace than joy. After securing her spear to her back, she looped a tendon over the log as Hawk did, crossed sweat-slick ankles over it, and moved out. One shaking hand at a time, her body hanging over nothing but air, only tendons and a tree trunk— and her trust in Hawk—stood between her and a painful death. Her gaze locked onto the fluffy clouds above, not the maelstrom below, and then her eyes closed, preferring to hear and not see.

Her foot slipped. Trying to swing it back over the log dislodged the other. Only her hands prevented her from dropping.

"Sling your leg over the log!" Hawk's bark was calm but insistent.

"I don't need you to tell me that," she growled to herself as both legs regained their hold and her slow journey continued, foot by foot. Her arms burned, her legs ached, and her hands bled from slivers shoved deep into her palms and fingers. Her neck throbbed from the effort to keep her head up.

When her feet hit solid ground, Hawk grunted and jogged to a pool by the chasm. His back to her, he drank deeply and then trotted off. It took a moment before Xhosa stopped shaking and another to let her breath calm and the pounding in her chest slow. She slaked her thirst and then trotted after Hawk, not looking forward to crossing this chasm again on the way home.

When she caught up, he was digging up a drooping dry plant. Attached to the roots were tiny bulbs.

"Mulch this and give it to Shadow every day. If it doesn't work quickly, let her die. The burden of a sick female is not the responsibility of my People nor yours."

When Xhosa collected as much as her neck sack would hold, leaving enough to regrow for future harvests, she speared a hare and they settled to eat.

"You are a good Leader, Hawk. I suspect you are a formidable warrior but you balance this with compassion."

Hawk's face softened. "I hope I lead well and with respect. My People are loyal and we are rarely challenged."

They ate in companionable silence. As they prepared to leave, Hawk put a hand on her arm. "I have met many Leaders, as I am sure you have. They either meet my gaze or look elsewhere. Which it is tells me all I need to know about whether they will be friend or foe. You Xhosa, are a friend.

"I'm not sure about your Lead Warrior."

Hawk joined a long line of Leaders who doubted Nightshade.

She motioned, "I know him my entire life. My father hand-picked him to lead our People. Be patient. He will be worth it."

"How are you the Leader if Nightshade was ordained?"

Xhosa offered a blank gaze. "That story is complicated."

"Is he your pairmate?"

This surprised Xhosa. She looked away, trying to determine his meaning. Hawk hadn't mentioned a pairmate or child of his own. One female—Clear River—tried to join him after his loss to Pan-do but he brushed her away. Xhosa fidgeted, trying to decide the best answer, and picked honesty.

"There is no time. Nightshade deserves better. And you—is it Clear River?"

She'd seen Nightshade eying this female. He liked to mate with the mates of other Leaders but not pairmate.

Hawk shook his head. "Your Lead Warrior is welcome to her."

The trek back went quicker and the log not nearly as frightening. She could see herself soon scampering across with Hawk's confidence. As they passed the last clearing before the final homeward trek, Xhosa heard the pad of paws over dry tinder.

"Cat stalks us."

Hawk grunted and continued without looking.

When Cat emitted a hungry growl, Xhosa added, "It sounds unfriendly."

"So am I."

The predator advanced toward them, crouched low, one step at a time. Xhosa smelled not only feral Cat but milk. A quick glance and she discovered tiny balls of fur poorly hidden in a grass hollow.

"She wants to feed her cubs."

Hawk ignored her.

When they entered a boulder bed, Cat's claws scratched against stone. After a breath, her ears peeked over a boulder ahead of them.

Xhosa motioned, "We go around," but Hawk shook his head.

"Wait here," and he moved away, as though oblivious to Cat's presence. Only the tightened grip on his spear and warclub told Xhosa he prepared.

Instead of waiting as ordered, she joined Hawk, spear ready, attention on Cat. Or rather, her ears. A growled purr announced Cat's intention.

Before Hawk could react, Xhosa yelled, "If you attack, Cat, Hawk will kill you and your kits will starve."

Xhosa tossed the remains of their hare toward the cubs. Mother watched, nose twitching, and then turned back to her prey. Hawk roared in a voice that would scare mammoth and stared into Cat's eyes. The feline shook her head and fled. Xhosa stared, stunned, panting as sweat prickled her forehead, proud of Hawk's raw courage, honored to be with him.

Hawk continued as though nothing happened.

Hawk never watched even anyone bravely face down danger as Xhosa did. She hung from the slippery log where some of his own warriors wouldn't. She smelled mother's milk, located the cubs, and created a plan that protected their lives without wasting the mother. Xhosa would be an asset to his People.

# Chapter 44

Hawk returned to his camp and Xhosa to hers. Pelts lay in the clearing, one for each family. Unlike the one Xhosa wore, these smelled like rotting carrion. The females were settled in the shade, moving as the shadows lengthened, scraping the inside of the skins to remove the spoiled remnants of meat and sinew that would attract the white worms.

Nightshade hurried to her. "We harvested firestones as well as hard rocks for choppers, cutters, cleavers, flakes, and hand axes." He motioned wide-eyed, just noticing her stone-tipped spear. "Did you run into Big Heads?"

"No. I will show you later how to attach a hand axe to the spear. Let everyone know we will join Hawk's People for the meal." She ignored his curious look and headed toward Shadow.

The female bent over a skin like the others but looked up at Xhosa's scent.

"Pan-do gave this to me."

Xhosa ignored her. That was none of her business.

"Eat this," and handed her the healing plant Hawk had found.

Shadow tried to smile at the noxious taste but it ended as a grimace.

"Thank you. If not for you and Siri, I would die. What would my son do?"

Xhosa suspected Shadow knew the answer to that. Many among the People would willingly help a child. They were the future.

As she rose to leave, Spirit tore into camp and raced toward Nightshade. The Lead Warrior yanked his spear up causing Spirit to whine and sprint to Lyta. He pawed her chest, mouthing her hand as though to pull her, and growled in wolfspeak. The girl stiffened as Spirit pivoted toward the open field. Just outside of the clearing, he reversed direction and fixed his blue eyes on first Lyta and then Nightshade.

The wolf was more agitated than Xhosa had ever seen him, pads dark with mud, fur saturated with the smell of pig, and something red stuck to the top of his head.

"Where are your minders," Nightshade snarled, spear still at the ready.

Lyta batted it away. "Don't hurt him! He is asking that we follow him."

Xhosa jerked her head around, searching. "Has anyone seen Zvi and Seeker?"

Spirit bounced, paws slamming the ground, tail tucked, hackles up.

Shadow motioned, "They were about to show us how to use the firestones when Spirit ran off and they chased him."

Lyta tugged at Xhosa. "They need help. Spirit would not leave them if not for trouble. Please!"

Spirit howled, sprinted away and then loped back to Xhosa, howled again and ran again.

Xhosa clutched her spear as memories of Big Heads drawing her warriors away so they could invade the homebase swirled through her head.

Pan-do crouched in front of his daughter. "We will find them." He held her shoulders but that did nothing to stop her shaking.

Xhosa motioned, "Stay, Pan-do. If this is a distraction, you must defend our People. Tell Snake and Sa-mo-ke to be prepared! If Nightshade and I don't reappear soon, warn Hawk." She faced Spirit who pranced impatiently, tongue hanging. "Take us to Seeker and Zvi, Spirit!"

Without another word, Xhosa and Nightshade dashed after Spirit. He sped forward, leaping over crevices and plunging into grass beds. No unfamiliar smells wafted across her path but the silence—of the birds and insects—could only mean they sensed a threat. She should move cautiously but the frantic wolf wouldn't run slower than a full-out sprint.

Shadows stole over the foothills. Coyote whined plaintively, frogs croaked, and Owl hooted. The night hunters were already out. Ahead was a sprawling tree that must be Spirit's destination, its leaves rustling in the cooling breeze.

At the base circled one of the largest pigs Xhosa had ever seen. It was taller than Spirit and stretched wider than the tree. It pawed the trunk leaving deep gouges in the supple bark, snorting, its horn glistening red in the fading light.

Beneath the tree was a bloody pool the size of Xhosa's hand.

With a throaty growl, Spirit tackled the surprised pig, pulling away before the deadly tusk stabbed him.

"Spirit!" Xhosa barked. "You are no match for this monster. You did your part leading us here. We will take over."

She patted his head and made a shooing motion which the wolf ignored. His neck bristled, bared fangs gleaming, saliva dripping as he continued a throaty growl.

From the leafy boughs, a voice called, "Ah. Spirit brought you. Of course. Don't worry, friends. We are both fine," Seeker waved, chewing on a root, seemingly unconcerned.

"Seeker." Zvi. "We're treed by a massive pig who prefers to eat us than allow escape."

Zvi shared little of her friend's peacefulness, probably to do with the leaf around her foot that dripped blood.

"Is it painful, Zvi?" It looked bad to Xhosa—long and jagged, cutting the skin to the white tissue beneath.

The bulky female shrugged. "I climbed too slowly," and with her size, not often either.

Spirit flapped his ears and spread his legs with a glare that asked, "What's the plan, pack?"

Nightshade motioned to Xhosa, "You go that way."

Spirit huffed, announcing his intention to join them, and the group separated, now covering more sides than the pig could see. The hunter became the hunted.

With everyone in position, Spirit raced in and nipped the pig's hoof, his reward a bruising kick. The wolf flew backward, crashing upside down with a whine, and tumbled to his paws as Xhosa loosed her spear. It lodged in Pig's shoulder. Not a death strike but painful enough to enrage the beast. It snorted, forgetting the assailants in its desperation to bite lose the spear. With a thunk, Nightshade's spear pierced the pig's throat, protruding like a heavy bristle. The stricken creature wheezed and groaned, and fell over dead.

Seeker jumped from the boughs nimbly and Zvi clunked, twisting a knee as she tried to balance on her good foot, finally falling over with an oomph. Both hugged the massive wolf, petting the spot where Pig kicked him. Seeker tried to lick away the blood stuck to the crown of Spirit's head but it clung obstinately, dry and cracked.

Nightshade regarded Spirit with new respect. "His bravery makes him a worthy partner."

Zvi motioned, "He saved me many times by alerting to a sound or smell, but never before has he gone for help."

"Where is your spear? Nightshade snapped. "You endanger all of us if we must rescue you for something you could handle alone!"

Zvi drooped and Seeker giggled. "We left without them. Spirit needed us."

Seeker pulled Spirit up on his rear legs and swirled in a circle. Amazingly, the wolf kept up, tail wagging so hard it jiggled his rear legs.

Xhosa shook her head but tried to see things as this odd male might, finally giving up.

Nightshade motioned, "The pig will feed everyone this night," and swung the carcass around his neck one-handed, hooves draping to his waist, and tromped angrily away.

Sun dropped, sucking out whatever heat remained in the air, and Xhosa shivered as she ran, slowing to accommodate Zvi's injury. The bulky female limped awkwardly, leaning heavily against Seeker's slender shoulder as the boy exulted nonstop about the strength of the pig, its prowess as a hunter, and its sacrifice in feeding the People. By the time they reached the caves, most of the People were snugged into the new skins and cuddling their children beneath them for warmth. Zvi's was large enough for herself, Spirit, and Seeker. When the wolf tried to eat the pelt, they pushed him away.

Xhosa led the People to Hawk's camp. They covered the distance faster than the day before. The Hawk People were gathered around the fire with room open by the Leader for

Xhosa. When they saw the massive pig covering Nightshade's shoulders, space was made for him to Hawk's other side as the hunter who brought the meat, the spot Pan-do sat in the night before.

Xhosa motioned to Pan-do. "Here, with us, Leader."

Hawk beckoned also. "Come. Make our circle complete."

Lyta plopped down next to Zvi, rubbed her injured foot with a sticky sap and then, applied it to Spirit's bruised ribs. The wolf tried hard to lick it off but gave up, whined, and exposed his vulnerable belly.

"You deserve this, Spirit," and rubbed and scratched until the wolf fell asleep. When she stopped, he awoke with a start and eyed her as though to say, *that's it?* When she ignored him, eyes on Seeker, Spirit rolled onto his belly and rested his head on his paws. Only the twitching of his pointed ears and sharp nose indicated his continued vigil protecting his pack.

"Eat first, and then we hear the stories."

As they ate, Spirit sidled over to Nightshade, hungry drool dribbling from his jaws, pleading for a share of the pig bone the male held.

Xhosa laughed. "He considers himself your warrior, Nightshade."

The Lead Warrior grunted. "He did help," and tossed him a rib. The wolf ripped it out of the air and settled by Nightshade, chewing, just another part of the group gathered to eat and share stories.

Food completed, Xhosa and Hawk started the stories by telling of crossing the log, saving the life of mother Cat, solving the riddle of attaching a stone to a spear, and finding the healing plant for Shadow. Nightshade eyed Hawk, hiding his admiration, but to Xhosa it was clear.

Seeker and Zvi offered to demonstrate how to use the firestones the next day.

Xhosa searched the crowd and found whom she needed. "Siri, tell us about the skins."

Silence settled over the group, all eyes on Hawk. Few females spoke at these meals but if Xhosa hoped to meld with the Hawk People, that must change. Females would be judged on their merits, not childbearing abilities.

Siri opened her mouth but nothing came out. Her face reddened and she began to shake.

Hawk waved toward her. "Stand so all can hear." His voice was firm but friendly.

Siri stood, hands clutched in front of her, wobbling from one foot to the other. "The Hawk females showed us how to slit the carcass down the belly and up each leg to peel the skin from the flesh beneath. We scraped and pounded the hides to remove the remaining meat and tissue and rubbed dirt and salt into the underside to preserve them. It will take several nights but they say the skins will last a long time."

One female beamed encouragingly.

"The Hawk females—they are helpful and patient."

"Remember the urine." Zvi spoke calmly though rubbing her injured foot.

"Urine?" Hawk asked. "Why?"

In answer, Zvi took the pelt from Seeker's waist, the one that hid his dangling parts, and handed it to Hawk. "Compare this scent to the one you wear. Urine keeps the hide from rotting and washes out after several days."

Hawk inhaled and tossed the loin-skin to his Lead Warrior who passed it to his pairmate who after a thoughtful moment, nodded.

"Good," was all he responded.

Nightshade seethed. Did Xhosa not see how much Hawk wanted her? Of course he would be drawn to her energy and the towering height that made her so commanding but possessing Xhosa meant controlling the People, her father's People. Knowing that, Nightshade didn't understand why she responded to Hawk as she did.

Anger closed in like a storm, seething deep inside him, burning and growing. His face hardened.

Spirit growled.

# Chapter 45

Xhosa found the Hawk People like hers in many ways. They respected elders. Members specialized in tasks suited to their abilities. All valued females for providing and nurturing children. Everyone ate what they wanted while scavenging and hunting, sharing what remained at the meal.

No one owned anyone.

The nightly gatherings by the warm fire were always friendly. The groups blended well, traded knowledge, and helped each other.

"It is time."

Shadow would probably take her daily herbs without Pan-do's reminder but he enjoyed the visits. Since everyone had become accustomed to avoiding her for fear of catching the bloody cough, he brought food, sharpened cutters, and did what she couldn't.

Shadow showed her teeth, lips curling, something that happened often now that the cough no longer bled. Her beauty awed Pan-do as it did several of Hawk's warriors. They talked about visiting her when their Leader declared her cured.

"You are kind to me—and everyone. Why do you not find a pairmate?"

Pan-do considered the possible answers. He still missed his pairmate and wondered if Lyta would accept a new mother but the real reason, he was not yet ready to talk about to Shadow.

"I have," and then changed the subject. "Your child does well?"

After a quizzical moment, she smiled. "We visit often though at a distance. I appreciate you spending time with him. Xhosa says I am soon cured." Sadness tinged with happy flitted across her face.

While Shadow chewed, Pan-do watched as Lyta talked with Spirit, her movements unusually calm and clear. The wolf quietly listened, head cocked as his tail wagged. Only one person remained unhappy with the new arrangements and that had nothing to do with the abundance of hunting, the lack of enemies, or the selection of mates.

Xhosa still confused Pan-do. From Shadow, he heard the story of how she tried to save her father and then her victorious leadership challenge against Nightshade. The People respected her. All assumed Nightshade would become her pairmate, as did Pan-do until Hawk arrived. Soon, Xhosa must choose between Nightshade and Hawk, free her Lead Warrior to move on.

Pan-do motioned, "Nightshade mates with a female from Hawk's People."

Shadow snorted. "Because no one here will risk his temper. Look at Clear River. Every day, her body bears a new injury. Today, it's her eye."

Pan-do attributed Nightshade's abuse of Clear River to resentment toward Hawk. Clear River had been the favorite of Hawk until Xhosa. Hawk must be angry at the maltreatment of a female he once cherished but didn't interfere. A female chose her mates and as Leader, he would only get involved if the female was too damaged to work. That had not happened.

Yet.

Pan-do thought back to the furtive conversation between Nightshade and some unknown person. Whatever they discussed wasn't likely to happen with Hawk supporting Xhosa, but Pan-do trusted the Lead Warrior less the longer he knew him. In rare unguarded moments, when Nightshade thought he was unobserved, his antipathy for Hawk was more deadly than the best-thrown stone. He hated the male who stole Xhosa from him.

But what bothered Pan-do most was Nightshade's uncharacteristic patience. He was waiting for the right moment.

# Chapter 46

"Not yet. My first responsibility is a new home for my People."

They crouched on an outcropping at the crest of a hill that overlooked Hawk's encampment. The People's caves barely showed in the distance.

Hawk motioned, "Everyone is happy."

"Almost."

One of Hawk's hunters beckoned him.

This abundance did feel like home. Her People slept in Hawk's cave, enjoying the warmth of many bodies and well-tended fires. They had learned the best places to forage, the location of waterholes, and where Cat and her cousins denned. There was much to like and few problems.

She gazed to the horizon, subconsciously looking for dust trails or out-of-sync movement. The vastness humbled her, its silence arousing fear and peace in equal amounts. Hawk wanted her as his pairmate, to make both groups stronger, but Nightshade wanted to move on. The longer Xhosa remained silent, the further away he moved from her. He used to appear at her side before she knew she needed him and they would talk about the People's problems. As it should be with Leaders, now that strategizing occurred with Hawk. Her Lead Warrior reacted by shutting her out, so much so Xhosa worried he would leave as Rainbow did, taking most of her warriors. Hawk would control the loyalty of the remaining warriors and the group. She would lose her father's People which would break the promise made to him.

Hawk treated Nightshade as Water Buffalo's equal which antagonized his Lead Warrior and did nothing to placate Nightshade. If the choice became keeping Nightshade with the People or pairmating with Hawk, well, there was only one answer.

Hawk trotted up, grinning. "Your Ant—with Dust—brought down a buffalo. It seems his leg is finally healed."

"He has become what I saw in him."

Hawk guffawed. "We eat well this night."

"Zvi tells me cold comes soon."

"How does she know?"

"From Seeker."

They took their places in Hawk's cave, with Pan-do to the one side, Dust and Ant to the other. The young males had never before been invited to eat with the Leaders. Their chests puffed and they nudged each other like children.

As everyone finished eating, preparing for the story of the hunt, Seeker broke in. "Coastline tidal ponds, so much food!"

Zvi translated, "Seeker's homeland included extensive seacoasts and shorelines filled with plants and small animal communities—very different from here—"

"Tsunamis!"

Zvi motioned, "Tsunamis are uncontrolled storms that flood the land further inland than you can throw a spear. I have no idea why he has brought this up." Zvi scratched her head, looked to Spirit for help but got none.

Seeker added, "A raft sailed out and never reappeared."

Which confused everyone. Xhosa focused on what Seeker called a "raft" that did something called "sail".

"What is this 'raft'?"

Zvi explained, "It is logs tied together with vine... Zvi has always promised to show me how to make one but the time never seemed right..."

Xhosa motioned, "Why would anyone make one?"

Zvi opened her mouth, closed it, and stuttered for an explanation. Seeker leaped up and danced in an energetic circle. Zvi motioned, "Yes, of course. To cross... say, Endless Pond..."

"To escape!" Seeker threw himself in the air, leaping higher than he should be able to.

Xhosa caught Nightshade's eye. "We could avoid the cannibals by floating across Endless Pond?" She could hardly believe this was possible.

"Yes! No!" Seeker and Zvi answered together and explained, finishing each other's ideas as though they had one thought. Spirit yipped at all the right times. Lyta sang and pounded her hands together.

Zvi motioned between Seeker and herself and Spirit. "We must leave. You should come with us."

Everyone fell silent until Xhosa motioned, "To search for his stars? We—"

"No, Leader," Zvi interrupted. "To save your lives. You—and we—are in peril."

Seeker added with unexpected clarity, "We can build rafts for everyone, to escape this place before we die."

Xhosa shivered. Lyta paled, her light complexion even more ashen. Heads spun as they tried to see who wanted to leave.

Zvi continued, "They have too many warriors to stop. We must leave—very soon—or all die."

Seeker motioned, "And I can't die without finding the stars."

He and Zvi spoke evenly as they might discuss curing hides with urine.

Xhosa motioned, "That can't be true, Zvi—"

Lyta interrupted, "It's not your enemy, Xhosa. It's Hawk's, from long ago. I am going with my future pairmate."

"My People go with my daughter."

Xhosa grabbed Zvi, "What does Seeker mean by 'coastline tidal pools'?"

"It's where we can eat once the rafts land."

Xhosa awoke the next morning shaking. Another dream of Lucy that pointed this time to Seeker and Zvi. She scanned the clearing in front of the caves but didn't see them.

Shadow called out, "They're by Endless Pond."

The female was with her son, healed enough to be out among the People.

Hawk caught up as she approached Endless Pond. "I sent scouts to see if Seeker is right, that we are to be attacked. While they are gone, you and I can test these floating logs and then hunt."

Endless Pond bustled with activity. A vast expanse of logs packed the shoreline, many on top of each other. Some of the People were aligning a group while others tied them together with tendons and vines. No one spoke or rested. Xhosa ticked off most of Pan-do's People and a considerable number of hers and Hawk's.

"I am surprised so many listen to the words of Seeker."

Hawk motioned, "My People have grown to trust Lyta who trusts the strange one, Seeker."

"Where did the logs come from?"

He pointed down the coastline. "Around that bend. They've been collecting them for days—"

Zvi approached and interrupted, "We wanted to know there were enough before suggesting our plan."

Xhosa chewed her lip. "These are all for one raft?"

Zvi shook her head. "Many. Each will carry this many people," and ticked off all fingers on both hands.

Xhosa mentally watched her People board the rafts, followed by Pan-do's and Hawk's. They all fit.

She motioned, "Zvi, why is Seeker so sure we will join him?"

"This danger we face, soon, will roll over us like a tsunami. You have never experienced such a violent storm but I have. Our only chance is to run."

Zvi wrung her hands and bounced. "Seeker is more frightened than I have ever seen him, in all our journeys. I've learned to trust him. You should, too."

"How does he know we face this tsunami danger?" But Xhosa too had known when the Big Heads would attack. Some terror inside of her built day to day until it couldn't be ignored. Zvi didn't need to answer for Xhosa to know that also happened to Seeker.

Zvi's eyes softened and her body filled with a quiet confidence, somehow knowing Xhosa's thoughts, and then she turned to Hawk. "Seeker wants me to tell you that he knows you won the last time you fought this enemy but if you fight again, you will lose."

Hawk gulped. "But we exterminated every one of their warriors. How did they regain their strength?"

Zvi motioned, "You allowed the children to live—"

Hawk's face paled and sweat prickled his forehead.

Zvi continued, "And they grew up hearing how you killed their fathers. Now, they burn with vengeance."

Xhosa fixed her eyes on Hawk. "We can't cross Endless Pond. That's where the Big Heads live."

Zvi touched her arm. "We aren't *crossing* Endless Pond, Xhosa. We are sailing along the shore until we find a new home. Then, we land."

Hawk grunted. "My scouts were forced to stop at the mountains. There is no way over them. If we can sail—is that what you called it?—beyond those, we are safe."

Zvi bobbed her head. "And we can stay on the rafts a long time by carrying food and water. We can even fish from them."

After a shallow halting breath, Hawk motioned, "How do we guide it—this raft? Leaves float but aimlessly. We must sail beyond the mountains. How do we make that happen when leaves can't?"

Zvi dropped a leaf into Endless Pond and swished the water. The leaf bobbed but went nowhere.

"As you say, Hawk, but watch how I change that," and Zvi swept her hands through the water on both sides of the leaf. This time, it moved forward. "We make long spears wide enough to move the water on either side. The raft will then glide the direction we point it."

Xhosa crossed her arms and shifted from foot to foot. "You're sure these logs float? Many of the People can't swim." Would they trust a few limbs lashed together?

"These are special trees. We are lucky they grow here."

Xhosa shook her head. "I don't know…"

Zvi looked away. "My people never left the forests. Seeker is c-confident. H-his People did th-this often," but her stuttering worried Xhosa more than ever.

Seeker stepped to Zvi's side, his young face radiant. "I can do this," he motioned with such confidence Xhosa squared her own shoulders.

Hawk motioned, "How many have you made, Seeker, before these?"

He scratched his head. "Well, none. That was someone else's job. But I've seen many built."

Xhosa's insides dropped.

"Zvi and Spirit and I go first. If we die, you can stand and fight."

When Zvi and Seeker left, Xhosa motioned to Hawk, "If you stay, we stay."

Hawk gazed into the distance, across the sandy shoreline to the edging forests and beyond to where the People's caves lay. "If there's any way, we will but either decision will require meat," and they headed back to the camp to gather the hunters.

Heat washed over everyone as they crossed a shallow valley, up a slight rise to a plateau to where they could see the fullness of the surrounding country, its naked peaks of ridges and hills, and a massive herd gathered at a waterhole.

Nightshade motioned to Hawk, "Some hunters will drive those that become separated from their herd toward you and Pan-do or other groups."

When Hawk said nothing, Nightshade motioned, "Ask what you will. Leader. I've been expecting this."

Hawk motioned, "You do not mate with Xhosa?"

"She mates with no one. It interferes with her leadership." After a breath, he added without looking at the Leader, "We will pairmate when the time arrives."

A warble halted further discussion and the Leaders separated, heading toward their positions.

From the start, it didn't work as planned. Someone threw a spear at the lead Wild Beast. It squealed, shook enough to dislodge the lance, and galloped toward Hawk and Pan-do. Pan-do could easily avoid him but not the slower Hawk so Pan-do stood his ground and bellowed in the voice of the she-cat. The Wild Beast skidded to avoid its primary predator as Pan-do flung a stone the size of a coconut at the terrified animal. It hit, perfectly, and the beast collapsed.

Pan-do shouted to Hawk, "It's only stunned," and sped toward the downed Wild Beast, Hawk trying to keep up. The beast rose to its knees, shook its head, and roared toward Hawk. Pan-do leaped in front and stabbed it in the chest while Hawk thrust at the throat and eyes.

With a final bellow, its chest sank and its bowels released.

Hawk panted, muscles bulging from the effort. "There was no reason for it to head our direction." He searched the edges of the group as the hunt raged on around them. "Who threw that branch?" His motions, choppy and stiff.

Pan-do suspected what happened but had no proof. What he did know was that Nightshade was out of position. It could be either to avoid some unidentified danger or by accident. Or he might have moved on purpose, knowing the wounded animal would focus on the slow Hawk. In all his hunts with Nightshade, the warrior never fought any way but perfect. It chilled Pan-do to consider that Nightshade might believe others should die to achieve the end he desired.

As Pan-do and Hawk chopped the carcass into portable pieces, Pan-do watched Nightshade, trusting him even less than he had this morning. Nightshade watched Hawk.

And Hawk's Lead Warrior, Water Buffalo, watched Nightshade.

Xhosa breathed out when the hunters returned, laden with meat.

She approached Hawk. "The scouts are back. The invaders, they're here."

"How many?"

"They cover everything the scout could see."

"How far away?"

"Less than a moon."

Hawk beckoned her away from the group until they were far enough, no one would hear or see their hand motions. "We are leaving. You must also."

Xhosa stared at him, digging beneath the worry, the stress of being responsible for so many, and his concern for her. There was something more he wasn't telling her.

"Hawk, why would this enemy risk their finest warriors for vengeance?"

Hawk stepped closer to her, his back to the group. "After their defeat last time, we tracked them a Moon and another, to their homeland. Ice mountains covered the land like water fills a lake, and it was so cold, we couldn't stop shivering even with our pelts. They either take our land or freeze to death in theirs."

"In my homeland, the Big Heads needed our land for the food. Without it, they would starve."

"Come with us, Xhosa. My People respect you. And Nightshade," and Hawk dipped his head but not before Xhosa saw trouble in his eyes.

"What happened on the hunt?"

Hawk wouldn't look up. "I suspect if not for my interest in you, Nightshade would be a loyal friend."

When he finally met her gaze, she saw what he didn't say. He would give her up to protect his People.

As she would him.

Xhosa gazed across the lofty mountains, the sweeping valleys, and the mighty canyons that dwarfed the flat hills, nowhere seeing her boundless open savannas where mammoth's trumpet soothed her to sleep. Moreover, everything here was cold.

She turned away, motioning over her shoulder, "I will convince my people."

From then on, building the rafts, collecting food and weapons became what the People did.

That is, until they ran out of time.

# Chapter 47

Xhosa bolted upright, eyes unblinking, senses alert. Around her were the gentle snores of her People but Nightshade was not by her, nor Hawk. That must be what awakened her.

She rubbed her hands down her face, awakening from another dream of Lucy. Bits floated to the surface, of the ancient female running, her small pack—Garv, Voi, and the wolf Ump—frightened but hopeful, and then Lucy's dream gaze met hers, conveying hope, energy, and confidence—

Xhosa shook her head, ridding herself of sleep's webs.

Nightshade appeared, face grim, lips white. "A field of warriors, armed with spears and warclubs, advances toward us."

He spread his fingers to indicate how many more of the barbarians there were than the People.

Xhosa's head pounded, her ears ringing so loudly it was all she heard. As it used to be, Xhosa heard Nightshade's thoughts. *If the rafts are ready, we flee. If not, we fight.*

"Hawk's warriors engage them now, to slow them so his females and children can escape with us."

Hawk had agreed to this, part of a much larger plan to ensure as many of the combined People as possible survived. Water Buffalo, familiar with the invaders' strategies, would lead the group, thin the invaders' ranks, and tire them out. Then, Nightshade's warriors would take over, giving the exhausted fighters time to reach the rafts.

They also had a few surprises the invaders wouldn't expect.

"Siri—get the females and children to the rafts."

Since arriving at the new homeland, she performed the duties of Primary Female well. Now, when it mattered most, Xhosa depended upon her energy, leadership, and support.

Xhosa hurried to endless Pond, joined by Pan-do, Nightshade, Sa-mo-ke, and Hawk. If the rafts weren't ready, everyone would die, but the shore was lined with them. Some bobbed as though eager to leave while others sat on the sand, waiting. The thunderous noise of the attack could be heard even this far away.

Sun beat down but in the distance rose great black thunderheads, like mountains. Between them floated grayish-white, fluffy clouds. Still more flanked these, moving gradually and majestically but pushed away by some irresistible force.

Xhosa strode toward Zvi. "We must leave."

Zvi's face, always pleasant, was today grim, body tense, and there was an urgency in her voice that had never been there before. "Everything's ready."

Xhosa and Siri thrust everyone aboard the rafts, shoved paddles in two sets of hands, and forced them to push away from the shore faster than should have been possible. No warriors boarded because they would fight when the enemy arrived at the Pond.

Xhosa loaded the last female onto a partly filled raft as a bloodcurdling scream echoed, followed by the wet thunk of a spear penetrating flesh. Xhosa wondered who died. Nightshade, Snake, Stone, and all of the People's warriors charged toward the sounds. Xhosa heard grunts of pain and screams of death just beyond the trees and brush that shrouded the coastline as the invaders were stalled by the fresh fighters, letting Hawk's exhausted warriors stumble onto the rafts. Nightshade would withdraw before he lost too many. The People needed enough warriors to defend themselves wherever they ended up.

The sky over Endless Pond darkened to slate, the clouds ominous, the chilled air making her shiver. Her pelt had been forgotten in the cave. Despite Seeker's warning, the storm caught her by surprise.

Another raft pushed off the shore as Nightshade's warriors burst from the edging trees, howling and shrieking as they fought, backs to her, withdrawing one bloody step at a time, giving ground only when they must. All suffered wounds, some limped, and many carried injured groupmates.

Nightshade bellowed, "Hold on!" wanting to add, *for the next part of the plan.*

Pan-do's warriors were hiding to the side in the sedge grasses, their spears and warclubs unblooded. With a mighty howl, they drove into the surprised intruders, Sa-mo-ke the loudest, flinging his deadly cutter that never missed. They were fresh, the invaders tired and injured. Nightshade's exhausted fighters staggered to the rafts, tumbled onboard, and pushed away. Xhosa would board the last one, with Hawk's warriors.

Lyta lurched toward her father but Xhosa stopped the girl. "He's OK, Lyta."

Pan-do locked eyes with his daughter, brandished his spear in victory, as his group finished their part in the plan and raced toward the rafts, covered by the last squad of warriors, led by Hawk and a handful of the combined group's best warriors. They had hidden along the shoreline, waiting to surprise an enemy that would think the People had been routed. The surprise was complete and many more were killed but the enemy flood seemed never-ending. Finally, Hawk's small group raced for the final rafts.

Away from the sandy shore, too far for swimming but close enough for spear throws, drifted the warriors' rafts, ready for their next part in this drama.

"Spears!" Xhosa howled at the same moment Nightshade did and every warrior who still held a spear flung it toward shore, protecting Hawk's retreat.

That's when she saw that Shadow, her daughter, and Siri, had been left behind. They raced toward the rafts but were too far away.

"They won't make it!"

Then, a yowl resounded over the battle, more of a savage roar.

"Spirit!"

There, amidst the fray, biting and clawing his way toward the trapped females, was the wolf's plumed tail, broad furry head, and flat ears. No one expected the attack of a wolf.

"Spirit is going for them! They'll kill him!" Seeker wailed, the first time Xhosa had ever seen the boy distressed.

Xhosa trusted Spirit to take care of himself and focused instead on Shadow.

"Hurry! You're almost here!" Shadow pushed harder, driving herself forward, hand gripping her daughter. The girl pitched forward, almost dragging Shadow down with her. Shadow screamed ferociously and yanked the child to her feet but the invaders snatched the girl. Spirit snarled a fulsome growl and bit the warrior's arm so hard, the bone snapped. He yowled but grabbed with his other arm so Spirit mauled that one, ripping and shaking until the warrior had to drop the child. She scrambled to her feet and fled, Spirit with her. Hawk appeared out of nowhere, threw Siri over his shoulder, snagged the child's hand, and raced away faster than Xhosa had ever seen him run. When a final warrior tried to stop them, Shadow jumped in front of him.

It was a suicide move but bought Hawk the breaths he needed to escape with Siri and Shadow's child.

Shadow screamed as they hit her and Spirit stopped, confused. He looked over his shoulder when she screamed again. His tail stiffened, hackles up. He smelled his pack in front of him but the voice behind him—that too was pack.

"Spirit!" Seeker yelled, voice breaking. Spirit turned to the sound and huffed. His legs spread as he sniffed again, listening. The screams he had heard, behind him, were gone.

"Spirit—she's gone! We need you!"

The wolf whimpered and responded to his pack's alpha but by this time, he'd been overrun. The savages rushed past the wolf, not recognizing the danger he presented, and lined the shoreline, hurling spears at the last of the People.

"Spirit! Get over here!" This time, Seeker's voice was commanding. Xhosa had never before heard him order Spirit to do anything but it worked. Spirit streaked through the savages along the shoreline, knocking several down, and flung his massive body into the water with a loud whump.

"Can he—well, I guess so." Spirit, among his other skills, could swim like a fish.

The wolf locked onto Seeker like a biting insect does blood, legs paddling, paws churning the water to a frothy white. Shouts erupted behind him as the savages swung at him and missed. They finally recognized the People wanted this wolf so hailed spears on the fleeing animal. One tried to grab his paw and got a vicious bite for his efforts. A spear punctured the wolf's rear leg but fell out, coloring the water red. A stone hit him in the temple and another above the eye. He whined and stopped, shook his head, and almost sank but pulled himself up.

One leg dangled loosely, unable to paddle, and his eyes drooped. He whined again and then moaned, his body dead in the water. He was too deep for the attackers to grab him but close enough for their weapons.

"Ant, paddle us back! We can't leave him!" Xhosa motioned in between flinging stones at Spirit's assailants.

Suddenly, mammoth's trumpet saturated the air followed by another and another. It seemed to come from beyond the trees. The battle seemed to have riled a herd of the behemoths and they did the only thing they knew how to do when attacked. They charged.

On one of the rafts, Hawk roared a laugh. "Your Pan-do—he is as clever as you said, Xhosa!"

As others joined Pan-do's voice, the invaders screeched, flailing their arms, and fled down the shoreline away from what they thought were charging animals. Those in the water gave up their chase of Spirit and floundered away.

Seeker dove toward Spirit calling him. That seemed to snap the wolf out of whatever confusion he was in. He whined with excitement at the sight of his packmate and paddled madly toward Seeker with his two working legs until the boy grabbed Spirit's front paws, looped them over his shoulders, and dragged him to a raft. The sharp claws dug into his skin as he leaped onto the logs but he didn't seem to notice. The wolf plopped onto the deck and panted happily, tail whapping, clearly saying nothing about life was wrong when he had his pack.

They were safe from Other enemies but not from the thick dark clouds that covered most of the sky nor the light rain that now dropped constantly. Xhosa stroked the water but the logs moved slowly.

"Seeker! We must move to land until this storm passes. How do we do that?"

Xhosa waited for his answer and was dismayed to get only a shrug. "Those who guided them made it look simple so I thought it was."

"Did they go out in weather like this?"

"Well, no. They waited for clear skies."

Within a finger of Sun's passage, the soft rain deepened to torrents that pelted Xhosa's skin in vicious, stinging slants. The sky fire boomed. Fingers clenching the paddle, Xhosa pulled with every ounce of strength she possessed. Ant on the opposite side did the same. With the two of them working together, the craft cut a jagged course forward through the churning water.

"Like this!" Xhosa demonstrated to anyone who could hear over the crack of sky fire, her voice muted further by deafening explosions and torrential rains.

"Pull like this!" Xhosa tried again but no one heard.

She swiped at a lock of dripping hair as the connected logs bucked and dropped. Freezing waves sloshed over it, drenching her already frigid skin.

As though sensing their weakness, the raging waves bounced the platform high above the Pond and then threw them toward shore. Xhosa snatched for her paddle but lost it when a swirling wet wall slammed against her, hurling her overboard. Her head broke the surface but just long enough for a quick gulp before being pulled under. The next time she clawed her way to the surface, someone called her name, a frantic voice, and then she sank again. By the time she surfaced again, the voice was further away, a squeak, and then another wave tumbled her down and across the Pond's bottom. It seemed forever before her feet—really, her knees—hit ground. She crawled forward, sludge filling her mouth, until an arm wrapped her torso.

"I have you," Nightshade shouted in her ear as he dragged her to shore. "I have you, Xhosa. You'll be fine."

"Nightshade?"

"We made it."

Xhosa smiled to herself at yet another strange land to conquer in search of their new home. With her People safe, any challenge was doable. She was her father's daughter. She would never give up.

Then, she passed out.

## Preview of *The Quest for Home*
## Book 2 in the *Crossroads* Trilogy

# Chapter 1

*Northern shore of what we now call the Mediterranean Sea*

Pain came first, pulsing through her body like cactus spines. When she moved her head, it exploded. Flat on her back and lying as still as possible, Xhosa blindly clawed for her neck sack with the healing plants. Her shoulder screamed and she froze, gasping.

*How can anything hurt that much?*

She cracked one eye, slowly. The bright sun filled the sky, almost straight over her head.

*And how did I sleep so long?*

Fractured memories hit her—the raging storm, death, and helplessness, unconnected pieces that made no sense. Overshadowing it was a visceral sense of tragedy that made her shake so violently she hugged her chest despite the searing pain. After it passed, she pushed up on her arms and shook her head to shed the twigs and grit that clung to her long hair. Fire burned through her shoulders, up her neck and down her arms, but less than before. She ignored it.

A shadow blocked Sun's glare replaced by dark worried eyes that relaxed when hers caught his.

"Nightshade." Relief washed over her and she tried to smile. Somehow, with him here, everything would work out.

Her Lead Warrior leaned forward. Dripping water pooled at her side, smelling of salt, rotten vegetation, mud, and blood.

"You are alright, Leader Xhosa," he motioned, hands erratic. Her People communicated with a rich collection of grunts, sounds, gestures, facial expressions, and arm movements, all augmented with whistles, hoots, howls, and chirps.

"Yes," but her answer came out low and scratchy, the beat inside her chest noisy as it tried to burst through her skin. Tears filled her eyes, not from pain but happiness that Nightshade was here, exactly where she needed him. His face, the one that brought fear to those who might attack the People and devastation to those who did, projected fear.

She cocked her head and motioned, "You?"

Deep bruises marred swaths of Nightshade's handsome physique, as though he had been pummeled by rocks. An angry gash pulsed at the top of his leg. His strong upper arm wept from a fresh wound, its raw redness extending up his stout neck, over his stubbled cheek, and into his thick hair. Cuts and tears shredded his hands.

"I am fine," and he fell silent. Why would he say more? He protected the People. He didn't whine about injuries.

When she fumbled again for her neck sack, he reached in and handed her the plant she needed, a root tipped with white bulbs. She chewed as Nightshade scanned the surroundings, never pausing anywhere long, always coming back to her.

The sun shone brightly in a cloudless sky. Sweltering heat hammered down, sucking up the last of the rain that had collected in puddles on the shore. Xhosa's protective animal skin was torn into shreds but what bothered her was she couldn't remember how she got here.

"Nightshade, what happened?"

Her memories were a blur—terrified screams and flashes of people flying through the air, some drowning, others clinging desperately to bits of wood.

Nightshade motioned, slowly, "The storm—it hit us with a fury, the rain as heavy and fierce as a waterfall."

A memory surfaced. Hawk, the powerful Leader of the Hawk People, one arm clutching someone as the other clawed at the wet sand, dragging himself up the beach.

*He was alive!*

It was Hawk who offered her People a home when they had none, after more than a Moon of fleeing for their lives through lands so desolate, she didn't know how anyone survived. Finding Hawk and his People, she thought she'd found a new homeland.

Her last hunt with Hawk flashed through her mind—the stone tip they created like the Big Head's weapon, how she had hung by her ankles from a tree trunk to cross a deep ravine. How he grinned when she reached the other side, chest heaving but radiant with satisfaction. He told her many of his warriors shook with fear as they crossed. His pride in her that day glowed like flames at night.

For the first time in her life, she felt Sun's warmth inside of her.

She looked around, saw quiet groups huddled together, males talking and females grooming children. Pan-do bent over a child, whispering something in her ear but no Hawk.

*Where is he?* But she didn't ask Nightshade. The last time she'd seen the two together, they had fought.

She couldn't imagine a world without Hawk. They had planned to pairmate, combine their groups into one so strong no one could ever again drive her away. She hadn't known there were enemies worse than Big Heads until Hawk told her about the Ice Mountain invaders. They attacked Hawk's People long before Xhosa arrived. Hawk had killed most and chased the rest back to their home, icy white cliffs that extended from Sun's waking place to its sleeping nest, bereft of plants and animals. When he saw where they lived, he understood why they wanted his land.

The children of those dead invaders grew up and wanted revenge.

Someone moaned. She jerked to find who needed help and realized it was her. She hoped Nightshade didn't hear.

He glanced at her and then away. "All the rafts were destroyed."

She shook, trying to dislodge the spider webs in her brain. Hawk's homebase was squashed between a vast stretch of open land and an uncrossable pond. They should have been safe but the Ice Mountain invaders attacked in a massive horde. Her People—and Hawk's—were driven into the water. The rafts became their only escape. Floating on a log platform to the middle of a pond too deep to walk across was something no one had ever done but they must or die. The plan was the rafts would carry the People to safety, away from the Invaders.

That hadn't worked.

"There were too many enemy warriors, Xhosa," and Nightshade opened and closed his hands over and over to show her. "More than I have ever seen in one place."

Images of warclubs slashed through her thoughts, flying spears, the howls of warriors in battle. Many died, beaten until they stopped moving, children dragged screaming from mothers. The giant female—Zvi—sprinting faster than Xhosa thought someone her size could, the children El-ga and Gadi in her arms, a spear bouncing off her back. Her size stunned the enemy, immobilized them for a breath which gave Zvi the time she needed to reach safety.

Almost to himself, Nightshade motioned, "I've never seen him this brave."

Xhosa didn't understand. "Him?" Did he mean Zvi?

"Pan-do. His warriors attacked. They saved us." Nightshade locked onto the figure of Pan-do as he wandered among the bedraggled groups, settling by an elder with a gash across his chest and began to minister to the wound.

"I remember," Xhosa murmured. When the People were trapped between the trees and the water, prey waiting to be picked off, Pan-do's warriors pounced. That gave Xhosa precious time to push the rafts out onto the water. It seemed none of the enemy knew how to swim. Pan-do sliced through the Ice Mountain invaders without fear, never giving ground.

Nightshade motioned, "He isn't the same Leader who arrived at our homebase, desperate for protection, his People defeated."

Xhosa's hands suddenly felt clammy. "Is Lyta alive?"

Since the death of his pairmate, before Xhosa met him, Pan-do's world revolved around his daughter, Lyta. He became Leader of his People to protect her. When he arrived at the People's homebase, Lyta stood out, unusual in an otherwise homogenous group. First, it was her haunting beauty, as though she shone from within, her hair as radiant as Sun. Awe turned to shock when she walked, her gait awkward on malformed feet. She should have been destroyed as a child but Pan-do said he had never considered it. He explained that in Moons of migration, before joining Xhosa's People, Lyta had never slowed them down. He didn't expect that to change if the two groups traveled together.

And then she spoke. Her voice was like bird's song and a gift to People exhausted from the day's work. It cheered up worried adults and put smiles on the faces of children, its melodic beauty convincing them that everything would work out.

It was more than a Moon after his arrival before Pan-do told Xhosa what he valued most about his daughter. Lyta could see truth simply by watching. No one could hide a lie from her, and she never hid it from her father. Pan-do kept it secret because the people it threatened might try to silence her. He only told Xhosa because Lyta had witnessed a conversation about a plan to kill Xhosa.

One of the people Lyta didn't recognize but the other, he was someone Xhosa trusted.

When Nightshade nodded, *Yes, Lyta lives*, Xhosa relaxed but only for a moment.

"Sa-mo-ke?"

Nightshade nodded toward a group of warriors. In the middle, eyes alert and hands energetic, stood Sa-mo-ke.

She sighed with relief. Pan-do's Lead Warrior was also Nightshade's greatest supporter outside of the People. When he first arrived, Sa-mo-ke spent Moons mimicking her Lead Warrior's fighting techniques until his skill became almost as formidable as Nightshade's with one critical difference. While Nightshade liked killing, Sa-mo-ke did so only when necessary.

Nightshade motioned, "Escape came at a tremendous cost, Xhosa. Many died, the rafts were destroyed, and we are now stranded in an unfamiliar land filled with nameless threats."

*It doesn't matter,* she whispered to herself. *We are good at migrating.*

She jerked her head around, and then motioned, "Where's Spirit?"

The loyal wolf had lived with people his entire life. He proved himself often while hunting, defending his packmates, and being a good friend. An image flitted across her mind, Spirit streaking toward the rafts, thrusting his formidable body like a spear through the shocked hordes. The enemy had never seen an animal treat People as pack. Then, the wolf swimming, paws churning the water into whitecaps, gaze locked onto Seeker. Endless Pond was too deep for him to touch the bottom so his head bobbed up and down, feet paddling like a duck's as he fought to stay above the surface.

Nightshade gestured, "The attackers almost killed Spirit."

She bit her lip, concentrating. "I remember Mammoth's trumpets."

The rare hint of a smile creased his mouth. "Another of Pan-do's tricks. It saved Spirit and probably all of us. He brayed like a herd of Mammoth thundering toward the shoreline. The invaders fled for their lives."

*Pan-do is clever.*

Nightshade grimaced. "But the storm worsened and the rafts foundered. Many of the People managed to cling to logs long enough to crash onto this shore. Then, they saved others. But many died."

He opened and closed his hands to show how many.

A stillness descended as Nightshade's gaze filled with a raw emotion he never showed. It shook Xhosa. Nothing frightened her Lead Warrior.

She gulped which hurt her insides. Shallow breaths worked better. Rolling to her hands and knees, she stood, making her head swim, and she threw up.

Finally, the dizziness subsided and Xhosa asked, "Hawk?"

Nightshade peered around, hands fidgeting. He examined something on the ground, toed it with his foot. "When the tempest destroyed the rafts, he dragged many to shore, to safety. The last time, he did not return. I tried to find him."

Soundless tears dampened her face. Nightshade touched her but Xhosa focused on a trail of ants and a worm burrowing into the soft earth. Her vision dimmed and she stumbled, fell, and then crawled, happy for the pain that took her mind off Hawk. When she forced herself up, everything blurred but she inhaled, slowly, and again, until she could finally see clearly.

*How dare Hawk die! We had plans.* Xhosa shoved those thoughts away. Later was soon enough to deal with them.

"His People—do they know?"

# Preview of *Born in a Treacherous Time*
## Book 1 in the *Dawn of Humanity* Trilogy

# Chapter 1

The scene replayed in Lucy's mind, an endless loop haunting her days and nights. The clear sun-soaked field, the dying Mammoth, the hunters waiting hungrily for its last breath before scavenging the meat, tendons, internal organs, fat, and anything else consumable—food that would nourish the Group for a long time.

But something went horribly wrong. Krp blamed Lucy and soon, so too did Feq.

*Why did Ghael stand up? He had to know it would mean his death.*

Lucy wanted to escape, go where no one knew what she'd done, but Feq would starve without her. He didn't know how to hunt, couldn't even tolerate the sight of blood. For him, she stayed, hunting, scavenging, and outwitting predators, exhausting herself in a hopeless effort to feed the remaining Group members. But one after another, they fell to Snarling-dog, Panther, Long-tooth Cat, Megantereon, and a litany of other predators. When the strangers arrived, Feq let them take her.

By this time, Lucy felt numb, as much from the death of her Group as the loss of Garv. Garv, her forever pairmate, was as much a part of her as the lush forests, Sun's warmth, and Snarling-dog's guidance. Now, with all the other deaths, she could leave his memory behind.

Forests gave way to bushlands. The prickly stalks scratched her skin right through the thick fur that layered her arms and legs. The glare of Sun, stark and white without the jungle to soften it, blinded her. One step forward became another and another, into a timeless void where nothing mattered but the swish of feet, the hot breeze on her face, and her own musty scent.

Neither male—not the one who called himself Raza nor the one called Baad—had spoken to her since leaving. They didn't tell her their destination and she didn't ask, not that she could decipher their intricate hand gestures and odd body movements. She studied them as they talked to each other, slowly piecing together what the twist of a hand and the twitch of a head meant. She would understand it all by the time they reached wherever they headed.

It was clear they expected her to follow. No one traveled this wild land alone but her reasons for joining them, submissively, had nothing to do with fear. Wherever the strangers took her would be better than where she'd been.

Lucy usually loved running through the mosaic of grass and forest that bled one into another. Today, instead of joy, she felt worry for her future and relief that her past was past. She effortlessly matched Raza's tread, running in his steps at his pace. Baad did the same but not without a struggle. His sweat, an equal mix of old and stale from the long trip to find her and fresh from trying to keep up, blossomed into a ripe bouquet that wafted over her. She found comfort in knowing this strong, tough male traveled with her.

Vulture cawed overhead, eagerly anticipating a meal. From the size of his flock, the scavenge must be an adult Okapi or Giraffe. Even after the predator who claimed the kill—Lucy guessed it to be Megantereon or Snarling-dog— took what it needed, there would be plenty left. She often hunted with Vulture. It might find carrion first but she could drive it away by brandishing a branch and howling. While it circled overhead, awaiting a return to his meal, she grabbed what she wanted and escaped.

Feq must smell the blood but he had never been brave enough to chase Vulture away. He would wait until the raptor finished, as well as Snarling-dog and whoever else showed up at the banquet, and then take what remained which wouldn't be enough to live on.

Sun descended toward the horizon as they entered a dense thicket. They stuck to a narrow lightly-used animal trail bordered by heavy-trunked trees. Cousin Chimp scuffled as he brachiated through the understory, no doubt upset by the intruders. Only once, when a brightly-colored snake slithered across her path, did Lucy hesitate. The vibrant colors always meant deadly venom and she didn't carry the right herbs to counter the poison. Baad grumbled when her thud reverberated out of sync with Raza's, and Cousin Chimp cried a warning.

Finally, they broke free of the shadows and flew through waist-high grass, past trees laden with fruit, and around the termite mound where Cousin Chimp would gorge on white grubs—if Cheetah wasn't sleeping on top of it.

*I haven't been back here since that day...*

She flicked her eyes to the spot where her life had changed. Everything looked so calm, painted in vibrant colors scented with a heady mix of grass, water, and carrion. A family of Hipparion raised their heads but found nothing menacing so turned back to their banquet of new buds.

*As though nothing happened...*

Lucy sprinted. Her vision blurred and her head throbbed as she raced flat out, desperate to outdistance the memories. Her legs churned, arms pumped, and her feet sprang off the hard earth. Each step propelled her farther away. Her breathing heaved in rhythm with her steps. The sack around her neck smacked comfortingly against her body. Her sweat left a potent scent trail any predator could follow but Lucy didn't care.

"Lucy!"

Someone far behind shouted her call sign but she only slowed when the thump in her chest outstripped her ability to breathe. She fell forward, arms outstretched, and gasped the damp air into her tortured lungs. Steps thumped louder, approaching, but she kept her eyes closed. A hand yanked her head back, forcing her to look up.

Despite the strangeness of Raza's language, this she did understand: *Never do that again.*

Feq followed until Lucy had reached the edge of her— Feq's—territory. Here, he must let her go. Without Feq, the Group's few children and remaining female would die. She threw a last look at her brother's forlorn face, drawn and tired, shoulders slumped, eyes tight with resolution. Lucy dipped her head and turned from her beleaguered past.

Maybe the language difference made Raza ignore Lucy's every question though she tried an endless variety of vocalizations, gestures, and grunts. Something made him jumpy, constantly, but Lucy sniffed nothing other than the fragrant scrub, a family of chimps, and the ever-present Fire Mountain. Nor did she see any shift in the distant shadows to signal danger.

Still, his edginess made her anxious.

*What is he hiding? Why does he never relax?*

She turned toward the horizon hoping whatever connected sky to earth held firm, preventing danger from escaping and finding her. Garv credited Spider's web with that task, said if it could capture Fly, it could connect those forces. Why it didn't always work, Garv couldn't explain. Herds and dust, sometimes fire, leaked through, as did Sun at the end of every day. Lucy tried to reach that place from many different directions but it moved away faster than she could run.

Another truth Lucy knew: Only in Sun's absence did the clouds crack and send bolts of fire to burn the ground and flash floods to storm through the canyons. Sun's caring presence kept these at bay.

A grunt startled her back to the monotony of the grassland. At the rear of their column, Baad rubbed his wrists, already swollen to the thickness of his arm. When she dropped back to ask if she could help, his face hardened but not before she saw the anguish in the set of his mouth and the squint of his eyes. The elders of her Group suffered too from gnarled hands. A common root, found everywhere, dulled the ache.

Why bring a male as old and worn as Baad without that root?

Lucy guessed he had been handsome in his youth with his commanding size, densely-haired body, and brawny chest. Now, the hair hung gray and ragged and a white line as thick as Lucy's finger cut his face from temple to ear. In his eyes smoldered lingering anger, maybe from the shattered tooth that peeked through his parted lips.

Was that why he didn't try to rut with her? Or did he consider her pairmated to Raza?

"Baad," she bleated, mimicking the call sign Raza used. "This will help your wrist," and handed him a root bundle from her neck sack. "Crack it open and swallow the juice."

Baad sniffed the bulb, bit it, and slurped up the liquid. His jaw relaxed and the tension drained from his face, completely gone by the time they passed the hillock that had been on the horizon when Lucy first gave him the root.

"How did you know this would work?" Baad motioned as he watched her face.

Why didn't *he* know was a better question. Lucy observed animals as they cared for their injuries. If Gazelle had a scrape on her flank, she bumped against a tree that wept sap so why shouldn't Lucy rub the thick mucus on her own cut to heal it? If swallowing certain leaves rid Cousin Chimp of the white worms, why wouldn't it do the same for Lucy? Over time, she'd collected the roots, blades, stems, bark, flowers, and other plant parts she and her Group came to rely on when sick.

But she didn't know enough of Baad's words to explain this so she shrugged. "I just knew."

Baad remained at her side as though he wanted to talk more.

Lucy took the opportunity. "Baad. Why did you and Raza come for me?"

He made her repeat the question as he watched her hands, body movements, and face, and then answered, "Sahn sent us."

His movement for "sent" was odd. One finger grazed the side of his palm and pointed toward his body—the backtrail, the opposite direction of the forward trail.

"Sent you?"

"Because of the deaths."

Memories washed across his face like molten lava down the slopes of Fire Mountain. His hand motions shouted a rage she never associated with death. Predators killed to feed their families or protect their territory, as they must. Why did that anger Baad?

"Can you repeat that? The deaths?"

This time, the closest she could interpret was "deaths without reason" which made no sense. Death was never without reason. Though he must have noticed she didn't understand, he moved on to a portrayal of the world she would soon live within. His location descriptions were clear. In fact, her Group also labeled places by their surroundings and what happened there—stream-where-hunters-drink, mountains-that-burn-at-night, and mound-with-trees. Locations were meaningless without those identifications. Who could find them if not for their surroundings?

His next question surprised her.

"Why did you come?"

Bile welled in Lucy's throat. She couldn't tell him how she failed everyone in her Group or explain that she wanted a better life for the child she carried. Instead, she grunted and pretended she misunderstood.

That night, Lucy slept fitfully, curled under a shallow overhang without the usual protection of a bramble bush barrier or a tree nest. Every time she awoke, Raza and Baad were staring into the dark night, faces tight and anxious, muscles primed.

When Sun reappeared to begin its journey across the sky, the group set out, Lucy again between Raza and Baad. She shadowed the monotonous bounce of Raza's head, comforted by the muted slap of her feet, the thump in her chest, and the stench of her own unwashed body. As they trotted ever onward, she became increasingly nervous. Though everything from the berries to the vegetation, animals, and baobab trees reminded her of home, this territory belonged to another group of Man-who-makes-tools. Before today, she would no sooner enter or cross it as they would hers. But Raza neither slowed nor changed direction so all she could do to respect this land-not-hers was to move through without picking a stalk of grass, eating a single berry, or swallowing any of the many grubs and insects available. Here and there, Lucy caught glimpses of the Group that called this territory theirs as they floated in the periphery of her sight. She smelled their anger and fear, heard them rustling as they watched her pass, reminding her she had no right to be here. Raza and Baad didn't seem to care or notice. Did they not control territories where they lived?

Before she could ponder this any further, she snorted in a fragrance that made her gasp and turn. There on the crest of a berm across the savanna, outlined against the blue of the sky, stood a lone figure, hair puffed out by the hot breeze, gaze on her.

"Garv!" Lucy mouthed before she could stop herself. *He's dead. I saw it.*

No arm waved and no voice howled the agony of separation.

"Raza!" Baad jerked his head toward the berm.

"Man-who-preys?" Raza asked with a rigid parallel gesture.

Lucy's throat tightened at the hand movement for *danger*.

"Who is Man-who-preys?" Lucy labored with the call sign. "We don't prey. We are prey." Why did this confuse Raza?

Raza dropped back and motioned, "I refer to the one called Man-who-preys—upright like us but tall and skinny." He described the creature's footprints with the distinctive rounded top connected to the bottom by a narrow bridge.

She knew every print of every animal in her homeland. These didn't exist.

"No. I've never seen those prints."

He paused and watched her face. "You're sure Mammoth slaughtered your males? Could it have been this animal?"

"No. I was there. I would have seen this stranger."

Raza dropped back to talk to Baad. She tried to hear their conversation but they must have used hand motions. Who was this Man-who-preys and why did Raza think they caused the death of her Group's males? Worse, if they followed Raza from his homeland, did that bring trouble to Feq?

Lucy easily kept up with Raza, her hand tight around an obsidian scraper as sharp and sturdy as the one the males gripped. Her wrist cords bulged like the roots of an old baobab, familiar with and accustomed to heavy loads and strenuous work. Both males remained edgy and tense, often running beside each other and sharing urgent hand motions. After one such exchange, Raza diverted from the route they had been following since morning to one less trodden. It's what Lucy would do if worried about being tracked by a predator or to avoid a group of Man-who-makes-tools. They maintained a quicker-than-normal pace well past the edge of her world. That suited her fine though she doubted that Man-who-preys could be more perilous than what preyed in her mind.

*Click to purchase*

# About the Author

Jacqui Murray lives in California with her spouse and the world's greatest dog. She has been writing fiction and nonfiction for 30 years and an adjunct professor in technology-in-education.

You can find Jacqui Murray on her blog:
https://worddreams.wordpress.com

Twitter:
https://twitter.com/WordDreams

LinkedIn
https://www.linkedin.com/in/jacquimurray

# Bibliography

Allen, E.A., The Prehistoric World: or, Vanished Races
Central Publishing House 1885

Brown Jr., Tom, Tom Brown's Field Guide: Wilderness
Survival  Berkley Books 1983

Caird, Rod  Apeman:  The Story of Human Evolution
MacMillan  1994

Calvin, William, and Bickerton, Derek  Lingua ex Machina:
Reconciling Darwin and Chomsky with the Human
Brain MIT Press, 2000

Carss, Bob The SAS Guide to Tracking Lyons Press Guilford
Conn. 2000

Cavalli-Sforza, Luigi Luca and Cavalli-Sforza, Francesco  The
Great Human Diasporas: The
History of Diversity and Evolution  Perseus Press  1995
Conant,

Dr. Levi Leonard The Number Concept: Its Origin and
Development  Macmillan and Co. Toronto 1931

Diamond, Jared  The Third Chimpanzee  Harper Perennial
1992

Edey, Maitland Missing Link  Time-Life Books  1972

Erickson, Jon Glacial Geology: How Ice Shapes the Land
Facts on File Inc. 1996

Fleagle, John Primate Adaptation and Evolution  Academic
Press 1988

Fossey, Dian  Gorillas in the Mist   Houghton Mifflin  1984

Galdikas, Birute Reflections of Eden: My Years with the
Orangutans of Borneo Little Brown and Co. 1995

Goodall, Jane In the Shadow of Man  Houghton Mifflin
1971

Goodall, Jane The Jane Goodall Institute 2005
http://www.janFriendshipegoodall.com/chimp_central/
chimpanzees/behavior/communication.asp

Goodall, Jane Through a Window Houghton Mifflin 1990

Grimaldi, David, and Engel, Michael Evolution of the Insects
Cambridge University Press 2005

Human Dawn: Timeframe Time-Life Books 1990

Johanson, Donald and Simon, Blake Edgar From Lucy to
    Language Simon and Schuster 1996

Johanson, Donald and O'Farell, Kevin Journey from the
    Dawn: Life with the World's First
Family Villard Books 1990

Johanson, Donald and Edey, Maitland Lucy: The Beginnings
    of Humankind Simon and Schuster 1981

Johanson, Donald and Shreve, James Lucy's Child: The
    Discovery of a Human Ancestor Avon 1989

Jones, Steve, Martin, Robert, and Pilbeam, David The
    Cambridge Encyclopedia of Human Evolution
    Cambridge University Press 1992

Leakey, Richard and Lewin, Roger Origins E.P. Dutton
    1977

Leakey, Richard The Origin of Humankind Basic Books
    1994

Leakey, Louis Stone Age Africa, Negro Universities Press
    1936

Lewin, Roger In the Age of Mankind Smithsonian Books
    1988

McDougall, J.D. A Short History of the Planet Earth John
    Wiley and Sons 1996

Morris, Desmond Naked Ape Dell Publishing 1999

Morris, Desmond The Human Zoo Kodansha International
    1969

Rezendes, Paul Tracking and the Art of Seeing: How to Read
    Animal Tracks and Sign Quill: A Harper Resource Book
    1999

Savage-Rumbaugh, Susan, et al Kanzi: The Ape at the Brink
    of the Human Mind John Wiley and Sons 1996

Spencer Larson, Clark et al Human Origins: The Fossil
    Record Waveland Press 1998

Stringer, Chris, and McSahn, Robin African Exodus: The
    Origins of Modern Humanity Henry Holt and Co. NY
    1996

Strum, Shirley C. Almost Human: A Journey into the World
    of Baboons Random House 1987

Tattersall, Ian  Becoming Human: Evolution and Human Uniqueness  Harvest Books 1999

Tattersall, Ian et al  Encyclopedia of Human Evolution and Prehistory, Chicago: St James Press 1988

Tattersall, Ian Fossil Trail: How We Know What We Think We Know About Human Evolution Oxford University Press 1997

Tattersall, Ian  The Human Odyssey:  Four Million Years of Human Evolution  Prentice Hall 1993

Thomas, Elizabeth Marshall, The Old Way: A Story of the First People Sarah Crichton Books 2008

Tudge Colin Time Before History  Touchstone Books  1996

Turner, Alan, and Anton, Mauricio The Big Cats and Their Fossil Relatives:  An Illustrated Guide to Their Evolution and Natural History Columbia University Press NY  1997

Vogel, Shawna Naked Earth: The New Geophysics  Dutton 1995

Vygotsky, Lev  The Connection Between Thought and the Development of Language in Primitive Society 1930

Walker, Alan and Shipman, Pat  Wisdom of the Bones: In Search of Human Origins  Vintage Books  1996

Waters, JD Helpless as a Baby http://www.jdwaters.net/HAAB%20Acro/contents.pdf 2001

Wills, Christopher Runaway Brain: The Evolution of Human Uniqueness  Basic Books 1993

# Reader's Workshop Questions

## Setting

- What part did Nature and the land play in Xhosa's ability to survive and thrive?
- How does the setting figure as a character in the story?

## Themes

- Discuss Xhosa's respect for all animals. Why do you think she felt this way?
- Why did Xhosa and her kind survive Nature's challenges? Discuss how her brain offset the ineffectiveness of her physical attributes?
- We know *Homo erectus* died out, replaced by the more-advanced human, Archaic *Homo sapiens*. What characteristics and traits in this story help to explain why?

## Character Realism

- What traits made Xhosa a survivor?
- Do you relate to Xhosa's predicaments? To what extent does it remind you of yourself or a woman you know struggling to attain respect, fit into a "man's" world, or survive a toxic environment?

## Character Choices

- What moral/ethical choices did the characters in this book make? Discuss why the animals are referred to as "who" rather than "that" and why often they are addressed by proper nouns rather than simple nouns.
- Discuss the dynamics between Xhosa, Nightshade, Hawk, and Pan-do. How did the People raise children? Do other primitive tribes handle families in this way?
- What events triggered Xhosa's evolution from passive to warrior?

## Construction

- Discuss how Xhosa communicated—with body language, gestures, facial expressions, and the rare vocalization. How effective do you think it was? How is it relevant today? What present-day animals communicate with methods other than words?
- Discuss why Xhosa's People didn't use proper nouns to describe places.
- Discuss Xhosa's lack of a number system and how she described quantities (such as "Sun traveled a hand" or "ticked them off on her fingers"). Discuss the limited number systems used by some primitive tribes even today.
- How did early man make sense of the moon disappearing and reappearing over and over?

**Reactions to the Book**
- Did the book lead to a new understanding or awareness of how man evolved to be who we are today? Did it help you understand something in your life that didn't make sense before?
- Did the book fulfill your expectations? Were you satisfied with the ending?

**Other Questions**
- What do you think will happen to the characters in Book 2?
- Discuss books you've read with a similar theme or set in the same time period.

Printed in Great Britain
by Amazon